Amy & Roger's Epic Detour

Morgan Matson

SIMON & SCHUSTER BFYR

New York London Toronto Sydney

SIMON & SCHUSTER BFYR

An imprint of Simon & Schuster Children's Publishing Division
1230 Avenue of the Americas, New York, New York 10020

SIMON & SCHUSTER BFYR is a trademark of Simon & Schuster, Inc.
For information about special discounts for bulk purchases, please contact
Simon & Schuster Special Sales at 1-866-506-1949 or business@simonandschuster.com.
The Simon & Schuster Speakers Bureau can bring authors to your live event. For more
information or to book an event, contact the Simon & Schuster Speakers Bureau at
1-866-248-3049 or visit our website at www.simonspeakers.com.
Book design by Krista Vossen
The text for this book is set in Fournier.
Sunflower photo on page 183 copyright © 2010 by iStockphoto.com
Elvis impersonator photo on page 280 copyright © 2010 by iStockphoto.com
Manufactured in the United States of America
2 4 6 8 10 9 7 5 3 1
Library of Congress Cataloging-in-Publication Data
Matson, Morgan.
Amy & Roger's epic detour / Morgan Matson.—1st ed.
p. cm.
Summary: After the death of her father, Amy, a high school student and
Roger, a college freshman, set out on a carefully planned road trip from
California to Connecticut, but wind up taking many detours, forcing Amy
to face her worst fears and come to terms with her grief and guilt.
ISBN 978-1-4169-9065-9 (hardcover)
[1. Automobile travel—Fiction. 2. Guilt—Fiction. 3. Grief—Fiction.
4. Death—Fiction. 5. Fathers—Fiction. 6. Interpersonal
relations—Fiction.] I. Title. II. Title: Amy and Roger's epic detour.
PZ7.M43151Am 2010
[Fic]—dc22
2009049988
ISBN 978-1-4391-5749-7 (eBook)

FIRST EDITION

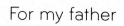
For my father

Acknowledgments

First and foremost, I owe huge and heartfelt thanks to Alexandra Cooper, every writer's dream editor. Thank you so much for your editorial brilliance, patience, kindness, and humor. I couldn't have taken this journey without you.

Thank you to Rosemary Stimola, agent extraordinaire and source of endless wisdom.

Many, many thanks and much gratitude to everyone at Simon & Schuster for going so far above and so far beyond. Thanks especially to Justin Chanda, Lizzy Bromley, Krista Vossen, and Julia Maguire.

This book, in its infancy, began at the New School's MFA program. I owe huge thanks and dozens of cupcakes to the faculty and my fellow students for their invaluable input: David Levithan, Tor Seidler, Sarah Weeks, Amalia Ellison, Lucas Klauss, Maude Bond, Lisa Preziosi, Zach Miller, and Reinhardt Suarez.

Thanks to my mother, Jane Finn, for all her support and encouragement — and for driving across the country with me in a '98 Volkswagen Cabrio. Twice.

Jenny Han and Siobhan Vivian—thank you for being my writing buddies in coffee shops all over Brooklyn, and for helping me to find words when I thought I was out of them. Also, for sharing your pastries.

Thanks to Jason Matson, Lola and Jesse Meyers, Laura Martin, Naomi Cutner, and Kate Stayman-London.

And above all, thanks to Amalia Ellison, my best friend. Without you, this book—and so much else—would never have been possible.

RAVEN ROCK HIGH SCHOOL
Raven Rock, CA

FINAL REPORT CARD

Student

AMELIA E. CURRY   JUNIOR/500 TRACK

Class	Final Grade
American Literature	A
American History	A
Chemistry	B-
French	B+
Physical Education	B
Honors Theater	A

Notes

This student's academic record will be transferred to STANWICH HIGH SCHOOL, Stanwich, Connecticut. Student will be matriculating as a senior in the fall.

Absences

1—Excused (A)
5—Excused (D)

Excused Absences

A Illness
B School-Sponsored Event
C Vacation
D Bereavement
E Other

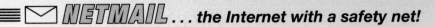

INBOX amycurry@netmail.com

FROM	SUBJECT	STATUS
Mom	Made it to Connecticut!	READ
Julia Andersen	**Worried about you**	**UNREAD**
Raven Rock HS	Final Report Card	READ
Mom	Hope the musical went well!	READ
Raven Rock Realty	Showing house this afternoon	READ
Julia Andersen	**Hello??**	**UNREAD**
Julia Andersen	**Plz write back**	**UNREAD**
Raven Rock Realty	Will be showing house at 4	READ
Julia Andersen	**Hoping you're okay**	**UNREAD**
Mom	The Trip	READ

FROM: Hildy Evans (hildy@ravenrockrealty.com)
TO: Amy Curry (amycurry@netmail.com)
SUBJECT: Will be showing house at 4
DATE: June 1
TIME: 10:34 a.m.

Hi, Amy!

Just wanted to let you know that I'll be showing the house to some prospective buyers today at four. Just wanted to make sure that you were aware of the time, so you could make arrangements to be elsewhere. As we've discussed before, we really want people to be able to imagine this as their HOME. And that's easier when it's just the family and me going through the house!

Also, I understand you're going to be joining your mother in Connecticut soon! You can feel free to lock up when you go—I have my copy of the keys.

Thanks bunches!
Hildy

FROM: Mom (pamelacurry@stanwichcollege.edu)
TO: Amy (amycurry@netmail.com)
SUBJECT: The Trip
DATE: June 3
TIME: 9:22 a.m.
ATTACHMENT 📄 : TRIP ROUTE

Hi, Amy,

Greetings from Connecticut! I was glad to hear that your finals went well. Also glad to hear that Candide was a success. I'm sure you were great, as usual—I just wish I could have been there!

Can't believe it's been a month since I've seen you! Feels like much longer. I hope you've been on your best behavior with your aunt. It was very nice of her to check in on you, so I hope you thanked her.

I'm sure all will go well on the drive. I'll expect you and Roger no later than the tenth, according to the itinerary I've mapped out for you (attached). You have reservations at the hotels listed. Pay for them, meals, and gas with your emergency credit card.

And please be safe! AAA information is in the glove compartment in case of emergencies.

I know you send your brother your love. He e-mailed me—he says hi. You can't call at his facility, but he can check e-mail. It might be nice for you to write him one of these days.

Mom

TRIP ROUTE

Start: Raven Rock, California

First Night: Gallup, New Mexico

Second Night: Tulsa, Oklahoma

Third Night: Terre Haute, Indiana

Fourth Night: Akron, Ohio

End: Stanwich, Connecticut

I will then drive Roger to his father's house in Philadelphia. Please drive safe!

Miss California

Eureka [I have found it]
—*California state motto*

I sat on the front steps of my house and watched the beige Subaru station wagon swing too quickly around the cul-de-sac. This was a rookie mistake, one made by countless FedEx guys. There were only three houses on Raven Crescent, and most people had reached the end before they'd realized it. Charlie's stoner friends had never remembered and would always just swing around the circle again before pulling into our driveway. Rather than using this technique, the Subaru stopped, brake lights flashing red, then white as it backed around the circle and stopped in front of the house. Our driveway was short enough that I could read the car's bumper stickers: MY SON WAS RANDOLPH HALL'S STUDENT OF THE MONTH and MY KID AND MY $$$ GO TO COLORADO COLLEGE. There were two people in the car talking, doing the awkward car-conversation thing where you still have seat belts on, so you can't fully turn and face the other person.

Halfway up the now overgrown lawn was the sign that had been there for the last three months, the inanimate object I'd grown to hate with a depth of feeling that worried me sometimes. It was a Realtor's sign, featuring a picture of a smiling, overly hairsprayed blond woman. FOR SALE, the sign read, and then in bigger letters underneath that, WELCOME HOME.

I had puzzled over the capitalization ever since the sign went up and still hadn't come up with an explanation. All I could determine was that it must have been a nice thing to see if it was a house you were thinking about moving into. But not so nice if it was the house you were moving out from. I could practically hear Mr. Collins, who had taught my fifth-grade English class and was still the most intimidating teacher I'd ever had, yelling at me. "Amy Curry," I could still hear him intoning, "*never* end a sentence with a preposition!" Irked that after six years he was still mentally correcting me, I told the Mr. Collins in my head to off fuck.

I had never thought I'd see a Realtor's sign on our lawn. Until three months ago, my life had seemed boringly settled. We lived in Raven Rock, a suburb of Los Angeles, where my parents were both professors at College of the West, a small school that was a ten-minute drive from our house. It was close enough for an easy commute, but far enough away that you couldn't hear the frat party noise on Saturday nights. My father taught history (The Civil War and Reconstruction), my mother English literature (Modernism).

My twin brother, Charlie—three minutes younger—had gotten a perfect verbal score on his PSAT and had just barely escaped a possession charge when he'd managed to convince the cop who'd busted him that the ounce of pot in his backpack was, in fact, a rare California herb blend known as Humboldt, and that he was actually an apprentice at the Pasadena Culinary Institute.

I had just started to get leads in the plays at our high school and had made out three times with Michael Young, college freshman, major undecided. Things weren't perfect—my BFF, Julia Andersen, had moved to Florida in January—but in retrospect, I could see that they had actually been pretty wonderful. I just hadn't realized it at the time. I'd always assumed things would stay pretty much the same.

I looked out at the strange Subaru and the strangers inside still talking and thought, not for the first time, what an idiot I'd been. And there was a piece of me—one that never seemed to appear until it was late and I was maybe finally about to get some sleep— that wondered if I'd somehow caused it all, by simply counting on the fact that things wouldn't change. In addition, of course, to all the other ways I'd caused it.

My mother decided to put the house on the market almost immediately after the accident. Charlie and I hadn't been consulted, just informed. Not that it would have done any good at that point to ask Charlie anyway. Since it happened, he had been almost constantly high. People at the funeral had murmured sympathetic things when they'd seen him, assuming that his bloodshot eyes were a result of crying. But apparently, these people had no olfactory senses, as anyone downwind of Charlie could smell the real reason. He'd had been partying on a semiregular basis since seventh grade, but had gotten more into it this past year. And after the accident happened, it got much, *much* worse, to the point where not-high Charlie became something of a mythic figure, dimly remembered, like the yeti.

The solution to our problems, my mother had decided, was to move. "A fresh start," she'd told us one night at dinner. "A place without so many memories." The Realtor's sign had gone up the next day.

We were moving to Connecticut, a state I'd never been to and harbored no real desire to move to. Or, as Mr. Collins would no doubt prefer, a state to which I harbored no real desire to move. My grandmother lived there, but she had always come to visit us, since, well, we lived in Southern California and she lived in Connecticut. But my mother had been offered a position with Stanwich College's English department. And nearby there was, apparently, a great local high school that she was sure we'd just love. The college had helped her find an available house for rent, and as soon as Charlie and I finished up our junior year, we would all move out there, while the WELCOME HOME Realtor sold our house here.

At least, that had been the plan. But a month after the sign had appeared on the lawn, even my mother hadn't been able to keep pretending she didn't see what was going on with Charlie. The next thing I knew, she'd pulled him out of school and installed him in a teen rehab facility in North Carolina. And then she'd gone straight on to Connecticut to teach some summer courses at the college and to "get things settled." At least, that's why she said she had to leave. But I had a pretty strong suspicion that she wanted to get away from me. After all, it seemed like she could barely stand to look at me. Not that I blamed her. I could barely stand to look at myself most days.

So I'd spent the last month alone in our house, except for Hildy the Realtor popping in with prospective house buyers, almost always when I was just out of the shower, and my aunt, who came down occasionally from Santa Barbara to make sure I was managing to feed myself and hadn't started making meth in the backyard. The plan was simple: I'd finish up the school year, then head to Connecticut. It was just the car that caused the problem.

The people in the Subaru were still talking, but it looked like they'd taken off their seat belts and were facing each other. I looked at our two-car garage that now had only one car parked in it, the only one we still had. It was my mother's car, a red Jeep Liberty. She needed the car in Connecticut, since it was getting complicated to keep borrowing my grandmother's ancient Coupe deVille. Apparently, my grandmother was missing a lot of bridge games and didn't care that my mother kept needing to go to Bed Bath & Beyond. My mother had told me her solution to the car problem a week ago, last Thursday night.

It had been the opening night of the spring musical, *Candide*, and for the first time after a show, there hadn't been anyone waiting for me in the lobby. In the past, I'd always shrugged my parents and Charlie off quickly, accepting their bouquets of flowers and compliments, but already thinking about the cast party. I hadn't realized, until I walked into the lobby with the rest of the cast, what it would be like not to have anyone there waiting for me, to tell me "Good show." I'd taken a cab home almost immediately, not even sure where the cast party was going to be held. The rest of the cast—the people who'd been my closest friends only three months ago—were laughing and talking together as I packed up my show bag and waited outside the school for my cab. I'd told them repeatedly I wanted to be left alone, and clearly they had listened. It shouldn't have come as a surprise. I'd found out that if you pushed people away hard enough, they tended to go.

I'd been standing in the kitchen, my Cunégonde makeup heavy on my skin, my false eyelashes beginning to irritate my eyes, and the "Best of All Possible Worlds" song running through my head, when the phone rang.

"Hi, hon," my mother said with a yawn when I answered the phone. I looked at the clock and realized it was nearing one a.m. in Connecticut. "How are you?"

I thought about telling her the truth. But since I hadn't done that in almost three months, and she hadn't seemed to notice, there didn't seem to be any point in starting now. "Fine," I said, which was my go-to answer. I put some of last night's dinner—Casa Bianca pizza—in the microwave and set it to reheat.

"So listen," my mother said, causing my guard to go up. That was how she usually prefaced any information she was about to give me that I wasn't going to like. And she was speaking too quickly, another giveaway. "It's about the car."

"The car?" I set the pizza on the plate to cool. Without my noticing, it had stopped being a plate and had become *the* plate. I was pretty much just using, then washing, the one plate. It was as though all the rest of the dishes had become superfluous.

"Yes," she said, stifling another yawn. "I've been looking at the cost to have it shipped on a car carrier, along with the cost of your plane fare, and well . . ." She paused. "I'm afraid it's just not possible right now. With the house still not sold, and the cost of your brother's facility . . ."

"What do you mean?" I asked, not following. I took a tentative bite of pizza.

"We can't afford both," she said. "And I need the car. So I'm going to need it driven out here."

The pizza was still too hot, but I swallowed it anyway, and felt my throat burn and my eyes water. "I can't drive," I said, when I felt I could speak again. I hadn't driven since the accident, and had no plans to start again any time soon. Or ever. I could feel my throat constrict at the thought, but I forced the words out. "You know that. I won't."

"Oh, you won't have to drive!" She was speaking too brightly for someone who'd been yawning a moment before. "Marilyn's son is going to drive. He needs to come East anyway, to spend the summer with his father in Philadelphia, so it all works out."

There were so many things wrong with that sentence I wasn't sure where to begin. "Marilyn?" I asked, starting at the beginning.

"Marilyn Sullivan," she said. "Or I suppose it's Marilyn Harper now. I keep forgetting she changed it back after the divorce. Anyway, you know my friend Marilyn. The Sullivans used to live over on Holloway, until the divorce, then she moved to Pasadena. But you and Roger were always playing that game. What's it called? Potato? Yam?"

"Spud," I said automatically. "Who's Roger?"

She let out one of her long sighs, the kind designed to let me know that I was trying her patience. "Marilyn's son," she said. "Roger Sullivan. You remember him."

My mother was always telling me what I remembered, as if that would make it true. "No, I don't."

"Of course you do. You just said you used to play that game."

"I remember Spud," I said. I wondered, not for the first time, why every conversation I had with my mother had to be so difficult. "I don't remember anyone named Roger. Or Marilyn, for that matter."

"Well," she said, and I could hear her voice straining to stay upbeat, "you'll have a chance to get to know him now. I've mapped out an itinerary for you two. It should take you four days."

Questions about who remembered what now seemed unimportant. "Wait a second," I said, holding on to the kitchen counter

13

for support. "You want me to spend four days in a car with someone I've never met?"

"I told you, you've met," my mother said, clearly ready to be finished with this conversation. "And Marilyn says he's a lovely boy. He's doing us a big favor, so please be appreciative."

"But Mom," I started, "I . . ." I didn't know what was going to follow. Maybe something about how I hated being in cars now. I'd been okay taking the bus to and from school, but my cab ride home that night had made my pulse pound hard enough that I could feel it in my throat. Also, I'd gotten used to being by myself and I liked it that way. The thought of spending that much time in a car, with a stranger, lovely or not, was making me feel like I might hyperventilate.

"Amy," my mother said with a deep sigh. "Please don't be difficult."

Of course I wasn't going to be difficult. That was Charlie's job. I was never difficult, and clearly my mother was counting on that. "Okay," I said in a small voice. I was hoping that she'd pick up on how much I didn't want to do this. But if she did, she ignored it.

"Good," she said, briskness coming back into her voice. "Once I make your hotel reservations, I'll e-mail you the itinerary. And I ordered you a gift for the trip. It should be there before you leave."

I realized my mother hadn't actually been asking. I looked down at the pizza on the counter, but I had lost my appetite.

"Oh, by the way," she added, remembering. "How was the show?"

And now the show had closed, finals were over, and at the end of the driveway was a Subaru with Roger the Spud Player inside. Over the past week, I'd tried to think back to see if I could recall a Roger. And I had remembered one of the neighborhood kids, one with blond hair and ears that stuck out too far, clutching a maroon superball and calling for me and Charlie, trying to get a game together. Charlie would have remembered more details—despite his extracurriculars, he had a memory like an elephant—but Charlie wasn't exactly around to ask.

Both doors of the Subaru opened, and a woman who looked around my mother's age—presumably Marilyn—got out, followed by a tall, lanky guy. His back was to me as Marilyn opened the hatchback and took out a stuffed army-style duffel and a backpack. She set them on the ground, and the two of them hugged. The guy—presumably Roger—was at least a head taller than she was, and ducked a little bit to hug her back. I expected to hear good-byes, but all I heard him say was "Don't be a stranger." Marilyn laughed, as though she'd been expecting this. As they stepped apart, she met my gaze and smiled at me. I nodded back, and she got into the car. It pulled around the cul-de-sac, and Roger stood staring after it, raising one hand in a wave.

When the car had vanished from sight, he shouldered his bags and began walking toward the house. As soon as he turned toward me, I blinked in surprise. The sticking-out ears were gone. The guy coming toward me was shockingly good-looking. He had broad shoulders, light brown hair, dark eyes, and he was already smiling at me.

I knew in that instant the trip had suddenly gotten a lot more complicated.

But I think it only fair to warn you, all those songs about California lied.

—*The Lucksmiths*

I stood up and walked down the steps to meet him in the driveway. I was suddenly very conscious that I was barefoot, in old jeans and the show T-shirt from last year's musical. This had become my de facto outfit, and I'd put it on that morning automatically, without considering the possibility that this Roger guy might be disarmingly cute.

And he really was, I saw now that he was closer. He had wide hazel eyes and unfairly long lashes, a scattering of freckles, and an air of easy confidence. I felt myself shrinking in a little in his presence.

"Hey," he said, dropping his bags and holding out his hand to me. I paused for a second—nobody I knew shook hands—but then extended my hand to him, and we shook quickly. "I'm Roger Sullivan. You're Amy, right?"

I nodded. "Yeah," I said. The word stuck in my throat a little, and I cleared it and swallowed. "I mean, yes. Hi." I twisted my hands together and looked at the ground. I could feel my heart pounding and wondered when a simple introduction had changed to something unfamiliar and scary.

"You look different," Roger said after a moment, and I looked up at him to see him studying me. What he mean by that? Different from what he'd been expecting? What had he been expecting? "Different than you used to look," he clarified, as though he'd just read my thoughts. "I remember you from when we were kids, you and your brother. But you still have the red hair."

I touched it self-consciously. Charlie and I both had it, and when we were younger, and together all the time, people were always stopping us to point it out, as though we'd never noticed ourselves. Charlie's had darkened over time to auburn, whereas mine stayed vividly red. I hadn't minded it until recently. Lately it seemed to attract attention, when that was the last thing I wanted. I tucked it behind my ears, trying not to pull on it. It had started falling out about a month ago, a fact that was worrying me, but I was trying not to think about it too much. I told myself that it was the stress of finals, or the lack of iron in my mostly pizza diet. But usually, I tried not to brush my hair too hard, hoping it would just stop on its own.

"Oh," I said, realizing that Roger was waiting for me to say something. It was like even the basic rules of conversation had deserted me. "Um, yeah. I still have it. Charlie's is actually darker now, but he's . . . um . . . not here." My mother hadn't told anyone about Charlie's rehab and had asked me to tell people the cover she made up. "He's in North Carolina," I said. "At an academic enrichment program." I pressed my lips together and looked away, wishing that he would leave and I could go back inside and shut the door, where nobody would try and talk to me and I could be alone with my routine. I was out of practice talking to cute guys. I was out of practice talking to anyone.

Right after it happened, I hadn't said much. I didn't want to talk about it and didn't want to open the door for people to ask me how I was feeling about things. And it wasn't like my mother or Charlie even tried. Maybe the two of them had talked to each other, but neither of them talked to me. But that was understandable— I was sure both of them blamed me. And I blamed myself, so it made sense that we weren't exactly sharing our feelings around the kitchen table. Dinners were mostly silent, with Charlie either sweaty and jumpy or swaying slightly, eyes glazed, as my mother focused on her plate. The passing back and forth of dishes and condiments, and then the cutting and chewing and swallowing process, seemed to take up so much time and focus that it was really amazing to think we'd once had conversations around the dinner table. And even if I did think about saying something occasionally, the silence of the empty chair to my left killed that impulse.

At school my teachers had left me alone, not calling on me for the first month afterward. And then after that, I guess it just became habit that they didn't. It seemed like people could revise who you were very quickly, and they seemed to have forgotten that I once used to raise my hand and give my opinions, that I once had something to say about the Boxer Rebellion or symbolism in *The Great Gatsby*.

My friends had gotten the message pretty quickly that I didn't want to talk to them about it. And without talking about it, it became clear that then we really couldn't talk about anything. After not very long, we just stopped trying, and soon I couldn't tell if I was avoiding them or they were avoiding me.

Julia was the one exception. I hadn't told her what had happened. I knew that if I told her, she wasn't going to let me off the hook. She wasn't going to go away easily. And she didn't. She'd found out, of course, and had called me constantly right after, calls I let go to voice mail. The calls had tapered off, but she'd started e-mailing instead. They came every few days now, with subjects like "Checking In" and "Worried About You" and "For God's Sake, Amy." I let them pile up in my in-box, unread. I wasn't exactly sure why I was doing it, but I knew that if I talked to Julia about it, it would become real in some way I couldn't quite handle.

But as I looked at Roger, I also realized that it had been awhile since I'd had an interaction with a guy. Not since the night of the funeral, when I'd invited myself to Michael's dorm room, knowing exactly what was going to happen. When I left an hour later, I was disappointed, even though I'd gotten exactly what I thought I wanted.

"It's not true, you know," said Roger. I looked at him, trying to figure out what he meant. "Your shirt," he said, pointing. I glanced down at the faded blue cotton, emblazoned with ANYONE CAN WHISTLE. "I can't," he continued cheerfully. "Never have been able to."

"It's a musical," I said shortly. He nodded, and silence fell, and I couldn't think of anything else to say on the subject. "I should get my things," I said, turning to the house, wondering how the hell we were ever going to get through four days.

"Sure," he said. "I'll load my stuff in. Do you need a hand?"

"No," I said, heading up the stairs. "The car's open." Then I escaped inside, where it was blessedly cool and dark and quiet and I was alone. I took a breath, savoring the silence, then continued into the kitchen.

The gift my mother had sent was sitting on the kitchen table. It had arrived a few days ago, but I hadn't opened it. If I opened it, it meant that the trip was actually going to happen. But there was no denying it now—the proof was making comments about my T-shirt and putting his duffel bag in the car. I tore open the package and shook out a book. It was heavy and spiral-bound, with a dark blue cover. *AWAY YOU GO!* was printed in white fifties-style script. And underneath that, *Traveler's Companion. Journal/Scrapbook/Helpful Hints.*

I picked it up and flipped through it. It seemed to be mostly blank pages, with a scrapbook section for preserving "Your Lasting Memories" and a journal section for recording "Your Wandering Thoughts." There also seemed to be quizzes, packing lists, and traveling tips. I shut the book and looked at it incredulously. This was the "present" my mother sent me for the trip? Seriously?

I tossed it on the counter. I wasn't about to be tricked into thinking this was some sort of fun, exciting adventure. It was a purely functional trip that I was being forced to take. So I didn't see any reason to make sure I'd always remember it. People didn't buy souvenirs from airports they'd had layovers in.

I walked through the rooms on the first floor of the house, making sure that everything was in order. And everything was—Hildy the Realtor had made sure of that. All our furniture was still there—she preferred not to sell empty houses—but it no longer even felt like ours. Ever since my mother hired her, she'd taken over our house to the point where I sometimes had trouble remembering what it used to feel like when we were all just living in it, and it wasn't being sold to people as the place where they'd always be happy. It had started to feel more like a set than a house. Too many deluded young marrieds had traipsed through it, seeing only the square footage and ventilation, polluting it with their furniture dreams and imagined Christmases. Every time Hildy finished a showing and I was allowed to come back from walking around the neighborhood with my iPod blasting Sondheim, I could always sense the house moving further away from what it had been when it was ours. Strange perfume lingered in the air, things were put in the wrong place, and a few more of the memories that resided in the walls seemed to have vanished.

I climbed the stairs to my room, which no longer resembled the place I'd lived my whole life. Instead it looked like the ideal teen girl's room, with everything just so—meticulously arranged stacks of books, alphabetized CDs, and carefully folded piles of clothing. It now looked like "Amy!'s" room. It was neat, orderly, and devoid of personality—probably much like the imaginary shiny-haired girl who lived in it. Amy! was probably someone who baked goods for various sports teams and cheered wholeheartedly at pep rallies without contemplating the utter pointlessness of sports or wanting to liven things up with a little torch song medley. Amy! probably babysat adorable moppets up the street and smiled sweetly in class pictures and was the kind of teen that any parent would want. She probably would have giggled and flirted with the cute guy in her driveway, rather than failing miserably at a simple conversation and running away. Amy! had not, in all probability, killed anyone recently.

My gaze fell to my nightstand, which had on it only my alarm clock and a thin paperback, *Food, Gas, and Lodging*. It was my father's favorite book, and he'd given me his battered copy for Christmas. When I'd opened it, I'd been disappointed—I'd been hoping for a new cell phone. And it had probably been totally obvious to him that I hadn't been excited about the present. It was thoughts like that, wondering if I had hurt his feelings, that ran through my head at three a.m., ensuring that I wouldn't get any sleep.

When he'd given it to me, I hadn't gotten any further than the title page. I'd read his inscription: *To my Amy—this book has seen me through many journeys. Hoping you enjoy it as much as I have. With love, Benjamin Curry (your father).* But then I'd stuck it on my nightstand and hadn't opened it again until a few weeks ago, when I'd finally started reading it. As I read, I found myself wondering with every turn of the page why I couldn't have done this months ago. I'd read to page sixty-one and stopped. Marking page sixty-two was a note card with my father's writing on it, some notes about Lincoln's secretary, part of the research he'd been doing for a book. But it was in the novel as a bookmark. Page sixty-one was the place he'd gotten to when he'd last read it, and somehow I couldn't bring myself to turn the page and read beyond that.

Food, Gas, and Lodging

slam without saying good-bye or leaving a note. In the paper sack Walter had packed a change of clothes, a paperback John D. MacDonald and the postcard that Nancy had sent with a picture of Central Park on the front. There was an address on it, an address in New York City, and that's where he was headed.

He had seventy-six dollars of his own and fifty-five dollars of his father's that he'd taken off the dresser that morning while his father was down the hall shaving. He figured that the money would be missed sooner, and for longer afterward, than he would be.

He walked to the car, the car that had been his ever since his grandfather had left it to him in the will that had been read forty-eight hours before. He was going to get on the highway and just drive, like all those songs and books and movies had urged him to do. And at the end of it, after all those miles passed, there would be Nancy waiting at the end of it.

You got one chance to take a trip like this, he thought as he put his grandfather's keys into the ignition, dice keychain dangling, coming up snake eyes. You had to do it when you were young and had the energy to drive all night and didn't care about the quality of the motel and it didn't even really matter where you ended up. This is what he'd thought about, working in that museum every day, surrounded by the artifacts carefully labeled, everything that the young braves had taken on their spirit quests. He just figured that this would be his. He started the car, pressed his foot down on the gas, and drove away, resolving not to look back but breaking it immediately, seeing his own eyes in the rearview mirror, seeing his

I still had no idea what Walter saw. I wasn't sure I was ever going to know. But I wasn't about to leave the book behind. I picked it up and tucked it carefully in my purse. I gave the room a last look, turned out the light, dragged my rolling suitcase out into the hall, and closed the door behind me. It was actually a relief not to see the room anymore. In the past month, I'd spent almost no time in it, crashing downstairs on the couch most nights and just heading up to get clothes. It was too stark a reminder of my life Before. And it still didn't make any sense to me that absolutely everything in my life could have changed, that it all could have become After, but the pictures on my walls and the junk in the back of my closet remained the same. And after Hildy's Amy! makeover, it seemed like the room had become a version of myself that I would never live up to.

I was about to drag my suitcase downstairs, but I stopped and looked down the hall to my parents' bedroom. I hadn't been in it since the morning of the funeral, when I'd stood in the doorway so my mother could see if the black dress I'd chosen was appropriate.

I walked down the hall, passing Charlie's bedroom, which was adjacent to mine. The door to Charlie's room had been closed ever since my mother slammed it behind her after she had literally yanked him out of it one month earlier. I opened the door to the master bedroom and stood on the threshold. Though tidier than it once had been, this room was at least still recognizable, with its neatly made king-size bed and stacks of books on each nightstand. I noticed that the books on my father's side, thick historical biographies alternating with thin paperback mysteries, were beginning to gather dust. I looked away quickly, reminding myself to breathe. It felt like I was underwater and running out of oxygen, and I knew I wasn't going to be able to stay there much longer. The door to my father's closet was ajar, and I could see inside it the tie rack Charlie had made for him in fifth-grade woodshop with his ties still hanging on it, all preknotted to save him time in the morning.

Trying to quash the panicky feeling that was beginning to rise,

I turned away from my father's side of the room and crossed to my mother's dresser. On an impulse, I pulled open her top drawer—socks and stockings—and reached into the very back, on the left side. The drawer was emptier than usual, but even so, it took me a second to find it. But when my fingers closed around something smooth and plastic, I knew that Charlie had been telling the truth. I pulled it out and saw that it was an ancient pantyhose egg, with L'EGGS printed on the side in gold script that was flaking off. I cracked the egg open and saw, as promised, that the egg was stuffed with cash.

Charlie had told me that he'd found it sometime last year—I hadn't wanted to ask how or why. But there was a piece of me that registered how desperate he must have been to have found the money my mother kept hidden in her sock drawer. That was about the time I started noticing just how far gone he actually was. Charlie had told me that he only dipped into it in case of emergencies and was always careful to put the money back, since he was sure Mom would notice. It always had six hundred dollars in it, mostly hundreds and fifties. Maybe Charlie had been too out of it by the end to care, or maybe he hadn't had time to replenish it before he found himself on a plane to North Carolina, but there was only four hundred dollars in it now.

I heard the front door slam downstairs and realized that Roger was probably wondering why it was taking me so long to get my suitcase. Not stopping to think about what I was doing, I pocketed the cash, snapped the egg shut, and put it back in its place. A piece of me was running through justifications—you couldn't trust these house hunters and shady Realtors, really I was just helping my mother out—but I knew none of them were the real reason I'd taken the money. So then why had I?

I pushed the thought away and hurried out of the room, closing the door behind me and dragging my suitcase down the stairs. When I reached the kitchen, I saw Roger standing in front of the fridge, staring at it. He looked at me as I thumped my suitcase onto the landing.

"All set?" he asked.

"Yep," I said, then immediately wondered why I'd just started talking like a cowboy. I pulled the suitcase toward the door and glanced back at Roger in the kitchen. He was back to looking at the refrigerator, which gave me a moment to study him undetected. He was tall, and the kitchen, which had been so quiet and still lately, seemed filled up with his presence. My mother had told me that he was nineteen and that he'd just finished his freshman year. But there was something about him that made him seem older than that—or at least made me feel young. Maybe it was the hand shaking.

"These are incredible," Roger said, pointing at the refrigerator.

"Oh, yeah," I said, crossing into the kitchen, knowing he was talking about the magnets. The fridge was covered with them, many more than were needed to hold up Classic Thai takeout menus and grocery lists. They were all from different places— cities, states, countries. My parents had started collecting them on their honeymoon, and they'd kept it up until a few months ago, when my mother spoke at a conference in Montana and came back with a magnet that was just a square of bright blue with BIG SKY COUNTRY printed on it.

"My parents—" I heard my voice catch a little on the word. Words I'd always taken for granted had turned into landmines, traps for me to stumble over and fall into. I saw that Roger had averted his eyes to the fridge, pretending he hadn't noticed any-thing. "They, um," I continued after a moment, "collected them. From all the places they'd been."

"Wow," he said, stepping back and taking in the whole fridge, as though it was a piece of art. "Well, it's impressive. I've never been anywhere."

"Really?" I asked, surprised.

"Really," he said, eyes still on the fridge. "Only California and Colorado. Pretty lame, huh?"

"I don't think so," I said. "I've barely been out of California." This was incredibly embarrassing, something I had told nobody

24

except Julia. I'd been out of the country once—we'd all spent a very damp summer in the Cotswolds, in England, while my mother did research for a book. But California was the only state I'd ever been in. Whenever I had complained about this, my mother had told me that once we'd seen all there was to see in California, we could move on to the other states.

"You too?" Roger smiled at me, and as though it was an automatic reaction, I looked down at my feet. "Well, that makes me feel a little better. The way I justify it is that California's a pretty big state, right? It'd be worse if I'd never been out of New Jersey or something."

"I thought," I started, then regretted saying anything. It wasn't like I really wanted to know the answer, so why had I started to ask the question? But I couldn't just leave that out there, so I cleared my throat and continued. "I mean, I thought my mother said your father lived in Philadelphia. And that's why you're, um, doing this."

"He does," said Roger. "I've just never been out there before. He comes out here a couple times a year, for business."

"Oh," I said. I glanced up at him and saw that he was still looking at the fridge. As I watched, his face changed, and I knew he'd seen the program, the one held up by the ITHACA IS GORGES! magnet in the lower left corner. The program I tried to avoid looking at—without success—every time I opened the fridge, but hadn't actually done anything about, like removing it or anything.

It was printed on beige card stock and had a picture of my father on the front, one that someone had taken of him teaching. It was in black and white, but I could tell that he was wearing the tie I'd gotten him last Father's Day, the one with tiny hound dogs on it. He had chalk dust on his hands and was looking to the left of the camera, laughing. Underneath the picture was printed BENJAMIN CURRY: A LIFE WELL-LIVED.

Roger looked over at me, and I knew that he was about to say a variation on the same sentence I'd been hearing for the past three months. How sorry he was. What a tragedy it was. How he didn't know what to say. And I just didn't want to hear it. None of the words helped at all, and it's not like he could have possibly understood.

"We should get going," I said before he could say anything. I grabbed my suitcase by the top handle, but before I could lift it, Roger was standing next to me, hoisting it with ease.

"I got it," he said, carrying it out the front door. "Meet you at the car." The door slammed, and I looked around the kitchen, wondering what else I could do to delay the moment when it would just be the two of us, trapped in a car for four days. I picked up the plate from where I'd left it to dry in the empty dishwasher, put it in the cupboard, and closed the door. I was about to leave when I saw the travel book sitting on the counter.

I could have just left it there. But I didn't. I picked it up and, on impulse, pulled the program out from behind the Ithaca magnet and stuck it in the scrapbook section. Then I turned out the kitchen lights, walked out the front door, and locked it behind me.

Away You Go!

YOUR JOURNEY BEGINS . . .

Congratulations! You are embarking on a JOURNEY! You might be traveling by plane, train, automobile, ship, bike, or foot! Whatever your means of transportation, you are sure to encounter new people, see new sights, and return home again a changed person with new experiences!

The tips, guidelines, and lists contained in this book will help you to document and organize your trip, ensuring you maximize your experience to the fullest!

But the greatest joy of traveling can never be planned for. And that is the element of SURPRISE! Be open to this, as it will make your trip much richer. After all, you never know where the road will take you!

HAPPY TRAILS!

Where I've Been . . .

State #1: CALIFORNIA—The Golden State

Motto: Eureka—"I have found it"

Size: BIG

Facts: California actually means "hot oven."
Who knew? Thanks, rest-stop info kiosk.

Notes: It is so big that it is entirely
possible that someone might not have left
the state AT ALL until the age of seventeen.
The same is probably not true of Rhode
Island.

California is a garden of Eden, a paradise to live in or see. But believe it or not, you won't find it so hot, if you ain't got the do-re-mi.

—*Woody Guthrie*

I got into the passenger seat and slammed the door. Roger was already sitting in the driver's seat, moving slowly up and down, then back and forth, as he played with the seat adjustment. He must have found the setting he liked, because he stopped moving and turned to me. "Ready?" he asked, drumming his hands on the wheel and smiling at me.

"Here," I said, taking my mother's itinerary out of my bag and thrusting it at him. It had the list of towns she'd chosen for us to stop in, MapQuest directions, and a list of hotel reservations—for two rooms in each place—along with the estimated driving time and mileage for each leg of the journey. And if she had tried really hard, she wouldn't have been able to pick less interesting places to break up the trip: Gallup, New Mexico. Tulsa, Oklahoma. Terre Haute, Indiana. Akron, Ohio. "That's what my mother mapped out," I said, as I pulled on my seat belt and snapped it in, taking a deep breath and then letting it out. I could feel my heart hammering in my chest, and we weren't even moving yet, which didn't seem to me to be a good sign.

"Do you have GPS?" he asked, flipping through the pages. I saw his expression grow less cheerful as he did so, and I figured that he must have reached the part about Tulsa.

"No," I said. We'd had it in the other car, but we no longer had the other car, and I didn't really want to go into why. "But I'm a pretty good navigator," I said, reaching around to the backseat and grabbing the road atlas. "And I think she printed out the directions for each location."

"She did," Roger said, still frowning down at the papers. "Do you know why she planned the trip this way?"

I shook my head. "I think she did it by mileage."

"Oh," he said. He looked through the pages again, at the maps and lists of hotel reservations, and seemed a little disappointed. "Well, that makes sense."

"You know that I don't . . . ," I started. I wanted to find out what he knew without actually telling him anything. I cleared my throat and started again. "You know I'm not driving, right?"

"That's what my mother told me," said Roger, putting the stack of paper on the console between us. "Do you not have your license?"

I look at him, shocked. I studied his expression for a moment, trying to figure out if he was asking this question genuinely. He seemed to be. I felt my heart start to beat a little faster, but with relief this time. *He didn't know*. He hadn't heard the details. He had no idea what I'd done. It felt freeing, like I could breathe just a little bit easier. "No," I said slowly. "I have my license. I'm just not . . . driving right now." Which was a terrible explanation, but it was all I could come up with on the spot.

"That's too bad," he said. "I love driving."

I had once too. It had once been my favorite thing to do. Driving was when I organized my thoughts and listened to music, my therapy on wheels. It seemed wrong that in addition to all the things that had been taken from me, that had to go as well. I gave a shrug that I hoped seemed nonchalant. "I guess it's just not my thing."

"Well, okay," Roger said, handing me the stack of papers. I flipped through to the first set of directions, which would take us to Gallup in approximately nine hours. "Ready?" he asked again, seeming much less enthusiastic now.

I nodded. "Let's go." I handed Roger the keys, and he started the car. I closed my eyes for a moment as the car moved forward, trying to tell myself that I was fine, that everything would be okay. I opened them in time to see the garage door closing, as Roger signaled to pull around the cul-de-sac. I took a last look at the house, realizing that the next time I saw it—if I ever saw it again—it wouldn't be mine anymore. WELCOME HOME, the sign exclaimed, and it was the last thing I saw before the house disappeared from view.

I turned to face forward, reminding myself to keep breathing and taking in the neighborhood flashing past my window. I glanced over at Roger, feeling that the reality of this situation hadn't hit me until now. I was going to be stuck sitting very close to a guy I didn't know, constantly, for the next four days. A really cute guy I didn't know. I looked out the window as Roger made his way toward downtown Raven Rock. It was the all-day-every-day aspect of this that was troubling me. I knew I could seem like I was actually doing okay, so long as you didn't talk to me for too long. I wasn't an actress for nothing. But I knew that if anyone looked too closely, they would see that I was so far from being okay that it was laughable. And I was just worried that so much time together would give Roger the opportunity to see that.

As we headed to the main street downtown, and Roger sped up to match the traffic, I found I couldn't help wincing and pressing my foot down, hard, on the phantom brake every time it seemed like he got too close to the car in front of us. And the cars in the other lane and across the intersection were just flying by. Why did everyone have to go so *fast?*

The car behind us honked, loud, and I felt myself jump a little. I saw Roger glance over at me as he put his turn signal on to make the right onto Campus Drive. "You okay?" he asked.

"Fine," I said quickly, staring at the small green arrow blinking on and off, fighting down rising panic as I realized how he intended to get us to the freeway. "But you know, it's faster if you take Alvarez."

"Really?" he asked. "But we can just cut over to—"

"No," I said, more loudly than I'd meant to. "If you just go straight here, you can get to the 2 that way. It's faster."

The light changed, and Roger paused for a moment before

turning his signal off and going straight. "Sure," he said.

I stared out the window, taking deep breaths and trying to calm myself down, trying not to think about how close I'd just come to seeing the intersection at University. I had no idea if the ribbons and signs were still there, or if they'd disappeared into recycling bins and birds' nests. I didn't want to know. I just wanted to get away from it as fast as possible.

As we got closer to the freeway, it struck me—probably a little late—that this would be one of the last times I would see my town. Raven Rock wasn't going to be my home anymore. And I'd never even really taken the time to think about it. It was just the place I'd always lived, kind of boring, kind of confining. But *mine*, with all my history, good and bad, wrapped up in it. I saw landmarks from my life passing the window at faster speeds than I was comfortable with. The Fosters Freeze where Charlie and I used to walk to get shakes, and the Jamba Juice where he deeply humiliated me when we were twelve. He told me that if you yelled out "JAMBA!" at full volume, all the employees would yell back "JUICE!" He lied.

I turned in my seat to try to see as much as I still could, but then Roger was turning onto the freeway's on-ramp, and thankfully not saying anything about the fact that we'd taken the scenic route to get there. I looked in my side mirror to see Raven Rock getting farther away, turning into just another dot on a map, just another anonymous town to be driven past. And as I watched, it disappeared from view until all I could see behind me were the other cars on the freeway.

We drove for about twenty minutes in silence. Once we were out of Raven Rock and off the surface streets, being in a car was bothering me less. On the freeway, where there were no stoplights or people who ran them, I could feel myself relax a little bit.

And Roger seemed to be a good driver, much more comfortable in my mother's car than I had expected him to be. I kept sneaking glances across the car at him. I had never realized just how small the front seats of cars were. We seemed to be in closer proximity to each other than I had anticipated. Every time he moved, it caught my attention, and I was sitting at the very edge of my seat, pressed practically into the door, so that we wouldn't bump elbows on the console or anything. Roger just seemed to take up a lot of space, driving with the seat pushed far back, his long jeans-clad legs looking like they were almost fully extended. He drove with one hand on the wheel, the other resting on the glass of the window. This hadn't been my style—when I'd been driving I'd been a strictly ten-and-two girl. But he was in control of the car, not driving too fast, but fast enough to keep up in the carpool lane. Traffic was moving, thankfully, since on the other side of the freeway it was bumper-to-bumper—for no apparent reason, at noon on a Thursday.

"Hey," Roger said, breaking the silence in the car. He tapped the glass on the driver's side. I looked and saw a familiar yellow arrow and red sign across the freeway. "What do you think?" he asked. "You hungry?"

←——→

"I'm going to miss this," Roger said, reaching into the white paper bag sitting between us and pulling out a french fry. "I love fast food in all its forms, but nothing really compares to In-N-Out."

I took a careful bite of my burger and nodded in agreement. We were in the back of the Liberty, what Charlie and I had always called the way-back, the open space designed for storing things. The door was raised, and we were sitting with our legs dangling over the edge. The sun was getting strong, and the glare made it harder to look

directly at Roger. But my sunglasses had shattered three months ago, and I'd gotten used to squinting. The cars on the freeway rushed past to the right of the car, and to the left of us an In-N-Out employee seemed to be breaking up with her boyfriend—loudly—over the phone.

We'd taken the food to go, but when Roger struggled to take a bite of his burger while pulling out of the parking lot, it became clear that this was an eat, then drive situation, and he'd pulled back into the parking lot. I hadn't realized until Roger told me, after we'd ordered, that In-N-Out was a West Coast–only burger chain. There was no In-N-Out in Connecticut, because clearly that state was an inhospitable wasteland.

"It's annoying," Roger said, shaking the paper sack. We'd long since finished our individual containers of fries, but apparently there were still a few stragglers rolling around the bottom. Sure enough, he pulled out a small handful. "Because I missed this all year while I was at school. The closest one to Colorado is in Utah, which is a little far to go for a burger. But it might have been doable. Except for the fact that I didn't have a car."

I took a sip of my milk shake to buy myself some time to think about a response. "Colorado?" I finally asked, remembering the bumper sticker. "That's where you go?"

He nodded. "Colorado College, in Colorado Springs. It's a good school. And I have a lot of great friends. . . ." I thought I saw something pass over Roger's face for a second when he said this, but then it was gone. "Anyway, I'd planned on being here all summer. But after finals, my father began insisting that I spend the summer with him in Philly."

"That's where your father lives?" I regretted the sentence as soon as I'd said it. First of all, he'd told me that back in the kitchen. Second of all, I'd already known it. Third of all, I had a feeling that it was going to be a very long four days unless I could stop acting like such a moron.

But if Roger noticed, he wasn't letting on. "Yeah," he said, shaking the bag again and coming up with more fries. "He lives there with his new wife and her son. He freaked out when he saw my grades and said he wanted me there so I can, and I quote, 'learn some discipline.' Which sounds like a great way to spend a summer. I don't know anyone there. And what am I supposed to do in Philadelphia?"

"Eat cheesesteak?" I asked, on impulse.

Roger laughed for the first time, a loud, reverberating laugh that seemed to fill the whole space. "Right," he said. "Cheesesteak and cream cheese."

I guess neither of us could think of any more Philadelphia-related foods after that, because silence fell between us. I took another long sip of my milk shake and could feel Roger looking at me. I glanced over at him and saw that he was reading the back of my T-shirt, with the list of the cast members printed on it.

"This musical," he said. I noticed he pronounced "musical" like it was in a foreign language, like it wasn't a word he'd said very often. "You were in it?" He sounded surprised.

"Yeah," I said, turning to face him so he would stop reading my back. "I was, um, the lead." I saw Roger's eyebrows shoot up, and I looked back down at the plastic lid of my milk shake cup. I could understand his surprise. Even before it had happened, people had always seemed surprised to hear I was an actor. But I'd always loved the chance to become someone else for a few hours. Someone for whom the words had been written, every gesture and emotion plotted, and the ending figured out. Almost like life. Just without the surprises.

"So," I said after a moment, "we should probably get back on the road, right?"

Roger nodded. "Probably." He took a sip of his root beer and looked out at the freeway. "You know," he said thoughtfully, "I don't think it's going to take us four days. Some friends of mine drove cross-country, and they did it in thirty-six hours."

"Seriously?"

"Yeah. Though I don't think they ever stopped—I think they

just drove straight through. And they probably sped a lot," he added.

"Huh," I said, not exactly sure how to respond to that. It hit me that, while I didn't want to do this, Roger probably wanted to do it even less. Why would a college almost-sophomore want to spend four days transporting a high schooler across the country? Maybe this was Roger's way of saying that he wanted to get it over with as fast as possible.

"Have you ever taken a road trip?" he asked.

I turned to squint at him and shook my head, feeling very lame. I knew that he didn't mean a family excursion to see a historical landmark. He meant a *road trip*, the kind that cool people took in college. "Have you?" I asked, even though I had a feeling the answer was yes.

He nodded. "Just in-state, though. Up to San Fran, down to San Diego. And I don't know . . ." He paused and peered into the bag. He shook it hopefully, fished around inside, and came up with three fries. He took one and offered the rest to me. "Last two," he said. "Go for it." I took one, leaving one for him. He smiled and ate it, looking pensive. "I guess I just thought that this trip might be more of a real road trip," he said. "I don't know. More interesting places. And at least a route we could pick ourselves."

I took a sip of my shake, hoping my relief wasn't obvious. So it wasn't *me* he had a problem with, just my mother's version of the trip. Which was entirely understandable, given the places that she'd chosen for us to stop.

I thought about what I'd just reread in my father's book. About going out and just driving, and how you can only do it when you're young. For the first time, it struck me that this trip could be something worth recording in the scrapbook, after all. "Well," I said, not entirely able to believe I was about to suggest this. "I mean, I guess we could go other places. As long as we're there in four days, does it really matter which way we go?"

"Really?" Roger asked. "What about your mother's reservations?"

I shrugged, even though my heart was pounding. It was a

legitimate question. Knowing my mother, she'd probably be calling every hotel to make sure we'd checked in. But there was a tiny, reckless piece of me that wanted to be the difficult one for once. That wanted to make her worry about *me* for a change. That wanted to show her what it felt like to be left behind. "I don't care," I said. This wasn't exactly true, but I liked the way it felt to say it. It was something Charlie would have done. And something Amy! would never do in a million years. And as I thought about the four hundred dollars in my front pocket, it occurred to me that we might be able to use it to buy just a little bit of freedom.

Roger blinked at me. "Okay," he said. He turned to face me more fully and leaned back against the window. "So where should we go?"

"We'll still get there by the tenth, right?" I asked quickly. My mother was not going to be happy we were ignoring her route, but I knew she would have a conniption if we took longer than the allotted time. "This is just a detour," I clarified.

"Just a detour," Roger agreed, nodding. He smiled at me, and I felt the impulse to smile back. I didn't, but the feeling was there, for the first time in months.

The In-N-Out employee to our left suddenly raised her volume and began screaming at her soon-to-be-ex. Apparently, his name was Kyle, and he knew exactly what he'd done. Feeling like I was overhearing something I probably shouldn't, I jumped to my feet and began to walk around to the front of the car when I saw that Roger hadn't moved. He was still listening to the breakup with a slightly nauseated expression on his face.

"Roger?" I asked.

"Right," he said quickly, getting up as well and crumpling the white paper bag. We buckled ourselves in, and Roger started the engine. "So if this is going to be a real road trip," he said, backing out of the parking space and heading toward the exit, "we need to get some road trip essentials."

"Like gas?"

"No," he said. "Well, yes," he amended, looking down at the

gauge. "But there are two things that are absolutely necessary if you're going to be hitting the road."

"And what are those?"

Roger smiled at me as he paused at a stoplight. "Snacks and tunes," he said. "Not necessarily in that order."

←——→

"How do you feel about Billy Joel?" Roger asked, scrolling through his iPod. We were still sitting in the parking lot of the Sunshine Mart, as Roger insisted that we couldn't start driving until there was a soundtrack. He'd offered to play one of my mixes, but I had put him off, letting him pick the music. Most of what was on my iPod was Broadway musical soundtracks or oldies, and it didn't seem like Roger was a secret Andrew Lloyd Webber fan.

I looked up from the road atlas. "Fine, I guess." I didn't want to tell him that most of my knowledge of Billy Joel came from the musical *Movin' Out*. I retrieved my snacks from the plastic bag, placed my cream soda in the back cup holder, and opened my Red Vines. Roger had loaded up on Abba-Zabas, telling me that they could only be found in California—making me wonder yet again why on earth anyone would ever choose to live in Connecticut. I pulled out his root beer and placed it in the front cup holder for him, then placed the snack bag behind me in the backseat.

"So Billy's in," said Roger, spinning his track wheel and clicking on the center button. "Excellent."

I focused back on the map, tracing my finger over all the freeways that crisscrossed and bisected the state of California, which seemed impossibly huge. In the atlas, it took up five pages. Connecticut, I'd seen when I flipped past it, shared a page with Rhode Island. I turned to the page that covered central California, and as soon as I saw it, I knew it was where I wanted to go: Yosemite National Park. It was a six-hour drive from Raven Rock, and part of it had been founded by my ancestors on my father's side. We used to go up every summer for two weeks—my father, Charlie, and me. We'd stopped going a few years ago, not for any specific reason. It just seemed like none of us had the time anymore. I hadn't realized how much I'd missed it until I saw it on the map, just up the interstate, half a state away. "I think," I started, then cleared my throat. Roger looked up from his iPod and at the atlas on my lap.

"Do we have a heading?" he asked, smiling.

"Maybe," I said. I looked down at the map, at my finger resting on the blob of green that represented the national park. What if he didn't want to go? What if he thought it was stupid? I wasn't even sure why I wanted to go. Lately I'd been doing my best to avoid places that reminded me of things I didn't want to be reminded of. But it was suddenly the only place I wanted to be. I took a breath. "Have you ever been to Yosemite?"

Travel Scrapbook

SUNSHINE MART
****
Santa Bonita's
Oldest Convenience Market...
since 1972!

GAS SALE 87 GRADE	42.95
CREAM SODA	1.95
ROOT BEER	1.95
2 RED VINES	4.00
5 ABBA-ZABA	6.95
TOSTITOS	3.95
DORITOS	3.95
SKITTLES	1.99
REESE'S PIECES	1.99

TOTAL: 69.68
DATE: June 06
PAYMENT:
CREDIT
AMELIA E. CURRY
XXXX XXXX XXXX 8766
WE APPRECIATE YOUR BUSINESS!
COME BACK SOON!

*You ain't never caught a rabbit, and
you ain't no friend of mine.*
—*Elvis Presley*

NINE YEARS EARLIER

"Are we there yet?" Charlie whined, kicking the back of my seat. I turned around to glare at him, slouched in the backseat and staring out the window.

"Stop it," I said. "It's annoying." Charlie responded by kicking my seat again, and harder this time. "Daddy!" I said, turning to my father, who was driving.

"Yes?" he asked. He was tapping his fingers on the steering wheel in time with Elvis, totally oblivious to what was going on behind him.

"Charlie's *kicking* me."

"Is he really?" My father shifted his eyes to the rearview mirror. "That's an impressive reach, son!"

"I mean," I said, frustrated, "he's kicking my *seat*."

"Ah," my father said. "Well, in that case, please refrain. Your mother isn't going to want footprints on the upholstery."

Charlie muttered something I couldn't hear and, I saw in the rearview mirror, slumped even farther down in his seat. On these trips, I was always allowed to sit in the front seat, because when I was little I'd gotten carsick. I no longer did, but now it was habit. When my mother drove with us on long trips, she sat in the back with Charlie, and the two of them read their respective books the whole time, the only sound being an occasional burst of laughter from something one of them had read. I'd see Charlie pass my mother whatever he was reading at the time, his finger on the page to mark what had made him laugh, and I'd see my mother smile in return.

But when we were in the car, their private world of books didn't bother me for once. Because my father and I had our own routine in the front seat, and I had responsibilities.

He had taught me to read a map about the time I was learning to read, and I was always the navigator. "All right, my Sancho Panza," he'd say. "Tell us our course." I had no idea what he was talking about, but I didn't care. I was important. I was in charge of making sure we were going the right way and, if there was traffic or a road closed, finding an alternate route. When a CD needed changing, I was in charge of putting in the next one. But it wasn't like there was a lot to choose from. Generally, when my father was driving, it was all Elvis, all the time.

He'd put two packs of Life Savers in the cup holder, and I was allowed to have as many as I wanted, provided that when he held out his hand, I was ready to unwrap one and drop it in his palm.

Charlie kicked my seat again, this time a repetitive pattern that grew increasingly annoying. Rather than giving him the satisfaction of turning around again, I just stared straight ahead and helped myself to another Wint-O-Green.

Whenever it was just the three of us, Charlie became especially annoying. He was always more fidgety than I was, and reading was the only thing that had ever calmed him down.

The kicking grew harder, and I whirled around in my seat again. "*Stop* it!"

"Come on, son," my father said, looking behind him. "Tell you what—you can pick out the magnet this time, how about that?"

"Whatever," Charlie muttered, but he sat up a little straighter and stopped kicking.

"And do we see it approaching?" asked my father, turning down "Hound Dog" for the occasion. I looked out the window to my left, and there it was. Yosemite. There was the small wooden guardhouse, and the guard in his green uniform outside it, collecting twenty dollars from every car that passed through and giving them a permit and a map. Then he would wave us through the gate, allowing us to enter another world. I tipped my head back as far as it would go to look up at the trees.

"We see it," Charlie called from the backseat, and I held my breath, waiting for my father to say what he always said when we passed through the gates.

"We're back," he said, "you glorious old pile of rocks. Did you miss us?"

ROGER PLAYLIST #1

"Leaving California" aka "Hitting the Road" aka "Snacks Are Important, But Not Quite as Important as Tunes"

SONG TITLE	ARTIST
"Going to California"	Led Zeppelin
"Drive Away My Heart"	Ida Maria
"California in Popular Song"	The Lucksmiths
"I See You"	Mika
"Travel Song"	Someone Still Loves You, Boris Yeltsin
"Miss California"	Jack's Mannequin
"The General Specific"	Band of Horses
"I'm Movin' Out (Anthony's Song)"	Billy Joel
"Life in the Fast Lane"	Eagles
"Birds of a Feather"	The Rosenbergs
"Limelight"	Rush
"All My Stars Aligned"	St. Vincent
"Unhurried Hearts"	Harlem Shakes
"The Wild"	Princeton
"I Stand Corrected"	Vampire Weekend
"In California" (Live)	Neko Case
"Nobody Lost, Nobody Found"	Cut Copy
"Vanilla Twilight"	Owl City
"Adrift"	Jack Johnson

CALIFORNIA REPUBLIC

CAMP CURRY
YOSEMITE NATIONAL PARK

GUEST SERVICES

June 6 / 8:21 p.m.
Number of guests: 2
Reservation: No

Accommodation Requested:
Cabin with Bath
Cabin without Bath

Accommodation Available:
Canvas-Tent Cabin/ 1 bed

Note:
Guest(s) gave specific instructions to contact them
immediately if any of the cabins with more than
one bed became available.

Duration of guest stay: 1 night
Cost: $40.00
CASH

BE BEAR AWARE!!

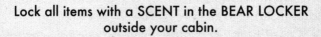

Remove ALL objects that have a scent from your car.
This includes: soap, shampoo, toothpaste, trash,
makeup, perfume, drinks, food, coolers,
EVEN IF THEY ARE EMPTY.

Lock all items with a SCENT in the BEAR LOCKER
outside your cabin.

Yosemite is NOT RESPONSIBLE for loss of,
or damage to, your property.

I'd like to dream my troubles all away on a bed of California stars.
—*Wilco*

"Wow," Roger said as we stepped out of the reservations office. "Bears, huh?"

"Bears," I confirmed. I was relieved that there had been a cabin available at all. Apparently, most people made reservations for their cabins months in advance, something that hadn't occurred to me, as my father had always taken care of that. But they'd had a cancellation, and we'd gotten the last available cabin. Not the kind of cabin we always used to stay in, but one of the canvas-tent cabins. It had only one bed, which I was trying not to think about at the moment. But it had taken us so long to get there—and then an hour just to get to Camp Curry once we'd reached the Yosemite gates—that having to turn around would have been really depressing.

After we'd paid for the room, we'd had to watch a video of a bear mauling a station wagon, then sitting on the ground and eating the chips the owners of the station wagon had left behind at their car's peril. Watching it, I actually wondered why the camera operator didn't do something, or at least send someone to warn the station-wagon family. But the message we were meant to take away was that bears at Yosemite were dangerous, especially to vehicles. And then we'd had to sign releases saying that we wouldn't sue if our car got mauled, even if we *had* taken the chips out.

We walked back over to the main parking lot, down by the Curry Dining Pavilion—what we'd always called the lodge.

Although it was growing dark, there was still enough light to see to get around. Which was a good thing, because when it got dark at Yosemite, it got *dark*. There were no lights around anywhere, except by the lodge. Which made it easier to see the stars, but harder to find your cabin. As we walked down the paved path, I noticed Roger looking up, mouth hanging slightly open. I looked up as well, at the scenery that I could still make out. Even though it wasn't my first time there, Yosemite was still stunning. There were mountains and huge, ancient trees everywhere, making you feel tiny. The air was clearer, and crisper, and had always made me want to take more deep breaths. It had always seemed to me to be a place apart, with none of the normal rules that applied elsewhere. For example, having to take your shampoo out of your car to stave off hungry wildlife.

We packed up all the snacks, and took my one suitcase and Roger's two out of the car. Then we set off to find Cabin 9. I soon realized, when the paved path turned to gravel and wood chips, that there was a reason most people coming to Yosemite didn't bring big rolling suitcases. Mine kept getting caught on the wood chips and flipping over, and refusing to roll. Not to mention the fact that the people walking by—the ones who'd prepared to be at Yosemite, carrying flashlights and wearing fleece vests—probably thought I looked ridiculous. But I finally got it up to the cabin, where Roger was standing outside, looking down at his phone.

"All set?" he asked, looking a little distracted.

"Yep," I said, then inwardly cursed myself. The cabin, as advertised, was made of white canvas, with a green-painted door. A set of four steps and a railing, also painted green, led up to it. The bear locker was at the bottom of the steps. Roger and I went through our things and locked anything that bears might think was food—that is, *everything*—inside the metal box, making sure that it was latched closed. I looked at it a little dubiously. The cabins we used to stay in hadn't had these, and I wasn't confident that this little metal box could withstand hungry bears, especially when station wagons were no match for them. I also didn't like the fact that it was so close to the cabin. Wasn't that kind of like setting the appetizer right next to the main course?

Trying not to follow this line of thought to its conclusion, I took the small brass key they'd given me and opened the cabin door. I found the light switch just inside and turned it on. The cabin was very small, with the one bed taking up most of the room. The bed was metal, painted white, and unmade, with a set of sheets and two gray scratchy-looking blankets resting on top. Clearly these were not luxury accommodations. But the bed looked *small*. I doubted it was even queen-size.

"Rustic," Roger said, looking around at the cabin, which was the same white canvas on the inside, with green-painted wooden beams crossing it. There was a chair in the corner, and a wooden dresser with a wood-framed mirror. And that was it. "But I'd expect nothing less," he added, setting down his duffel bag and backpack and taking out his phone again.

I looked back at the bed, which seemed to be drawing all my attention. "Look," I said haltingly, not exactly sure where I was going with this. "About the bed situation . . ." I didn't want him to think that I'd *wanted* a cabin with only one bed. "I'm really sorry about it."

"Why?" asked Roger. "Do you snore?" He smiled as he asked this, but I could see that he was blushing a little. "And it's just for tonight."

"Right," I said. Since we hadn't actually left the state of California, but had just moved up it—when we were supposed to be in New Mexico—I knew we were going to have to do a lot of driving tomorrow. But presumably, wherever we ended up, there would be two separate hotel rooms.

"My only thing is that I have to sleep on the right side," he said. "My girlfriend—" He stopped and cleared his throat. After a moment, he continued, "Well, I mean my ex-girlfriend, she always had to sleep on the left. So I guess it's just ingrained."

"Oh," I said, turning over what he'd just said. That right now he was single. But that there had been a girl in the picture, one who'd changed his sleeping habits. And that the way he said "girl-friend" sounded a lot like the way I said "parents."

Even though I hadn't realized I'd formed an opinion, I guess I'd just assumed that Roger had a girlfriend. He seemed too cute and too nice not to have one. And there was just something about him that made him seem taken. The fact that he wasn't suddenly made me a little nervous.

"Well, the left is fine for me," I said, hoping it would be. I had never stayed the night in Michael's dorm room, so I hadn't shared a bed with anyone since Julia, when we were in seventh grade and sleeping over at each other's houses every weekend. I had no idea what it would be like to share a bed with a guy. Especially a cute, older, apparently single guy.

"Awesome," Roger said, still sounding distracted. "So, I'm going to make a phone call." He headed for the door.

"You can make one here," I said, taking my own cell out of my pocket to check for bars and seeing I had a missed call from my mother. "There's reception."

"No, that's okay," he said, speaking quickly. "I'll give you some time to get settled, and then I'll meet you down by the lodge, okay?"

"Oh," I said, realizing a moment too late that he obviously wanted privacy to make the call. "Sure."

He was out of the cabin a second later, raising one hand to me in a wave and letting the door bang shut behind him. I waited a moment, then snapped off the lights and stepped out of the cabin, locking it behind me. Then I sat on the top step and looked around, shivering slightly. I'd forgotten how cool it could get, even in the summer. It was almost totally dark out, but the trees were casting their shadows on the ground because the moon was out—and it was incredibly bright and clear. I could see Half Dome, Yosemite's most famous mountain, to my left, and it was all achingly familiar.

It was just me—and who I was with—that was completely different. "I'm back," I said softly, "you glorious old pile of rocks. Did you miss me?"

←——→

"Hi, you've reached Pamela Curry. Please leave a message with your name and number, and I will return your call as soon as I am able. Thank you."

Beep.

"Hi, Mom, it's Amy. I guess I missed you. Darn. But things are fine. The drive was fine. And now we are at our hotel and checked in and everything. So everything is going according to plan! I'll try to talk to you tomorrow. Tell Grandma hi for me."

←——→

I stood on the steps outside the cabin and tried to make myself go inside. This had been going on for a while now. I knew that with every minute that passed, Roger was probably thinking I was having some sort of intestinal problem, since I'd left to walk to the bathrooms to get ready for bed about twenty minutes ago.

I thought I'd be okay with the whole sleeping-in-the-same-bed thing when the moment came. I really did. I'd met Roger at the lodge, where we'd had dinner and been talked at by two incredibly loquacious dentists from Palm Desert. Then we'd watched the evening entertainment, an informational video on *Yosemite and Its History*, and then we'd headed back to Cabin 9 to go to bed.

I'd even been fine with it when Roger had gone out to the bathrooms to get ready. It was only when he came back, wearing a blue and gray Colorado College T-shirt and a pair of black mesh shorts, that the reality of it hit me. Not only would I have to sleep next to Roger, but I would have to sleep next to him while he wore pretty much just his underwear.

I gaped for a moment, then grabbed my own sleep things, retrieved my toiletries from the bear locker, and headed to the bathrooms to get changed. The bathrooms were located down the path from our cabin, and I walked down it, keeping an ear out for the sound of bears and trying to seem as unappetizing as possible. I put on the least-revealing sleepwear I had—sweatpants and a long-sleeved shirt—then brushed my teeth and washed my face, taking my time, hoping against all odds that by the time I got back, the reservations office would have miraculously found another cabin.

But I knew this wasn't really a possibility. I'd locked my things in the bear locker and was now trying to get myself to open the door and go inside.

I just didn't *want* to. I didn't want to have to sleep in the same bed with someone I barely knew. I wanted to be back home, in my own bed, with my parents down the hall and Charlie next door. I'd just always assumed those constants, so basic, would never change. I hadn't even realized they were anything special at the time. And now I would have given anything to be back there again.

Amy! was probably having a burger right now with her football-playing boyfriend, and her biggest concern was that zit on her cheek that just *wouldn't* go away, darn it!

I heard Roger moving around inside the cabin, and I knew I was going to have to go in eventually. I took a breath and opened the door, feeling my palms get sweaty. I saw that Roger had made the bed, and neatly, the top blanket folded down. He was sitting on the bed, on the right side. I set my clothes down on top of my suitcase and walked around to the left side of the bed, feeling incredibly self-conscious and wondering what it was that I normally did with my hands. As I got to my side of the bed, I saw that Roger's T-shirt had risen up a little, exposing a strip of his back above his shorts. I looked away quickly, wondering what to do. Should I sit on the bed as well? Pull back the blanket? Wait for him to get under the covers first?

Roger turned to me. "Everything okay?" he asked. "I was starting to get worried a bear got you."

"Oh, ha ha," I said, trying for a light laugh but, even I could hear, failing miserably. "No, I'm fine. I was just, um . . ." I had no idea how to finish that sentence, so I didn't even try, and it just hung there in midair between us. "Thanks for making the bed," I said finally. "You didn't have to."

"It was no big deal," Roger said with a smile. He stood and looked at me for a moment, taking in my outfit. "You look hot."

"What? Me?" I stammered, completely flummoxed.

"Yeah," he said, still looking at me.

What? Was this some kind of come-on or something? Right before we were about to sleep in the same bed? Like this wasn't complicated enough already. "Oh. Um, thank you. I mean, not that you don't, but I'm not sure that you should—I mean . . ."

"Oh, no," Roger said quickly, and I could see that he was blushing again. "No. I mean—I meant what you're wearing. Are you going to be too warm?"

Oh. I momentarily wondered if it would be possible to get one of the bears lurking outside to come in and kill me. "Oh, right," I said, trying to force my voice to stay upbeat. "Um, I think I'll be okay. I always get pretty cold here at night." Roger nodded and stretched, revealing a flat strip of stomach this time, and I looked away again, wishing that he could have worn a slightly longer shirt. "Are you going to be okay?" I asked. "Warm enough, I mean?"

"Oh, sure," he said, pulling back the covers on his side. Relieved to have some direction, I pulled them back on my side as well. "I'm always hot at night. Hadley used to call me the space heater."

I walked over to the door, checked that it was locked, and turned out the light. But because of the white walls, and the moonlight filtering in, there was still enough light to see to get back to my side of the bed. Roger got in, and I climbed in as well, staying as far over as possible on my side while still actually being on the bed. I kept both arms pressed against my sides and looked up at the ceiling, acutely aware of how close together we were. I could have reached out and touched him without even extending my arm. I could feel the rhythm of his breathing. "Hadley?" I asked after a moment, figuring this was the ex-girlfriend—the one whose side of the bed I was now occupying.

"Yeah," said Roger, and I could hear a strain in his voice. "My girlfriend. My *ex*-girlfriend," he corrected immediately, sounding annoyed with himself. "She . . . she was just . . ."

I waited, turning my head slightly to look over at him, but apparently what Hadley was wasn't going to be articulated. Roger sighed deeply, then tucked his arms behind his head. I took in the gun show for a moment, then looked fixedly up at the ceiling.

"What about you?" he asked, turning his head toward me. "Is there anyone in the picture?"

I immediately thought of Michael, but wasn't sure how he fit into any picture I wanted to tell Roger about. "Um, not really," I said. Then, thinking that made me sound too pathetic, I added, "I mean, there was this guy, but it was just . . . I mean it was mostly just . . . I mean, it wasn't really . . ." I stopped, wondering where all my adjectives, nouns, and verbs had gone. Mr. Collins would not have approved. "I don't know," I finally concluded brilliantly. "Not really."

I looked over and saw that Roger was now on his side, facing me, curled up a little bit. I usually slept—or tried to sleep—on my side as well. I looked up at the ceiling, mentally preparing myself for another long night. I'd started having insomnia for the first time in my life over the last month. I'd lie awake for hours before finally giving up and going to watch the Weather Channel. For whatever reason, I found it soothing—the preciseness of it, the way it essentially predicted the future. I liked that the meteorologists could tell people across the country what their days and weeks would bring. They were preparing people, letting them know that a storm might be coming toward them. And that way, you weren't caught totally off guard and unprepared when it finally hit you. After watching the Doppler radar for a while, I could usually doze off for an hour or two. But here, without the seven-day forecast, with bears potentially hanging around outside, and sharing a bed with Roger, I knew I wouldn't be getting any sleep.

"Well, good night, Amy," Roger said.

"Good night. Sleep tight. Don't let the bears bite," I added automatically. It was how my father and Charlie and I had always said good night when we were here. I hadn't thought about it in years, and yet there it was, just waiting for the right prompt.

Roger laughed, a quieter version of the laugh I'd heard earlier. "Right," he said. "You too." I saw his eyes close and figured he'd probably be asleep immediately. I felt irrationally envious of him—someone who could just drift off, someone whose thoughts didn't keep him up. Someone like I'd once been.

Roger's breathing got more even, and slower, and I could feel myself start to relax a little on my side of the bed. There was a little stretch of bed between us that Roger didn't seem to be drifting toward. Moving as incrementally as I could, I turned myself over to lie on one side, facing Roger, and curled up.

And even though I knew that sleep was going to be impossible, I let my eyes close as well.

←——→

The next thing I knew, I was awake again. I squinted at my watch and was shocked to see that it was three a.m. I'd fallen asleep—even without the benefit of the Doppler radar. I sat up and looked around. The cabin was darker than it had been before—maybe the moon was behind a cloud—and I was alone in bed. I immediately felt myself begin to panic, which was ironic, considering how much I hadn't wanted to share the bed in the first place. But now it felt much too big. I was starting to run though a list in my head of where Roger could have gone—the bathroom, off to do a little late-night stargazing—when I heard his voice outside. I looked to the door and saw that it was slightly ajar, and I could hear him talking.

"Hey, Hadley," I heard him say, "it's me again." I looked around and wondered what I should do. Turn on my iPod? I knew I wasn't supposed to hear this, but at the same time, I really, really wanted to. Before I could make a decision, Roger continued. He sounded nervous.

"So I guess you're not in. Or maybe you're sleeping. I guess it's pretty late there. Or early. So if this woke you, I'm sorry. . . ." He paused. "I'm up in the mountains in California, and the stars are so beautiful here. I wish you could see them. I'm . . ." His voice trailed off. "I just don't understand what happened, Had. Or why you haven't been in touch. It's not really like you. So I . . . I don't know. Anyway, give me a call if you get this, okay?"

I waited to hear him say good-bye, but nothing followed that. Figuring that he'd be heading in soon, I lay back down and closed my eyes, pretending to be asleep so he wouldn't know I'd heard him.

But the next time I opened my eyes, it was fully light out, and I could hear birds—some chirping, some squawking—all around me. I looked at my watch and saw that it was eight o'clock. I looked across the bed at Roger, his head just a hand's distance away from mine. He was sleeping soundly, the covers falling off his shoulder. I watched him for a moment, hoping this wasn't creepy, just taking in what it was like to see someone when they looked so peaceful, when all their defenses were down. I looked away, then rolled out of bed and stretched. I'd just slept more soundly than I had in months.

Travel Scrapbook . . .

This is what
I had for
breakfast

This is what Roger
had for breakfast

Curry Dining
Pavilion

Yosemite in the morning

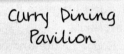

CURRY MARKET

1 Yosemite mug—"AMY"   4.95
1 Skittles   1.95
1 Postcard   1.24
1 Disposable camera   9.99

TOTAL: 18.13

CURRY MARKET

1 Yosemite mug—"ROGER"   4.95
1 Reese's Pieces   1.95
1 "Bear Necessities"
T-shirt   12.99

TOTAL: 19.89

You'll be missed, Miss California.

—Jack's Mannequin

After Roger woke up, we headed to the lodge, a building I'd always loved. It was stone, with an enormous fireplace where people tended to congregate. Between the wooden decor and the constantly burning fire, it was the kind of place that made you want to curl up with hot chocolate, even in July. And decorating it were pictures of my long-ago ancestors, who'd descended on Yosemite more than a century before and set up a camp for profit. Eventually it had been made part of the park. It seemed like the main thing my ancestors had been responsible for was the "Firefall," in which flame was poured, nightly, down a chute carved into a mountain. The Firefall was stopped in the sixties, mostly because people were amazed that it hadn't killed anyone yet. After I'd given Roger the brief tour of my family history, we ate breakfast.

Or, more accurately, *I* ate breakfast. Roger ate the kind of meal usually reserved for holiday dinners and people with tapeworms. Luckily, it was a buffet, and all-you-can-eat, a policy I had a feeling they might be revising after our visit. As Roger came back with his third heaping plateful—this one focused on various meat groups—he raised his eyebrows at my plate. "Is that all you're eating?" he asked.

"It is," I said, taking a sip of orange juice. I'd already had oatmeal, two muffins, and a banana, which seemed like more than enough for me. "I'm pretty full."

Roger shook his head. "You should carb up," he said. He settled into his chair, picked up the *Yosemite Guide* we'd taken on our way in, and began reading it while eating a piece of sausage. "There's a lot going on today—hiking, walks, something called Badger Pass—and you're going to need the energy."

He handed me the paper, and I pretended to read it as I looked at him over the top of it. "So how'd you sleep last night?" I asked as casually as I could.

"Great," Roger said, but I noticed that he was concentrating very hard on his Canadian bacon. "I was out like a light. How about you?"

"Oh, fine," I said lightly. I looked across at him and realized that there was more to Roger than I'd assumed. And that I was not the only liar sitting at the table.

←——→

"Hi, it's Amy's phone. Leave a message and I'll get back to you. Thanks!"

Beep.

"Hi, Amy, it's your mother. I guess we're playing phone tag. Glad you made it to New Mexico, and I hope by now you two are well on your way to Oklahoma. I called the Gallup Holiday Inn to make sure you'd checked in, but they had no record of you. But I didn't get the impression the desk clerk really knew what she was doing. So just call me back so I'll know everything's on track."

←——→

"This is beautiful," Roger said, stretching his legs in front of him and looking around. We were sitting on the outside patio of the Curry lodge, taking in the scenery—the enormous pines, the stunning mountains, the sunlight filtering through the trees. We'd checked out of the cabin and put our things back in the car, but we were close enough to it that we would be able to see if some hungry-looking bears came wandering by. Roger held up his hand to block out the sun and pushed himself to his feet. "Sunglasses needed," he said, pulling the car keys out of his pocket. He looked down at me. "Want me to get yours?"

YOSEMITE
DAILY ACTIVITIES!

—— **June 7** ——

- **Half Dome Climb***
- **Hike Around Yosemite Valley**
- **Ranger Rob's Nature Lecture: "Which Roots and Berries Are Your Friends?"**
- **Act like Ansel!—Photographic tour of Yosemite**
- **Wildflower Viewing Walk**
- **Hike-u!**

ACTIVITY CHOICES:
~~Half Dome Climb~~
~~Ranger Rob~~
~~Wildflowers~~
Hike-U

* Please note that this is a three-day, Class-3 climb recommended for experienced hikers only. Be prepared to use grappling hooks and to carry your refuse. Please join us! A waiver will be required exempting Yosemite in the unlikely event of death or dismemberment.

Name: | Cabin/Tent Number: 9
Amy Curry/Roger Sullivan

Yosemite Hike-u
Led by Ranger Carl

Welcome to this place of Serenity and Natural Beauty! The Hike-u tradition has been around for seven years now, and it is one of our favorite parts of the Yosemite hiking program. Throughout the hike, we will have designated stopping times where you can record your Feelings on the paper below.Please try to keep to the 5/7/5 pattern. Keep longer Pieces and Ideas for the Sunset Sonnet Stroll or the Couples' Couplet Constitutional.

ENJOY!

Yosemite Hike-u
Led by Ranger Carl
WORKSHEET

This is so stupid
Haikus are so very dumb.
Plus, getting blister.
—Amelia E. Curry

You were the one who
Wanted to go on the hike
Of Half Dome, 'member?
—Roger H. Sullivan

That was before I
Read the fine print, which was
Very very very very very scary.
—A.E.C.

Amy, I don't think
Haiku are supposed to rhyme
Or repeat same words.
—R.H.S.

Yosemite Hike-u
Led by Ranger Carl
WORKSHEET

Is the plural of
Haiku really haiku, Rog?
I doubt it somehow.
—A.E.C.

Like mice, like moose, like
Aircraft, plural is the same.
And "Rog"? Stretching, "Ame."
—R.H.S.

Ranger Carl is mad
His face turns red when he yells,
"Don't hold up the group!"
—A.E.C.

Ranger Carl needs to
Allow some slow people more
Time to count meter.
—R.H.S.

Yosemite Hike-u
Led by Ranger Carl
WORKSHEET

Was that referring
To me? I take some offense
I just don't like Carl.
—A.E.C.

Poor, poor Ranger Carl
Yelling, red-faced, and sunburned
And fly is open.
—R.H.S.

Wait, is it really?
I had not yet noticed that—
Oh my God. Hee hee.
—A.E.C.

"That's okay," I said, but I had a feeling this statement was belied by the fact that I had to squint to look up at him.

"Really?"

"Well," I said, trying not to squint, but finding it physically impossible, "I don't actually have any right now."

"They had some in the gift shop," Roger said. I'd seen them—they were mostly the sporty mirrored wraparound kind that people who were actually going to be climbing mountains bought. But I didn't want any sunglasses.

"I'm okay," I said firmly. Roger looked at me for another moment, then shrugged, heading to the car.

I closed my eyes and tipped my head back. It felt nice, like it had been awhile since I'd felt the sun on my face.

"Amy?"

I opened my eyes and saw an older woman standing in front of me, looking at me intently. She was standing right in front of the sun, and I could barely make her out. I stood up to see her more clearly. She was wearing hiking gear with a windbreaker tied around her waist, and she had close-cropped, curly gray hair. I took in all these details before something clicked into place in my memory. This was Cathy . . . Something. By coincidence, she and her husband had followed the same schedule as us for years. We'd always run into them when we were here, and we'd usually all end up sitting together in the dining hall. I think they'd even sent us a Christmas card once. Happy Holidays from the Somethings.

"Hi," I said, trying to look like I hadn't been just trying to place her. "Cathy," I said, hoping that I'd remembered her name right, and dropping my voice a little on the last syllable in case I hadn't.

"It is you," she said, reaching out and hugging me quickly before I realized what was happening. "I'd recognize you anywhere, though my goodness, you've grown up! You're such a beautiful young lady!"

Why were older people always saying things like this? Even

after they were always telling us not to lie. I just nodded, because what was I supposed to say to that?

"So where are the rest of you?" Cathy asked, looking around. "Your brother and father? Are they inside?"

I could feel my heart begin to hammer, and I was starting to get the panicky feeling that I always got whenever I thought I might have to Tell Someone. I hadn't had to say the words out loud yet, and I honestly didn't think that I could. Even the thought of saying them made me feel panicky.

"Oh," I said, hearing how my voice was already strained, feeling like my throat was closing around the words even as I tried to force them out, and hating myself and the fact that I couldn't even form a simple sentence. "They're not here this trip." I was blinking very quickly, looking down at the scratched wooden deck, hoping against hope that Cathy Something would leave it at that and go away. In my peripheral vision, I saw Roger, sunglasses on, heading toward me from the car, slowing slightly when he saw me talking to someone.

"Oh, that's too bad," she said. "Your dad was always such fun to have at dinner! How's he doing? He's well?"

"Um," I said, feeling my breath come shallowly and furiously blinking back tears. I wanted nothing else than to just disappear, go back home where I was alone and there was nobody to make me feel these things. I could feel myself very close to losing it, breaking down right on the spot, in front of Cathy. But it wasn't like I could escape—I had to stand there and let it happen. And knowing that was only making it worse. I could feel my pulse beating in my throat, and it was getting harder to breathe. The underwater feeling was creeping in. "Um," I said again, my voice breaking. Cathy seemed to notice that something was wrong—her eyebrows went up, and she frowned slightly. "He's actually . . . he's . . ." A strangled sob escaped my throat, and I looked away, knowing I wasn't going to be able to continue.

"Hi," I heard Roger say, as he approached Cathy's other side.

He stuck his hand out, turning her away from me. I noticed, even though my vision was blurred, that he was watching me over her shoulder. "Roger Sullivan. I'm a friend of the family."

"Cathy Summers," said Cathy, and I registered the last name dully in my head, crossing my arms and pressing my lips together as hard as I could. Despite this, I could still feel how they were shaking, how my chin was trembling uncontrollably. "I was just asking about the other Currys," Cathy said, her voice rising on the last word, making it a question.

Roger looked over at me, and I looked straight ahead, blinking fast, trying to force this back into retreat, trying to find the edge of okay and hang on to it. Roger took a step closer to Cathy and lowered his voice a little. "It's actually . . . ," he said, then paused and cleared his throat. "Unfortunately, Mr. Curry passed away recently."

It was all I could stand to hear. I walked toward the lodge, keeping my head down, and yanked the door open, but not before I heard Cathy's shocked gasp and the sympathetic sounds that followed. I walked as fast as I could toward the bathroom, not needing to be there to know what would follow. How shocked she was. How it was such a tragedy. And then, of course, the Question: How had it happened? Roger, at least, didn't know the answer to that one.

I pushed open the door to the bathroom, which was thankfully empty, and locked myself in the nearest stall. Then I leaned back against the cold metal door and let the crying take over. I cried into my hands, big, horrible sobs that seemed to come from somewhere deep inside. I'd never cried like this until it happened, and I hated it. This crying was huge and uncontrollable, and it also never made me feel any better. It only reminded me that I hadn't cried much yet, and so of course when I did, it was wrenching and violent. The crying attacks just seemed to point out that as much as I might want to pretend otherwise, there was a big, gaping hole in my chest, one I'd tried to cover over with leaves and a few branches. The pathetic camouflage that wasn't even fooling myself.

When the worst of it seemed to be over—when my breath was coming more regularly, with only an occasional hiccup in the rhythm—I wiped my hands over my face. Then I unlocked the door and stepped out, wincing when I saw my reflection. My eyes were bloodshot and puffy, my nose red, and my skin blotchy. I ran my hands under the water, as cold as I could get it, and splashed some on my face. Then I patted it dry with the scratchy brown paper towels, which actually seemed to make things worse.

The door swung in, and a mother entered, shepherding her little girl toward the sink. She stared at me, then looked away quickly, and I knew hiding in the bathroom all day—appealing as it sounded—wasn't really an option. I pushed open the door and almost tripped over Roger, who was sitting on the floor to the right of it.

"Hi," he said, standing, and I saw he had my purse with him. "Um, you left this outside."

I nodded and took it, staring down at the gray-brown carpet. "Thank you," I said, hearing that my voice still sounded raw. But thankfully, no longer out of control.

"Are you okay?" he asked.

Since the answer was so clearly *no*, there didn't seem to be any point in telling him that I was fine. I didn't think I was that good an actress. I just shrugged.

"Well," he said, then paused a moment before going on. When he did, it was hesitantly, like he was searching for each word before speaking it. "If you ever want to talk—or just want me to listen—I mean, I could . . ."

"Who told you?" I asked, saying the words very quickly, as that seemed to be the easiest way to get them out. "Was it your mom? Or the program on the fridge?" I didn't trust myself to look up yet, so I asked the carpet these questions.

"My mom," Roger said after a moment. "I think she went to . . . to the service." She might have. She might have ridden into St. Andrew's on an elephant and I wouldn't have had a recollection of it.

I nodded. "Do you . . ." I took a breath and forced myself to say it. I didn't think he knew. But I needed to be sure. "Do you know how it happened?"

"No," he said. "Do you want to tell me?" I shook my head, just once to either side. I could feel my lip begin to tremble again, and I bit down on it, as hard as I could. "Well," he said, after a moment. "We should probably hit the road, don't you think?"

I nodded, and when I looked up, I saw that Roger was holding out his sunglasses to me. I didn't even think about refusing, just took them and slipped them on. They were too big for me, heavy square guy sunglasses, and they slid down my nose. But at that moment, I was just grateful to have a bit of a barrier between my face and the world, if only so I wouldn't frighten Yosemite's children. We headed out of the lodge, and I gave it one last look before I stepped outside. It no longer seemed like the cozy place it had this morning. I let the door slam behind me and followed Roger to the car.

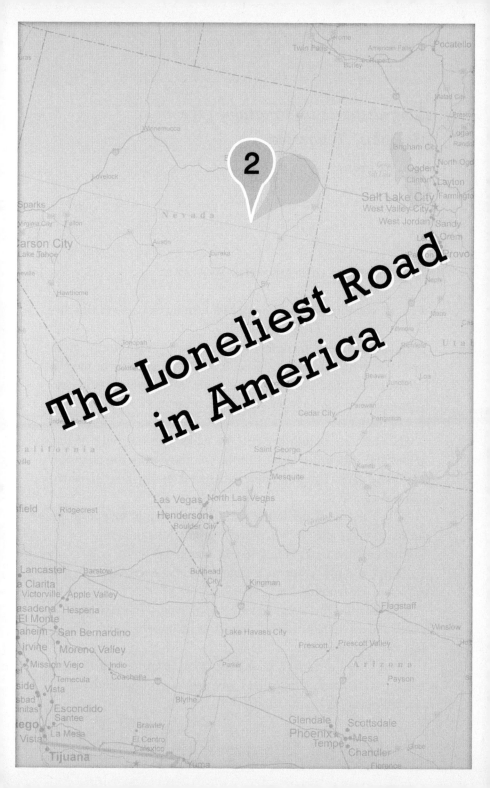

The Loneliest Road in America

2

*Long-distance information, give me
Memphis, Tennessee.*
—*Elvis Presley*

February—four months earlier

What do you think?" my father asked, turning from me to Charlie, looking incredibly proud of himself.

I glanced across the dinner table at Charlie, then to my left at my father, who was smiling wide. Then I looked down at the gift I'd just unwrapped—a Frommer's guide to Memphis, Tennessee. Charlie looked similarly puzzled by his present, a book on the history of the blues.

My mother, coming back to the table with her mug of tea, smiled and shook her head. "I told you they were too abstruse, Ben," she said. I didn't know what that meant but, as usual, Charlie seemed to.

"They're *clues*," my father said, not seeming to be put off by our reactions at all. "To where we're going this summer."

I held up my book. "I'm guessing Memphis?"

"Yes," said my father with exaggerated patience. "But not just anywhere in Memphis. . . ."

Charlie rolled his eyes and set his book down. "Graceland?" he asked, and my father nodded. *Seriously?* he mouthed to me across the table. I ignored him.

"Yes!" my father said, taking the book from me and flipping through it. "I was thinking about July. So clear your calendars, you two, we're calling on the King."

Charlie shook his head and pushed the book away. "No offense, Dad, but Graceland's kind of lame."

"Lame?" my father asked, mock-outraged. He turned to my mother for support, but she just smiled and shook her head, already flipping through the *New York Review of Books*, staying out of the conflict like she always did.

"It's not lame," I said, taking my present back from my father and paging through it.

"Have you been there?" Charlie asked.

"Have you?" I retorted, glaring at my brother. I didn't know why Charlie always had to be so difficult, and why he couldn't just go with something for once. It wasn't like Graceland was the first place I wanted to go either, but clearly it was important to Dad. Which, as usual, Charlie didn't seem to care about.

"Your sister makes an excellent point," my father said, and I heard Charlie mutter, "Of course she does," under his breath. "As the only one sitting at this table who has been to Graceland, I can attest to its non-lameness. It's an American institution. And we're going. We'll pack up the car—"

"Wait a second." Charlie sat up straight. "We're driving? To *Tennessee?*"

"We're going to discuss that," said my mother, looking up from her paper. "It's a long way, Ben."

"No better way to see America," my father said, leaning back in his chair. "And when we get to Memphis, we'll see Beale Street, and the ducks at the Peabody, and get some barbecue. . . ." He turned to me and smiled. "You ready to navigate, pumpkin?"

She's gonna make a stop in Nevada.
—*Billy Joel*

"Are we headed the right way?" Roger asked, glancing over at me. I pushed his sunglasses up and rotated the map. I had directed us out a different way, since it had looked easier to leave through the other side of Yosemite, rather than retrace our path to the park entrance.

"I think so," I said, looking at a sign as we neared it. But it was completely covered by the branches of the tree next to it. I could only see a strip of green at the top. "Oh, good," I muttered.

"I'm just a little turned around," said Roger, peering ahead of him.

"We're okay," I said, seeing, relieved, a sign that wasn't overgrown with branches and told us which way to get to the highway. "Just take the right up here."

"I'm glad you're on top of this," he said, making the right. "I'm not the greatest with directions. And I can never tell when I'm lost, either. It's a bad combination, because I always think that if I just stick with the road long enough, it'll all work out."

"Well, I'm good with maps. So I'll navigate," I said, speaking around the lump that was threatening to form in my throat.

"Excellent," he said. "You'll be my Chekov."

I looked over at him. "Anton Chekhov?" I asked. "The playwright?"

"No, Chekov, the navigator of the Starship *Enterprise*," he said, looking back at me. "From *Star Trek*."

"I've never seen *Star Trek*," I said, breathing out a tiny sigh of relief. Maybe Roger wasn't quite as cool as he'd first seemed.

"Now that's a tragedy," he said. "Though I must admit, I've never read your Chekhov."

The road, as we left Yosemite, became more winding and more deserted. It was just a two-lane road, and as we made increasingly sharp turns, it became clear that we were in the mountains. As I looked at the pine trees surrounding us, it seemed impossible that we were still in the same state we'd been in yesterday, with freeways and palm trees.

"You ready to put on some of your music?" Roger asked, as his mix started over again.

"That's okay," I said. My suspicions that Roger didn't like musicals had been confirmed when I'd seen his playlist. He seemed to like the kind of music that the in-the-know people at school always seemed to be talking about, the kinds of bands with names that didn't even sound like real names at all. Someone Still Loves You, Boris Yeltsin? That was a band? A real band, with fans other than Roger? So I had a feeling he wasn't going to be into my selection of Jason Robert Brown and Elvis. And I wasn't listening to Elvis anymore, anyway.

"Really?" he said. "I don't want to keep hogging the DJ job."

"It's fine," I insisted. I didn't want to have to watch him pretending to enjoy my music, or just tolerating it, waiting until he could switch back to his stuff. It was easier to keep listening to his. And I found that I actually liked a lot of it.

"Want to at least give me an indication of what you like?" he asked.

I shrugged, wishing he would stop grilling me about this already. "I like everything."

Roger shook his head. "Such a cop-out," he said. "If you like everything, that's basically just saying that you don't really like anything."

"I like stuff," I snapped, sharper than I meant to sound. "I just don't care, okay?" I stared out the window, immediately regretting my words. I did this a lot lately—I would suddenly get angry for no reason. That was why it was easier just not to talk to anyone.

"Well, okay," he said after a moment. "When we reach civilization, I'll make a mix."

"Just no Elvis," I said, looking out the window.

"Not a fan of the King?" he asked, and I could feel him looking at me.

I shrugged and pulled my knees up, wrapping my arms around them and staring out at the scenery passing by. "Something like that," I said.

←—→

Two hours later we had passed through the towns surrounding Lake Tahoe and were heading toward the Nevada border. When it had become clear after about an hour or so that civilization was not going to appear right around the corner, we had pulled over to the side of the road and Roger had compiled his new mix. While I had known California was big, I had never realized just how big until now. It seemed impossible that we were still in the same state. We'd had a lot more mountain scenery for a while, more rocks and pine trees and sharp turns. But things had begun to flatten out a bit, and Highway 50, the winding two-lane highway we'd been on since leaving Yosemite changed to four-lanes, with two going each way.

As Roger's new mix started for the second time, he slowed the car down and pulled it over to the side of the road. I looked over at him, and he nodded ahead of the car. "I thought we had to stop and mark this moment," he said, pointing. "Check it out!"

I looked, and there it was—a smallish white sign, with blue letters that spelled out WELCOME TO NEVADA. And then, below that, THE SILVER STATE. "Wow," I said, staring at it.

"Leaving California," Roger said. "How's it feel?"

"Good," I said, without even stopping to think about my answer.

ROGER PLAYLIST #2

"What Do You Mean We're STILL in California?!" aka
"The Very Long and Winding Road" aka
"The Ballad of Amy's Lost Sunglasses"

SONG TITLE	ARTIST
"Wine Red"	The Hush Sound
"Heartbeats"	The Knife
"16, Maybe Less"	Calexico/Iron and Wine
"Human"	The Killers
"West Coast Friendship"	Owl City
"Forest for the Trees"	Alright Alright
"Buildings and Mountains"	The Republic Tigers
"Transcontinental"	Pedro the Lion
"It Won't Be Long"	The Smithereens
"Drive Away"	The All-American Rejects
"She's the One"	Caribou
"Next Exit"	Interpol
"We Are Lost"	The Like
"Get Back (Where we Started From)"	Army Navy
"Get Gotten"	Ben Lee
"Wandering"	The Hidden Cameras
"What Else Is There?"	Röyksopp
"Can't Go Back Now"	The Weepies

ARE WE THERE YET?

CALIFORNIA

NEVADA

(bear locker)

It did feel good. It was what I'd been thinking ever since I'd felt the desire to get out of Yosemite. It was the impulse to turn a new page, to put some distance between myself and California and everything that had happened there.

"So," said Roger, reaching into the backseat and picking up the atlas, "do we know which way we're going?"

"Yes," I said, taking the atlas from him and flipping to the page for Nevada, which suddenly looked worryingly big. And we were crossing it at the widest point, not the little tip of it you'd drive across if you went the southern route. "So here's the thing. There are only two interstates that run through Nevada. Eighty up by Reno, and 15 down by Vegas."

"Vegas?" Roger asked, peering at the map.

"Right," I said. "The Reno one is closer to us at this point, but it's still out of the way. And that puts us way up by Salt Lake City, which seems really far out of the way."

"So what's the plan?" he asked.

"Well," I said, tapping my finger on where we were, "right now, we're on Highway 50. And it looks like that will take us all the way across Nevada and into Utah. And then a little ways into Utah, we can get onto Interstate 70."

"There are no interstates that go through the middle of Nevada?" Roger asked, looking over at the map. "Huh," he said, after staring at it for a moment. "There really aren't, are there?"

"But I think that's our best bet," I said, studying the map. As I did, I realized that in terms of logistics, Yosemite hadn't been a great pick. It had taken so long to get to, and so long to get out of, and now it seemed it was going to be challenging crossing Nevada. Apparently, not many people chose to leave California by way of a national park. "Think we're still going to be okay with the time-line?" I asked, acutely aware of the fact that we were supposed to be closing in on Tulsa at the moment, not just venturing out of California.

"Probably," said Roger, still looking down at the map. "I'm

sure we'll be able to make up the time. And I think your mother will understand if we're a day late."

I wasn't so sure about that, but I nodded. "So where should we head?" I asked. "I picked Yosemite. Where do you want to go?"

"Well," Roger said, glancing up at me for a moment, then back down at the map, and flipping to the page for Colorado. "It looks like if we get on the interstate in Utah, and follow that through Colorado, we'll hit Colorado Springs."

"Pretty close," I said. It wasn't, exactly, but it was close-ish. I looked up at him, surprised that he would want to go someplace he'd already been. "Is that where you want to go?"

"Well, it might make sense," he said, not looking at me but fiddling with the volume on the iPod. "We'll definitely have a place to crash, free. And I can show you around the campus, see which of my friends are around. . . ." He said this last part very quickly.

"Sure," I said, turning the pages back to Nevada. "That's fine with me."

"Great," he said, looking incredibly relieved. "So, Highway 50?" he asked. "Shall we?"

"Let's," I said, nodding, and Roger signaled and pulled back on the road.

After two hours, we realized something was wrong. The highway had switched from a four-lane road to a two-lane road at some point, with one lane going in each direction. But that in itself wasn't worrying, as we'd encountered several stretches of those near Yosemite. What was different was that suddenly there just wasn't . . . anything. The road stretched out ahead of us, a straight line extending as far as I could see. There were mountains in the distance in front of us and mountains in the distance behind us, but mostly there was just a huge, open, deserted landscape, cut down the center by the two-lane highway. And nothing else. The flatness of it was a big change from the winding mountainous roads near Yosemite. There were what looked like scrub brushes on the side of the road. I found it hard to believe that only a few hours ago, I'd been surrounded by pine trees.

We continued to drive, and I noticed that Roger was sitting up a little straighter, looking around as well. There was just *nothing*. No gas stations, no mini-marts, no fast-food restaurants. And there were almost no other cars. Occasionally there would be one behind us, but it would inevitably pass us. It wasn't like there needed to be a passing lane—you could see ahead of you for what looked like miles. Very occasionally a car or semi came roaring up the opposite lane. But in two hours, we'd only seen about three other vehicles.

"Um," I said when I couldn't take it any longer. "Is it just me, or is this kind of strange?"

"Very," said Roger. His expression was troubled, and it made me realize for the first time how cheerful he normally looked.

"Should we . . . ," I started. I looked out at the road, which seemed like it just continued on, more of the same, for miles. "Should we turn around?" My heart sank a little at the thought of having to retrace our steps, lose those two hours, and still not be where we wanted to be.

"I don't know," Roger said. He was sitting up very straight now, both hands on the wheel, and his brow was furrowed. We drove without speaking for a while, just the sounds of Roger's mix playing. Finally he said, "Look, we'll have to hit a town soon, right? And once we do, we can go from there."

"Okay," I said, figuring that he had to be right. Civilization hadn't totally disappeared. At some point, we would meet up with a highway town. We had to.

An hour later we hit a town.

I had never in my life been so excited to see a gas station. It was a tiny little place, two pumps and a mini mini-mart. We pulled in, and I used my mother's card to pay for the gas. As Roger filled up, he told me what he hadn't wanted to tell me before—that we'd actually been getting pretty low, and if we hadn't come upon this town of Fallon, Nevada, when we did, we might have been in serious trouble.

When the tank was full, we used our respective bathrooms and met up inside the tiny mini-mart, which actually looked more like a house. But I didn't care. I figured that we'd just hit a strange, deserted stretch of Nevada, but soon we would be back in the happy world of roadside amenities and Golden Arches and other cars on the road.

I grabbed a cream soda from the glassed-in case against the back wall, then, after hesitating a moment, grabbed a root beer as well. Roger was studying the chip selection, but I caught his eye and held up his soda, raising my eyebrows. He nodded and gave me a small smile. I passed the candy aisle, picking up my Skittles and grabbing Roger a bag of Reese's Pieces a little grudgingly, as I'd always hated any kind of peanut butter candy. Peanut butter, in my opinion, belonged in sandwiches and nowhere else. I saw something I'd never seen before, a candy bar in a red wrapper called LOOK! It worked, because I did, and decided to try it. I met Roger up at the counter, where he was setting down a bag of BBQ chips. I added my armful of snacks, and the woman behind the counter, who was tiny and white-haired with slightly weathered skin, rang us up.

"So we just drove in," Roger said, as she punched numbers into the register using the eraser end of a pencil. "It was kind of . . . deserted."

"Course it was," she said, not looking up from her register and continuing to punch in numbers. "What did you expect?"

"Well," said Roger. He looked at me. I didn't know how to answer this either, but I jumped in anyway.

"I guess we were just surprised that there wasn't more stuff," I said. "But that stops now, right?"

She looked up at Roger, then at me, then out at the car. "California?" she asked a little dismissively, reading the white plates. I nodded. "Figures," she said. "You kids even know where you are?"

"Fallon?" I asked tentatively, hoping she hadn't meant the name of her gas station, as I'd already forgotten it.

She shook her head. "For about another minute you're in Fallon." She rang up our total, $13.11. I dug in my pocket for my mother's cash and handed her a twenty. She gave me back my change and scooped our snacks into a plastic bag. "But you've got miles and miles of road ahead of you with not much there." She handed me the bag across the counter. "Welcome to the Loneliest Road in America."

←——→

Roger and I slammed our doors and looked at each other. "Well," he said.

"Yeah," I agreed. I could hear that I sounded as shell-shocked as he did. Maybe it had been my horrified expression, but the woman behind the counter had softened slightly after she'd told us exactly what road we'd ended up on. She explained to us that Highway 50 was famously deserted, and she couldn't believe that we'd managed to make our way to it by accident. She told us to always make sure we had enough gas, as there were a few towns, but they were all more than a hundred miles apart. Then she wrote down her phone number and told us her name was Barb, and that her brother-in-law was a state trooper, and that if we had car trouble, to give her a call and she'd let him know. Then she'd sent us on our way.

Roger put the keys in the ignition but didn't start the car. "I don't know what to do," he said, rubbing his hand over his face. The worried expression was back. "I mean . . ." He looked over at me. I'd long since taken his sunglasses off, but I played with them in the cup holder when his direct look began to make me uncomfortable. He let out a breath. "Your mother is trusting me. My mother is trusting me. And they both expect me to get you across the country, and soon, and safe. And now we've gone way off course, and we're on the saddest road in the country—"

"Loneliest," I corrected, but Roger kept on going.

"And I just don't know what the best thing to do is. Should we turn around and find an interstate? And call your mother and tell her exactly where we are? Because I'm not feeling so good about this anymore. I think we might have found the Highway to Hell. We really might be in an AC/DC song at the moment." I looked up and met his eyes, then looked right back down again. "What do you think we should do?" he asked.

"I think . . . ," I said. I looked down at Barb's phone number and thought about the road we'd just driven on. I thought about facing more of it. Much more of it—according to Barb, at least eight more hours on Highway 50 before we would make it to the interstate in Utah. But to my surprise, it didn't bother me. Now that I knew why we weren't seeing any cars or people—that we hadn't actually entered some kind of *Lost*-esque purgatory—I was much more okay with it than I had been before. "I think we should keep going," I said. Roger sighed and gripped the wheel, and then let it go. "I mean, time-wise, it doesn't make sense to go back," I continued.

"But what if something happens?" he asked. "I mean, normally I stick with a road and hope it gets better, but I don't know if I can handle eight more hours of that. Do you know how to change a tire?" I shook my head. "Me neither. And despite what Barb says, I don't want to have to rely on her brother-in-law in case we have car trouble in what *literally* seems to be the middle of nowhere."

"But we'd have to go back two hours to get on the interstate anyway," I pointed out. "And there are other people driving this road. It's an American highway. It's not like we're in the outback or something."

"No," said Roger, starting the car. "But we are on the most depressed road in the country."

"Loneliest," I said. "There is a difference."

He looked over at me. "We're doing this?" he asked. And for the first time since the trip began, it felt like *we* were doing something. The two of us, making a choice, taking a leap, together.

I nodded. "We're doing this."

Roger gave me a small smile. "Well, then," he said, pulling out of the gas station. "Let's hit it."

I glanced back and saw Barb standing in the doorway, watching us. On impulse, I waved to her, and she waved back, and I looked back at her small figure until we turned a corner and she was gone from view.

Barb had been telling the truth, and Fallon ended almost as quickly as it had begun. As we left, there were signs warning that there would be no more "gas or services" for a hundred miles, and to make sure we were prepared. I saw Roger frown as he read that, but he kept going, and we were back on Highway 50.

We drove. Time seemed to pass a little differently when there was nothing to mark how far you had come, or what you were heading to. I would look at my watch, thinking an hour had passed when it had been five minutes. Or I would catch the car's clock and realized forty-five minutes had gone by in what I would have sworn was fifteen. Now that I knew what to expect from this road, it wasn't so stressful. There were still moments when the sheer aloneness of it all would cause me to have a momentary panic. But then it would subside, and I would look out the window, take in the view, and feel myself calming down.

Maybe it was because I'd never really seen anything like it before. But even though it was scary and isolated, the scenery out the window was the most beautiful thing I had ever seen. It was just stunning. I could see much more of the world than I was used to. It was like someone had opened the pages of a pop-up book, where the pop-up was our car, and everything else all around us was totally flat. It was sunny, but not squint-inducing, and Roger had since reclaimed his sunglasses. The sky was a bright, clear blue, and the few clouds that filled it seemed too picturesque to be real. There were mountains in front of us, way off at the horizon, and we never seemed to be getting any closer to them. But I didn't mind. They just added to the picture—how I'd imagined the desert looking, even though I probably wouldn't have been able to put it into words until now. And even the isolation was beginning to seem kind of cool—the shadow our car made was the only thing on the road. It was like the two of us were getting to see something nobody else was, and something that not many other people had seen.

After an hour, my butt beginning to hurt from sitting in the same position, I kicked off my flip-flops and placed one foot on the dashboard, then the other, looking over at Roger to see if he was bothered by this. But he didn't seem to be. He just looked over at me and gave me a small smile before turning back to the road. He'd put on cruise control, and it looked a little strange to see both his legs bent at the same angle, feet flat on the car's mat, like the car was driving itself into the endless horizon. I slid down a little farther in the seat and looked out the window.

We drove. Just outside a mini-town called Middlegate, we passed an enormous cottonwood tree that had hundreds—or thousands— of shoes dangling from it, casting shadows on the highway. Roger slowed down to look at it—which was easy to do, since there were no cars behind us. "You know, I've always wanted to do that," he said, looking at the tree.

"Go for it," I said, looking at the sheer oddness of the spectacle, all these sneakers and shoes and boots, joined by their laces and tossed over the branches. The car slowed even more, and I thought Roger was going to stop and do it. But then he shook his head. "It's probably pretty wasteful," he said. But I noticed him looking back at the tree in the rearview mirror as we sped up again.

About half an hour after the shoe tree, I made Roger pull over so that I could take a picture, and I realized that there was no way to ever capture the entire landscape. So I turned in a circle, taking a picture in every direction, knowing that was the only way I could come close to capturing what it looked like. I lowered my camera and stood still for a moment, just taking in the silence. Even though it probably should have been scary, standing by the side of a deserted desert highway, it wasn't. It felt strangely peaceful.

There were no other cars on the road. Just the sound of the wind, and the motor idling, and through his open window, the faint clicking sounds of Roger making another mix. I closed my eyes and let the wind whip my hair around my face, letting out a breath I hadn't known I'd been holding.

State #2: NEVADA—The Silver State

<u>motto</u>: All for Our Country

<u>Size</u>: Also big

<u>Facts</u>: Could use a restructuring of their highway system, in my opinion. Where's the love for the middle-of-the-state people?

<u>Notes</u>: State highway signs have a drawing of the shape of the state, and the highway number is inside it. Also, it's best not to drive on lonely roads unless you are AWARE you are going to be doing this.

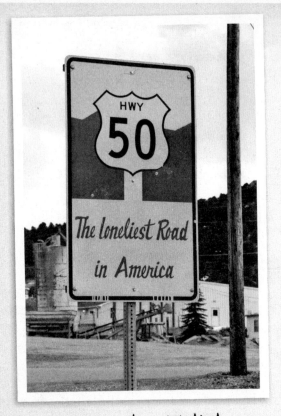

EUREKA, NEVADA.
"The Friendliest Town on the Loneliest Road!"
(It's very true.)

Travel Scrapbook

Call if you get into trouble.
(775) 555-2847
Remember to FILL UP!
      -Barb

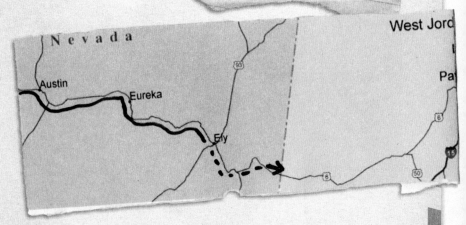

ROGER PLAYLIST #3

"Road to Nowhere" aka "Cruise Control on Highway 50"

SONG TITLE	ARTIST
"Long, Lonesome Highway Blues"	Steve Earle and the Del McCoury Band
"Go Places"	The New Pornographers
"I'm With You"	The Ponys
"Live to Tell the Tale"	Passion Pit
"Highwayman"	Willie Nelson
"Stunner Shades in Heaven"	Princeton
"Fake Empire"	The National
"They Are Night Zombies!! They Are Neighbors!! They Have Come Back from the Dead!! Ahhhh!"	Sufjan Stevens
"Moonshine"	Feeder
"Familiar Landscapes"	A New Found Glory
"Show Me What I'm Looking For"	Carolina Liar
"Le temps perdu"	Carla Bruni
"Sons and Daughters"	The Decemberists
"Strangers"	The Kinks

We're on the road to nowhere. Come on inside.
                                    —*Talking Heads*

When we reached Eureka, one of the little mini-towns, it started to get dark. We hadn't stopped to eat dinner—partly because there didn't seem to be anywhere *to* stop and get dinner, but mostly because Roger seemed to want to get across Highway 50 as quickly as possible. We loaded up on more snacks at another little gas station mart, and I added some granola bars and trail mix this time, feeling like we should have something that was closer to real food than, say, Fritos.

We headed back on the highway, the sunset beginning with a line of pink at the bottom of the horizon, and then slowly taking over the whole sky. The car's shadow was lengthening far in front of us, and I leaned my head back and took in the sunset.

"Amy?" Roger asked. I looked over to see that he was playing with the various buttons and levers around the steering wheel. "I don't know what happened—the lights came on automatically last night. Maybe I turned that off. . . ."

He was right; it was dark enough now that the headlights should have come on. "Let me see," I said, looking over to see, but soon realizing I wasn't going to be able to get close enough with my seat belt on. I unbuckled it and leaned over to Roger's side, fully aware of how close together we now were. "Um," I said. I looked at the buttons on my side of the steering wheel but didn't see the light controls anywhere. "I think they might be on your side," I said.

"Really?" he asked, looking down, causing the car to swerve slightly.

"Yeah," I said. I took a breath and leaned over him, making sure to keep looking straight ahead, very aware that if I turned my head, we'd be close enough to kiss. I saw the dial that controlled the lights on Roger's side of the steering wheel. "Hold on," I said. I reached over, being careful not to touch him, and turned the dial to the setting for the automatic lights, and they came to life immediately, two spots of light on the dark road. I moved back to my side of the car and buckled my seat belt, feeling my heart beating a little faster than usual.

"Thanks," Roger said, turning his brights on. The headlights were absolutely the only light on the road, but it wasn't pitch-black out, because the moon was huge and bright above us in the clear, enormous expanse of sky. And the stars were even better than they were at Yosemite, because there seemed to be more of them, as the sky seemed much bigger than normal. Roger reached around behind his seat, and seeing what he was looking for, I reached back and grabbed his backpack.

"This?" I asked.

"Thanks," he said. "Would you mind grabbing my glasses? They're in a brown case."

I unzipped his backpack and reached in, wishing it was light enough to see what was in there. But I found the glasses case, opened it, and handed him the glasses.

He put them on and adjusted them a little self-consciously. "I know," he said. "I only wear them for driving at night. Well, and movies. Things in the dark that are far away, I guess."

"They're nice," I said, taking in this new version of him. And they were—he now seemed a little more approachable, a little dorkier, and a lot less perfect.

"They make me look like a substitute math teacher," he said ruefully. "According to some people, that is," he added after a moment.

"But like the really *cool* substitute math teacher," I said, and was rewarded with another of his booming laughs.

"Thanks," he said. "I appreciate the support."

I put the empty case back in his bag and went to zip it when a small sketch pad at the bottom caught my eye. "You draw?" I asked, then realized he probably thought I was snooping. Which I kind of was, but unintentionally. "Sorry—I just saw it in there. . . ."

"It's fine. I draw," he said, nodding. "Not well, though. It's just something I do for fun."

"Do you mind?" I asked, lifting out the sketch pad.

Roger laughed. "Sure," he said. "But don't mock me." I held the sketchbook over the dashboard, flipping through the pages by moonlight. Almost every page was filled with small sketches. Roger had a cartoon-ish style, unless he was doing little mini-portraits, when the drawings became more realistic. Most of the portraits seemed to be of a stunningly beautiful girl with long, light hair. I figured that this was Hadley but didn't want to ask about it, feeling I'd pried enough for one night. I closed the book and zipped it back inside his bag.

"They're good," I said, but Roger just smiled and shook his head. "Are you an art major?"

"Definitely not," he said. "I'm leaning toward a history major, political science minor."

"Oh," I said. Normally, this would have been when I would have said that my father was a history professor. I pushed away the impulse. It wasn't even an option—I wasn't talking about that. But the fact that I couldn't even manage to make this simple statement caused a wave of sadness to hit me. I turned away from Roger and curled up, facing my window. I looked outside, to the endless empty landscape and zillions of stars above. Then I rested my head against the cool glass of the window and closed my eyes.

"Amy. Hey, Amy."

I started and jerked awake—I'd been dreaming. It had been March, and warm, the grass freshly cut and sticking to my bare feet. I blinked at Roger, driving in the dark, the deserted highway stretching on and on forever in front of us. Right. I was on the Loneliest Road in America. Naturally.

I tried to turn my head, immediately feeling the pull in my neck. "Agh," I muttered. It seemed that I had managed to find the most uncomfortable sleeping position possible. "Hey," I murmured, rubbing my eyes. I looked at the clock and saw that it was two a.m. "Jesus," I said, sitting up straighter. "Roger, shouldn't we stop so you can get some sleep?" The road in front of us was still dark, and still utterly deserted, the stars shining as brightly as they had been a few hours ago. It felt a little bit like we were the only two people on earth at that moment, like it was just us and our car under all that sky, the stars shining for us alone.

"That's why I wanted to wake you up," he said. Even by dashboard light, I could see he looked exhausted. His eyes seemed bleary behind his glasses. "I want to make it to Utah tonight. I'm ready to be off this road, and if we can get to Delta, we should be almost to the interstate, and then we can definitely make Colorado Springs tomorrow." Even though I appreciated this urgency, it was surprising, since he'd been the one saying we had lots of time. I wondered where this rush to get to Colorado Springs was coming from. "But I'm going to need you to keep me awake," he said.

"Oh," I said. "Sure." I looked at him, waiting for more instructions. "How should I do that?" I saw the headlights of another car coming toward us. It looked miles off in the distance, but as the only light on the horizon, it was easy to spot. Roger turned his brights down, even though the car was probably a good five minutes from reaching us.

"Just talk to me," he said, rubbing a hand across his forehead. "Make sure I answer your questions. And if you could put some new music on, that would be great."

"Okay," I said, picking up his iPod. "But we can always stop in Ely and get some sleep." On the map, it had looked like Ely was the last mini-town in Nevada before hitting Utah.

Roger shook his head. "We need to make it to Utah," he said. Since it was my choice of detour that had gotten us off schedule, I wasn't going to argue with him. "Something upbeat," he said, gesturing to the iPod. "I didn't make a new customized playlist, but I should have some older ones saved on there."

I scrolled through it and saw that most of the playlists had very generic titles—"Mix #1," "Mix #2." I scrolled up to the top, figuring I would just have to look at them and try and guess what kind of music went with his oddly named bands, when I saw a mix titled "Had to be there . . . ☺" Figuring the smiley face was a good sign, I selected it and put the iPod back in the cradle. The first song that started playing was pretty and slow, with lyrics about a love-struck Romeo.

"What mix is that?" Roger asked sharply, and I turned to him, surprised.

"The smiley-face one," I said. "I thought—"

"Something else," he said, the edge still in his voice. I noticed his hands were clenching the wheel, and he no longer seemed tired at all.

"Sure," I murmured. I hit pause, and the song stopped playing, leaving silence in the car. As I scrolled through the other mixes, the clicking of the trackball suddenly seemed very loud. I found one called "Mix #4," hoped that was safe, and selected it. Some very upbeat horns started playing, and Roger's hands unclenched. "Better?"

"Much," he said. "Sorry. I should have deleted that one."

I figured it had something to do with Hadley—which I now realized was probably part of the title—but I wasn't about to ask. So I just nodded.

"It was a mix she made me," he said after a moment. "Hadley." Her name floated between us in the car for a moment, and I couldn't help but notice that he'd pronounced her name differently, like her name, and only her name, contained all the good letters. "My ex," he added unnecessarily. But maybe it was for his own benefit, since he seemed to be having trouble remembering that part.

"Ah," I murmured, not sure what else to say. Amy! probably would have known exactly what questions to ask. She would have been sympathetic and kind, inviting Roger to talk about his feelings without reservation. She probably would not have sat silently next to him, looking out the window, afraid to ask him anything in case he returned the favor.

"Utah," Roger said, pointing out the window at the sign. We slowed, and I leaned over and looked at it. WELCOME TO UTAH! it read. And then in smaller letters underneath that, MOUNTAIN DAY-LIGHT TIME ZONE.

As we drove past it, I thought about the imaginary line we'd just crossed, and how even though I was two states out of California, nothing felt any different. Not that I'd really been expecting it to.

"So!" said Roger, turning to look at me. "You're falling down on your job here. I need to be kept awake. Ask me questions. Recite poetry. Whatever you've got."

—←———→—

"Is it a person?" I asked, yawning, six rounds of Twenty Questions later.

"Yes," Roger said. "Nineteen. Stay with me, Curry!"

I smiled at that, and it happened automatically, surprising me enough that I stopped immediately. "Are they alive?" I asked.

"No. Eighteen."

"Are they male?"

"Yes. Seventeen."

I looked at Roger, who no longer seemed in danger of falling asleep at the wheel. I had learned the hard way that history majors had a distinct advantage when playing games like Twenty Questions. But I was beginning to get a sense of the kind of answer he was continually choosing. "Is he an explorer?"

Roger glanced over at me, one eyebrow raised, looking maybe a little impressed. "Yes. Sixteen."

He'd already chosen Drake, Livingstone, and Sir Edmund Hillary. I took a guess and hoped it was right, as I wasn't sure how many more explorers I knew. "Is it Vasco da Gama?"

He sighed, but seemed happy. "Got it in five," he said. "Well done. Your turn."

"What's with the explorers?" I asked, figuring that four in a row had to be something of a theme, not just a strategy to keep beating me.

Roger shrugged, looking a little embarrassed. He ran his hand through his hair, and it stood up in little tufts all over his head. I had an impulse to reach over and smooth it down. But it was an impulse I immediately squashed. "I've always been interested in them. Since I was a kid. I loved the idea that people could discover things. That you could be the person to see something first. Or see something that nobody else had been able to."

"Is that why you're a history major?"

He smiled without looking at me. "Probably. I started reading history like an instruction manual when I was a kid, trying to figure out what all these explorers did so that I could do it too. I used to be convinced that I was going to find something really important."

"But everything's been found by now," I said. I turned to face him a little more, pulling out my seat belt to give it some slack and leaning back against my window.

"Well, technically," he said, not seeming bothered by this. "But I think there are lots of things still to be discovered. You just have to be paying attention." I pulled one knee up and rested my chin on it, thinking about this. "God, I've been talking a lot," he said with a laugh. "Your turn. Tell me something about you."

That was absolutely the last thing I wanted to do, now or ever. "Oh, I don't know," I said. "I haven't discovered anything."

"Yet," Roger said emphatically, and I felt myself smiling again. But I looked over at him, with his substitute math teacher glasses and hopeful expression, and my smile faded. He hadn't learned yet that things didn't work out just because you wanted them to.

"Right," I said, reaching over and turning up the music, a song about a fake empire that, on the second listen, I'd found I really liked.

"But I'm serious," he said. "Tell me something about you. What is your . . . biggest regret?"

I hadn't been expecting that question, but I knew immediately what the answer was, and I closed my eyes against it. The morning in March, carrying my flip-flops, my feet covered in grass clippings. The one thing I really, really didn't want to think about.

I opened my eyes and looked at him. "No idea."

Yesterday, when you were young . . .
—*The Weepies*

MARCH 8—THREE MONTHS EARLIER

"So then what happened?" Julia asked breathlessly.

"Stop it," I said, laughing into the phone. I was sitting on the front steps of the house, talking to her while my father mowed the lawn. My mother and I were always teasing him about the lawn. He tended to be kind of a slob with everything else, but about the lawn, he was beyond fastidious. It never looked like it needed mowing, mostly because he spent every Saturday morning doing just that. "There's an art to it," he always insisted. "I'd like to see you try!"

As I watched, he pivoted the mower at a sharp 90-degree angle to get the corner of the lawn. "There's really nothing to tell," I said, turning my attention back to Julia.

"Yeah, right," she said, and I could hear she was laughing too, which always made me happy, as Julia was usually a little too composed, always considering her words before she said them. "I need details, Amy."

I could feel myself smile. I'd had a date—and a pretty epic make-out session—with Michael the night before. And Julia was always the first person I told about these things. Somehow, if I didn't talk to her about it, it didn't seem real. "It was good," I said, and could hear her sigh loudly over the phone, all the way from Florida.

"Details!" she said again.

"My *dad* is out here," I said into the phone, lowering my volume. "I can't talk about this now."

"Tell Julia I say hi," my father called, as he pivoted the mower again.

"Put your back into it!" I called to him, and he smiled as he headed in the other direction, for an overgrown patch invisible to everyone but him.

"Come on," Julia said. "Give me the scoop. Things are going well with you and the college boy?"

I looked over to check that my father was out of earshot. "Yes," I said, settling back against the step, preparing for one of our marathon conversations. "Okay. So last night he picked me up at eight."

"And what did you wear?" she prompted.

"Amy," my mother said, in the doorway behind me. I lowered the phone and looked at her. She seemed stressed, and usually Saturday was the one day she took off from that.

"Yeah?" I asked.

"Have you seen your brother?"

I could feel my pulse begin to race a little bit at that, as I tried in an instant to figure out what the right answer would be. Charlie hadn't sent me an alibi text, so I was in the dark as to what he'd told Mom and Dad he was doing, and what he'd actually ended up doing. "No," I said, finally.

"He's not upstairs," my mother said. She frowned, staring out at the cul-de-sac. "I'm going to check again," she said, heading back inside.

"Sorry," I said to Julia. "Charlie drama."

"How is he?" Julia asked. Julia had had a huge crush on Charlie back in middle school, but it has faded out during high school, when he headed down a very different path than we did.

"About the same," I said. This was to say, not very well. I knew

Julia would understand what I meant. I looked back to the house and realized I should probably do some recon, to try and get in front of this before it got worse. "I should go."

"Okay," Julia said. "But call me later? Promise?"

"Of course," I said. I hung up with her and pulled the door open, taking just a moment to look back at my father, in his element, puttering along behind the mower, whistling to himself.

Beehive Inn
DELTA, UT

Arrival Date: June 8, 3:35 a.m.
Projected Departure Date: June 8.
CHECKOUT TIME IS ELEVEN A.M.

Name:
Edmund Udell/Hillary Udell

Address:
1 Salt Lake City Boulevard
Salt Lake City, UT
Zip Unknown

Phone: No phone.

Room:
Honeymoon Suite

Payment Method:
Cash

Projected cost of room:
$99 + tax

ENJOY YOUR STAY!!

A love-struck Romeo sings a streetsuss serenade.
—*Dire Straits*

I sat on the edge of the king-size bed, trying not to disturb the rose petals scattered on it, waiting for Roger to come out of the bathroom and trying to figure out how, exactly, this had happened. Again.

It had taken longer than we'd thought it would to reach Delta, the first town in Utah on Highway 50. By that point I was truly concerned about Roger, who had been driving for the better part of a day. Most of the motels we passed had the NO in their vacancy signs illuminated, and I had begun to worry what would happen if we couldn't find somewhere to stay in Delta. On the map, it looked like the next town was probably another hour away, and I had a feeling Roger just wasn't going to be up for that.

We'd finally pulled into the Beehive Inn to see what the situation was. As it looked a little nicer than the roadside motels, it wasn't advertising its occupancy in neon on its sign. We'd gotten out of the car, and as I walked to the entrance, I felt the tightness in my leg muscles, and how much my butt was aching from sitting for that long. I could feel myself getting nervous as we stepped through the automatic glass doors and into the lobby, which seemed jarringly bright after the night's drive. I'd never tried to check in by myself at a hotel before. Was I even allowed to? Did you have to be eighteen? Was that why my mother had made reservations for us—because I wouldn't be able to do it alone?

My heart was pounding as I reached the front desk. The hotel itself seemed nice, if a little aggressively homey, with quilts covering every available surface. Before I could look around too much, though, we were greeted by a frazzled-looking desk clerk.

"Are you the Udells?" he asked, looking from me to Roger.

"What?" I asked, thrown, as this wasn't a question I'd been expecting. And Roger, who was literally swaying on his feet at this point, didn't seem in a state of mind to answer it.

"I've been saving our last room for you," he said, frowning at me and typing on his computer. "Even though I got that message that you were canceling the reservation. I've been holding it open, since you booked in advance."

"And that's the last room available tonight?" I asked, looking over at Roger, whose eyes were drifting shut, then snapping open again.

"Yes," the clerk said a little testily.

"Right," I said, thinking fast. If these Udells had canceled, they most likely weren't coming. And it was three thirty in the morning, and Roger clearly needed to crash as soon as possible. "That's us," I said smiling brightly. "The Udells." That seemed to wake Roger up a little, and he blinked at me, surprised.

"Finally," the clerk muttered. "All right. Names?" he asked, fingers poised over his keyboard.

"Oh," I said, "Well. That's . . . Edmund. And I'm Hillary." Roger glanced over at me, a little more sharply, and I tried to shrug as subtly as possible.

I think the clerk began to doubt us when I wasn't able to tell him the zip code of Salt Lake City, and when Roger, who'd joined in the conversation by this point, explained that we didn't have a cell number to give, because those things were just fads. But I think at that point the clerk just wanted us to go. I paid in cash from my mother's sock-drawer fund, so that the Udells, whoever they were, wouldn't be charged. Then he'd handed us a key—not a key card, but a real old-fashioned brass key, with a small heart charm dangling from it.

"Enjoy your stay," he said, with an odd smile and a raised eyebrow. I thanked him, and Roger and I headed off to find the room.

Which turned out to be the Honeymoon Suite.

I stared at the plaque with its curly writing for a moment, hoping that it was a joke. But it wasn't—the key fit into the lock, and it explained the clerk's leer and the heart charm. I pushed open the door and stepped inside, and could feel myself blushing as I took in the room. The white quilt of the king-size bed was covered in rose petals, and to the side of the bed was a bottle of champagne bobbing in a bucket of water. This seemed weird until I realized it had probably been ice a few hours ago. Roger closed the door behind us and I looked up at him, hoping my face wasn't the same color as my hair.

"So . . . ," I started, incredibly embarrassed, and not even sure what I *could* say about this. "Um . . ."

"Nice choice of rooms, Hillary," he said with a faint smile. Maybe he was too tired to be embarrassed, but he wasn't even blushing.

"I'm really sorry," I said. "But they only had this one left—"

"It's fine," he said. "I'm going to change first, if that's cool." He headed toward the bathroom, carrying his duffel.

"Sure," I said, still staring at the bed. When Roger closed the bathroom door, I looked in the mirror and saw that my blushing had more or less subsided. Then I checked out the room. It had been awhile since I'd been in a real hotel—the cabin in Yosemite didn't count. It was nice, too—there was a memo pad on the desk in the corner of the room, with a yellow and black BEEHIVE MOTEL pen, and I took both, stashing them in my purse. As I did, it occurred to me that this was the first time I was staying in a hotel without my family. And I was in the honeymoon suite. With a college guy.

Just as I had this jarring thought, Roger came out of the bathroom, yawning, dressed in the same shorts-and-T-shirt combo he'd worn the night before. It wasn't so startling, now that I'd known to expect it. Roger looked at the bed as well. "It seems a shame to wreck it," he said, and I looked down at the rose petals and realized that they'd been arranged in the shape of a heart.

I looked away, grabbed my own suitcase, and headed for the bathroom. "I don't think the Udells will mind," I said as casually as I could. I closed the door behind me and leaned back against it, letting out a breath. I knew Roger was tired, but clearly he hadn't been too tired to notice that the whole room had been set up with the expectation that the people staying in it would be having sex.

We were in the *honeymoon suite*. The expectation of sex was in the very atmosphere, like perfume, but less subtle. This was worse than sharing a bed in Yosemite, even if this bed was bigger. It was like there was an elephant in the room. An elephant that expected us to have sex. I could feel myself blushing again, and thanks to the bathroom mirror, I was able to have visual proof as well. Trying to think about other things, I looked around the bathroom and saw that the tub was built for two, with complimentary bubble bath and a small dish of rose petals waiting on the tub's edge.

Stalling, and also taking advantage of the fact that this bathroom was in-suite, and not a five-minute walk through bear-friendly territory like it had been last night, I took a long shower. Then I got changed for bed, swapping the long-sleeved shirt I'd worn the night before for a T-shirt, figuring that it wouldn't be as cold here. As I combed out my hair, I tried not to focus on how much hair was left behind in the comb when I finished. I just packed up my toiletries, adding in the bubble bath, the complimentary shampoo, the sewing kit, and the hand lotion.

When I came out of the bathroom, I saw that Roger was already under the covers on his side, with his eyes closed. So maybe he wasn't bothered by any of the weird room pressure at all.

Roger had turned off all the lights but one, the small chintz-covered bedside lamp on the left side—my side. Trying to make as little noise as possible, I slipped under the covers and snapped off the light. I turned on my side and looked across at Roger, who was curled up, facing me. Sleeping next to him didn't seem as scary to me as it had yesterday. Had it only been yesterday?

I watched him for a moment. Then, even though I was sure the night before had been a fluke, and I wasn't going to get any sleep, I let my eyes close. "Good night, Roger," I murmured.

After a moment, Roger surprised me by replying—I was sure he'd fallen asleep. "'Night," he said. "But the name's Edmund."

FYI—
at mom's cafe,
a scone is a
HUGE
FUNNEL CAKE.
Roger had four.

The Best in Home Cooking
MOM'S CAFE
Corner of State & Main
Utah

DINERS!
Why doesn't
Raven Rock have
diners?

Roger mocked me for taking pictures of trees

Where I've Been...

State #3: UTAH—The Beehive State

motto: Industry

Size: Again with the big. Very, very big.

Facts: The Beehive State! All the signs that tell you what highway you're on have pictures of beehives on them.

Notes: A sign on the side of the interstate: OPEN RANGE CAUTION. But what does this mean? Seriously, what does this mean?? But Utah is SO beautiful. Even the trees are beautiful enough to take pictures of, and this is NOT stupid. Also, the Salt Lake City zip code is 84148.
Just in case.

Utah is STUNNING!!!!

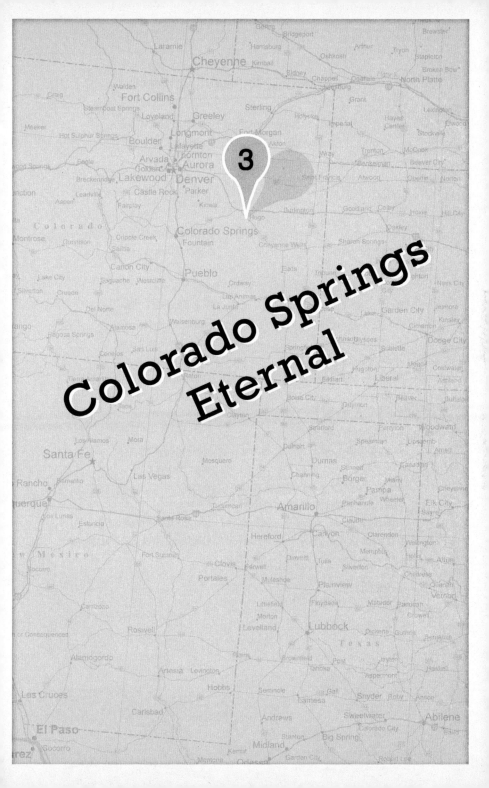

3

Colorado Springs Eternal

ROGER PLAYLIST #4

"Hillary & Edmund Hit the Highway" aka
"People Who Take Pictures of Trees"

SONG TITLE	ARTIST
"Colorado"	Grizzly Bear
"Young Folks"	Peter, Bjorn and John
"I Am John"	Loney, Dear
"Unknown Legend"	Neil Young
"Break It Out"	The Rocket Summer
"No You Girls"	Franz Ferdinand
"Surf Colorado"	Bowling for Soup
"Just Like Heaven"	The Cure
"The First Single (You Know Me)"	The Format
"Gravel"	Ember FX
"Rootless Tree"	Damien Rice
"I Figured You Out"	Elliott Smith
"Baby, It's Fact"	Hellogoodbye
"Free"	Cat Power
"Don't Forget to Breathe"	Beulah
"Love Like a Sunset, Part I"	Phoenix
"Nobody Move, Nobody Get Hurt"	We Are Scientists
"A Year in the Past, Forever in the Future"	Dashboard Confessional

LOOK! A TREE! I MUST STOP AND TAKE A PICTURE OF IT!

LOOK! ANOTHER TREE!!

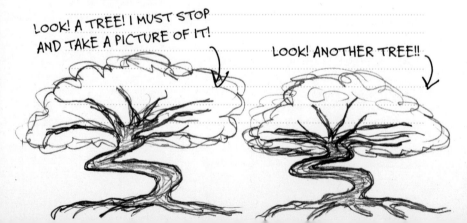

There's no surf in Colorado.
—*Bowling for Soup*

"Hi, it's Amy's phone. Leave a message and I'll get back to you. Thanks!"

Beep.

"Amelia. This is your mother. I'm not happy that you didn't call me back yesterday. I'm getting concerned, especially since none of the hotels seem to have a record of you checking in. Call me immediately."

←——→

"Hi, you've reached Pamela Curry. Please leave a message with your name and number, and I will return your call as soon as I am able. Thank you."

Beep.

"Hi, Mom. Wow, I guess we keep missing each other. Weird. But things are fine! There's no need to be concerned. We, um, hit traffic outside of . . . Oklahoma, which we are way past by now. So we've been a little behind. But we've been finding hotels with no problem. And the driving is fine, and everything is going okay. So no need to worry!"

←——→

"Is it a man?" Roger asked me.

"Yes," I said. "Sixteen."

"Is he alive?"

"No. Fifteen."

"Is he an explorer?"

"Only you would ask that. No," I said.

"*You* ask me that every time."

"Because you keep choosing explorers."

"Fair point. Is he famous?"

"Yes. Fourteen."

"Hmm." Roger drummed his fingers on the steering wheel, and I curled my legs up under me and looked out the window.

The sun was just beginning to set—we'd been driving all day. We'd gotten a later start than we wanted because, to my shock, I had slept through the night again and was still fast asleep when the irate desk clerk called us at what I thought was ten. But since neither of us had adjusted for the time change, it was actually eleven, and we were in danger of getting charged for a late checkout. We'd hit the road and actually stopped along the way to sit down and eat both breakfast and lunch. I'd discovered that I loved diners, and Roger loved diner jukeboxes.

The drive through Utah—during which I'd learned that John Cabot had possibly discovered Canada and Roger learned who Stephen Sondheim was—was absolutely breathtaking. The scenery was even more stunning than it had been on Highway 50, mostly because there was now something to look at. And what there was to look at took my breath away. It was strangely otherworldish—these huge red plateaus and fantastic little driftwood trees that I couldn't stop taking pictures of, much to Roger's delight, since he thought that taking pictures of trees was the most ridiculous thing he'd ever heard of. As it had been the day before, it was as though someone had opened up the landscape and you could just see forever, underneath a sky that, I swear, was bigger and bluer than it had been in Nevada.

Now that we were back on the interstate, we were seeing road signs again, and most of them were new to me. In addition to the inexplicable OPEN RANGE CAUTION, there were animal signs I'd never seen before—an antelope, a cow, and a cow with horns. There were deer signs too, but I'd seen those for the first time near Yosemite. But it worried me that, without warning, a cow with horns might be running across the interstate. And that this had happened frequently enough that they'd had to erect a sign to warn people about it.

As we crossed into Colorado, slowly but surely the landscape changed again. The open flatness we'd had in Nevada and Utah became more mountainous, and suddenly the pine trees were back. The grades of the incline were now posted on signs on the side of the road, and the road was getting more winding and much steeper as we crossed actual mountains. We'd climb and climb, and then go downhill sharply. The Liberty was fine with this, but it seemed that the steep grades were an issue for the truckers—especially the downhill grades. There were signs that I couldn't believe were real, that seemed to offer truckers stream-of-consciousness support for these roads. STEEP GRADE AHEAD, TRUCKERS! USE CAUTION! and TRUCKERS! IT'S NOT OVER YET! MORE 6% GRADE AND WINDING ROADS! The one that I stared at the longest, however: IF BRAKES FAIL, DO NOT EXIT. STAY ON INTERSTATE. I mean, what? That seemed like terrible advice to me, and whenever we were behind a truck, I found myself watching its brake lights, making sure they were flashing red.

Roger had been getting quieter the closer we got to Colorado Springs. At both diners, he'd left during the meal to make phone calls, calls he made clear he didn't want to talk about when he returned to the table and immediately changed the subject. I'd almost asked, the first time, if he'd been calling Hadley, but then realized that would involve admitting I'd heard his conversation at Yosemite.

I'd used one of his absences to send a message to my mother's cell. Charlie had figured out how to do this years ago, but I'd never done it until now. It meant that a voice mail showed up on her phone without it ringing. Charlie was sure that Mom had never figured out her cell had this feature, as she always just assumed that she had missed the call. I didn't think I was up for having a

conversation with her that would either involve a lot of uncomfortable truth telling, or would be a parade of lies. I knew that I would
probably have to tell her the truth soon—we were supposed to be
in Indiana at the moment, and we were pretty far from Indiana.
But I tried to tell myself that maybe we could make up the time by
driving all night, or something. I also wasn't exactly excited about
the prospect of being in Connecticut in a day or two—I didn't
want to have to start that life yet. I also hadn't seen my mother in a
month, and the thought of seeing her again made me nervous, for
reasons I didn't want to explore.

I took a sip of my cream soda and checked my watch, now
adjusted to mountain time. It was getting close to seven, and it
felt like we'd been in the car for a very long time. "Well?" I asked,
propping my feet on the dashboard and looking over at Roger.

"Sorry," he said. He picked up his phone, looked at it, then set
it back down in his cup holder. "Um. Is he alive?"

"No," I said, glancing over at him again. "And you asked that
already."

"Sorry," he said, giving me a quick smile, then turning back
to the road, which was getting windy again. "I think I'm just a
little . . . distracted. Want to just put on some music?"

"Sure," I murmured, trying not to feel hurt. It was just a stupid
game, anyway. I turned up Roger's mix, and we drove the next six
songs without speaking.

I started seeing Colorado Springs on the signs that told you
how far you were from various destinations. And when we were
about sixty miles outside it, it was like we joined the world again.
We must have been through the mountains, because the landscape
was more open, and there were suddenly three lanes of traffic we
could drive in, then four. The sense of remoteness fell away, and
there were Targets and Wal-Marts and Starbucks and fast-food restaurants on the side of the road again. All those things I'd missed
on Highway 50 that now seemed too big and brightly colored. I
found myself missing the little mini-marts.

We stopped for gas when we were about twenty miles outside of town. While Roger filled up, his cell rang—I was squeegee-ing the windshield, which had turned into a dead bug graveyard, and I could see it, lighting up and dancing around as it vibrated in the cup holder. I opened the passenger door and grabbed it, seeing the display read BRON CALLING. I had no idea what this meant, but I handed the phone to Roger, who suddenly looked very nervous. I put the squeegee back, even though the window was only half-cleaned, and got back in the car so I could avoid hearing Roger's conversation. But I couldn't help slouching down a little in my seat to see him in the side mirror. I could only see him in profile, but he didn't look too happy. Even though he was smiling, it seemed a little forced. It struck me, a moment after I thought this, that I could now tell the difference with him.

Roger got back in the car and slammed his door a little harder than necessary. He didn't put the keys in the ignition, just played with them, resting on his knee. He looked tired, and some of the energy that was always humming around him seemed to have faded a little. "You okay?" I asked.

"Sure," he said to the keys, still not looking at me. "So I have good news. I got a place for us to crash. It's one of the houses off campus. It's the International House during the year, but right now, it's just for people who are taking summer courses."

"Great," I said. I looked at him more closely. He did not look happy. "That's a good thing, right?"

Roger just sighed. "So here's the thing," he said. I immediately felt myself tense up. "I should tell you something. I should have told you before, actually."

"Okay," I said, really beginning to get worried now. Was he sick of me, and just planning on staying here with his friends? Was he backing out of the trip?

"So the reason we're here," he said, still not looking at me, "is that . . . I heard Hadley was here."

"Oh," I said. Suddenly it made sense that Roger had been so

focused on his phone all morning. "Is she?" I asked, as casually as possible.

"No," he said, and I felt myself relax a little bit. "I'd heard from one of my friends that she was here taking summer courses. But apparently, she's back home in Kentucky."

"Oh," I said again, feeling out of my depth.

"She hasn't been returning any of my calls or e-mails. So I just thought that maybe if I came here, and saw her, we could talk, and we could maybe . . ." His forehead creased. "I don't know."

Amy! would have known exactly what to do here. She wouldn't have felt so tongue-tied and awkward and annoyingly young. "Um," I finally said. "What . . . I mean, what happened with you two?"

There was a honk behind us, and I turned and saw a minivan waiting for the pump, clearly wondering what we were doing just sitting in the car. Roger started the car and steered us back onto the interstate. We'd been driving in silence for a few minutes when he started talking again. "I don't know what happened," he said. "If I knew that, I don't think we'd be here."

"Well," I said. I wondered if we should do this like Twenty Questions, with The Reason Hadley Broke Up with Me being the answer. "So what did she say?"

Roger clenched and unclenched his hands on the steering wheel, his forehead still furrowed. He looked preoccupied and unhappy, which only highlighted just how cheerful he normally seemed. Like so much else, I hadn't fully realized this until it was gone. "It was during finals. We were supposed to meet at the library—I was going to help her study for her history final. I'd made note cards," he said, sounding disgusted with himself. "But she came to my dorm and . . ." Roger paused, and I noticed a muscle pulsing in his jaw as he clenched his teeth. "She said," he continued, "that it was over between us. That she'd been feeling this way for a long time, and she needed to get it off her chest, because it was interfering with her studying."

"She said that?" I asked, stunned.

"Yeah," he said, with a small, unhappy laugh. "Hadley never really was one for sentiment. Well, needless to say, I didn't do so great on my finals. And then she left me a voice mail saying that she was sorry about the way she left things, and told me when I could come by her sorority house, so we could say good-bye."

"And?"

"Oh, I didn't go," said Roger, changing lanes. "I don't say good-bye. And she *knew* that. I'd told her a hundred times."

I sat up a little straighter. "You don't say good-bye?"

"Nope," he said. "Not since I was eleven. It's a superstitious thing," he added, a little unnecessarily. "Three of my grandparents died that year—bam, bam, bam. And each time, it was almost immediately after I talked to them. And said—guess what? Good-bye. So now I don't do it. It's stupid. But the one grandparent I have left is still alive and kicking and I haven't said good-bye since. So there you go."

"But," I said, as Roger took exit 143 for Uintah Street/ Colorado College, "what does saying good-bye have to do with it?"

"It has everything to do with it!" Roger said, some of his old energy coming back into his voice. Things were starting to look less developed now, and I could see the mountains again. And they were stunning. They were backlit by the setting sun, so I could basically only see their outlines—but the mountains actually looked purple, just like in the song. Roger was driving down what seemed like a main street—clothing boutiques and pizza parlors and record stores. It could have been Raven Rock—it had that college-town feel to it—except for the mountains in the background, which were far more impressive than California's. "Saying good-bye is basically an invitation not to see a person again. It's making it okay for that to be the last conversation you have. So if you don't say it—if you leave the conversation open—it means you'll have to see them again." I just stared at him, and Roger looked over at me and laughed, a normal-sounding laugh this time. "I know it doesn't actually make sense," he said. "But it's pretty much ingrained now."

"But sometimes," I said, feeling my throat begin to tighten, but forcing the sentence out anyway, "sometimes you don't say good-bye and you never see the person again anyway. Sometimes that happens."

"I know it does," he said quietly, and from his expression, I knew he knew what I was talking about. "I guess it's just my resid-ual guilt for the grandparentcide."

I felt myself smile at that. "You didn't kill your grandparents."

"I know that now. But you try telling that to eleven-year-old me."

I looked out the window at the darkening purple mountains and thought about that. Good-byes didn't seem as important to me as they once had—I'd found out that when you're never going to see someone again, it's not the good-bye that matters. What matters is that you're never going to be able to say anything else to them. And you're left with an eternal unfinished conversation.

"Anyway," Roger said, turning down a street that was lined with small houses, most with Greek letters nailed to their doors, "I'm sorry to lay all this on you. I should have told you earlier why I wanted to come here."

"It's fine," I said.

Roger smiled at me, then pulled the car over to the side of the street and parked in front of a dilapidated two-story house with peeling white paint and a half-inflated plastic palm tree drooping on the lawn. "Want to check out our digs?"

We found the common area of the Colorado College International House deserted, except for a skinny, shirtless guy sprawled on the couch. He had spiky black hair and appeared very involved in a video game. It seemed to be set in a forest and featured a much more buff version of the guy on the couch.

"Hey, Leonard," Roger said.

"Hey, Sullivan," the guy—presumably Leonard—said, raising

one hand for a fist bump without looking up from the screen.

"How's Honour Quest treating you these days?" Roger asked.

"I made it to the Forest of Doom," he said.

"I see that," Roger said, leaning over the couch to look at the TV screen. "Impressive."

"What are you doing here?" Leonard asked. "I thought you were in California for the summer. Are you here till school starts?"

"No," said Roger. "Spending the summer in Philadelphia."

"Bummer," Leonard said. The virtual him stomped around a bit, waving his sword.

"So we're crashing here tonight," Roger said. "I talked to Bron and she said it was fine. Mind if I take the extra bed in your room?"

"Sure," said Leonard. "The more the merrier, and all that. Just put your stuff anywhere. And I heard there's going to be a little fiesta tonight at the Quiet Dorm. Should be pretty rocking." He glanced up and seemed to notice me for the first time. "Oh. Hey," he said. "Leonard Cho."

"Amy Curry," I said.

"Charmed," he said, turning his attention back to the screen. "Whatever you do, Sullivan, avoid Conrad's room. He's been keeping a rabbit in his closet, and it's turned on him."

"A rabbit?" I asked, not sure I'd heard right.

"It's *turned* on him?" Roger echoed.

Leonard shook his head. "It's not pretty. Just do yourself a favor and avoid the whole sitch."

"Sure," said Roger. "Thanks, man." He raised his eyebrows at me and headed into the kitchen. I followed, looking around. There were signs that a number of people shared this kitchen, and not all harmoniously, with charts on the wall for trash and cleanup duties, cabinets secured with padlocks, and the words JUST EAT YOUR OWN GODDAMN FOOD AND NOBODY GETS HURT painted on the wall.

"So," Roger said, crossing the kitchen, "welcome to the International House. My friend Bronwyn's the RA here for the summer, and she said we could crash for the night. She said you could stay with her." He headed up a narrow, dark stairway with shoe treads worn into the carpet, and I followed.

"She won't mind?" I asked, realizing that I now understood the BRON CALLING on his phone earlier. Roger stopped in front of a door with a whiteboard attached to it. It was covered in messages, most of which seemed to have to do with a rabbit.

"Not at all," he said. "I'm across the hall in Leonard's room." He pointed it out. "He's barely ever off the couch, so I'll probably get the room to myself." Roger opened Bronwyn's door to reveal a small, messy room that seemed to be one giant closet—clothes were hanging everywhere, and the small set of drawers was over-flowing and stacked with piles of shirts. There was what I assumed was a bed pushed against one wall, but it was hard to know for sure, as it was covered in clothing.

"Wow," I said, looking around.

"I know," he said. "She's got a bit of a shopping problem." He looked down at me. "Are you okay with this?" he asked. "I mean, we can always get a hotel if you'd be more comfortable. . . ."

I shook my head. "It's fine," I said. It wasn't, really. I didn't want to have to stay with a stranger, some college girl who was probably going to resent the fact I was there. But this was so clearly where Roger wanted to be, I didn't see any way I could get us out of it without disappointing him.

He smiled at me, seeming relieved, and I knew that had been the right answer. "Great. Well, I'll go get the bags out of the car. Be right back." Before I could reply, Roger was out the door.

Even without the stacks of clothes, it would have been a tiny room. The stuff everywhere just made it feel that much more claustrophobic. There was basically just the bed, a tiny space of floor next to it, and a desk with science textbooks piled around and on top of it. There was another bulletin board above the desk, and, recognizing Roger in a picture, I stepped inside the room to look at it.

"Hey there!"

I turned around at the sound of the voice and saw a girl standing in the doorway. She had long brown hair and bangs that swept almost into her eyes, and she was around my height and build, if maybe a little curvier. I assumed this was Bronwyn, only because she was wearing the outfit of someone who cared about clothes deeply, as the owner of this room clearly did. She had on jeans and a T-shirt, like me, but that was where the similarity ended. She seemed to have that thing that I'd noticed in girls at school—a way of putting together clothing so that everything just *worked*, and seemed special and pulled together but also casually effortless. Her white T-shirt was fitted but somehow also loose. She had a few delicate gold necklaces layered on top of each other, and these seemed to coordinate perfectly with her gold flats. I looked down and saw that on my own T-shirt, there was what looked like a blob of jam from the toast I'd had at lunch.

"Hey," I said, sticking my hands into my pockets, hoping she wouldn't notice the jam.

"Are you Amy?" she asked, looking at me closely. She walked over to me, somehow managing to avoid stepping on any clothes or shoes. She was looking at me with the friendliest expression I'd ever seen on anyone who wasn't a flight attendant.

"Yes," I said, sticking out my hand to shake hers, figuring that maybe this was the thing to do at college. "Hi."

She didn't even acknowledge my hand, just took a step closer and hugged me tight. I immediately felt myself stiffening. I hadn't really hugged anyone in a long time. A few people had hugged me at the funeral, but those had been quick, barely touching, two-pats-on-the-back hugs. This girl wasn't letting go. After a moment, I tried to extricate myself, but that only seemed to make her hold tighter. It was strange to feel, since we were about the same height, but it seemed like I was being hugged by a much bigger person. I felt something inside me weaken, a splinter or two popping off the dam I'd put up in front of everything I didn't want to feel. The second I felt this, I took a step back. Bronwyn took a step back of her own and smiled at me.

121

"So nice to meet you!" she said, and I heard a faint, twangy Southern accent in her words. "You," for example, seemed to have more syllables in it than I was used to hearing.

"You too. Um . . ." I said, just to check. "Are you Bronwyn?"

"Oh my goodness!" she said with a laugh. "I'm so sorry! Yes, I am. Bronwyn Elizabeth Taylor. Pleased to make your acquaintance."

"Elizabeth Taylor?" I repeated, not sure I'd heard correctly.

Bronwyn laughed again. "Yes, I know. Blame my older sister. She was obsessed with *National Velvet* around the time I was born. Girls and horses, you know," she said, and I nodded, like I was able to follow this. "So she suggested it as a middle name, and here I am. That's why you don't let a five-year-old pick your name, am I right?"

"Right," I said, a bit stunned. She spoke *fast*, seeming to go against all the things I'd heard about the slow Southern drawl. Reeling a bit, I tried to drag the conversation back to familiar ground. "Thank you so much for letting me stay here tonight."

"Oh, pshaw!" she said. I had never heard anyone actually say this word aloud before, but there it was: puh-shaw. "I'm thrilled you all are staying here. I am just starved for some good conversation. And Roger is one of my top ten favorite people in the world." She said this like it was truly an honor. I believed her immediately.

"Oh," I said. "Yeah. He's really—"

"And I am just sick," she continued on, "about what that girl has done to him. Such a sweet boy. Nothing but practice to someone like Hadley." I noticed that Bronwyn pronounced her name in the opposite way that Roger had, practically spitting out the syllables. "She took one look at him and saw someone she could sharpen her claws on." I nodded dumbly, feeling a bit like I'd just walked into a tornado. I tried to sift through what she'd just said, tried to think of a proper response to any of it. "So . . . ," I began.

"My goodness, where are my manners? Please sit down."

I didn't see any place where this seemed possible, but Bronwyn swept some clothes off the bed and patted it, then crossed the room and hopped up on her desk. I lowered myself carefully onto the space she'd cleared. She was looking at me expectantly, so I decided to try again. "So," I said, then waited a moment. When she didn't jump in, I continued, "So you're the RA here for the summer?"

"I am," she said with a groan that somehow managed to also seem good-natured. "It's free room and board, keeps me from having to be home all summer and provide slave labor at my aunt's day care. But enough about me!" She leaned forward. "I want to hear all about you! How's the drive been so far?"

"Oh," I said, feeling a little uncomfortable now that the full force of her attention was turned to me. "Good, I guess. So far."

"Has *she* come up yet?" The way Bronwyn said "she," I had no doubt who she meant.

"No," I said. "Not really. He hasn't really talked about it."

Bronwyn nodded. "I thought as much. No worries, darling. I'll get it out of him."

"Um," I said, "I think that's why we're here, though. One of the reasons," I added quickly. "He said he was looking for Hadley—he thought she might be on campus this summer."

Bronwyn snorted. "Well, she's not. Believe me, I'd have known about it and sent out an all-points bulletin." She turned to her desk and lifted a framed photo off it. "You want the visual?" Before I could reply, she crossed the room and handed it to me.

There were four people in the picture: Bronwyn on the left, standing next to a cute, stocky guy with close-cropped curly black hair, then Roger standing next to a striking blond girl. I figured this had to be Hadley, and not only because someone had drawn horns on top of her head with red marker. I looked closer. She was almost as tall as Roger, willowy, with small, perfect features, evenly tanned skin, and pale blond hair. She was smiling absently and looking off-camera, but Roger, who was smiling right at her, hadn't seemed to notice. "Huh," I said, not sure what the proper response to this was.

"I know," Bronwyn said. "Totally, right? Can't you just see it on her face?" She took the picture back from me. "But look at Jaime," she said, smiling at it, her finger resting on the guy standing next to her. "Isn't he just the sweetest? Don't you just want to eat him up?"

"Mmm," I said, as neutrally as possible, figuring this was probably not something to agree to with too much enthusiasm. "Is he your boyfriend?"

"He is," she said, sighing happily. "And pretty much Roger's best friend around here. That's how I got to know him, you see. And her," she added darkly, after a moment.

"So," I said, feeling like I was on the verge of uncovering a mystery, "what exactly happened between them?"

Bronwyn shoved another armful of clothes onto the floor and sat down next to me. "Honey, if I knew that I could have fixed this two months ago. I think the problem is that there isn't any *there* there. I think she just got bored and wanted to be free in Kentucky for the summer. But I don't know," she said. "We'll have to ask RS. . . ." She paused and looked around, as though she had just noticed Roger wasn't in the room. "Speaking of, where is that boy?"

"He's getting the bags," I said. I realized that he really should have been back by now, and I wondered if he was taking his time on purpose, so that Bronwyn and I could talk.

"Gotcha. Well, we should start getting ready anyway. There's a party at the Quiet Dorm tonight. You're coming," she said, and I noticed that she didn't phrase it as a question, or wait for my answer. "We'll get dressed, and . . ." Her eyes shifted to my outfit. "Well, maybe you can borrow something of mine. It'll be fun!"

And you're doing fine in Colorado.

—*Jackson Browne*

The Quiet Dorm did not live up to its name. Roger had explained, on the walk to the party, that the houses that were for specific things during the school year—like the International House—became just regular housing during the summer for the students staying on campus. Apparently, the wildest parties over the summer happened at the Substance-Free Dorm.

We could hear the party when we were still down the street from it: the steady, pounding beat of music mixed with laughter and the occasional yell. The Quiet Dorm was walking distance from the International House, in another run-down house—this one looked like it might have been an old Victorian. When we got closer, I could see that there was a fake beach in front of the wrap-around porch, an expanse of sand with a volleyball net strung up across it. It didn't seem like anyone was going to be playing tonight, though, as a small campfire had been made next to the net. There were people standing around it, couples talking on the porch, and a guy passed out over the railing, still clutching his bottle of beer. It was all very familiar—replace the bottles of Mile-High Ale that were scattered around with Dos Equis, and it could have easily been the parties I'd been to at College of the West. I'd only been to a handful, and always with Michael. I had tended to stick next to him, sipping the warm keg beer out of my red plastic cup and smiling when someone spoke to me, trying not to say anything that would identify me as a high school student.

Charlie, on the other hand, had been going over to campus since we were in middle school, when he was apparently treated like a mascot at the parties. By the time we were in high school, he was just accepted as a fixture. And often, he was the one who was providing the party, or at least the one who knew who was holding. It had always been jarring to look across a dorm room or a house as I sat on the sidelines and see my brother, front and center, holding court.

As I followed Bronwyn and Roger up the stairs, I grabbed onto the railing, avoiding the passed-out guy, trying not to lose my balance. I was perfectly sober, but I was not wearing my own shoes. This had not been my choice, but apparently "no" was not a word Bronwyn readily understood.

$\longleftrightarrow$

"Of course you're coming!" she'd said after I'd protested and Roger had reappeared with my suitcase. She'd said hello but then shooed him out again so we could begin to get ready. Which is when I found out that I was, most likely, not getting out of going to the party.

"It's really okay," I said.

Bronwyn, who had been humming something under her breath and rummaging in one of her drawers, turned and looked at me. "Of course you have to go," she said. "Don't be silly."

"I'm fine here," I said. *Really.*

She waved my words away again. "You're coming, sugar," she said. "And what's more, it's going to be fun." She straightened up and looked at me closely. "I think we could change this up a bit," she said, gesturing to my flip-flops, loose T-shirt, and jeans. "I understand you had to dress for travel and all."

"Right," I murmured. I didn't want to tell her that this had become my uniform. It wasn't planned, just what I kept gravitating toward. Somehow, clothes that were too fitted felt like they were suffocating me, skirts made my legs feel too cold, bright colors drew too much attention. So I'd ended up with an ensemble that let me hide a little, and let me fade into the background, and it was working just fine.

"But," she continued, "to every season. Am I right? A time to be casual and a time to dress up. And this is the latter." She pulled out a pink one-shouldered top, looked at it, then me, then tossed it on the bureau. She rummaged farther in, gave a little gasp of triumph, and came out with a long, sky-blue top edged with yellow. "Perfect," she said.

"Bronwyn," I started, not wanting to offend her, but not wanting her to make all this effort for nothing. "Not that I don't appreciate this, but I just don't think I feel like going to a party tonight." That was an understatement, but I wasn't sure how else to put it. I was only just getting used to spending time with Roger. I had spent almost three months barely talking to anyone, and the thought of seeing so many people, and being around that many strangers, made me feel like the only thing I wanted to do was crawl into bed. Once, I'd happily gone to parties. It had never been an issue. But that, of course, had been Before. That had been Old me.

"I know," said Bronwyn with a sigh, surprising me. "Half the time I don't want to go out either, darling. But you know what? You go anyway. It's the Taylor family motto: You get up, you dress up, you show up. And usually have a pretty good time by the end of it." She threw the blue shirt at me, and I caught it. "And sometimes," she added, in slightly hushed tones, like she was letting me in on a secret, "if you don't feel great on the inside, just look great on the outside, and after a while you won't be able to tell the difference." She smiled at me. I guess I didn't look totally convinced, because she shrugged and said, "But if you're miserable, I promise you can leave early, 'kay? Now put that on and I'll find you a skirt."

I realized that resistance was futile and pulled off the jam-stained T-shirt as Bronwyn emerged from a pile of clothing with a denim skirt. She glanced up at me, and I tried to turn away—I was only wearing my bra—to put the blue shirt on. As I felt the softness of the material, I could tell that this was a really nice shirt. After spending the last few months in preshrunk cotton, I'd almost forgotten what it felt like, and I ran my fingers over the neckline, which was delicately scalloped.

"This too," she said, and a bra whacked me in the head.

"Um," I said, holding it up, "I think I'm okay. . . ." This just seemed to be taking the clothes borrowing a little far.

"Don't worry, it's new," she said. "I bought it for my roommate last year. I mean, the girl lived in her sports bra. Such a shame. But she told me she didn't want it. And that I was being *inappropriate*. Can you believe it? Try it on."

"Um," I said, wishing I could just get dressed, "it's really all right. . . ."

"No, it isn't," she said. "If you're going to dress, you have to do it all the way. I think that good underwear is so underrated."

I turned the bra over in my hands. It, like the shirt, was obviously well made. It was a pale green with underwire and delicate lace, and definitely a lot sexier than any of the bras I currently had. "Well, thanks."

"Of course. And," she said, grabbing something else and throwing it at me, "here." It was a matching pale green thong with the tags still attached.

"You bought your roommate underwear?" I asked.

"Well, it was a set!" she said, a little defensively. "You don't want to separate a set. And you can just save it for special occasions, if you like." She winked at me, and I tried not to blush. The first—and last—time anyone had seen me in my underwear, it certainly hadn't been anything this impressive. But then, Michael hadn't really seemed to care, so maybe it didn't make a difference after all. "So you get changed and then we'll see how it looks!" she said, grinning and clapping her hands together as she headed out the door.

When the door closed behind her, I got dressed, then had to sit down on the bed for a moment and try to wait out the wave of sadness that had just clobbered me. I hadn't realized how much I'd missed hanging out with another girl—how much I'd missed Julia—until now. We always got ready for parties together. She was a genius with hair, and loved doing mine, since hers was so curly she said she could never do anything fun with it. Sometimes the getting ready part—in my room, music blasting, choosing clothing—was much more fun than the party itself. And then after the party, I'd drive her home and we'd recap the night.

"All right," Bronwyn said, returning to the room, checking her watch. "We have to hurry if I'm going to do your hair and makeup. We only have about an hour."

←——→

Which was how I ended up at the party, wearing almost nothing that was my own, including the shoes. Bronwyn had picked out a pair of slingback heels for me that were a little too small, but she had refused to let me leave her room in my flip-flops.

It had been startling to look at myself in her mirror after she'd finished. I looked . . . not like my old self, since I'd never looked this fashionable. But I looked more like I remembered myself looking. Like I had somewhere to go and would have a story to tell about it afterward. I knew it was all artifice and would disappear as soon as I washed off the makeup she'd put on me—but it was nice to see, at least for a night, someone I'd thought wasn't coming back.

We ended up in the Quiet Dorm's noisy kitchen, with Bronwyn talking to someone she recognized from her organic chemistry class. I stood off to the side, next to Roger, sipping warm beer out of a red cup and feeling a strong sense of déjà vu.

"You look really nice," Roger said. I looked at him, surprised, and saw that he was looking down into his cup.

"Oh," I said. I turned this over for a moment in my head, trying to figure out if this was another "you look hot" moment and I was misunderstanding him. But I didn't see how I could be, in this case. I touched the hem of Bronwyn's shirt self-consciously. "Thanks," I said.

"Sure," he replied, swirling the beer around in his cup. He glanced up and smiled at me. I had the feeling that he was going to say something else, when three guys in various stages of drunkenness stumbled into the kitchen.

"Sullivan!" the tallest one of them yelled, and made a beeline for Roger. "Hey!" He stopped when he saw me, and looked from me to Roger. "Dude," he said, shoving Roger's shoulder, still looking at me. "You've got *fire*."

I looked up at Roger, who had flushed. I had no idea what the guy meant, but I figured it was probably a comment about my hair. "Be right back," I muttered, and walked across the kitchen to stand next to Bronwyn. I tried to stay at the edge of her group, but she grabbed me by the arm and pulled me next to her, making room for me in the circle.

"This is Amy," she said to everyone, as she straightened my shirt, smoothed down my hair, and poked me in the back, making me stand up straight. She had interrupted a guy with thick, trendy glasses who had been talking about Kant, and he did not look happy about having to yield the floor. "She's from California." I blinked at Bronwyn as she said this. I hadn't told her that—but I realized that Roger must have. I felt a momentary drop in my stomach, wondering what else he'd told her about me.

"Oh yeah?" the guy with the glasses asked. "That's cool. What's your major?"

"She's undecided," Bronwyn said smoothly, before I could reply. She gave me a tiny wink, then turned her attention back to the conversation.

Two hours later, I was actually having fun. My feet ached in Bronwyn's shoes, and I was tired of hearing arguments about which sociology professor was the best, but I'd gotten to see Bronwyn absolutely decimate in a game of Quarters, and when he lost some kind of bet, the glasses-wearing guy do a pretty fantastic set of dance moves, including the Worm. I stepped out on the porch to get some air, and was sitting on the bottom step, just taking in the sight of the smoke rising up to the stars, the fire, and the drunk people who were now trying to play volleyball around it, occasionally singeing themselves.

"Hey," a voice to my left said. I looked over and saw that a guy was standing on the ground, leaning on the railing and looking down at me. He was blond and red-faced, but whether from the sun or beer—or both—I couldn't tell.

"Hi," I said, then turned away again .

"Do you go here?" the blond guy asked me.

"Um, no," I said. Not liking being forced to look up at him, I pushed myself to my feet, wobbling a little in Bronwyn's shoes.

"Careful there," he said, stepping closer, grabbing my arm to steady me, and then leaving it there. "You okay?" he asked, running his fingers up and down my arm.

"I'm fine," I said, taking a step back and starting to put my hands in the pockets of my jeans, before I remembered I wasn't wearing them.

"Yeah, I didn't think I recognized you," the guy said. "And I know I would have remembered you." He took a step closer and smiled at me. "I'm Bradley. What's your name, pretty girl?"

I blinked at him, feeling my heart beat a little faster, startled by a memory that had suddenly intruded with such force I wanted to shut my eyes against it.

"Pretty girl?" he asked again, his smile growing, taking another step closer. "You do have a name?"

"Hillary Udell," I stammered. "I have to go." I walked down the last step, stumbling slightly, and across the fake beach. I saw Roger walk onto the porch and look around, possibly for me. He caught my eye, and I pointed in the direction of the International House, trying to force a smile on my face, so he would think I was okay, before turning back and walking on.

"Hey!" I heard Bradley yell behind me. "Where are you going?"

But I didn't turn around to look at him, and thankfully, he

didn't follow me. I made it to the sidewalk and took off Bronwyn's shoes, looping the heel straps over my wrists. The stars above were beautiful, the sky was amazingly clear, and I could smell the fire faintly, but I barely registered any of it.

I kept my head down, trying very hard not to think about anything but avoiding broken glass on the pavement, as I walked barefoot back to the dorm.

Mistakes become regrets.

—*Carolina Liar*

MARCH 11—THREE MONTHS EARLIER

I stood in front of Michael's door and knocked. I straightened my skirt and pulled down the stretchy purple tank top that I'd borrowed from Julia back in November. I hadn't been sure what to wear for this, but I'd figured that leaving very little to the imagination was probably the way to go. I'd changed out of the black dress I'd been wearing all day, from the funeral in the morning to the reception afterward. Even though it had been unusually hot all week, in the seventies, my mother had insisted that I wear black tights. Throughout the service, I'd concentrated on feeling how itchy they were, and how they made my legs feel compressed, so I wouldn't have to hear anything that was being said.

Everyone had gathered at our house after the service, the living room filled with relatives, friends, colleagues, and my father's thesis students looking uncomfortable in jackets and ties. The caterers walked around discreetly with passed appetizers that everyone grabbed at, as though food was one thing that was still understandable. Everyone clutched their drinks a little too tightly and talked in small groups, in low tones. My mother circled the room, making sure that everyone had food and drinks, directing the catering staff, replenishing the napkins, not really stopping to speak to anyone. It was as though she was simply organizing an event that had nothing whatsoever to do with her. Charlie had disappeared halfway through the reception and returned an hour later, glassy-eyed. I had stood in the kitchen, off to the side. I'd nodded and agreed with relatives and family friends who approached and told me what a terrible loss it was, and thanked them when they told me that I was bearing up well. I was just waiting to wake up from this surreal dream that I'd somehow landed in. Nothing seemed to be making sense. It was like a bomb had just gone off in the kitchen, and instead of cleaning up the rubble, people were stepping around it and eating mini-quiche.

But eventually everyone had trickled out, the last pair of head-lights swung around the cul-de-sac, my mother had locked the front door, and the three of us were alone. We'd all ended up in the family room. My mother was sitting in her armchair, but for some reason looking very small in it, like it might swallow her up. Charlie was sitting in the middle of the couch, hunched over his knees, ripping threads off the cuffs of his navy suit jacket. I was standing against the back wall, looking down at my black heels. The last time I'd worn them—to the winter formal in January— I'd been dancing.

"So," my mother said, and Charlie and I both turned to look at her. We hadn't talked about it yet. There had been things to organize—the service, the reception, the relatives, the caterers. But now there was nothing left to take care of. I'd been waiting for her to do something since it happened. I didn't even know what— to talk to me about it, or give me a hug, or just look me in the eyes. What I really wanted was for her to take charge, like she always did, and somehow make this okay again. To show us how we were going to get through it.

She glanced at Charlie, then at me, before looking away and standing up. "I'm going to bed," she said, rubbing her neck. "You two should probably get some sleep as well. We've all had a long day." She left the room without looking back at us, and I heard her steps, unusually slow, going up the stairs.

I stared at the door she'd left through, feeling a little bit like I'd been punched. I'd been waiting for her to fix this. I'd never even considered the possibility that she might not. I had no idea what to do now. Was it because it had been my fault? Was that why she was doing this—as a punishment?

I felt my throat tighten and I looked down at the floor, which was blurring in and out of focus as my eyes filled with tears that felt hot. I blinked them back, hard. I had a feeling that if I let myself start crying, there was a very real possibility I would never stop. The need to cry was so strong that it scared me, and I pushed back against it as hard as I could. I looked over at my brother. The days when we'd known everything about each other had ended years ago, but maybe there was a chance we could talk about this and acknowledge the fact that it had actually happened.

"Fuck this," Charlie said, taking off his jacket and dropping it on the couch. He stood, heading for the front door, already loosening his tie. "I'm going out."

"Where?" I asked, hearing how strangled—how needy—my voice sounded.

"Out," he said, unlocking the door and pulling it open. "I have no fucking idea where." He slammed the door behind him, and I felt myself flinch, even though I'd known it was coming.

Not sure what else to do, I crossed to the door and locked it. Then I picked up Charlie's jacket from the couch to fold it. I could feel panic rising up inside me, the kind of nerves I would get before I went onstage, but these were somehow worse, stronger, and I could feel my heart beginning to pound. I put the jacket down, then picked it up again and crumpled it in my hands, wishing I was strong enough to tear it in two. Seeing what I was doing, I dropped the jacket again.

I knew couldn't stay there. I needed to go somewhere, and do something, that would push this away for a while. I headed up to my room to change, taking the stairs two at a time. I was also going out. But unlike Charlie, I knew exactly where.

←→

"Hey, pretty girl," Michael said, opening the door and smiling. This was his name for me, what he'd started calling me after our first makeout session. I always just called him Michael. He was from Oregon, an inch taller than me, and always smelled faintly of Irish Spring.

"Hey," I said, putting a smile on my face. "Can I come in?"

"Of course," he said, opening the door wider. I stepped into the room he shared with Hugo, a German exchange student who kept his side of the room immaculate. Michael's side was always a mess, his bed piled high with clothes and books. But those could easily be moved.

"Is Hugo here?" I asked.

"No," said Michael, shutting the door. "He's at a study group." He stuck his hands in his pockets. "Look, I know I'm probably going to say the wrong thing here. But I'm really sorry, Amy."

I nodded, as though these words meant something, as if they hadn't just bounced off me. "Thanks," I said, walking over to him. "I really appreciate that." I slid my arms around his neck and kissed him, lightly at first, then more intensely. He kissed me back, but then pulled away.

"Um," he said. "Are you sure we should be . . . I mean, don't you want to talk or something?"

"No," I said. I was there to forget I wanted to talk, there so I would have something else to feel for a while. "It's fine. I prom- ise." I kissed him again, just wanting to think about something else. Or not think about anything at all. And this was the perfect solution. I tugged at the bottom of his College of the West T-shirt, pulling it over his head and tossing it on Hugo's bed. And then, before I could change my mind or lose my nerve, I pulled my own tank top off.

"Wow," Michael said, looking at me. "Um." I struggled with my skirt's zipper with fingers that were trembling slightly. But I got it undone and stepped out of it and stood facing him. "Really?" he asked, sounding incredulous.

"Absolutely," I said, as though I was sure. And to prove it, I started kissing him again. We stumbled backward together until we hit his bed. I sat on the edge of it while Michael cleared it off hurriedly, then stepped out of his khakis and yanked off his tube socks. "The light?" I asked, trying to keep my voice even.

"Right, sure," he said, crossing back to the door, locking it, then flipping the switch and throwing us both into the dark.

Have you ever been down to Colorado? I spend a lot of time there in my mind.
—Merle Haggard

I let myself in the front door of the International House. I wanted to go to Bronwyn's room, clear a spot on the floor for myself, and go to sleep. I just wanted to close my eyes and make it all go away for a little while.

"Sullivan?" a voice called from the TV room. I paused, one foot on the stairs that would lead me to peace and quiet. "That you?" the voice asked, sounding a little desperate this time. I sighed, turned, and walked toward it.

Leonard was still on the couch, and it looked like he might not have moved in the last few hours, except that he had put on a T-shirt, a faded yellow one that read CALL ME KEVIN. "Hey," I said. He was still playing his game, only now it seemed the terrain was different. It looked rockier now, and less sylvan.

He turned his head and looked at me. "Oh," he said. "I thought you were Roger."

"I think he's still at the party," I said. "I left early," I added unnecessarily, just to have something to say. "I was just . . . tired."

He kept looking at me, as the game continued on behind him. "You look different," he finally said.

"Oh," I said, tugging the hem of Bronwyn's skirt down. "Yeah, I guess."

"It's good," he concluded after looking at me for a moment longer. "Nice." He nodded once more, then turned back to the game, jumping out of the way of some kind of wolf creature just in time to avoid being killed. As I watched, words in flourishy type flashed across the screen. **Quickly! You must save Princess Jenna!**

"Princess Jenna?" I asked, and saw the tips of Leonard's ears turn red.

"Yeah," he said, with an embarrassed laugh. "Her real name is Princess Arundel. But I figured out how to hack the game and change it."

"So who's Jenna?" I asked, as he flushed again.

"Nobody," he said with a shrug. "Just this girl in my chem class. Whatever."

"Okay," I said, but I noticed that he suddenly wasn't playing as well, as three gnomes appeared and began kicking him in the shins. I stared at the screen, as buff virtual Leonard shook off the gnomes and began dashing across the rocks again. "What's the appeal?" I asked.

"Of Honour Quest?" he asked, not looking away from the game, fingers jabbing the buttons on the controller.

"Yeah," I said. "You just run around and try not to let the wolves get you?"

"Lupine were-demons," he corrected me. "And it's not just running around. I'm on a quest."

"For what?"

"We think it's to save Arundel. Or, you know, Jenna."

"You think?" I asked, leaning over the back of the couch.

"The end of Honour Quest is a carefully guarded secret. Nobody I know has finished it yet. And really, it's not about the destination. It's getting there that's the good part. But there have been rumors that the princess isn't the final goal. That at the end of it, the game reboots and you're on a new quest. And you've actually just spent this quest gaining knowledge and strength and faerie acorns in preparation for it. Which would be *sweet*."

"Got it," I said, watching him onscreen for a moment longer, running full-out toward an ending he wasn't even sure of. I shook my head. "'Night, Leonard," I said, as I headed toward the stairs.

"Totally," he said. "You too. Goddamn orcs," he muttered as he began slaying again with a vengeance.

I headed up the stairs to Bronwyn's room and pushed open the door. The room was dark, and I was about to turn the lights on when I saw that Bronwyn was in bed, sleeping, her breath slow and rhythmic. I hadn't even realized she'd left the party. Using the light spilling in from the hallway, I looked around the room and saw that alongside her bed, she'd laid out a sleeping bag for me, with a neatly folded green T-shirt and sweatpants on top of it.

It seemed easier to just change into these rather than try to deal with my suitcase in the dark. I closed the door and changed, trying to make as little noise as possible. But Bronwyn seemed to be a pretty deep sleeper, which was a good thing. Because I'd just wanted to go to sleep, anyway. If she'd been awake, we probably would have had to talk about the party, and I could have told her about Bradley. But now I didn't have to, so it worked out.

I pulled the sleeping bag around my shoulders, hoping that whatever magic had worked the last two nights would work tonight, and I could just go to sleep. I wanted to block out the memories of Michael and stop remembering that night. But as soon as I closed my eyes, all I could see was his face, and I knew that probably wasn't going to happen.

Those memories so steeped in yesterday.
Those memories you couldn't run away.

—*Ember FX*

MARCH 11—THREE MONTHS EARLIER

I sat on the edge of Michael's bed and put my bra back on, getting the hooks wrong but not really caring. Michael was rubbing my back in slow circles, and I moved away from him under the pretense of getting my shirt. But mostly, I just didn't want him to touch me anymore. I pulled on the tank top with hands that were shaking slightly.

"You okay?" he asked from the bed, where he was sitting up, still under the sheet. I wondered why I'd never noticed before that the whole room smelled like pizza.

"I'm fine," I said brightly, but I could hear the edge of hysteria in my voice. I found my skirt balled up under the bed and I smoothed it out, then pulled it on, standing to zip it.

"Hey," Michael said, sounding concerned. He held out his hand to me. "Come here."

I didn't want to go there. All I wanted was to get out of his room as soon as I could, and, if possible, go back in time and erase the last twenty minutes. "I should get going," I said, trying to keep at bay whatever was threatening to break apart inside me. I looked around for my black heels, but they seemed to have vanished.

Michael pulled his khakis back on and walked over to stand in front of me. "Amy," he said, reaching out to smooth down my hair.

"Have you seen my shoes?" I asked, trying to step around him.

"What's the matter?" he asked, taking my hands in his. "Look, I promise the second time will be better." I pulled my hands away, reasoning that I really didn't need my shoes. I could get home barefoot. It would be fine.

Michael pulled me into a hug, running his hand over my hair, and I felt myself stiffen. It was all just too much. Everything was too much. What we'd just done, and how I hadn't known that I would feel so vulnerable while it was happening, which was the last thing that I wanted to feel. How when it was over, I'd realized what a huge mistake it had been. But a mistake that was impossible to take back. How, suddenly, with his arms around me, I felt like I couldn't breathe. I pushed him away and stepped back. As I did, I saw a hurt look flash over his face, but I didn't care. All I knew was that I had to get out of there.

"I have to go," I said, hearing how unsteady my voice sounded, and feeling like something inside me was crumbling. I couldn't believe I'd ever thought this was a good idea. I just needed to go someplace where I could be alone, and try to handle the fact that everything in the world seemed to be broken.

"Let's talk about this," he said, sitting down on the bed and patting the spot next to him.

"*I don't want to talk!*" I yelled this, not even knowing I was going to, and my voice broke on the last word.

"Okay," said Michael, now looking a little freaked out. "Um. That's okay. You don't have to."

I turned away from him and forced myself to take a breath, even though I could feel how jagged it was. "I just . . . I just want to be alone, okay? I'm sorry. I shouldn't have come here." I headed for the door, leaving behind in his messy room my shoes, my virginity, and the last semblance of the girl I'd once been.

"Amy," Michael said. "Don't—"

But I never found out what he was going to say, as I slammed the door behind me and walked down his dorm hallway, keeping my eyes on the industrial brown carpet, not looking back to see if he followed me. I felt tears pricking the inside of my eyelids. My eyes felt like they were burning, and two tears escaped from my right eye. I could feel just how much there was—everything that had happened, the enormity of it all. There weren't enough tears to cry. I didn't have enough voice left to scream. And it wasn't like anything was going to change. No matter how much I cried, even if I let myself yell, things were never going to get better. So I pushed back as hard as I could against the feelings inside me that were crying out for release. I concentrated on breathing, and taking one step, then another, and not thinking about what had happened, or the house I would have to go back to, or how it felt that my heart was beyond broken—how it felt so shattered that it was ground down to powder. I pushed these feelings away with everything I had left.

And by the time I stepped outside, into the still warm evening, I had stopped crying.

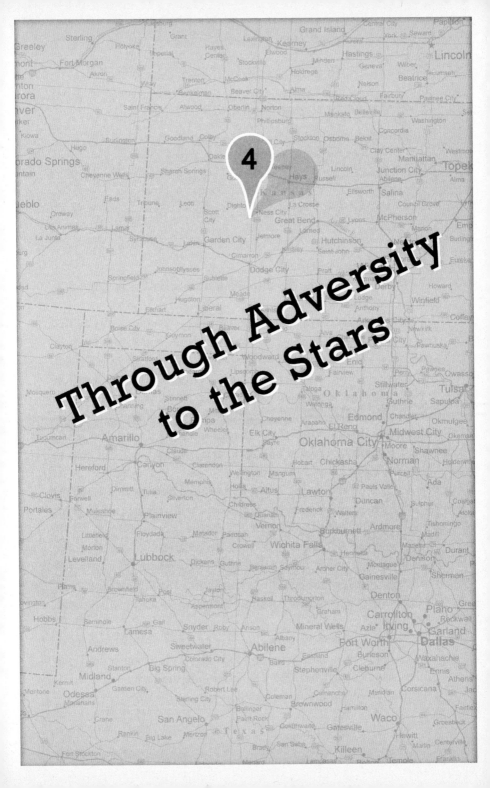

4

Through Adversity
to the Stars

I've reached the point of know return.
—*Kansas*

We were going to Kentucky.

Well, first we had to go through Kansas and Missouri, but then we were going to Kentucky.

When I'd woken up at ten that morning—having finally drifted off to sleep around four—Bronwyn was gone, and so was my suitcase. My jeans were folded on her bed, along with a white T-shirt, very like the one she'd worn the day before. There was a yellow Post-it lying on the clothes that read *For Amy*, and a pink Post-it next to the yellow one that read *Wear Me*. Confused, but not seeing any other options, I got changed, feeling the softness of the fabric as I did so. It was a nice shirt, and it was white—I'd have to be sure to stay far away from jam.

I rolled up the sleeping bag and headed downstairs. Leonard was asleep on the couch, snoring softly, controller resting on his chest. As I headed to the kitchen, Roger came out of it, wearing the "Bear Necessities" T-shirt he'd bought at the Yosemite gift shop. He must have just showered, because his hair was still wet and I could see the comb tracks through it, the cowlick in the back struggling valiantly to stand up. "Hey," he said. "Morning."

"Hi," I said quietly, even though there was probably no need, as the game was blaring some kind of pan-flute music and that didn't seem to be disturbing Leonard in the slightest.

"Did you have fun last night?" he asked.

"I did," I said, a fact that still surprised me. But I had actually been having fun, until the end.

"Good," he said, smiling at me. "I wasn't sure, when you left early . . ."

"Oh, that," I said, looking down at the ground. "I was just tired."

"Yeah," he said, stretching a little. "It's been an intense couple of days."

"It has," I agreed, realizing as I said this that it had only been three days. And that my life before the trip was beginning to seem very far away.

"Ready to hit the road?"

"Yep," I said, not registering my word choice until it was too late to take it back. But we were in Colorado, after all, so maybe cowboy speech was more acceptable. Or at least less random. "I need to find my suitcase, though. It wasn't in Bronwyn's room."

"That's okay," Roger said as he grabbed his duffel from the doorway. "Bron brought it down this morning."

"Really? That was nice of her."

"Mmm," he said vaguely. We walked past Leonard on our way to the door, and Roger fist-bumped the hand that was draped across the back of the sofa. "Later, dude," he said, continuing out to the car.

"Totally," Leonard mumbled.

I looked up at the screen and noticed that it was now flashing 𝔐𝔞𝔨𝔢 𝔥𝔞𝔰𝔱𝔢! 𝔜𝔬𝔲 𝔪𝔲𝔰𝔱 𝔰𝔞𝔳𝔢 𝔓𝔯𝔦𝔫𝔠𝔢𝔰𝔰 𝔄𝔪𝔶!

I watched the words as they faded, feeling myself smile. "Bye, Leonard," I said softly. "Good luck with your quest." I stepped outside and pulled the door to the International House shut behind me. Then I followed Roger out to the car.

"Bron had a meeting early this morning," he said as he put his duffel in the backseat, not making eye contact with me. He walked to the driver's side door, and I got in the passenger seat and buckled up. "But she said to tell you good-bye."

"Oh," I said, a little surprised and trying not to be disappointed.

"I, of course, told her I wouldn't," Roger said, shooting a quick smile at me. He started the car, signaled, and we pulled out onto the street. "But she wanted me to give you this." He handed me an envelope that was made of thick, cream-colored paper. AMY was written across the front in the same handwriting that had been on the Post-its. "She told me to wait until we were moving."

"Okay," I said, completely confused. I took the envelope and opened it.

From the desk of

BRONWYN E. TAYLOR

Hey Amy!

Sorry I wasn't able to say good-bye to you in person. I have to go to a mediation for two people in the house, who are both being pigheaded beyond all reason, and it's—well, never mind. Anyway, you should come back and visit us real soon! I hope you and Roger have a great rest of your trip. If you go through Texas, give it a six-clap for me.

Give old RS a hug for me. And keep in touch! Contact info is on the back.

xoxo, Bron

P.S.—Don't be mad about the suitcase! I did what I had to do. Taylors do not hide their light under a bushel. And neither should you! I promise you'll thank me someday!

I stared down at the note. It was sweet, except for the P.S., which was, to say the least, troubling. "Roger," I said, glancing toward the back of the car, "is there something wrong with my suitcase?"

"Um, what?" he asked, face slightly flushed as he fiddled with the iPod. "Oh, look, the interstate."

"Roger!"

"I don't know anything," he said. "I swear. I am merely a pawn in all this. She just brought down your suitcase this morning and told me not to open it, or let *you* open it, until we were on the road."

"And you just agreed?" I asked, turning in my seat and looking to the way-back, where my suitcase was.

"Well, she threatened to turn the rabbit on me if I didn't."

I didn't want to, but I couldn't help laughing at that. Roger laughed too and sounded relieved. "Look, we're almost at Fran's. If it's something truly unfixable, we're still close enough to go back and do something about it."

As he said this, Roger took an exit off the interstate, and then pulled into a parking lot that seemed almost to be filled with as many huge commercial trucks as cars. "Wow," I said, as we parked in the shadow of a huge semi.

"Yeah," he said. "This place is pretty popular with truckers and students. It makes for an interesting mix. Welcome to Fran's Pancake House."

I got out of the car, walked quickly around to the back, and lifted the door. I unzipped my suitcase and stared down into it. All my clothes were gone.

Well, that wasn't quite true, I realized as I dug through it. Bronwyn had left me my underwear—and given me the green thong and matching bra. She'd also left my "Anyone Can Whistle" T-shirt. But my other clothes were gone, and everything else was hers—the outfit I'd worn to the party, tank tops, dresses, skirts. I finished searching through the clothes and just stared down into the suitcase, not sure what to say.

"What?" Roger asked, hovering behind me. "Is it bad?"

"No," I said. "She's just given me an entirely new wardrobe, that's all."

"Oh." He stepped closer, maybe figuring that it was safe, now that I didn't seem mad enough to strike him. "But that's a good thing, right?"

I looked down at all the beautiful things that were suddenly mine and realized that Bronwyn hadn't given me clothes—she'd taken away my camouflage. She'd made it impossible to keep hiding. I wasn't exactly thrilled about this, or the fact that she'd hijacked my suitcase without asking me. But the clothes *were* lovely. I'd felt prettier last night than I had in a long time. Basically, it was all just a lot to take in before breakfast. "It is," I said, zipping the suitcase closed again, and then closing the back. "I think. Let's eat. I'm starving."

As we walked to the restaurant, Roger waxed rhapsodic about their pancakes, but I was only half listening. In the gleaming silver of a fuel truck, I caught my reflection in Bronwyn's—now my—white shirt. I couldn't help but notice that I was, in fact, standing up a little straighter.

⟷

I pushed away my empty pancake plate and looked across the table at Roger. The atlas was between us, open to the map of the country. There was still a long way to go before we reached the East Coast, but I was amazed to see how much ground we'd covered. We were a long way from Ohio, though, which was where we were supposed to be heading at this very moment. As I looked at where we were versus where we were supposed to be, I realized that I would have to call my mother—probably tonight—and tell her that we weren't in Akron. The thought of this conversation made my stomach plunge a little, but it wasn't nearly as nerve-wracking as it had been a few days ago.

Roger traced a path with his finger across the states that sat between Colorado and Connecticut. As I watched, he moved across to Kansas, through Missouri, then to Kentucky, and stopped.

Orig. route: Gallup—Tulsa—
Terre Haute—Akron—Stanwich
Our route: Yosemite—Delta—
Colorado Springs—Wichita—
Louisville—Stanwich??

Fran's Pancake House

Colorado Springs, CO
"Right off the interstate!"
Breakfast served 24/7/365"

• BREAKFAST •

All breakfasts served with coffee or tea.
Choice of potato: hash browns/home fries/fries
Choice of bread: wheat, white, multi, sourdough, bagel, English muffin

Francakes 5.99	2 Eggs, 2 Bacon, 2 Sausage 5.99
2 Eggs Any Style 3.99	Waffles 4.99
Francake Short Stack 3.99	Orange Juice 1.50
2 Eggs, 2 Bacon 4.99	Waffles Deluxe 5.99
Multigrain Francakes 5.99	Apple Juice 1.50
2 Eggs, 2 Sausage 4.99	Blueberry Waffles 6.99
Blueberry Francakes 6.99	Grapefruit Juice 1.50

"You want to go to Kentucky," I said. Roger looked up at me, surprised, then looked down to where his finger was resting on the map.

"Oh," he said. He sighed, tapping his finger on the state. "I don't know. It's just what I've been thinking about this morning." He ran both hands through his hair, and the cowlick in the back, as though happy to be freed, stood up jauntily.

"Hadley?" I guessed. It felt strange for me to be saying her name, especially after seeing the picture and hearing Bronwyn's take on her.

"It's obvious, huh?" he asked. "I just thought she'd be here, and I could talk to her. I was all prepared for it. And then she wasn't. . . ." He looked out the window, at the cars rushing by on the interstate. "I swear I don't want to stalk her," he said. "I just need to know what happened. And she's not returning my calls. . . ."

"Well," I said, looking down at the map, "I've never been to Kentucky."

Roger smiled at that, then turned back to me. "We don't have time," he said. "We're supposed to be in . . ."

"Akron," I supplied.

"Akron," he repeated. "And then in Connecticut by tomorrow. I don't think we can make it to Kentucky."

I stared down at the map. I wasn't ready to be in Connecticut yet. For some reason, I really wasn't in any hurry to see my mother again. And if we were a day—or two—late, what could my mother do about it? It seemed like Roger was on a quest of his own, just like Virtual Leonard. And who was I to stop that? "I think we should go," I said, making a decision.

"Really?"

"Really," I said. "It's just a detour, right?"

"It's a big detour," he said. "Your mother—"

"Will just have to deal with it. I'll just . . . tell her we hit lots of traffic in the mid-Atlantic states." I could barely believe that I was saying these things. My mother was going to kill me. She'd left another message on my phone that morning, and I hadn't listened to it yet, or responded. Even though I had been trying to push these thoughts away, I knew she was probably worried. Guilt twisted my stomach and made my Francakes churn. But Roger looked up at me, and I tried to shake off these feelings. After all, she was the one who had gone off and left me for a month; I couldn't do the same to her for four days?

"Let's do it," I said as firmly as I could, even though my heart was pounding. "Kentucky."

Roger stared at me for a moment longer, then nodded and offered me his pencil. "Want to figure out our route, Chekov?" he asked. He peered at the map. "I don't think it's actually going to take us long. And if we go through Kansas, we can meet up with my friend Drew. . . ."

"I think we'll go through Kansas," I said. As I flipped through the state maps, looking at the interstates we'd have to take, a thought occurred to me that made my stomach clench a little bit. "Roger," I asked, not really wanting to know the answer, but making myself ask it anyway, "is this—the Hadley thing—why you agreed to come on this trip in the first place?"

He looked up at me and met my eyes, a little guiltily, and I knew the answer was yes. This shouldn't have bothered or disappointed me, but it did. "It's okay," I said quickly. "I mean—"

"Well, yes," Roger said, interrupting me. "It was, at first. I mean, my mother asked me, but I didn't have to agree. I could have gotten my father to pay for my flight. But I thought it would be a good way to see the country, and I thought that Hadley was here, and if I could just see her, and talk to her . . ."

I nodded, telling myself not to be bothered by this. Of course he hadn't been excited about taking a trip with a high schooler he barely knew. I hadn't been happy about the trip; why was I suddenly upset that he hadn't been either?

"But seriously," he said, with enough gravity in his tone that I looked up at him. "It's not what I thought it was going to be. I'm having fun. I mean, it's an adventure, right?"

"Right," I said, looking down at the country. "An adventure." And since he'd just put his cards down on the table, I thought that I should probably return the favor. "I didn't want to do this at all," I said. "I mean, at first. But now . . . I mean, I'm glad. That we're doing this, I mean."

"Me too," he said, smiling at me. A busboy came and cleared away our plates with a loud sigh, which I took as our cue to leave. We headed out of Fran's, causing the bell at the top of the door to jingle, and stepped out of the way of two bleary-eyed truckers who were stumbling in.

"One thing," I said, as he unlocked the car with the clicker from a few feet away. "The guy last night at the party," I went on, as we walked around to our opposite sides of the car and looked at each other across the hood. This had been bothering me since it happened. "The one who said that you had fire. What—what did he mean?"

"Oh," Roger said, and I noticed that he wasn't looking at me. "I guess that must be a guy thing. It's stupid." He looked down at the key chain, fiddled with it.

"Was it about my hair?" I asked, sure that this was the answer and dreading it.

"What?" he asked, looking up at me. "No. Your hair's great. It meant that he thought you were hot. And he thought that we were . . . together."

"Oh," I said, understanding Roger's reaction now and feeling my face get warm.

"Yeah," he said with a laugh, opening his door and getting in. I stood outside the car for a moment longer, trying to get my face to cool down and feeling a small smile start to form on my face. Because if I remembered correctly, Roger hadn't told the guy that it wasn't true. This shouldn't have made me happy. But it did.

←——→

As soon as Roger steered the car toward Kansas, the landscape began to look much more Kansas-like, even though we were still in Colorado. Soon the mountains were gone, and everything was flatter, dry-looking, straw colored—and we had our big open skies back again. As expected, the land was very, very flat. But it was just as arresting, in its own way, as the mountains had been. There was an expansiveness, a peacefulness to it, and I propped my feet on the dashboard, leaned my head back against the headrest, and just took in the scenery.

When we crossed the state line into Kansas, I noticed that signs with lights attached to the top began appearing at the side of the road, reading WHEN FLASHING, TURN TO WEATHER ADVISORY CHANNEL. I hadn't paid much attention to these at first—I felt that after Colorado, it was going to take a lot to surprise me, sign-wise—until I realized that the weather advisory that the sign was referring to was most likely a *tornado*. Suddenly the skies didn't seem so peaceful anymore, but at least, as far as I could see, they were still clear.

←——→

"Is it a person?" Roger asked.

"Yes," I said. "Nineteen."

"Is it a man?"

"No. Eighteen."

"Is she alive?"

"No. Seventeen."

"Is she famous?"

"Very. Sixteen."

←——→

When we headed into the Sunflower Mart, without even asking, Roger grabbed a cream soda for me and a root beer for him, then made a beeline for the tiny apparel section.

"Amy!" he yelled, even though the mini-mart was empty.

"What?" I asked quietly, coming over to join him.

155

Where I've Been . . .

State #4: COLORADO—The Centennial State

motto: Nil sine numine (Nothing without Providence)

Size: Again, big. And mOUNTAINOUS. And this apparently causes lots of problems for truckers.

Facts: "America the Beautiful" was written IN Colorado Springs! There was a reason the mountains looked purple-they were the actual ones from the song!

Notes: Sign on highway: call *CSP IN CASE OF ROAD RAGE. But is this your road rage? Or someone else's? Unclear. But maybe this road rage is due to the fact that if brakes fail, you're supposed to remain on the interstate. I could see how that could lead to road rage.

ROGER PLAYLIST #5

"No Place Like Home" or "Why Won't Amy Buy Sunglasses?"
or "The Sunflower State"

SONG TITLE	ARTIST
"Where Is Home?"	Bloc Party
"Jolene"	The Weepies
"Somewhere Over the Rainbow" (cover)	Call Me Kevin
"Brand New Day"	Joshua Radin
"Starlight"	Muse
"Even Fairy Tale Characters Would Be Jealous"	PlayRadioPlay!
"Daylight"	Matt and Kim
"The Dark in You"	Plushgun
"100,000 Fireflies	The Magnetic Fields
"Wake Up"	The Secret Handshake
"Dust in the Wind"	Kansas
"Goodbye Yellow Brick Road"	Elton John
"I'll Do the Driving"	Fountains of Wayne
"Time After Time" (cover)	Quietdrive
"Faith in Fast Cars"	The Format
"Wonderful You"	The Dandy Warhols
"Take a Chance on Me"	Erasure

"Behold," he said, spinning the black plastic display, causing the sunglasses, priced at $4.99, to whirl around. *"Sunglasses."*

I tried to figure out if this was his way of telling me that I'd been wearing his too much, even though I thought I'd been careful not to. I resolved not to wear them at all in the future. "Okay," I said, embarrassed, walking over to the chip section and grabbing some Doritos.

"You can get some! And for a reasonable price, too."

"I'm okay," I said, picking up some candy. "But I won't borrow yours anymore."

"No, I don't care," Roger said, coming to join me by the counter, tossing down two mini Paydays by the register, and plunking down a quarter for them. "I just don't want you to have to keep squinting into the sun."

"I'm fine," I said shortly, and I saw Roger blink at this, then nod and head back to the car as I handed over my credit card.

←——→

"Okay. So it's a she. And she's dead. And famous. *Very* famous. And she's not Queen Isabella."

I shook my head. "I can't believe that was your first guess. Fifteen."

"How do you do this?" I asked, looking across Roger at the speaker box outside something called a Sonic Drive-In, where we were attempting to have lunch.

"There's a cherry-lime soda on the menu," Roger said, staring at the huge, illuminated menu adjacent to the covered area we'd pulled the car under. "I have no idea what that is, but I might just have to try it."

"Oh my gosh," I said, also staring at the menu, which was almost too much to take in. There was grilled cheese. There were tater tots. There was chili—*several kinds*. "They have mozzarella sticks. I have to get some."

A crackling sound came out of the speaker near Roger's side, then died away again. Roger tapped it tentatively. "Hello?" he asked. "We need mozzarella sticks out here!"

←——→

"So," Roger said. His mix was playing for the third time, and I mouthed along to the lyrics of the Fountains of Wayne song I had already memorized.

Our Sonic lunch had come with two mints stapled to the brown paper bag, and I unwrapped one and dropped it into his palm, then realized what I'd done and sat back hard against my seat.

"To recap. She's dead, very famous, and not Queen Isabella, Margaret Mead, or Queen Elizabeth."

"Correct," I said, staring out the window. "Thirteen."

←——→

When we were an hour outside of Wichita, the skies began to darken. I thought I'd known what cloudy skies looked like. We did get them occasionally in California. But I'd never seen anything like this. There was just so much sky, and all of it started to look cloudy, and I got the sense that things might turn on us, very quickly.

"Um. Roger?"

He glanced over at me, looking stressed. "I'm thinking," he said. "Don't rush me. I only have one question left."

"Not that. I was just wondering . . . do you know when tornado season is?"

"Oh." I saw him peer outside, as though noticing the cloudy skies for the first time. "Hmm. No. Do you?"

"No." I looked out at the clouds, which were now covering the entire landscape, hanging low, and stretching on for as far as I could see.

"Well," he said after a moment, "the signs aren't flashing yet. So maybe we don't need to think about it."

"Okay," I said, but I stared out the window, worried about what might be headed our way.

←——→

Roger stared at me in disbelief. *"Who?"*

"Ethel Merman," I said, helping myself to some Skittles. "She's female, dead, famous."

159

"Well, I've never heard of her," he said, frowning at the road.

"She's a renowned actress! She originated most of the major musical theater roles."

Roger just shook his head. "I think you made her up. I want a do-over."

"All right," I said, turning in my seat and facing him. "Your turn." As I said this, we crossed the city limits into Wichita, and I let out a sigh of relief. Even if a tornado did show up, at least we weren't in the middle of the highway, totally vulnerable.

"Wichita," said Roger. "Finally." He extricated his cell phone from the cup holder, where it had been buried under the collected detritus of the day—candy wrappers, white Sonic napkins, empty soda bottles. "I should call Drew."

Roger had started talking about Drew more as we got closer, mostly trying to stall as he pumped me for Twenty Questions clues. He didn't think we'd need to stay the night in Wichita— and we really didn't have time for that, if we were going to make it to Kentucky—but he thought it would be a good place to take a break. And seeing how tired Roger was looking, how he kept shifting in his seat, I realized that he was probably ready for a rest. I was too, actually. My butt was starting to go numb, and my leg muscles were feeling tight. "Drew's a friend from college?" I asked.

"Yes," Roger said. "He lived on my floor last year, and was always crashing in my room because he kept getting locked out of his. He lost his key more than anyone in the dorm's history. The RA finally stopped charging him for replacements, because she was starting to feel bad about taking all his money." Roger pressed a number, listened for a moment, then shook his head. "Voice mail," he said to me. "Hey, Cheeks," he said into the phone. "Listen, dude, I'm with a friend in Kansas, and I was wondering if you wanted to meet up. Call me if you get this, it's almost eight." He then hung up without saying good-bye, which I was getting more used to now, and placed the phone back on top of his empty M&M bag.

"Cheeks?" I asked.

"Oh," Roger said, laughing, "it's just a stupid nickname thing. All the guys on our floor had them."

"What was yours?" Roger didn't appear to hear me but looked out the window intently. "Roger?" I asked. "What was—" Before I could finish, his phone started vibrating in the cup holder. Roger glanced down at it, but on impulse, surprising myself, I grabbed it and saw that the display read CHEEKS CALL-ING. I ignored Roger's hand, which was motioning for me to give him the phone, and opened it. "Hello, Roger's phone," I said, sliding to the edge of my seat, out of his reach. Roger continued to try and grab for the phone, causing the car to weave slightly in the lane.

"Hey," a low-pitched voice on the other end said. "Is Magellan there?"

I turned to Roger, who was still trying to get the phone, feeling the smile taking over my face. *"Magellan?"* I repeated gleefully.

Roger sighed, and his hand drooped. Clearly, this was why he'd been trying to intercept the call. "Yeah," the voice on the phone said. "You know . . . Roger."

"Sure," I said, still smiling. "Just a second." I handed him the phone. "Magellan," I said, "you have a call."

"It's just a stupid nickname thing," he hissed at me, before taking the phone. "Cheeks, hey," he said. "Listen, we're in your neck of the woods . . . what?" Roger glanced over at me again. "Oh. No. That's just a friend. Hadley's in Kentucky."

Now it was my turn to feel embarrassed. I looked out the window until Roger waved at me to get my attention and mimed writing. I grabbed a pen and wrote the address and directions Roger dictated to me for the Wichita Country Club on a Sonic napkin.

When Roger hung up with Drew, he didn't look directly at me but instead stared ahead at the road, as though there was something to see besides endless highway and cloudy skies. "So Drew says it should take us about twenty minutes," he said. "I guess he's just finishing up work."

"Oh, that's great," I said. "Magellan?"

"Well, whatever," he said, and I noticed that he was blushing slightly. "I told you it was just a stupid nickname thing."

"I think it's funny," I said. "Because of your whole explorer thing?"

"Yes," said Roger. "But it's really gotten out of hand. I swear, some of the guys on the floor never even knew my real name. Hadley thought it was really stupid." He had the tone in his voice that came out whenever he said her name. A combination of wistful and resigned.

"I think it's funny," I repeated quietly.

Roger shot me a quick smile. "I did too," he said. "At first. It's less funny after six months when people are yelling it at you across the quad." He pointed to the napkin on the console between us. "Ready to navigate, Chekov?"

I picked up the napkin and smoothed it out, trying to decipher my scrawled directions. "Ready."

Twenty minutes later, as promised, we pulled up in front of the Wichita Country Club. There was a very intimidating guard in a small wooden house checking cars as they drove through, so we drove a little farther down the street and parked. We'd both gotten out of the car and Roger had taken out his phone to call Drew again when I heard a screech of tires. A tiny red car was careening out of the entrance and heading straight toward us.

"And that'll be Cheeks," Roger said, smiling. The car swung around and stopped next to the Liberty. The driver's side opened, and a round-faced, round-headed person emerged. He was wearing a teal polo shirt, pressed khakis, and loafers. "Dude," Roger said, walking over to the car. "You look like you're about to sell me insurance. Or trying to get me to rush your frat."

"Magellan," said Drew, and he and Roger did a quick guy hug

that seemed to mostly consist of hitting each other on the back. "You happen to be looking at the Wichita Golf Club's newest golfing assistant."

"You mean golfing assistant as in . . . caddy?" Roger asked.

"It's much more than that," Drew insisted. "There's an art to it. I have to choose the clubs. I have to read the greens. . . ." He gestured expansively and must have noticed me as he did so. "Well, *hello*," he said to me, giving me a big smile, and I noticed that his voice was suddenly deeper.

I registered all of this with surprise, and a growing sense of anxiety. He thought I was pretty. I knew it was probably because of Bronwyn's clothes, and I felt a flash of anger at her for doing this to me. I liked being invisible. Things were easier that way. I felt my heart pounding as I looked at him, smiling expectantly at me, hating how awkward even the simplest interaction now felt. Old me would have smiled back, and even flirted a little, just for fun. But I just stuck my hands in the pockets of my jeans and stared at the ground, wishing I was still in an oversize T-shirt. "Hi," I murmured. "I'm Amy."

"Andrew O'Neal," he said. "Pleasure." He looked over at Roger and raised his eyebrows, but Roger frowned and shook his head, and Drew sighed. "Nice to meet you," he said a little resignedly, his voice back to his normal register. I looked back and forth between the two of them, trying to figure out what had just occurred.

"Now that we've been properly introduced," said Drew, "let's move on to more important matters. Such as food."

I hadn't realized it until he'd said the word, but I was starving. Which was ridiculous, because we'd been eating and snacking all day and hadn't been doing anything except sitting in a car. Roger looked at me, and I nodded. "Sounds good," he said to Drew.

"Excellent," Drew said, heading back toward his car. He motioned for us to join him. "The foursome that I was assisting forgot, for some reason, to extend an invitation to the clubhouse for dinner. So I'm famished. And you probably need a break from driving, Magellan. I think New Way is really the only way to go."

"New Way?" asked Roger, as Drew opened the driver's door and Roger opened the passenger door.

"New Way," Drew agreed, pushing his seat forward so that I could climb into the back. "You'll see."

There's no place like home.
—The Wizard of Oz

New Way, we soon discovered, actually meant NuWay burgers, and was, according to Drew, a Wichita landmark. Wichita itself seemed kind of confusing, with a highway running across the city, dividing it in two. Drew pulled up in front of NuWay Café, the name spelled out in white on a red and yellow awning. We suddenly seemed a long way from the yellow and red arrows of In-N-Out, with palm trees on the cups. CRUMBLY IS GOOD! a sign on the window of the restaurant proclaimed.

We followed Drew into the restaurant, which was decorated with framed black-and-white pictures of NuWay and its customers through the years. It seemed Drew was telling the truth about the landmark thing. He took over the ordering for us and insisted on treating, and we emerged five minutes later with two brown paper bags that smelled delicious and were immediately dotted with faint translucent grease spots. We all got back in the car, and Drew drove us down the highway to Freddy's Frozen Custard.

"Frozen custard?" I asked. Unable to find a spot, Drew had double-parked and headed inside to get us dessert. I pulled on my seat belt to give it some slack and leaned forward into the space between the front seats.

"It's a midwestern thing," Roger said, turning his head to the left to talk to me. When he did, I sat back a little—I hadn't realized how close together our faces would be if he did that. "I discovered it this year. It's like ice cream, but a little thicker. It's good."

"I bet it's no Twenty-one Choices, though," I said, referring to the frozen yogurt place in Pasadena, taking a chance that Roger would know it too.

He smiled at the name. "Love that place," he said. I don't know what he was thinking, but I was thinking about home, about California, and how it seemed very far away at the moment. Roger leaned forward a little and turned around more toward me. "Frozen yogurt," he said, looking at me with a smile. "Such a California girl."

I smiled back, and silence fell between us. I took a breath to say something, when the driver's door opened again.

"And I'm back," Drew said, dropping into the car and handing three plastic Freddy's cups, red spoons sticking out of the top, to Roger. "Prepare to experience a Concrete," he said. "Nirvana contained in a frozen treat." He pulled out of the parking lot with a screech of tires and sped out into the intersection, throwing me back against the seat, causing Roger to slam against the passenger-side window, and prompting a cacophony of honking from all around us.

I felt myself begin to panic, and my stomach started to churn. I closed my eyes and tried to breathe, tried to block out the memory of a screech of tires and the terrible scraping metal sound, the feeling that I no longer had control of the car, the sickening spinning sensation and the way that time had seemed to slow down.

"Drew!" Roger said sharply. I opened my eyes and saw that he was looking at me, worried. "Could you slow down a little?"

"Why?" asked Drew, above the rap that he had cranked up.

"Just do it," Roger said, an edge I hadn't heard before still in his voice.

"Fine," Drew said a little petulantly, but he slowed down and started driving more calmly. I felt my own heart rate begin to decrease and my breath start to come more normally. It wasn't happening again. I was here, now. And Roger was here with me. I was safe.

You okay? Roger mouthed to me, and I nodded and tried to give him a smile. I'd thought that I was getting better at reading him, but I hadn't considered until then that it could be going both ways.

In about twenty minutes, we pulled into the staff entrance of the Wichita Country Club and swung around into the employee parking lot, which was almost totally deserted. It was fully dark out now, and clearer than it had been before. There were still clouds in the sky, but they were moving across the blackness, revealing the moon and stars, then blocking them out again.

"What are we doing back here?" Roger asked. "You putting in some overtime?"

"I promised you the ultimate Wichita experience," said Drew, putting the car into park. "I'm delivering." He got out, pushed his seat forward, and offered me his hand to help me out of the backseat. "Milady?"

I looked away from the hand and climbed out on my own. Old me would have smiled and taken his hand and said, *Why, thank you, good sir* and maybe made a *Camelot* reference. I just stared down at the ground while Drew locked the door.

Roger held out his free hand, the one that wasn't carrying our dessert, to Drew. "Keys," he said. "It's for your own good."

"Good call," Drew said, handing them over. "Where were you yesterday?" Drew led the way forward, and I fell in step next to Roger. Two of the cups were looking precarious, and I reached over and took them from him. He gave me a quick smile, and we hurried to keep up with Drew, who was a surprisingly fast walker. We crossed the parking lot and passed in front of what must have been the main country club building. It was imposing and white, with columns and bored-looking valets in red jackets, who were hanging out in front, smoking.

"Cheeks!" two of them called to Drew as he passed.

"I'm not here," he said. "Or on the back nine. You didn't see me."

"Got it," one of the valets called, and Drew gave him a salute as we walked by.

"They call you Cheeks here?" asked Roger.

"Word got out," he said, glancing back to where Roger and I were power walking behind him. "It caught on."

We had walked beyond the main building by this point and passed a large swimming pool that reflected the moonlight, a lone water wing bobbing in the shallow end. A little farther on, I could see deserted tennis courts and a practice wall with a white line painted across it to represent the net. The lights above the practice wall were turned on, and as we got closer, I could see that there was a girl there, playing. I slowed for a moment and watched her slamming the ball against the wall, and then returning her own hit as it came back to her, over and over again.

When Charlie had been playing, back when we were younger, when he'd been ranked and the hope of the local tennis coach, my father had painted the same line on the side of our garage, and on most nights, I'd hear the rhythmic smacking of the ball against the wall. When he quit two years ago—or was kicked off the team, I was never sure which—the absence of the sound was the hardest thing to get used to. It was like I kept listening for it, even though I knew it wasn't going to come back.

The girl missed one of her own shots and walked to pick up her ball, stretching a little as she did so. She saw us and waved with her racket. Then she turned back to the wall and continued playing, switching to her backhand. She was wearing all-white tennis clothes, and under the bright lights, she looked exotic and out of place, a large moth in a spotlight that shone directly down on her.

Drew made a sharp turn to the right, and Roger and I followed, as he led us onto the golf course.

"Dude, can we be here?" Roger asked.

"Of course not," said Drew, not slowing at all. "Have you a point?"

Roger glanced at me and shrugged, then hurried to keep pace with Drew. On impulse, I kicked off my flip-flops and carried them, walking barefoot. The golf course grass was dense and close-cropped, and it almost felt like I was standing on top of it, not sinking down at all. I dragged my toes back and forth across it for just a moment before running to keep up with the boys.

The three of us walked in a horizontal line across the fairway, empty open space all around us, the hills gently rolling, the woods close and dark on either side. It was utterly quiet, and very still, and none of us spoke as we walked. Every now and then we'd pass a sand trap, which seemed unnaturally bright against the darkness of the course. The traps must have been manicured recently; all of them had a complicated swirled pattern raked in. This made them look serene, like something I'd seen in pictures of Japanese Zen gardens, and not at all like the sources of great distress that they probably were. Even though it was dark out, we could easily see where we were going, lit by the course's occasional floodlight and the moon, bright in the huge sky, the stars shining through here with much more ease now that there were no streetlights or neon signs to obscure them.

Drew stopped at the tee by the twelfth hole, which was, according to the sign, a par four. He sat down on the grass, took the NuWay bag from Roger, and started spreading out a fast-food picnic. I sat down as well, dropping my flip-flops and setting down the Freddy's cups. When Drew handed me a burger, I took it a little doubtfully.

"Thanks," I said, trying to sound enthusiastic as I looked down at it. It was smaller than I'd expected, two halves in a white and red NuWay wrapper. It looked like a hamburger that had come undone—the meat appeared loose.

"All right," said Drew, rubbing his hands together. He gestured to the items he'd spread out on the flattened brown NuWay bags. "Now, we have tater tots, french fries, *and* onion rings. Ketchup, mustard, special sauce—"

"Tater tots?" Roger asked, grabbing one. "Seriously?"

"I told you NuWay was the way to go," he said. "They're amazing. Now, to the burgers. Do not be frightened of the crumbly. The crumbly is good."

"I read that on the sign," I said, clearing my throat. "But, um, why?"

"It's what NuWay is famous for. The burgers are loose. I don't know why. You'll have to try to believe."

Drew was just looking at Roger and me, waiting for us to begin. I looked down at my burger and took a bite. It wasn't bad. The hamburger was, as advertised, crumbly—almost more like taco meat. There were onions mixed in, giving it a little kick. I squeezed out a ketchup packet on top, and took a bigger bite. It was *good*. I looked up at Drew and nodded, giving him the thumbs-up with my free hand.

"Told you," he said, picking up his own burger, smiling.

"Dude," Roger said, looking up from his burger. "Amazing."

The burgers disappeared fast, along with the fries and tots. Feeling full and strangely peaceful, I stretched my legs out in front of me and leaned back on my elbows, looking up at the stars.

"So," Drew said, leaning back against his arms and crossing one ankle over his bent knee, looking at Roger. "You just happened to be passing through Wichita?"

Roger glanced over at me. "Well, kind of," he said. "We're driving Amy's mother's car from California, and—"

"We're headed to Connecticut," I said, feeling that this would simplify things, "eventually. Heading to Kentucky after this."

Drew sat up a little straighter. "Kentucky?" he asked, shaking his head. "Oh, man."

"What?" asked Roger, suddenly becoming very interested in gathering up the used ketchup packets. "I'm sure it's a fascinating state. I like bluegrass. I like fried chicken."

"You're going there for Hadley," Drew said matter-of-factly. "Come on, dude. I didn't just get here."

"Well, so what?" Roger said, stuffing the used napkins into the NuWay bag.

"Nothing wrong with that, exactly," Drew said, leaning back on his hands again. "A man on a quest. A Don Quixote searching for his Dulcinea."

"Drew used to be an English major before he decided philosophy would provide better job stability," Roger said, turning to me.

"But keep in mind, my good friend," said Drew, "Don Quixote never found his Dulcinea, did he? He did not. There sometimes isn't much difference between a knight's quest and a fool's errand."

Roger turned to me again. "I have no idea what he's talking about, do you?"

"Hadley never listened to you," Drew said. "Well, she never listened to me, either, but I wasn't dating her. I'm just saying. Think about if you really want to do this, okay?"

"Sure, Cheeks," Roger said with the air of someone who wants the conversation to end. But I could see that his expression was a little more troubled than it had been before.

"So. Amy," Drew said, turning to me. "What has brought you here, in the company of this foolish knave?"

I glanced over at Roger, who was now lying back on the tee, his arms folded behind his head. "It's a long story," I said.

"Can you give me the abridged version?" Drew asked.

"Oh," I said, looking over to Drew, "we're just taking a little detour." I saw Roger smile without moving his head, which was still tipped back, looking up at the sky.

"Well, that certainly was abridged," Drew said. "That was like *Reader's Digest* abridged. That was like *TV Guide* synopsis abridged. Can you give me a little more?"

Before I could respond, a roaring noise came from our left, shattering the stillness of the night. I turned and saw a riding mower cresting the hill one hole over. The person riding it was a guy, wearing big, DJ-style headphones, bobbing his head along to the music as he steered erratically around the course.

"Well, what do you know," Drew said. "Here comes Walcott." Drew waved, and the guy on the mower saw him, nodded, and steered over to the twelfth hole. When he got close to us, he killed the engine, which made the sounds of the cicadas suddenly seem much louder than they had before. He pulled his headphones back so that they hung around his neck.

"Hey, Drew," he said. "What's happening?" He climbed down from the mower and leaned back against it. He was thin and wiry, with curly blond hair, and seemed much smaller now that he was no longer sitting on top of the machine.

As I looked at the massive mower, it struck me how much my father would have loved to use it. Getting to mow this whole golf course would have been his idea of heaven. As soon as I thought this, I had to struggle to get my breath back. His idea of heaven was no longer so theoretical. Was he getting to experience it now, wherever he was? Was he mowing an endless lawn somewhere, listening to Elvis? Was he happy? I shut my eyes tight. How could he be, when we weren't there? When I wasn't there to give him Life Savers and make sure he didn't get lost?

I pressed my hands into the grass, struggling against the tide of feeling that threatened to pull me under. It finally subsided, but it didn't go easily.

"This is Derek Walcott," I faintly heard Drew saying, as though from someplace far away. "Walcott, this is Amy and this is Magellan."

"Roger," I heard him correct. "Hey."

I opened my eyes, glad for the camouflage of the darkness, and lifted a hand in a wave, not trusting my voice just yet.

"Did you guys get NuWay?" Walcott asked, walking over to us. "Got any left?"

"O rings," Drew said, holding them out to him. "Go to town."

"Thanks, man," said Walcott, taking the container from him. "I'm starving. I've been out here for, like, two hours and I'm only half done."

"I've told you," Drew said, tossing him a ketchup packet, which whacked him in the forehead, "if you do it in the morning, it'll go faster. You know, because it's light out then."

"It's hot in the morning," Walcott said, sitting down next to Roger. "We've talked about this."

Drew shrugged. "It's your funeral."

Walcott's head snapped up. "Now, *that* would be a good song title," he said.

"It already is," I said, without thinking. The three boys turned to look at me, and I felt my cheeks heating up a little. My throat felt tight, but I continued, feeling like I didn't have a choice. "From *Oliver!* You know, the musical?" Clearly, they didn't, as I got three blank stares in return. "Well, anyway, it's a musical. And 'That's Your Funeral' is a song in it."

"Bummer," Walcott said. "Still, we might be able to use it. I'm not sure we have a huge crossover audience with musicals."

"Walcott has a band," Drew clarified. "Please don't ask him about it, or he'll give you his demo."

"You have a band?" I asked. Drew groaned.

"I do," Walcott said, wiping his hands on his khaki shorts and leaving faint grease stains behind. "The Henry Gales. It's like emo-punk-alternative with a little hardcore edge. But we also do covers, you know, for weddings."

"Naturally," Roger said, smiling. "That's awesome."

"We played a show last night," Walcott said, a slightly dreamy expression coming over his face. "And it was so fresh. It's what it's all about, you know. You're telling your truth, to strangers, in the darkness. That's all. And when it works, it's *amazing*."

"Henry Gale," I murmured, only half-aware I was speaking out loud. The name meant something to me, but I couldn't remember what. "Why do I know that?"

"It's from *The Wizard of Oz*," Walcott said. "Dorothy's uncle."

"Walcott has a lot of Kansas pride," said Drew.

"As should you," Walcott said. "State traitor, going off to Colorado and abandoning the Hawks." Drew just shrugged. I got the feeling that they had this conversation a lot. "But check it out. Just got it done last week down at Sailor Gerry's." He lifted up the sleeve of his T-shirt to reveal a black tattoo that wrapped around his bicep. It just seemed to be a sentence, but the writing was stylized and gothic, and I couldn't make anything out.

"What does it say?" Roger asked.

"*Ad astra per aspera*," said Walcott. This meant nothing to me, but I saw Drew shake his head. "It's the Kansas state motto," he said to Roger and me. "To the stars through adversity."

"Wow," I said, turning these words over in my head. "That's beautiful."

"Isn't it?" Walcott asked, smiling fondly down at his tattoo, clearly thinking that was what I was talking about. "Gerry's a talented guy."

"Come on, Walcott," Drew said. Even with the lack of light, I could see he was rolling his eyes. "Aren't you taking this Kansas thing a little far?"

"No," Walcott said simply, rolling down his sleeve. "It's my home, man. You've got to have pride in your home. You are where you're from. Otherwise, you're always going to be lost."

"You just think that because you've never been anywhere," said Drew.

Silence fell, and I ran my hands over the blades of grass that, I now realized, Walcott had cut. I looked up at him, knowing how he felt. Until three days ago, I'd never been anywhere either.

But it didn't really seem to bother Walcott. He shrugged and brushed his hands off. "Well, I should get back to it," he said. "Thanks for the food. Nice to meet you guys." He headed toward the mower and started to climb up, then turned back to the three of us on the tee. "You don't have to go away to know where your home is," he said. "Everyone knows where their home is. And if you don't, you've got problems."

"If you have to look any further than your own backyard to find your heart's desire, you never really lost it to begin with?" asked Drew, a little sarcastically. I turned to him, trying to figure out why that sentence sounded so familiar.

"Yeah," Walcott said, starting up his mower shattering the stillness of the night. "Exactly." Then he turned the mower and steered it down the hill, raising one hand to us in a wave before he disappeared from view.

We all just watched him leave, the three of us looking where he'd gone, as though we were waiting for him to come back. Then Roger picked up his Freddy's cup, and I passed one to Drew. I took a cautious bite of mine, and then another. The frozen custard was thick and cool and sweet, and felt soothing on my throat. It was richer than ice cream, but had the consistency of frozen yogurt. And at that moment, it was exactly what I wanted.

"Sorry about Walcott," Drew said after a moment. "I probably shouldn't have said that. But he doesn't see that he's just wasting his life hanging around here. And he's never been anywhere, or done anything. . . ." He turned to Roger. "Back me up here, Magellan. I mean, you have to leave where you've come from. You have to go and see stuff. And that doesn't mean that I don't know where my home is. That's bullshit."

"But," I said, curling my legs up underneath me. I hadn't planned on joining in this conversation, but I found that the words were tumbling out before I could stop, or rehearse them. "But what if your home has disappeared?" I thought of the Realtor's sign, and the WELCOME HOME message that wasn't meant for me or my family—none of the people who'd actually lived there. "What then?" Roger looked over at me, forehead creased.

"I guess then your home is the people in it," Drew said. "Your family."

"But what if they're gone too?" I asked, looking straight ahead at the rolling greens and not at him or Roger, making myself say it, trying to keep my voice steady. "I mean, what if your family isn't there either?" Drew glanced over at me, and I saw surprise and a little bit of pity in his face.

"Then I guess you make a new home," he said. "Right? You find something else that feels like home."

After a few moments of silence, as though we'd agreed on a time to leave, we all began to pack up the last of the trash, and when the tee showed no evidence that we'd been there, we walked back across the golf course. We were almost to the end of it before I realized I'd left my flip-flops behind.

"Sorry," I said. "I forgot my shoes. I'll meet you back by the car?"

"Want me to come?" Roger asked.

I shook my head. "I'll just be a minute," I said, and headed back to the tee. Seeing the open expanse of green in front of me, I broke into a run, feeling the dense grass beneath my feet and the cool night air on my face, feeling my hair stream behind me as I ran faster, past sand traps and over hills, until I reached the tee of the twelfth hole and had to bend over to catch my breath. I picked up my flip-flops and turned back, walking this time, feeling my heart hammer from nothing except exertion. When I passed the seventh hole, I heard the sound of the mower again, and a moment later Walcott crested the hill behind me. He pulled up next to me and pushed his headphones back again.

"Want a ride?" he yelled over the sound of the mower. I shook my head, and he killed the engine, filling the night with silence. "Want a ride?" he repeated, apparently thinking I hadn't heard him.

"It's okay," I said. "Thanks, though." Walcott shrugged, then reached back to pull on his headphones again. "Walcott," I said quickly, before he left and before I could think about what I was doing. I rested my hand on the mower, which was surprisingly hot. "Do you like driving this? Is it fun?"

"Yeah," he said, smiling at me. "It's a good time. You want to give it a shot?"

I looked up, and heard my father's voice in my head clearly, as though it hadn't been months since I'd heard it at all. "There's an art to this, my Amy," I could hear him saying. "I'd like to see you give it a try."

"That's okay," I said, hand still on the mower. "My father—" My voice snagged on the word—it felt rusty. I forced myself to go on. "He would have wanted to. He would have loved that." I felt my breath begin to catch in my throat and knew that I'd reached the point of no return. I looked up at Walcott. "Can I tell you something?" I asked, hearing my voice shake, feeling a hot tear hit my cheek, and knowing there was no going back.

"Sure," he said, climbing down from the mower.

I closed my eyes. I hadn't said this out loud yet. To *anyone*. But now it wasn't that I couldn't say it—it was that I couldn't not say it any longer. "He died," I said, feeling the impact, the truth of the words hit me as I said them out loud for the first time. Tears ran down my face, unchecked. "My father died." The words hung in the night air between us. This wasn't ever how I imagined I'd say it for the first time. But there it was, like Walcott had said. A truth, told to a stranger, in the darkness.

"Oh, man," Walcott said. "Amy, I'm so sorry." I heard that there was real feeling in this, and I didn't brush it away, like I had everyone else's condolences. I tried to smile, but it turned trembly halfway through, and I just nodded. He took a step closer to me, and I felt myself freeze, not wanting him to hug me, or feel like he had to. But he just took his headphones off his neck and placed them over my ears.

Loud, angry music filled my head. It was fast, with a pounding beat underneath driving the electric guitars. There were lyrics, but no words I could make out, and after all my talky musicals, it was something of a relief. I placed my hands on the side of the headphones and just let the music sweep over me, pushing all other thoughts from my head. And when the song was over, I took the headphones off and handed them back to Walcott, feeling calmer than I had in a long time. "Thanks," I said.

He slung them back around his neck, then turned to his mower and pulled down a black patch-covered backpack. He unzipped it and dug around until he came out with a CD, which he extended to me. It looked homemade, in a yellow jewel case. "My demo," he said. I reached for it, but he didn't let go, looking right into my eyes. "You know what my grandma used to say?"

"There's no place like home?" I asked, trying again for a smile, this one less trembly than before.

"No," he said, still looking serious, still holding on to his end of the CD. "Tomorrow will be better."

"But what if it's not?" I asked.

Walcott smiled and let go of the CD. "Then you say it again tomorrow. Because it might be. You never know, right? At some point, tomorrow *will* be better."

I nodded. "Thanks," I said, hoping he knew I didn't mean just the CD. He nodded, climbed back up on his mower, started the engine, and headed off again.

I took a moment for myself, alone in the darkness by the seventh hole—par five—of the Wichita Country Club. Then I put my flip-flops back on and headed back. Drew and Roger were waiting for me where the course began and grass met gravel. Roger looked worried, and my face must have betrayed something of what had just happened, since he didn't stop looking worried when he saw me.

"You get lost?" Drew asked.

I held up the CD. "Ran into Walcott," I said, trying to keep my voice light. "He gave me his demo."

"Told you!" said Drew. We headed out, and I saw that the girl on the practice court was still there, now practicing her serve, tossing the ball high up above her head before slamming it back to the wall.

Drew insisted on driving us back to the car, saying that it was on his way out. It seemed that while I'd been gone, Roger had been telling him about Highway 50, and they picked up this conversation again.

"You can't believe it," Roger said. "It just goes on and on, and you think it's never going to end."

"But then it does," Drew said. "Wow. That's a great story, dude."

"I'm serious!" said Roger. "You think it's going to last forever."

"But nothing lasts forever," Drew said, and then he and Roger sang together, "Even cold November rain." I looked from one to the other, baffled.

"Seriously?" asked Drew, catching my expression in the rear-view mirror. "Magellan, get this girl some GNR."

I had no idea what he was talking about, but I didn't have time to ask, because a few seconds later, the car stopped outside the country club gates. I looked out and saw the Liberty, parked in a pool of streetlight. I was unexpectedly glad to see it again.

My house might be in the process of being sold by an overly friendly Realtor, and my family might be gone or scattered across the country, but the car seemed welcome and familiar and, mile by mile, more like home.

We all got out, Drew pulling the front seat forward for me. He extended his hand again, and this time I took it, giving him a small smile that he returned, broadly. Drew and Roger hugged and hit each other on the back a few more times, and then Roger walked to the Liberty, leaving me and Drew alone. "It was nice to meet you," he said.

"Thanks for the NuWay," I said. "Crumbly is good."

"Didn't I tell you? Do me a favor," Drew said, slamming the driver's-side door closed and leaning a little closer to me. "Keep an eye on my friend Magellan, would you? Be his Sancho Panza."

I stared at Drew, surprised. My father had suddenly intruded into this conversation, when I hadn't been expecting him. "What did you say?" I asked.

"Sancho Panza," Drew repeated. "It's from *Don Quixote*. The navigator. But listen. The thing about Magellan is the thing about all these explorers. Most of the time, they're just determined to chase impossible things. And most of them are so busy looking at the horizon that they can't even see what's right in front of them."

"Okay," I said, not really sure what he meant. Was he talking about Hadley? "Will do."

"Drive safe," he called to Roger, who, I saw, was already in the car and nodded in response.

I had just opened my door when I heard Drew let out an impressive stream of expletives. I turned to see him peering sadly in through the driver's-side window. "Keys?" Roger called. *"Seriously?"*

Drew sighed and pulled his phone out of his pocket. "Don't worry about me," he said with a shrug. "Go on. I'll be fine."

I climbed into the car, shut the door, and looked around its familiar gray interior and, most familiar of all, Roger sitting behind the wheel, smiling at me. "Ready?" he asked.

"Ready," I said. I took Roger's glasses out of his case. Seeing the smudges on the lenses, I gave them a quick polish with the hem of Bronwyn's shirt. He put them on, started the car, and we pulled out onto the road. In my side mirror, I could see Drew waving. He continued to wave as we drove away, until he got smaller and smaller and finally faded from view.

ROGER PLAYLIST #6

"Tornado Season??" aka "~~Ice Cream~~ Frozen
Custard Headache"

SONG TITLE	ARTIST
"Ghost"	Neutral Milk Hotel
"November Rain"	Guns N' Roses
"Sugar, We're Goin Down"	Fall Out Boy
"Route 66"	Chuck Berry
"Morning Calls"	Dashboard Confessional
"All My Days"	Alexi Murdoch
"Not the Same"	Ben Folds
"Heartbeats"	José González
"Here (In Your Arms)"	Hellogoodbye
"The Weight"	The Band
"The Bird and the Worm"	Owl City
"Cast No Shadow"	Oasis
"It'll All Work Out"	Tom Petty and the Heartbreakers
"This Time Tomorrow"	The Kinks

KANSAS / KENTUCKY

Where I've Been . . .

State #5: KANSAS—The Sunflower State

motto: Ad astra per aspera (To the Stars Through Adversity)

Size: Flat, with road signs that are worrying for their own reasons.

Facts: Tornado season is April to June. Oh, good.

Notes: But according to the rest stop info, if you see a tornado coming, you are supposed to pull over to the side of the road and lie down in a ditch.
Seriously.

FOR AMY

Travel Scrapbook

KANSAS

THE SUNFLOW

WEAR
ME

SUNFLOWER MART
Sunday, June 9
Gas & Go

Gas 87 Grade	34.99
Root Beer	1.50
Cream Soda	1.50
PB M&Ms	1.25
Skittles	1.25
Doritos	3.99
Postcards	3.25
Total:	47.73

Payment: Credit
Amelia E. Curry

Thank You!
Have a Nice Day!

Where they love me, where they know me, where they show me, back in Missouri.
—*Sara Evans*

Around midnight, it started to rain.

We'd been driving through Kansas in the dark for three hours, not speaking much. I'd been looking out the window, feeling the reverberations of what I'd told Walcott still coursing through me, like aftershocks following an earthquake. I'd said it out loud. I had. And it hadn't made things worse—the world hadn't ended. But I didn't feel a lot better, either. It was almost as though by saying the words out loud, I'd summoned it in a more real way, because I was now having a hard time thinking about anything else. My mind kept circling around and around the things I wanted to think about the least.

The rain was a welcome distraction. I leaned over and showed Roger how to adjust the wiper settings, and I looked ahead to the highway, obscured and made somehow beautiful by the rain streaking across the windshield, blurring the red lines of brake lights ahead of us and the white lines of headlights to the left of us, no sound in the car except Roger's mix and the constant, muted *thwap* of the windshield wipers.

The rain was light at first, just a few droplets, but then it was as though the endless sky above us had opened, and bucketful after bucketful was being tossed down onto the car. "Wow," Roger said, fumbling with the wiper settings again. I leaned over and turned them up so they were going at their fastest setting—*thwapthwapthwapthwapthwap*. "Thanks," he said.

"Sure." I leaned back and looked out into the darkness, at the rain droplets streaking diagonally across my window. I'd always felt safe driving inside cars at night when it rained. I knew most people—like Julia—had always hated being in cars when it rained, especially at night. She said it scared her. But it had never bothered me. Especially since I now knew that the worst could happen in broad daylight on a sunny Saturday morning, fifteen minutes from home.

"You used to drive this car?" Roger asked, glancing over at me.

"Sure," I said, propping my feet on the dashboard.

"If you ever want to drive," he said, a little tentatively, like he was considering each word before he spoke it, "I mean, you absolutely could. I would be fine with that."

I put my feet down and sat up straighter. "Should we stop?" I asked. "Are you too tired?"

"No, I'm fine," he said. "I've got at least two more hours in me tonight. I just . . . wanted to let you know that I'd be okay with you driving."

Something about the way he said this made me go still. Did he know what had happened? I'd thought he didn't, but maybe that was just what I'd wanted to think. And maybe he hadn't just been perceptive when Drew had been driving too fast for me. Maybe he'd known why it bothered me, and had known this whole time. "I don't want to drive," I said, trying to keep my voice steady, but hearing it quaver a little despite my best effort.

"Do you want to talk about why?" he asked. He glanced at me.

I stared at his profile, feeling my heart hammering. The car didn't feel so safe anymore. "Do you know what happened?" I asked, hearing that my voice was already sounding strangled.

Roger shook his head. "No," he said. "I just think that maybe you should talk about it."

My heart was pounding in my chest. "Well, I don't want to," I said as firmly as I could.

"I just . . ." He looked at me, and I saw that his glasses had gotten smudged again somehow. I could practically see a whole fingerprint on the right lens. I chose to focus on this, and not the way he was looking at me. Like he was disappointed in what he was seeing. "You can talk to me, you know."

"I know that," I said carefully. "Haven't I been talking to you?" I asked, deciding to deliberately misunderstand what he was saying. "Have we not been talking?"

He sighed and looked out at the road, and I knew he hadn't bought it. Of course I knew what he meant. But it was one thing to tell Walcott, since I knew I wasn't going to see him again. Opening up to Roger would be a wholly different thing. I'd have to sit with him in the car afterward, for miles and miles and hours and hours. And what if it was too much for him?

"I just . . . ," I said. I took a breath, so I wouldn't break down before I even started. "It's just hard for me. To talk about this. I mean." Or to complete full sentences, apparently. Amy! wouldn't have had this problem. Amy! would have had no issue with sharing her feelings and the things that scared her most with the person who was offering to hear them. But then again, Amy! probably had no issues. I really, really hated Amy!.

"I know it is," Roger said quietly. The mix ended, and he didn't start it up again. The iPod's tiny screen glowed for a moment, then faded, and the only sound in the car was the rhythmic thwapping of the wipers across the windshield, which remained clear for only a second before the rain engulfed it again.

"It's not that I don't want to talk," I said without thinking about it, and as soon as the words were out of my mouth I realized that they were true. I did want to talk. I'd wanted to talk for months. And here was someone who was offering to listen. So why did this seem so impossible? Like I was being asked to speak Portuguese, or something equally difficult? "I just . . ." I didn't even seem to possess the words to finish that sentence. I hugged my knees into my chest and looked out the window.

"All right," Roger said after a moment. "I'll start, okay? Twenty Questions."

"Oh," I said, a little surprised that we were switching topics so quickly. Because to be honest, I'd almost felt ready to talk to him. "Okay. Is it a person?"

"No," Roger said, smiling. "I mean, I'll ask you questions. And that way it might be easier for you to talk. Maybe?"

I was both relieved and anxious that we were staying on me, that I would have to talk. "Twenty seems like a lot," I said. "How about five?"

"Five Questions? Doesn't exactly have the same ring to it."

"And I get to ask you, too," I added on impulse. "It's only fair that way."

Roger drummed his fingers on the steering wheel, then nodded. "Okay," he said. "Ready?" I nodded. Mostly, I wanted to just get this over with. "Why don't you want to drive?" he asked.

I swallowed and concentrated on the wipers going back and forth. And even though Roger could see me and I him, I was suddenly glad for the darkness in the car. It made it easier to pretend that he couldn't see that I was trying hard not to cry, that my chin had apparently taken on a life of its own, and I no longer had any control over it. "There was an accident," I said finally, forcing the words out.

"A car accident?"

"Yes," I said. I was working very, very hard to keep control of myself, but I was on the verge of bursting into tears, and there was nowhere to go if that happened. No bathroom stall to hide in, nowhere to run.

"When was this?" Roger was asking me these questions gently, and quietly, but he might as well have been shouting them at me, that was how it felt to hear them, knowing I would have to answer.

"Three months ago," I said, and felt my voice crack a little on the last word. "March eighth."

"That's all?" Roger asked, sounding surprised, and sad.

"Yes," I said. I took a deep breath and tried to take a lighter tone. "That counts as one of your questions, you know." From the way my voice was shaking, and the way it sounded thick to me, I had a feeling that my lighter tone had not been successful.

"Last one," he said. He glanced at me again and asked, more quietly than ever, "Do you want to tell me what happened?"

I'd known this was coming, but that didn't make it any easier to hear him ask. Because there was a piece of me that wanted to talk about it. Deep down, somewhere, I knew that it would be better in the long run, to face it. That the bone would have to be set in order to heal properly, not weak and crooked. I had seen a flash of the Old me in Bronwyn's mirror in Colorado. I wanted to see her again. I wanted to try to get back to who I had once been. And the rational piece of me knew that not talking about it was keeping me from sleeping and was probably making my hair fall out.

But there was another piece of me, the part I'd been listening to for the past three months, that told me to turn away, not answer, pull the covers over my head and keep on hiding.

Because Roger didn't know what had happened. If he had, he wouldn't be looking at me the way he had been. Once he found out, he'd turn away from me, then leave me altogether, just like Mom and Charlie had done. And I didn't want to have to face the look in his eyes when I stopped being whatever he thought I was and turned into something else. I unclasped my knees, placed my feet on the floor, and looked at him. "No," I said quietly. But my voice seemed to reverberate in the silent car nonetheless.

Roger looked over at me, then back at the road, pressing his lips together, nodding. Then he brought the iPod to life again and turned up the music, beginning his mix again.

I felt like I'd let him down, but I knew that it was better, in the end, to keep this inside. I'd gotten good at that. And soon he'd stop asking. Soon this would just be who I was. Soon Old me would be dead too. I tipped my head against the cold glass of the window. When I felt myself begin to cry, I didn't fight against it. And when I caught my reflection in the dark window, I wasn't able to tell what was tears and what was rain.

I called your line too many times.

—*Plushgun*

MARCH 8——THREE MONTHS EARLIER

I headed back inside the house, pocketing my cell phone. My mother wasn't in the kitchen, but I could hear her in the family room, talking on the phone, her words clipped and anxious. *"Charlie,"* I muttered, hating that my brother was doing this to us.

I took the stairs two at a time up to his room and opened the door, and the strong scent of Glade Plug-Ins hit me. I always thought it might have raised my parents' suspicions that Charlie's room consistently smelled like potpourri, but they had never seemed to think anything of it. Or if they had, it was like they didn't want to deal with it, so they never said anything.

Charlie hadn't appeared in his room, and it looked just like it always did. His posters of James Blake and Maria Sharapova were tacked to the walls, and the bed, never made, was rumpled as usual. Charlie told me that he'd discovered if you never made your bed, it was harder for people to tell if you'd slept in it the night before. I closed the door and checked my phone again. Charlie was usually good at covering his tracks; it was how he'd been able to get away with things for so long.

I thought back to the conversation I'd had with him on our porch six months ago, my failed attempt at an intervention. When I'd threatened to tell Mom and Dad, I'd also threatened to stop covering for him. But I hadn't done either, just like he'd said I wouldn't, and here I was ready to try to fix the situation, if only he would give me some information. I sent him a text—WHERE ARE YOU???—and waited, staring down at my phone. But I didn't get a reply.

I headed back downstairs and heard my parents' voices in the kitchen. I sat on the bottom step, partially hidden but able to hear what was being said.

"Who else should we call?" my mother asked, and I could hear the raw worry in her voice. I couldn't help thinking that if it had been me who had disappeared, she wouldn't be worried. She'd be furious. But then, Charlie always had been her favorite.

"Maybe we should just hold tight," said my father. "I mean, he's sure to turn up. . . ."

The kitchen phone rang, and I stood up and stepped into the kitchen, leaning back against the counter. My father smiled at me when he saw me, but I could see how stressed he was. The whistling figure pushing the lawn mower was gone.

"Hello," my mother said, grabbing the kitchen phone. Her expression changed as she listened to what was being said on the other end. Genuine fear was now mixed in with the worry. "I don't understand," she said. "He's *where?*"

Fairfield Hotel

600 HAWLEY AVENUE, FAIRFIELD, MISSOURI

"Best in the Midwest"

Amy Curry Room: 245
2 Raven Crescent Room Type: GENR/ DOUBLE BED
Raven Rock, CA
Number of Guests: 2
90041 Rate: $95.00

Arrive: June 10 Time: 2:47 a.m.
Depart: June 10 BY NOON
Wake-up Call: 9:00 a.m.
Payment to Hold Room:
Credit Card/ Amelia E. Curry   XXXX XXXX XXXX 8766

WANDERING IS ENCOURAGED.

I hadn't been able to sleep. We'd checked into a hotel when it became clear that Roger was hitting his wall. He'd gone right to sleep, but I'd spent three hours lying awake, looking at the space between Roger's bed and my own, watching the clock. Roger was sleeping peacefully, and as I saw his back rise and fall, I envied him that sense of peace. I had taken my cell phone out and placed it next to me on the bed, and every time I opened it, I saw my voice mail icon illuminated. My sense of dread was growing. I knew I'd have to call my mother soon—in theory, we were supposed to be heading in from Ohio and getting to Connecticut that afternoon. We were not supposed to be in Missouri and heading for Kentucky. We were not supposed to be in a different time zone. When six a.m. rolled around, I gave up on the idea of sleep entirely. I grabbed the purple plastic room key card and my phone and headed out to the hallway, closing the door slowly behind me so it wouldn't slam and wake Roger.

I walked to the end of the hallway, where a large window overlooked the highway. Then I took a deep breath and pressed the speed dial for my mother's cell phone.

She answered on the second ring, sounding much more awake than I would have imagined she'd be at seven in the morning, her time. "Amy?" she asked. "Is that you?"

"Hi, Mom," I said.

"Hi, honey," she said. I felt myself blinking back tears, just hearing her voice. I knew that this was why I had avoided talking to her for as long as possible. Because I was feeling so many things right now, I wasn't even sure how to process them all. It was like I was in overload. It felt so good to hear her voice, but a second later I was furious, and I wasn't even sure exactly why.

"I'm so glad you called. I have to say, Amy," she said, and the sharpness was coming back into her tone, what Charlie called her "professor voice," even though she had hardly ever used it on him, "I've been very disappointed with how out of touch you've been during this whole process. I feel like I've barely heard from you, I hardly ever know where you are—"

"We're in Missouri," I interrupted her, which was something I almost never did, since I always knew her next words would be, *Don't interrupt me, Amy.*

"Don't interrupt me, Amy," my mother said. "It's just incredibly irresponsible, and—did you say Missouri?"

"Yes," I said. I felt my heart hammering again, the same feeling that I always used to get whenever I knew I was going to get in trouble.

"What," said my mother, her voice low and steady, always a bad sign, "on *earth* are you doing in Missouri?"

"Just listen for a second, okay?" I asked, swallowing and trying to get my bearings.

"Am I stopping you?"

"No. Okay." I held the phone away from my ear for a moment and looked out on the highway. I thought I could see a little tiny ribbon of light creeping up on the horizon, bringing the dawn. But it might have just been brake lights. "So Roger and I," I said, trying not to think about how mad my mother was probably growing on the other end of the phone, "we decided to take a little bit of a scenic route. We're fine, I promise, he's driving safely and we're stopping whenever he gets tired." There was silence on the other end of the phone. "Mom?" I asked tentatively.

"Did you just say," she asked, sounding more incredulous than angry, "that you're taking the *scenic route?*"

"Yes," I said, swallowing. "But I promise we'll be there before too long. We're just—"

"What you will do," she said, the anger now back in her voice, full force, "is get in the car and drive straight to Connecticut. I will put Roger on a train to Philadelphia, and then you and I will discuss your consequences."

"Don't interrupt me, Mom," I said. The words were out of my mouth before I even registered what I was saying. I held the phone away from my face as I stifled a shocked laugh.

"Amelia Curry," she said, saying the two words that inevitably meant a serious consequence was coming after them. "You are on very thin ice, young lady. This is not some sort of . . . pleasure cruise. This is not a vacation. You had one simple task to do. As though we haven't been through enough, you decide to . . ." her voice shook, and trailed off for a moment, but a second later she was back, sounding as in control as ever. "Why are you doing this?" she asked. "You're making my life much harder—"

"I'm making your life harder?" I repeated, feeling like I'd lost all sense of perspective, just feeling an overwhelming anger that seemed like it might take me over. "I'm making *your* life harder?" I could hear my voice coming out, loud and a little uncontrolled, sounding nothing like my normal voice. Tears had sprung to my eyes, and my hand that was holding the phone was shaking. I was furious, and the depth of it was scaring me. "Seriously?" I asked, feeling my voice crack and two tears slide down my cheek.

"Let me talk to Roger," my mother said. "You're clearly getting hysterical."

"He's sleeping," I said sharply, a tone I'd almost never used with anyone, and certainly not my mother. "It's six a.m. here. And I'm *not* getting hysterical."

"You will come home right now—"

"I don't think we will," I said. The scary, huge anger was beginning to ebb and was being replaced by a kind of recklessness that I hadn't felt in a long time, if ever. "I'll be there soon, but there's some stuff we want to see first."

"You will not," said my mother, and she was using the voice that usually ended any discussions. But now it just seemed to be egging me on. "You will come home immediately—"

"Oh, so you want me to turn around and go back to California? Because we can do that."

"I meant," she said, "come to Connecticut. You know that." She now sounded mostly tired and sad, like someone had let all the anger out of her voice. Hearing this shift, I suddenly felt guilty, on top of angry and scared and sad myself.

"We'll be there soon," I said quietly. I was crying now, and barely even trying to hide it from her. What was so terrible was that this was my *mother*, and she was so close, just on the other end of the phone. All I wanted to do was to just open up to her, tell her how I was feeling, and have her tell me it would be all right. Instead of this. Instead of how hard this was. Instead of any of the conversations we'd had over the past few months. Instead of feeling so far away from her. Instead of feeling so alone. "Mom," I said softly, hoping that maybe she'd feel the same way, and maybe we'd be able to talk about it.

"I am calling Marilyn and letting her know what her son has been up to," she said, her voice now clipped and cold. Taking care of things. I knew the tone well. "If you want to do this, good luck. Just know that you are totally on your own. And when you do get here, know that there will be serious consequences."

"Okay," I said quietly, feeling worn out. "All right."

"I am very," my mother said, and I heard her voice shaking a little now. With anger, or suppressed emotion, I had no idea. "*Very* disappointed in you." Then the phone went dead, and I realized my mother had just hung up on me.

I stared down at the phone and wondered if I should just call her back and tell her that I was sorry and we'd be there as soon as possible. I'd still get in trouble, but probably less trouble. I didn't want to do that, but I also didn't want to go the rest of the trip feeling guilty. I played with the room key, turning it over in my hands. And that's when I saw the message printed in white on the purple card.

WANDERING IS ENCOURAGED.

"Checking out?" the girl behind the front desk asked cheerfully. Roger and I nodded at her, both of us a little blearily. After I'd returned to the room, I'd gone back to bed but hadn't slept much at all, just staring at the gradually lightening ceiling and replaying the conversation with my mother. I must have drifted off a little, though, because the wake-up call at nine—the one I'd forgotten I'd left the night before—had startled me from sleep. When I had started to get dressed in the bathroom after a quick shower, I'd remembered that I no longer had my own clothes. I'd stared down at my suitcase, with no idea how to put outfits together like Bronwyn could. I'd finally just grabbed whatever was on top—a long black tank top and gray pants that were like a combination of jeans and leggings.

But it seemed that Bronwyn's clothes were magic, as I could see in the mirror behind the desk that I somehow managed to look more pulled-together than I had any right to. I yawned, feeling exhausted, and even though I covered my mouth, I saw Roger yawn as well about three seconds later.

"Okay . . . ," the girl said, typing on her computer. I wondered how many cups of coffee she'd had to be this awake, and this friendly, this early. Her name tag read KIKI . . . HERE TO HELP. "So no charges except the one night's stay, is that correct?"

"Right," I said, stifling another yawn.

"And was everything to your liking?"

"Fine," I said, figuring I should take this one, since Roger hadn't been conscious for almost any of the stay.

"All right," said Kiki, fingers flying over her keyboard. "Excellent. So I'll just put that on the card I was holding the room on?"

"Yep," I said, mentally rolling my eyes at myself, but feeling resigned to the fact that I was, apparently, going to occasionally speak like a cowpoke from now on. Kiki nodded, smiled, and headed off to the small room behind the desk. I turned to Roger, leaning my elbows on the counter. "Breakfast?"

"If breakfast involves coffee," he said, rubbing his eyes, "then yes."

"I'm sorry, Miss Curry," Kiki said when she returned, looking a lot less friendly than she had just a minute before. "I'm afraid your card has been declined."

I blinked at her. "What?" I asked, flummoxed.

"I've tried it twice," she said, sliding the card across the counter at me, touching it with only one finger. "It's not good. Do you have another card?"

"Well," I said, looking through my wallet, as though there would magically be another credit card in there. "Um . . ." I didn't understand how this could be happening. The card wasn't even attached to my bank account; it was linked to my mother's credit card. As soon as I thought this, I knew what had happened. I felt my stomach drop as I realized what my mother had meant when she told me I was now on my own. "Oh God, Roger," I said, turning to him. "There's something I should probably tell you."

←——→

Roger pushed our shared side of bacon toward me, and I took a piece. It was extra crispy, extra greasy, and really good. But that wasn't doing much to help the churning in my stomach. I wasn't sure we were going to be able to pull this off.

I had the atlas next to me on the table, open to the map of the country. The thought of facing all that road between Missouri and Connecticut—without the safety net of an emergency credit card—was making me feel a little sick. We'd pooled our funds, which left us with $440 to get to the East Coast. I'd provided the lion's share, thanks to my mother's drawer egg. When Roger had raised his eyebrows at my cash, I'd mumbled something about my mother giving it to me in case places didn't accept cards.

"What do you think?" I asked, looking down at the pile of money on the table between us. Our waiter, passing by, must have thought that we were assembling his tip, as he stopped and gave us both water refills, accompanied by a big smile.

Roger rubbed his hand over his forehead, which I now recognized was something he did when he was worried. "I think it might be enough," he said. "Hopefully." He pulled the plate of bacon back to him, took a piece, and crunched down on it. Then he looked out the window, which provided a beautiful view of the parking lot, for a long moment. "I guess I'm just surprised," he finally said. "When your mother told you to come back, you said no." He looked across the table at me and raised his eyebrows.

"I know," I said. I still couldn't believe that I'd done it—that we were now cut loose, and on our own in the middle of America. That my mother had basically washed her hands of me. I looked away from his direct gaze and down at the scratched surface of the table. Someone had etched into it RYAN LOVES MEGAN ALWAYS.

"Why?" Roger asked simply.

I glanced up at him. I hadn't asked myself this yet. Saying no had just been my first response. "Because . . ." I looked out the window as well, beyond the parking lot to the interstate, where the cars were rushing by, heading home, running away, all of them off to somewhere else. I suddenly had the most overwhelming urge to get into the Liberty and join them. "Because we're not done yet, right?"

Roger smiled but didn't say anything, choosing instead to eat a piece of bacon pensively, something I wouldn't have thought possible without seeing the proof.

"I mean," I said, watching his face closely, "you haven't seen Hadley yet." When he still didn't respond, I felt a sense of dread creep over me. I suddenly felt chilled in Bronwyn's tank top, even though sunlight was hitting the table and I had been too warm a moment ago. What if he wanted to end it? I had just assumed Roger would want to keep going. But maybe he didn't. Maybe we were going to change the route and head directly to Connecticut. The thought of being there, of having to begin my life there with my now furious mother, made me feel panicky. I wasn't ready to do that yet. "But if you want to stop it," I said, trying to keep my voice level, like saying this wasn't completely terrifying, "we can."

"No, it's not that," he said, looking across at me. He ran his hands through his hair, bringing it from its post-shower neatness to its normal messiness, and sighed. "I'm supposed to be the responsible one here. My mother is not going to be happy about this either. And I don't want to get you into trouble."

"You're not," I said quickly. "I did that on my own, believe me."

"I just feel guilty about this."

"Don't," I said. "Really." I looked at him closely. "Do you want to stop?" I held my breath, hoping for the sake of my health that he wouldn't take long to answer.

Roger looked across the table at me for a long moment, then shook his head. "I don't," he said, sounding a little surprised by the answer. I let out a long breath and felt my stomach unclench a little.

Our waiter passed by then, dropping our check and a handful of cellophane-wrapped mints on the table.

Roger took out his phone. "I should make some calls," he said. "I still haven't been able to talk to Hadley. And I should probably call my mother before yours does."

"I'll take care of this," I said, counting out money for the check.

"You want to hold on to that?" Roger asked, nodding at the rest of the money. "I'd be worried I'd lose it."

"Sure," I said, folding the bills and tucking them in my wallet.

"Meet you at the car," he said, grabbing one of the mints off the table and heading out the door, the bell above signaling his exit.

I looked down at the map and traced the route we'd take to Kentucky. We'd estimated about eight hours to get there, so we should be there by early evening, six or seven. I looked below Kentucky and saw Tennessee. And in the corner of the state, almost to Arkansas, was Memphis. I let my finger rest on the bolded name for a moment, thinking about the trip I was supposed to be on this summer—the trip that would have taken me there. To Memphis, but specifically to Graceland. It was strange to think how close we were going to be to it once we got to Louisville. Probably only a few hours away. But it would be backtracking. And I didn't want to go without my father. Which meant, then, that I never would.

I closed the atlas, trying to push this unsettling thought away. I paid the bill, placing the money on the check and securing the waiter's tip under my water glass. I figured I'd given Roger enough time to make his calls in private and got up to leave. As I did, my eyes caught the graffiti again. I wondered who Ryan and Megan were. And if, wherever they were, they'd made it. I wondered how anyone could have been so sure about a concept so tenuous and impossible as *always* that they'd be willing to carve it into a tabletop.

I glanced at it for a moment longer, then headed out of the diner, squinting against the sun.

```
          Fairfield Diner
          Fairfield, MO

     "Showing-You" a Great Meal!
              6/10
            Table 4
          Server/Kevin

Pancakes                    5.50
Waffle w/fruit              6.50
Side bacon/crisp            3.95
Root Beer                   1.95
Cream Soda                  1.95

Total:                     19.85

Paid CASH

     Have a N...
```

TRIP FUND

Amy: $335.25
Roger: $105.50

TOTAL: $440.75

Fairfield to
Louisville:
8 hours

I found my thrill on Blueberry Hill.
—Elvis Presley

SEVEN YEARS EARLIER

My father swung the car around into a spot in front of the Raven Rock tennis complex and leaned back so that I could reach over and honk the horn. I used the honk we always used for Charlie, *honk-honk-honkhonkhonk*, what my father for some reason called "shave and a haircut."

We sat back to wait, and a moment later, *From Nashville to Memphis*, the CD that had gotten us from home to 21 Choices and then to the tennis complex ended, and started over at track one. This was not permitted in my father's car. In his mind, once you started listening to a CD on repeat, you stopped hearing its nuances. "Maestro?" he asked, turning to me.

"I'm on it," I said, opening up the glove compartment and flipping through the Elvis CDs. I pulled out *Elvis at the Movies*, bringing us solidly to the sixties. "All That I Am" started playing, and my father tapped his fingers along to the rhythm of the song, smiling.

"Nice choice, pumpkin," he said, looking over at me with a nod of approval. "You know, I think this is my favorite of His songs?" The way my father said it, Elvis's name was always capitalized. He'd told us once, scandalizing my grandmother, who happened to be visiting, "I hope there's a God. I know there's an Elvis."

"It's my favorite song too," I said, making the decision on the spot.

My father laughed, leaned over, and ruffled my hair, causing me to scowl and smooth it down.

There was knock on the back window, and I turned to see Charlie tapping on the glass, his racket in its case slung over his shoulder, looking tired and grumpy. My father unlocked the car, and Charlie got in the back, buckling himself into the middle seat.

"Hey, champ," my father said as he started the car. "How was practice?"

"Lame," Charlie said.

"Why lame?" I asked, turning around to face him.

"It just was, okay?" he said, pushing his hair, dark with sweat, back from his forehead. "I don't know if I want to play anymore. I mean, what's the point?"

"The point," said my father, "is that you can do something extraordinary, and something that a lot of people can't do. And if you have the opportunity to work on your gifts, it seems like a crime not to. I mean, it's just weakness to quit because something becomes too hard. Am I right?"

Charlie slumped back against the seat. "How come Amy doesn't have to play tennis?"

I rolled my eyes. Charlie had been using variations on this argument whenever he threatened to quit, for about two years now, and it was getting old.

"Because Amy didn't like tennis," my father said with a sigh.

"I liked the clothes," I pointed out. I had stuck with it for a few years because my mother had bought me a new tennis outfit every year, and I'd really liked them. After a while, though, I'd decided that it wasn't worth spending hours trying to hit a fuzzy yellow ball just to get a white shirtdress.

"That's right," my father said with a smile and a shake of his head.

"Did you guys go to 21 Choices already?" Charlie asked, leaning forward, looking at the crumpled napkins on the console. "I thought we were all going to go after practice!"

"Sorry, champ," my father said, casting his eyes into the

rearview mirror. "Your sister wanted to go beforehand. But how about we make a quick stop right now?"

"Forget it," Charlie muttered, slamming himself back against the seat and staring out the window. "I don't want to go anyway."

I glanced in the rearview mirror and looked back at my brother. We'd never had that secret twin connection I read about in books, and more often than not, it felt like we were battling for something that had never even been named, so couldn't ever be won.

"Do we have to keep listening to this?" Charlie asked petulantly after a few minutes of Elvis's crooning. "We're always listening to Elvis. And I'm sick of it."

Saying this, in my father's car, was akin to swearing in front of your teacher, and I felt my pulse begin to quicken a little, wondering what Charlie thought he was doing.

"Hey now," my father said, as he made a left, and I realized that we were passing University, heading for downtown and away from our house. "You can't insult the King like that. You have to pay him his proper respect."

"I just think his music's stupid," Charlie muttered, but more quietly, and I had a feeling that he realized he'd gone too far.

"It's not just the music, son," my father said. "Though it's mostly the music. But it's what he represented. You'll see. Someday we'll all go down to Graceland, and you'll see."

"All three of us?" Charlie asked.

My father laughed, and I began to relax a little bit. "Maybe even all four of us, if we can talk your mother into it. I was there once years ago. I even wrote my name on the graffiti wall."

I turned to my father, and out of the corner of my eye, saw my brother grinning in surprise in the backseat. "You did graffiti?" I asked, shocked. "At Elvis's house?"

"Everyone does it," my father said with a laugh. He made another turn, and I realized where we were going, but I didn't think Charlie had yet. "It was probably sandblasted away years ago. But I'd like to go back and see if it's still there."

"Awesome," Charlie said. "Can I do it too?"

"Sure," said my father. "You too, Amy."

"No, thank you," I said firmly, causing both my father and Charlie to laugh. I didn't mind, though. Sometimes it seemed like the only time the three of us could all get along was when they were teasing me.

"All right," my father said. "You can be the law-abiding one. But I'm telling you, kids, when I die and go on to the great classroom in the sky, I want you to scatter some of my ashes at Graceland. Because that's where I'm going to be. Hanging out in the Jungle Room with the King."

"Don't talk about that," I said, more sharply than I'd intended to.

"I'm just kidding, pumpkin," he said, glancing over at me. "Don't worry." I nodded and let out a breath. When I looked up, I saw we were pulling into a parking space right in front of 21 Choices. "Why, look at where we are," he said with mock surprise. "Now, I think it'd be a shame to waste this parking spot. So who wants dessert?"

Where I've Been . . .

State #6: MISSOURI—The Show-me State

motto: SALUS POPULI SUPREMA LEX ESTO
("The welfare of the people shall be the supreme law")

Size: Again, big.

Facts: The Show-me State. Which basically means that people in Missouri don't trust you, and they demand you show them proof of things. Which is pretty awesome, but must make it hard to be a psychic here. Or a magician.

Notes: Seems to be pronounced both miz-OR-ee and miz-OR-uh.

Where I've Been...

<u>State #7:</u> ILLINOIS

<u>motto:</u> State Sovereignty-National Union

<u>Size:</u> Still pretty big

<u>Facts:</u> Prairie State. And residents are called "Illinoisans" which is awesome.

<u>Notes:</u> Kept an eye out for log cabins. Saw none, at least on the side of the interstate.

~~~~~~~~~~~~~~~~~~~~~~~

<u>State #8:</u> INDIANA—The Hoosier State

<u>motto:</u> The Crossroads of America

<u>Size:</u> Not quite as big as Missouri.

<u>Facts:</u> If you drive through Indiana with Roger, do NOT let him talk about the movie Hoosiers. YOU WILL REGRET THIS.

<u>Notes:</u> Feel like I am not giving Indiana its fair shake, since we just drove through. The roadside amenities, though, were EXCELLENT.

ROGER PLAYLIST #7

"Missouri-Illinois-Indiana-Kentucky" aka
"When will Amy be the DJ? WHEN?" aka
"1500 miles on 400 dollars . . ."

SONG TITLE	ARTIST
"Come On! Feel the Illinoise!"	Sufjan Stevens
"Going Back to Indiana"	Jackson 5
"The Trick to Life"	The Hoosiers
"No More Runnin'"	Animal Collective
"Globes & Maps"	Something Corporate
"All Hail the Heartbreaker"	The Spill Canvas
"Old Flames"	Harlem Shakes
"Don't Wake Me Up"	The Hush Sound
"My Beautiful Rescue"	This Providence
"Beating Heart Baby"	Head Automatica
"Song in My Head"	Sherwood
"Nightswimming"	R.E.M.
"Ulysses"	Franz Ferdinand
"Good Arms vs. Bad Arms"	Frightened Rabbit
"Late in the Evening"	Paul Simon
"After Hours"	Caribou
"The Good Ones"	The Kills
"Sunlight in a Jar"	The Lucksmiths
"Where the Story Ends"	The Fray

KENTUCKY FRIED ROAD TRIP

KFRT

We will sing one song for the old Kentucky home.
—*Kentucky State song*

"Snacks?" Roger asked, starting the ignition.

"Roger that," I said, lifting up the bag we'd just bought from MO Mart. I saw Roger roll his eyes at that, but I felt myself smile, realizing the bad pun had just slipped out, before I'd thought it over. It felt like something the Old me would have done.

"Drinks?" he asked.

"Check," I said, placing the cream soda and root beer in our respective cup holders, then loosening Roger's root beer bottle top a little for him, as we'd found out this was challenging to do without taking both hands off the wheel.

"Tunes?" he asked.

"Check," I said, looking at him. "Presumably."

"Check," he said, scrolling through his iPod. "But I'm seriously getting sick of my music. I wish you'd take a turn."

"I like your music," I said. And I did, to my continued surprise. It turned out that his strangely named bands made hummable, accessible music. I didn't know how I'd gone this long in life without the Lucksmiths. I was missing my musicals a little, though.

"Sunglasses," Roger said, slipping his on. He turned to me, raising an eyebrow above the frames. "You know, MO Mart had a lovely selection, for only three dollars plus tax."

"I'm fine," I said, shaking my head. Roger had taken my refusal to buy sunglasses as some kind of challenge. But I didn't want to buy any. It just didn't feel right somehow.

"All right," he said. "Shall we hit it?"

"Let's," I said, and Roger signaled to turn out of the mini-mart parking lot and back onto the interstate on-ramp.

←——→

"Is it a man?" I asked an hour later, as Missouri, slightly overcast, flew by the window.

"Nope," said Roger, picking up his phone from the cup holder and checking it, frowning. "Nineteen."

←——→

"I'm telling you, you can do this," I said encouragingly. "Just purse your lips and try."

"And I'm telling you," he said, smiling at me, "despite what your shirt said, not everyone can whistle. And I am that person."

←——→

"What do you think a Chick-fil-A is?" Roger asked, as we pulled off the interstate and into the parking lot.

"I don't know," I said. "So why don't we go to a nice diner instead?"

"You and your diners," he said, shaking his head.

I felt the same way about his fast-food restaurants, but kept that to myself. "Is it supposed to be 'filet,' and just spelled wrong?" I stared up at the red sign with its curly writing. "I don't know."

"Where's your sense of adventure?" asked Roger, swinging around into the drive-thru lane. Maybe the routine had been set after our first meal together at In-N-Out, but when Roger won and we ate fast food, we almost always got it to go and then ate it in the car. He pulled the car up to the speaker, which clicked on with a loud, staticky hiss. "Hello," he said, leaning forward. "This is our first time here. What would you recommend?"

Ten minutes later, back in the parking lot, I took a doubtful bite of my chicken sandwich. "Oh my God," I murmured around my mouthful. It was seasoned, breaded chicken on a soft roll. And we were sharing an order of spicy fries. I looked up and saw

Roger nodding, his sandwich almost all gone. "This is amazing."

Roger smiled. "I'm not going to say I told you so," he said. "But . . ."

←—→

"Okay," I said, once we were back on the road, and I'd taken a sip of my soda. "Let me make sure I've gotten this. She's female, *probably* dead, famous, and *kind of* an explorer?"

"Correct," he said, putting down his visor against the sun, which had started to peek out of the clouds. "The answer is closer than you think. Sixteen."

←—→

While I racked my brain so that I might have a chance of winning this round of Twenty Questions, Roger checked his phone. He'd go a few minutes, leaving it in the console behind the cup holders, but then would seem to lose some internal battle with himself and would flip it open, checking the screen for something that just wasn't there.

"How do you know if you don't try?" I asked him as Illinois flew past the window. "You just make an O shape with your lips. . . ." I demonstrated for him, whistling along with Paul Simon.

"I've tried," said Roger. "But not all of us can be as talented as you."

←—→

"Indiana," I said, pointing out the window, as we crossed another invisible state line. "The Hoosier State," I read off the sign.

"Hey," Roger said, putting his phone back in the console and turning to me. "Did you ever see that movie? *Hoosiers?*"

←—→

It started to get hot. The sun was beating down on the car, and I had flipped my visor down as well. I couldn't help wishing I hadn't grabbed a black shirt that morning. I stretched my arm out in the sun hitting my side of the car and saw that I was already starting to get a few freckles.

"So it's 1951," Roger said. "Gene Hackman is the coach of this Indiana high school basketball team. And they're the underdogs. And nobody expects them to win the big game, let alone the championship."

"But they do anyway?" I guessed.

Roger turned to me, surprised. "I thought you said you hadn't seen it."

←——→

"I just don't understand," I said an hour later, slouching down in the seat, putting my feet up on the dashboard and pulling my hair off my neck. It was getting really hot in the car now, and Roger and I had been having a battle as to whether we should have the AC on (his vote) or the windows down (my vote). But I had to admit, it was getting to be a little too hot to keep the windows down. I rolled up my window, and Roger cranked the AC.

"Don't understand what?" Roger asked. He drove up next to a huge truck, pulling the car into the shadow it cast and cooling us down considerably.

"How can someone be *probably* dead?"

"You know that counts as one of your questions, right?" he asked. "Fifteen."

←——→

"And then Shooter—I mean, Dennis Hopper—who everyone has written off, starts coaching along with Gene Hackman. And nobody thinks it's going to work out. Because they all think he's a loser."

"Maybe that's because his name is Shooter," I suggested.

Roger frowned at me. "Amy," he said gravely, "this is a very important movie."

"Then maybe I should see it for myself," I suggested. "Rather than just hearing about it. In detail."

"So it's the big game," Roger continued, undaunted. "And nobody thinks they're going to win. . . ."

←——→

211

I realized it after we'd been driving for an hour in Indiana. I'd learned that the underdogs had, shockingly, won the big game and proved all the naysayers wrong. But while Roger drummed on the steering wheel and checked his phone, I looked out the window—theoretically coming up with possibly dead females who were kind of explorers—and realized that we were free. I don't know why it had taken so long for it to hit me, but suddenly there it was, making my heart pound a little harder, with excitement this time. I no longer had to worry about how I was going to lie to my mother. I was in big trouble, yes, and we were more broke than I'd have liked, but the two of us were also on our own. The damage was done. We could do anything—go anywhere—that we wanted. We were crossing America. We had a car and gas money and a destination. The road was open ahead of us. I looked at the rolling green hills passing by outside my window and saw my smile reflected in the side mirror.

←—→

"Amelia Earhart?" I asked, staring at Roger, once I'd finally given up. *"Seriously?"*

"What?" he asked. "We don't know that she's dead, after all. It's just presumed. I like to think that she landed on some fabulous South Sea island and has been having a great time for the last seventy years." He looked over at me and smiled. "I told you the answer was closer than you thought. Amelia."

←—→

Four songs later, I leaned back against my window and looked over at him, running his hand through his hair, something I'd noticed that he did when he was nervous. I wondered if it had something to do with the fact that we were slowly, inexorably, getting closer to Kentucky. "So," I said, not sure how to begin. "Hadley." Which was a terrible segue, but I wasn't sure what else to say.

"Yeah," said Roger, running his hand through his hair again.

"Are you worried about it?" I asked. "About seeing her?"

"A little," he said, glancing over at me, as though surprised that

212

I'd picked up on this. "I mean, an unannounced visit is always a risk, you know?"

"But you've called her, right?"

"I have—repeatedly. In the last message I left, I told her I was going to be in her neck of the woods. But she's not calling me back."

"Maybe . . . ," I said slowly, trying to find the right words. "I mean, do you think it means something that she's not calling you back?"

"Of course it does," he said. "I got that. But I just have to try. And if she doesn't want to see me or talk to me, that's fine. But at least I'll have attempted it."

"You're on your quest," I said, thinking of Drew and what he'd said about Don Quixote.

"Something like that, I guess," said Roger. "I just really need some answers, that's all."

"Mind if I ask some questions?" I asked. "Like, say, five?"

Roger glanced over at me. "I had a feeling that was going to come back to haunt me," he said. He sighed and turned down the music. "Fine. Shoot."

"Are you sure?"

"That counts as one, you know," he said.

"All right," I said, realizing that I was going to have to be careful around him. And though I wanted to know more about Hadley, I also didn't want to hear him talk about her. But I felt like we had gone looking for this girl, and the only impressions I had of her were from Drew and Bronwyn. I decided to go for it. If he could ask these questions, so could I. "Do you love her?"

"Wow," he said, glancing over at me. "Jump right in, why don't you?"

"Sorry," I said, feeling like maybe I'd overstepped. "Was that too much?"

"That makes three, you know," Roger said. "No, it's okay. I . . . hmm." There was silence in the car for much longer than a normal pause. This one was at Harold Pinter levels. Amy! probably would have jumped in to fill the silence. Actually, Amy! most likely wouldn't have asked the question in the first place. I pressed my fingernails into my palm to make myself wait for the answer. But Roger kept looking out the window, and after a few more moments, I couldn't take it any more.

"Roger?" I prompted.

"That's four," he said. "You're really not very good at this."

"I think you're cheating," I said, mostly just glad that the silence had been broken.

"I'm just following your lead," he said. "Do I love her? You'd think it would be an easier answer, right?"

I was certainly not the person to ask this of. To ask of this. "I don't know," I said, careful not to let my inflection rise at the end of the sentence.

He sighed, and changed lanes. "I thought I loved her," he said. "If you'd asked me that a month ago, I would have said definitively yes. I even told her so."

"You did?"

"And that's five," he said. "Yeah. Not one of the best moments of my life." I wanted to ask why not, but I'd run out of questions. Roger glanced at me and must have realized this, because he smiled faintly and continued. "She didn't say it back," he said quietly.

"Oh," I said. Even though I'd never said it to anyone romantically, I could imagine that not hearing it back would feel pretty crushing.

"Yeah," Roger agreed. "She just smiled and kissed me, but didn't say anything. And I think that's when things started to change. I don't know, maybe I freaked her out. Hadley wasn't really one for big emotional displays. Maybe it was too much for her. . . ." His voice trailed off, and I waited as long as I could before jumping in again.

"One last one?" I asked.

"Fine," he said. "But I get a bonus question the next time it's your turn."

"Okay," I said. I looked at him and tried to figure out how to phrase it. I just wasn't sure that Roger had thought past our getting to Kentucky. I didn't know if he'd thought about what it would actually be like once we arrived. Maybe it was the navigator's job to think ahead, not the driver's. But it still worried me. "What do you want to happen when we get there?"

Roger looked at me, then back at the road. "I'm not sure," he said finally. "I don't know." That hung in the air between us for a moment, and then he turned up the music and we drove on.

←——→

When we were an hour outside Kentucky, Roger's phone rang. We both stared down at it, ringing and vibrating around the console. HADLEY CALLING read the display. I handed it to Roger, who looked paler than he had a moment ago.

He took a deep breath and opened the phone. "Hello?" he asked, his voice suddenly a little deeper.

I looked out the window fixedly, so it wouldn't appear that I was listening to his conversation, but it was impossible not to.

"Hey," he said. "So I'm actually almost in Kentucky. I didn't know if you were around. . . ." Roger looked over at me, then back at the road, clearing his throat. "With a friend," he said, and I felt myself deflate a little after he said that. I stared out the window and tried not to be ridiculous. I *was* a friend. I should be glad I'd accomplished that, not be inexplicably disappointed that he'd identified me correctly. "Okay," he said, then must have gotten cut off, because he frowned, listening. "But are you around?" he asked. "If so, it'd be good to see you—" He stopped again and was silent, listening. "So I should just call you when we get to Louisville?" he asked, sounding a little frustrated this time. "Fine," he said after another small pause. "Sounds good." And then he hung up without saying good-bye, something that no longer surprised me. He looked at me. "Hadley," he finally said. It sounded like he was pronouncing her name a little differently now, without the same kind of inflection he'd used a few days ago. It no longer seemed like her name was constructed solely from the alphabet's finest letters.

"I assumed," I said. I waited for Roger to fill me in on the conversation, but he was silent, staring at the road, frowning slightly. "Um, what did she say?"

Roger sighed. "She wasn't very clear. That never was one of her strong points. She's never really liked making plans. She said she might be around, she wasn't sure, but I should call when we got to Louisville."

"Is that where she lives?"

Roger shook his head. "A little ways outside it," he said. "Hummingbird Valley."

←——→

An hour later we crossed into Kentucky, THE BLUEGRASS STATE, according to the state sign. Roger pulled into a gas station—a Git 'n' Go, which was one I'd never seen before—and took out his phone. I stretched my legs, headed to the bathroom, then picked us up sodas and a Kentucky road map, just in case. When I headed back to the car, Roger was still sitting there, just staring down at his phone.

I slammed the door, settling into my seat, and handed him his root beer. "Well?" I asked.

"Now she's not answering," he said. He sighed and looked out at the highway. "I'd hate to have come this far for nothing." I wasn't sure what to say to that, so I just took a sip of cream soda. "I think we should go," he said.

"Okay," I said, a little surprised he was going to give up this easily. But I was willing to pick a new destination. I took out the atlas. "So where should we go?"

"No," he said, looking at me, "I mean, I think I should go to her house."

"Oh," I said. I wasn't sure that was such a great idea, but I didn't know how to tell Roger that without making him feel like a stalker. But I could only imagine what I would have felt if Michael had shown up on my doorstep. "I don't think that's the best idea, Roger."

Roger sighed, and his shoulders slumped a little. "I know that," he said. "But are we just supposed to hang around the Git 'n' Go? And wait for her to call?" He shook his head. "She was always doing things like this. . . ." His voice trailed off, and he looked down at his phone again. "I think we just swing by. And then at least I'll have given it my best shot. Because knowing her, she might not remember to call back for three days."

I opened my mouth to try and talk him out of this plan, then stopped when I saw the expression on his face. It was determined, and I'd never seen him look so set on anything—not even Chick-fil-A. And he probably hadn't wanted to go to Yosemite, either, but maybe I'd looked something like he looked now. "Okay," I said, opening up the Kentucky map. "Let's go."

Roger looked at me, surprised, then gave me a quick smile. "Thank you," he said.

"Sure," I said, focusing down on the map. "Hummingbird Valley?"

"Yes," he said, signaling and pulling back on the highway. He handed me his phone. "Hadley Armstrong. I have her address in my phone from when I sent her flowers over Christmas break."

"That was nice of you," I said, looking up at him.

"Well, I thought so," Roger said with a small smile. "But apparently, girls don't like red roses."

I had nothing against them. "Really?" I asked. "Because I'm a girl. And I've never heard that before."

"Seriously?" He raised his eyebrows. "The way she reacted, I thought I'd committed some crime against femalekind."

I shrugged. "I just think it's nice to get flowers," I said. "It's the thought."

"Even if the thought is trite and cliché? That's a quote, by the way."

"She said that?" I asked, a little stunned.

"She did," he said. "For Valentine's Day, I got her chocolate. I didn't even go near flowers. I don't know if I'm ever going to be capable of buying them again, and—"

"Get into the right lane," I interrupted him, seeing the sign for Louisville a little late, and hoping Roger would be able to make it.

"What, now?" Roger asked, already starting to cross lanes of traffic.

"Yeah," I said. "Sorry." I looked down at the map. "Okay, so I think we stay on this and go past Louisville, and then Hummingbird Valley should be a ways outside it—maybe half an hour."

"Loo-vulle," Roger said.

"What?"

"You said Lou-ee-ville. But it's pronounced Loo-vulle. Believe me, I got quite the education."

"Loo-vulle," I repeated. "That it?"

"Beautiful," he said.

We were now driving past downtown Loo-vulle; the highway was on an overpass above the city. It was nearing eight, and the sun had just set, leaving a blue, shadowy light over everything. It was lovely; it just made sightseeing harder. But I could see a big stadium outside my window: Slugger Field.

About twenty minutes outside Louisville, I saw the sign for Hummingbird Valley. I directed Roger off the interstate, and soon it was like we'd turned into an entirely different world. There seemed to be nothing but green rolling hills on either side of us, and everything was dark and quiet and fresh scented. Kentucky smelled great—like fresh grass. Like summer. I rolled down my window and breathed in, and realized with a little bit of a shock that it *was* summer. A new season had begun without my noticing.

I looked out the window but I wasn't seeing any houses; there just seemed to be long stretches of green land broken by occasional white fences. "What is this?" I asked, turning to Roger. "Is it a town?"

"It is," Roger said. "It's a town with only about two hundred people in it."

I turned away from what I could still see of the hills and looked at him. "Seriously?"

"Yeah," he said, laughing a little uncomfortably. "Welcome to the wealthiest town in Kentucky. One of the wealthiest in the United States."

"But I don't even see any houses," I said, peering outside.

"They're back there, from what I understand," said Roger, gesturing to the side of the road. "Way back." He squinted out the window. "I don't think these are properly called houses. I think they're actually estates."

"God," I said, looking outside, suddenly feeling nervous myself. "Something tells me we're not in Kansas anymore."

"You did not just say that."

I scrolled through Roger's phone, found Hadley's address—1205 Westerly Road—and pointed Roger in what I hoped was that direction. When we found the street, which was getting harder the darker it got, Roger slowed so we could start looking at the house numbers. But there weren't any house numbers. There were just endless white fences and the occasional gated entrance with a plaque with the house's—or estate's—name on it.

"Look," Roger said, slowing even more and pointing to his side of the road. "Do you see that?"

I looked. They would have been hard to miss. Animal-shaped topiaries stood on an expanse of lawn. But they were bigger and more detailed than any I had ever seen. Two bears, probably to scale, stood on their hind legs, raising paws in greeting to the passing cars. Below them, a fox waved a paw cheerfully. "Wow," I murmured. Roger rolled the car on slowly, and I turned back for a last look at them before they vanished from view. In the rapidly fading light, they somehow looked almost like sculptures, or enchanted creatures. Less and less like shaped shrubbery, at any rate. "Is that it?" I asked, catching sight of a sign outside a pair of gates. "On the left?"

The gates were wrought iron, and huge, and connected to two brick pillars on either side. ARMSTRONG FARMS ESTATES was carved on a silver plaque on the pillar on the left. HUMMINGBIRD VALLEY,

KENTUCKY was carved on a plaque on the right. The whole setup was intimidating. But lucky for us, the gates were open. "I think so," he said. Roger looked more nervous than I'd ever seen him. I watched as he clenched and unclenched his hands on the steering wheel and drove through.

True to his speculation, we did not reach the house for a long, long time. We drove up a gently winding driveway surrounded by green rolling hills. But I felt that at some point, this could not still be called a driveway. After this long, logically, it would seem to become a road again. As we drove, I thought suddenly with a pang about my house back in California, the Realtor's sign on the lawn and the driveway that had taken me, at most, ten seconds to cross.

We made another turn in the driveway, and then suddenly it was before us: huge and imposing and what immediately sprang to mind when you pictured a Southern mansion. It was large and white, with columns, dark green shutters on the windows, and side buildings that sloped down from the main house. There was a circular drive in front, but there were no cars parked around it. In the light that was still left, I could see beautifully landscaped flowers and white porcelain pots filled with blooms lining the steps. From what I could see along the side of the house, it looked like there was an expanse of manicured grounds in the back.

"Wow," I said, taking it all in.

"Yeah," said Roger, looking around as well. "I'd gotten the description, but I see now that she was downplaying it a bit." He put the car in park and killed the engine.

I turned away from the house and toward Roger. "So?" I asked. "Game plan? Are you just going to ring the bell?"

"I guess so," he said. "I hadn't really thought about this part. I'd thought about getting here, and what I'd say when I saw her, but not the bridge between the two." Roger cleared his throat and cracked his knuckles. "Okay," he said. "I'm going to go for it." He ran his hands through his hair again, making it stand up in all directions. Which was probably not the look he was going for, if he wanted to impress Hadley.

"Good," I said as encouragingly as possible. "But—if I could just do one thing . . ." I leaned forward, closing the space between us in the car, and reached over to him. I placed my hands firmly on his head, feeling the spring and softness of his brown hair against my hands, how on his left side it was warmer, from driving in the sun all day. I had an impulse to run my fingers through it, but pushed it away immediately. Instead I smoothed my hands forward over the cowlick in the back, flattening it down. "There," I said. "Better." I smiled at him quickly, then retreated to my side of the car.

"Oh," he said, looking in the mirror again. "Thanks."

I was about to wish him luck, when I was distracted by the sight of a person coming around the side of the house. It was a very large person wearing a white doctor's mask and brandishing a chain saw. And he was heading toward the car.

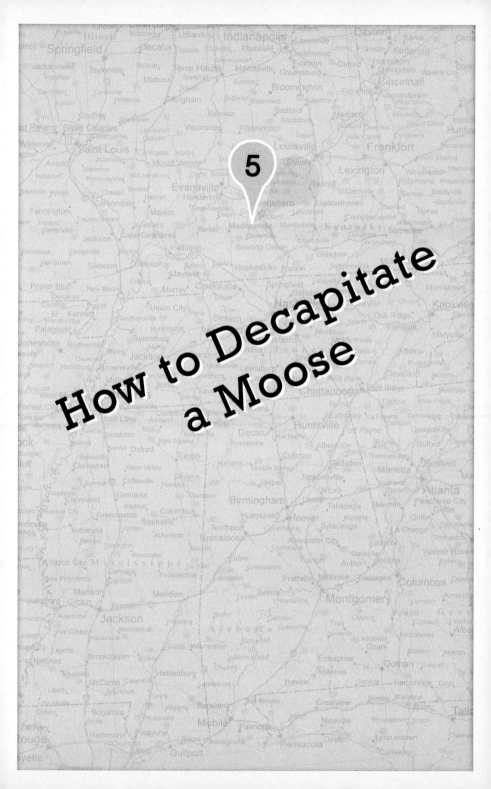

5

How to Decapitate a Moose

You'd better go on home, Kentucky gambler.
—*Dolly Parton*

"Okay," I murmured to Roger, my pulse pounding, "I think what you should do is turn the car on quietly and back down the driveway as quickly as possible."

"How," Roger whispered back to me, "do you turn a car on quietly? And you do remember that driveway, right? You expect me to back down it?"

"Roger, he has a chain saw," I hissed. "I am not going to die in Kentucky!"

Roger burst out laughing as the guy waved with his non-chain-saw-wielding arm. "Hey!" he called. "Y'all lost?"

"See?" Roger said. "He's friendly."

"That's probably how he lures his victims! They have made movies about this!"

"That was Texas," said Roger, still smiling, rolling his eyes at me and getting out of the car. "Hi," he called. "I was just . . . um . . . looking for Hadley Armstrong."

Coming closer, the guy took off his mask and had thankfully turned the chain saw off. We must have activated some kind of motion sensor, because the driveway was now softly lit, and I could see the guy actually looked fairly normal. He was wearing boat shoes, khakis, and a polo shirt. And though he was about the same height as Roger, he was just bigger. Not fat, exactly, just all-around big. Kind of like a teddy bear. Figuring this took him out of murderer territory, I opened my door as well and edged out slowly.

"I'm her brother," the guy said. "Lucien Armstrong." He held out his hand to Roger, and they shook. "Pleased to meet you."

"Roger Sullivan," said Roger. "Likewise."

"Oh!" Lucien said, snapping his fingers. "You're the guy who sent roses, right?"

Roger cleared his throat and gestured to me. "And this is Amy Curry," he said.

I stayed where I was, leaning against the car. "Hi," I said, lifting one hand in a wave.

"Hi," said Lucien, clearly not picking up on this, and crossing over to me. He held out his hand, and I shook it, feeling that I'd never shaken so many hands in my life as I had in the past few days. His hand was huge, and almost closed over mine. He didn't look anything like Hadley had in her picture. He had slightly overgrown blond hair that looked sun-bleached, and a sunburn across his cheeks. He was cute, I was surprised to see. I tried to take a step back, forgetting that I was already backed up against the car.

"Nice to meet you," I said, extracting my hand from his.

"Sorry about the chain saw," he said. "I was just cutting back some brush. So," he said, looking from me to Roger, "y'all are friends of Hadley's?" Roger nodded, and I nodded as well, thinking that it just seemed simpler than the truth.

"Yes," Roger said, sticking his hands in his pockets. "We were in the area, and I talked to her earlier, but then she stopped answering her phone. So I just thought I'd see if she was home. I left a message, but . . ."

"You know, this is awful," Lucien said. Unlike most people—and most people my age, which he looked near to—he actually seemed to really mean the things he said he felt. His brow was furrowed, and I could hear genuine regret in his voice. "I wish you could have gotten through to her, rather than coming all this way. Because Had left for a horse show a few hours ago and isn't getting back until tomorrow. I know she'll be sorry to have missed y'all."

"Oh," said Roger, nodding. "Right." I watched as he stuck his hands in his pockets, his energy ebbing away, looking a little lost. I found myself incredibly mad at this girl I'd never met. Why would she tell Roger to call when he got to Louisville when she had no intention of being there? I could only imagine how he felt—like if we'd traveled all the way to Yosemite, only to learn it was closed on Mondays or something.

"But," I said quickly, trying to cover the silence that was edging into uncomfortable territory, "I mean, maybe . . ." I looked at Roger and could see how much he didn't want to just turn around and go. "We could crash in Louisville tonight. . . ."

"Loo-vulle," Roger and Lucien said simultaneously.

"Right, there," I said. "I mean, we're pretty tired. We came from Missouri this morning and have been driving all day. So," I went on, trying to see how Roger felt about this plan I was inventing on the spot, "maybe we'll just head into town now, find a hotel, and come back tomorrow?" Roger met my eyes and gave me a small smile, and I had a feeling that I'd made the right call.

"Well, excellent," said Lucien, clapping his hands together, which made a surprisingly loud sound. "That sounds good. I would've hated for Had to have missed you if you've come all this way."

"Great," I said, turning back to the car. "So . . ."

"We don't want to keep you," said Roger.

"Nothing to keep me from," Lucien said. "The parents are down in Hilton Head for the week, Had's gone, I'm just holding the fort here by myself." He rubbed his hand over the nape of his neck, smiling a little fixedly.

There was something in his aspect that seemed startlingly familiar to me. It took me a moment, but then it clicked into place. He was alone in his house, with his sibling and parents gone. He had seemed so happy to talk to us. He was, most likely, as lonely as I'd been for the month I lived by myself in our house. There was something about being alone in places that were usually filled with people that made them seem particularly empty when it was just you.

"It was good to meet you, man," Roger said, extending his hand.

"Do you want to come to dinner?" I asked without even thinking about it, surprising myself. Roger glanced over at me, eyebrow raised, hand suspended in midair. "I mean, we were probably just going to grab something in town. And if you haven't eaten, I mean . . ."

Roger dropped his hand. "Yeah, you should come," he said. "I mean, if you don't have plans, that is."

Lucien looked from Roger to me. "Really?" he asked. "I don't want to impose on y'all."

"Not at all," I said, surprised that these words were coming out of my mouth. I had spent so long trying to avoid strangers, and now I was inviting them along? Apparently, I was. I wondered when that had happened. "You should come."

"Well, okay," said Lucien, smiling at us. "That's real nice of you. I appreciate it."

"Come on," Roger said, as he opened the driver's-side door. "I'll drive."

"Great," Lucien said, heading over to the Liberty. "All our cars are around back." Roger met my eyes as he said this, and we exchanged a tiny smile. I wondered how many cars he was talking about, how many there had to be to use the the the word "all."

Lucien opened the passenger-side door, and startled, I took a step back, figuring that maybe he really liked riding shotgun, or something. It took a silent, confused minute of him holding the door open expectantly for me to realize that he had opened it for me, and was just waiting for me to get in.

"Oh," I said, climbing in. "Um, thanks." I reached to close it, but a second later, he did it for me, shutting it gently.

He got into the backseat, buckling himself into the middle and leaning forward between our seats. "Have either of you ever been to Louisville before?" he asked.

"Nope," Roger said, and I shook my head.

"That decides it," he said, leaning back against the seat and smiling. "We're going to the Brown."

Travel Scrapbook

The Brown Hotel

We're in horse country

Travel Scrapbook

An authentic Hot Brown.
much better than it sounds

mmm, derby pie . . .

The Brown, it turned out, meant the Brown Hotel in downtown Louisville. Before we got there, Lucien gave us a quick tour of Louisville, which was lovely. It was the cleanest city I'd ever seen—certainly cleaner than Los Angeles. But it was beautifully landscaped, with trees in bloom all around us, making the air smell wonderful. The streets were wide, and nobody seemed to be in a particular hurry—another big change from L.A. There was horse stuff everywhere—which made sense, considering that this was the home of the Kentucky Derby. I noticed that some of the license plates in front of us even had horses on them, which seemed like a nice touch. Louisville just felt peaceful, which I hadn't expected.

Lucien had us drive past the Louisville Slugger Museum, which had a bat the size of the building leaning against it. I gawked at it and made a mental note to have Roger drive by in the morning again so that I could take a picture. Charlie would get a kick out of it—he'd always loved baseball. This thought jarred me a little bit, and made me realize how little I'd been thinking about my brother—or how much I'd been trying not to think about my brother. I had a suspicion that it was the latter. But I didn't want to think about Charlie. He was too tangled in everything that had happened, and then everything that had happened with him afterward. . . . I stared out the window, trying to concentrate only on Louisville passing by.

Lucien directed Roger to a very fancy-looking hotel. It had a huge red canopy, with THE BROWN written on it in gold lettering. It looked *nice*, and way out of our price range.

"This looks great," Roger said, glancing over at me, and I had a feeling he was also thinking of the four hundred dollars and change that was all the money we had. This place looked like it probably cost that much for one night. "But I'm not sure this is exactly the kind of place we were planning on staying tonight. . . ."

"No worries," said Lucien. "We're just eating here."

"Oh," Roger said. "Got it." It seemed like restaurants at this hotel might also be a little more expensive than the fast-food and diner dinners we'd been having, but I figured we could probably afford it for one meal.

Lucien's directions brought Roger around to the valet entrance, and before we could say anything, three doors were opened simultaneously by valets in white coats. I stepped out, glad once again I was wearing Bronwyn's clothes. I noticed that Roger was tucking his white T-shirt hurriedly into his jeans. Lucien stepped over to the valet who'd opened Roger's door and shook his hand, and I saw a flash of green pass from his palm to the valet's as he did this. Then he motioned us inside the hotel, as the doors were pulled open for us by two more valets, who seemed to appear out of nowhere. We stepped inside, and I looked around, my mouth hanging open a little. I was now certain this was out of our price range—this was an extremely nice hotel. There were chandeliers above us, and thick, patterned carpet on the floor, and there seemed to be a lot of shiny brass fixtures everywhere.

Lucien led us across the lobby—filled with antique-looking couches, Oriental rugs, and oil paintings of horses—and down three steps to J. Graham's Café and Bar. There was a crowd standing around the host's podium, but Lucien just walked up to the front, and we were seated right away, in a corner booth that looked out on the quiet street, lit with streetlights. "Enjoy your dinner, Mr. Armstrong," the host murmured as he handed us menus and departed.

I looked at Lucien, surprised. "They know you here?" I asked.

Lucien shrugged, looking a little embarrassed. "We've been coming here a long time," he said. "Every Derby season, the parents rent out a suite on the eleventh floor. So you get to know the staff."

"Right," I said, as though this was perfectly normal, and not at all intimidating. I looked around the tastefully decorated, clearly expensive restaurant and realized how long it had been since I'd been somewhere like this. Roger and I hadn't encountered cloth napkins in quite some time. I started to open up my menu, but Lucien laid his hand on top of it.

"If I may," he said, looking between Roger and me. "The Brown makes a famous dish that originated here, and if you haven't had it, you really should."

I thought about Roger asking me before where my sense of adventure was. I knew that he'd been kidding, mostly, but the question was now reverberating in my mind. Even Old me had always been a little cautious. I had to be, with Charlie not taking any caution at all. And I'd been reading maps too long not to want to follow some sort of plan and have an ending in sight. But I had told my mother off, and the world hadn't ended. And here I was, cut loose and in Kentucky, with Roger and a stranger, at a fancy restaurant, wearing someone else's clothes. Maybe my sense of adventure wasn't lost. Maybe it had just been lying dormant. I pushed my menu away. "Sounds good," I said, hoping immediately after I said this that the famous dish wasn't snails. Or anything to do with sweetbreads, which I'd found out the hard way in England were neither sweet nor breads.

I saw Roger give me a little smile across the table, though it faded when he heard Lucien order for all of us, something called a Hot Brown.

"You guys do eat meat, right?" he asked when three skillets were placed in front of us simultaneously by three waiters. "I should have checked, with you being from California and all." We'd done the basic introductions while we'd waited for the worrisomely named food to arrive. We'd found out that Lucien was eighteen and beginning college at Vanderbilt in the fall.

"No vegetarians here," Roger said.

"Good," Lucien said, "then dig in."

I looked down at the skillet that had been laid across my plate. One of the waiters had explained the dish: A Hot Brown was a turkey breast on big pieces of soft-looking bread, covered with parmesan cheese and a creamy sauce, flanked by tomato slices and finished with parsley and two pieces of bacon laid across the top. I had just been taking it in, wondering where to start, when

I realized Lucien hadn't started eating yet. He was looking at me expectantly, and only after I'd raised my fork did he raise his. I'd heard about Southern manners, but I'd assumed they'd died out a hundred years before. Apparently not. The proof was sitting in front of me, waiting for me to take a bite before he would begin to eat.

The silverware was surprisingly heavy, and I cut a small piece and took a bite. It was fantastic. I took another bite, and saw that across the table, Roger was eating with gusto. I realized as I ate more that these were all foods I liked—why had nobody except people in Kentucky realized how good they might be when combined and covered with melted cheese?

Roger had ordered a Coke, since root beer was not on the menu. But I'd taken Lucien's lead and ordered what he had, something called sweet tea. I took a small sip, then another one, realizing that cream soda might just have been eclipsed as my favorite drink. It was iced tea, but very sweet, with the sugar not grainy and mixed in, but part of the drink itself. Between this and the NuWay, I decided that from now on I would always follow the recommendations of the locals, as I hadn't been steered wrong yet. Lucien said that he would take care of ordering dessert, and I was happy to put myself in his hands.

I headed to the ladies' room, leaving the boys in an intense discussion of sports movies. I only hoped, for Lucien's sake, that he would have the sense not to bring up *Hoosiers*. As I washed my hands, I looked at my reflection. I thought back to the me reflected in the bathroom mirror at Yosemite. I looked different, and not only because I hadn't just been crying, then rubbing my face with paper towels that felt like they'd been made from some kind of bark. I was more tan now, and I had a new wardrobe. But it wasn't that, entirely. I looked at my reflection a moment longer, pulling my shoulders back.

When I returned to the table, the boys stopped talking immediately, which worried me. But before I could say anything, dessert

plates were presented. "Derby pie," Lucien said. "A Louisville tradition. Enjoy." He motioned the waiter to come closer, then said,
"And a glass of Maker's Mark, please."

The waiter looked from Roger to me and back to Lucien again,
who just stared back at him coolly. "Absolutely," the waiter said,
leaving.

"Did you just order a drink?" I asked, baffled, wondering if
Kentucky was somehow exempt from the drinking laws of the rest
of the country.

"Dude," Roger said reverently around a mouthful of dessert.
He saluted Lucien with his fork and went on eating. I took a bite
myself. The pie was a mixture of chocolate and strawberries and
pecans, and it was great. I found myself wishing that Kentucky was
better about exporting their local dishes to the rest of the country.

The waiter placed a short glass half-filled with two ice cubes
and a dark brown liquid in front of Lucien.

"What is this?" I asked. "Do they not card in Kentucky?"

"Not always," Lucien said with a smile. "We have in front of us
a glass of genuine Kentucky bourbon. You know that bourbon is
the only drink native to America?" Roger and I shook our heads.
"It is," he continued. "And unless it's made in Kentucky, it can't be
called bourbon. Otherwise, it's just called sour mash."

"Like champagne," I said, recalling the fact I'd once learned
while rehearsing a Noel Coward play. "Unless it's made in the
Champagne region of France, it's just called sparkling wine."

"Well, exactly," said Lucien. He set the glass of bourbon in the
center of the table. "So who's driving?" he asked. "I'm happy to, if
y'all are comfortable with that."

Roger glanced at me and took a sip of his soda. "I'll keep driving," he said. "Not a problem."

"Oh," Lucien said. "Okay."

"I'm not really driving right now," I said after a moment of
silence, feeling like some explanation was called for. But after
I said it, I realized this explanation hadn't actually clarified

anything. "Just . . . not," I said, stopping when I realized that without going into why, I wasn't going to be able to make myself any clearer.

"Well, whatever works," Lucien said. He gestured to the bourbon. "Would you like it?"

"That's okay," I said, drinking my second glass of sweet tea.

Lucien raised his eyebrows at me. "You're turning down a glass of our authentic local bourbon?" he asked.

"Oh," I said, glancing over at Roger, who for some reason was looking up at the ceiling, smiling. "Um, sure." With both of them watching me closely, I slid the glass toward me and lifted it up. It was surprisingly heavy, and I sniffed the liquid, then stopped, wondering if you were only supposed to do that for wine. At any rate, it smelled kind of like a stump. I took a tentative sip and almost spat the entire mouthful across the table. It tasted like stump too. Smoky stump. It was kind of like what I imagined it would be like to drink a forest fire. I forced myself to swallow it, and it burned my throat going down and made my eyes water. "Mmm," I choked out when I was able to speak again. "That's . . . smooth."

I looked up and saw that both Roger and Lucien were laughing. "Sorry about that," Lucien said, moving the drink away from me and into the center of the table again. "We just wanted to see if I could get you to drink it."

"What?" I asked, still coughing a little. Roger was still smiling. "Both of you?"

"Small side bet," said Lucien, slapping a twenty on the table. "Welcome to Kentucky."

"I thought I was going to insult you if I didn't drink it," I said, feeling flustered and betrayed, but also noticing how Roger looked like he was having fun as he leaned back against the booth, pocketing his twenty. I mentally added it to our current total.

"Nah," Lucien said. He edged my water glass toward me. "You'll probably need that." I grabbed the glass and took a big sip. "I think bourbon's disgusting. I have no idea how my mother drinks it. I think you actually can't drink it until you're in your fifties and can no longer taste anything."

"Sorry about that," Roger said to me, looking a little sheepish.

"Yeah, sure," I said. I tried to glare at him but found I couldn't keep the expression on my face.

"Cheers?" asked Lucien, holding up his water. I raised my sweet tea glass and Roger lifted his Coke.

"Cheers," I said, and we clinked.

Lucien looked across at Roger. "So. You and Hadley, huh?"

"Yeah," Roger said, clearing his throat. "I mean, we were dating this year at school. We broke up right as classes were ending."

"Let me guess," Lucien said with a sigh. "You haven't heard from her since?"

"Not really," said Roger. "I mean, we talked a little today, but . . ."

"Now she's not returning your calls?"

"No," he said slowly. "She's not."

Lucien shook his head. "I'm sorry, man," he said. "I'm afraid that's just her MO."

"What do you mean?" I asked.

"Modus operandi," Lucien said. "It's Latin."

"No," I said, rolling my eyes. "I know what that means. I mean, what do you mean?"

"One more guess," said Lucien, ignoring my question and turning again to Roger. "She didn't really give any explanation for why she was ending it either."

"Who," Roger said, a little blustery, "who said that she ended it? I mean, maybe it was my idea." Lucien just looked at him, and Roger sighed. "No," he said. "No explanation."

"Her MO," Lucien said, turning to me. "I've been watching her do this to suckers—no offense—"

"None taken," said Roger.

"Since she was in middle school. I'm afraid it's just what she does. You got caught in Hurricane Hadley. She comes in, shakes things up, and then leaves destruction and confused guys behind in her wake."

"This happens a lot?" Roger asked, his voice a bit strained.

Lucien nodded, and then there was a moment in which we all became very interested in our drinks. "But nobody's actually ever called her on this shit before," Lucien said, breaking the silence. "So good for you for coming here, man. Maybe you'll be the one to get through to her." He held his glass up to Roger. "I wish you luck."

I looked over at Roger, who was still staring down into his soda, and I felt like I was seeing something that I shouldn't have.

"But what do I know?" Lucien asked, a bit too loudly, maybe feeling the same way I did. "I mean, I'm just the younger brother. It's not exactly like she confides in me." He turned to me, and with the air of someone who is desperate to change the subject, asked, "Do you have any siblings?"

"One brother," I said, feeling like I'd already thought about Charlie more than I'd wanted to tonight, and wishing that Lucien had chosen almost any other subject.

"Older?"

"Younger," I said. "Three minutes."

Lucien's eyebrows shot up. "No shit," he said. "Twins?" I nodded. "So you guys must be super close, right?"

I felt my stomach clench a little when he said this. Charlie and I had had moments when we were younger when we'd been close, but mostly it seemed like we'd been battling our whole lives. Like there was always a wall between us that never came down. "Not really," I said, trying to keep my voice light. "No, not very close."

"Oh," said Lucien, and silence fell again. I had a feeling he wasn't going to be introducing any more topics of conversation tonight.

"Well, at least he's never bit you," Roger said, coming back into the conversation with a voice that was determinedly upbeat. He extended his wrist across the table, so we could all see a small, circular scar on his palm. "My stepbrother," he said. "Very hungry kid."

"That's nothing," said Lucien, rolling up his sleeve and showing us a faint scar on his forearm. "When I was eight, Hadley trained her horse to kick me. She always denied it, but our groom told me the truth."

Roger reached across to my plate to steal a strawberry, and Lucien excused himself, laying his napkin on the table, where it was immediately refolded by a waiter. "Sorry," I said once Lucien was gone, realizing we hadn't had an opportunity to talk yet, just the two of us. "About inviting him, I mean."

"No, it's fine," Roger said. "He's nice."

"He is," I said. "I just . . ." I hadn't told Roger about what it had been like, staying in our house by myself. I didn't think I'd even fully realized how it had made me feel until I'd seen something I recognized in Lucien's expression. "I think he seemed lonely, that's all."

"It's been fun," said Roger, giving me a faint smile that immediately disappeared. He shook his head. "Hadley had mentioned she had a brother, but no details, really. She hadn't told me what her house was like, or this town. It's weird." He drummed his fingers on the polished surface of the table, then continued, "Being here, it makes me feel like I didn't actually know her at all."

"Oh," I said. I looked at Roger's face to try and gauge what that meant for him. "But you still want to try to see her tomorrow, right?"

"Yes," he said, then nodded. "I do. I mean, we've come this far, right?"

Lucien returned to the table then but didn't sit back down. "Ready to go?" he asked.

"Don't we need to pay?" I asked, looking around for one of the many waiters who'd been hovering around us all night but now were nowhere to be seen.

Lucien simply shook his head. "Taken care of," he said, pulling my chair out for me. I stumbled a little as I stood, not having expected this.

"You didn't have to do that," I said, but Lucien just smiled.

"It was my pleasure," he said. "Thanks for the invite. It's no fun to eat alone." I saw Roger open his mouth to protest, but Lucien shook his head again. "Seriously," he said. "I appreciated the company."

As we headed out of the restaurant, we passed some of the same people still waiting for a table, and they glared at us as we left. We stepped into the hot, humid night that hadn't seemed to have cooled down from when we'd gone in. After California weather— desert weather—in which temperatures dropped sharply at night, this just felt odd to me, like something was unfinished. Like there was a switch that someone had forgotten to pull.

Lucien directed us back to Hummingbird Valley, and I kept looking over at Roger, who was unusually quiet. He looked pretty worn out. But whether it was the driving, or the prospect of seeing Hadley, I wasn't sure.

"Did you guys see the topiaries as you came in?" Lucien asked as we drove down his street, pointing outside the window to the figures we'd seen before, looking less ominous now that it was fully dark out and they were lit up by the huge moon. More like they were sentinels guarding the estates that stood just behind them.

"We did," I said. "They're amazing."

"They're a tradition," he said, leaning forward a little, between my seat and Roger's. "You should see this place at Christmas."

Roger signaled, and we pulled up the World's Longest Driveway. The house was all lit up as it came into view, and I turned back to Lucien. "It looks like someone else is here," I said, and noticed Roger's hands tighten on the steering wheel.

Lucien shook his head. "Timers."

I nodded and looked at the huge house, all those rooms, and thought about what it must be like to be alone in it. Roger pulled around in front, put the car in park, and turned to Lucien, extending his hand. "You showed us your town," he said. "Thanks for that."

"Sure," said Lucien, shaking Roger's hand. I noticed the fixed smile from earlier had returned. "I guess I'll see you guys tomorrow." I nodded and smiled. He unbuckled his seat belt and opened the door, but then turned back to us. "Listen," he said. "Y'all want to stay here tonight? We have tons of rooms, nobody's using the guesthouses." At this plural, I saw Roger's lips twitch in a small smile, probably imperceptible to anyone but me.

"We can't do that," I said automatically. "Thank you, though."

"Seriously," Lucien said. "They're always set up and ready for guests. And nobody's using them. It doesn't make any sense to drive all the way back into town and get a hotel for the night."

Roger and I glanced at each other, and I had a feeling we were both thinking the same thing. That it would help, money-wise, not to have to spend anything on a hotel tonight.

"Would that be weird for Hadley, though?" Roger asked, turning to Lucien. "I mean, her ex-boyfriend, staying in her house . . ." It registered that Roger hadn't had any problem with the "ex" part of that phrase this time.

"She doesn't have to know," said Lucien. "And so what if she has a problem with it? You guys are my guests, and I can invite people to stay if I want."

I glanced at Roger, who raised his eyebrows and nodded slightly. "If you're sure," I said. "But you've really done too much already."

"Not at all," Lucien said, closing the door, his smile relaxing into what I'd seen most of the night. "I'm happy to be able to do it. Now, what you're going to want to do is drive around the back." He directed Roger on a road that took us around the back of the house, and I rolled down my window, even though the air-conditioning was on, to try to get a closer look in the dark. The grounds seemed to continue on for miles, and they were gorgeously landscaped.

And there were more shaped topiaries, like the ones we'd seen on the side of the road. But there were lots of them here, scattered around—and they were amazing. I saw a bear peeking out from behind a tree, a few dogs, and what looked like a crane, before we made another turn and lost sight of those grounds. "Those are incredible," I said.

"You like them?" Lucien asked, leaning forward. "Really?"

"Absolutely," I said. "Are they done by the same person who did the ones on the road?"

"No," he said. "Someone different."

"I thought so," I said. "Those were better."

"I missed them," Roger said. "I was, you know, driving."

"I can show you guys tomorrow if you like. Roger, you're going to make a left here."

I understood why Roger had corrected me as we'd driven in—this really was an estate. I had totally lost sight of the main house by now, and we were driving on a paved path through what just seemed like woods. "You sure like to give your guests a lot of privacy," I said, as we continued on without seeing anything.

"It's not too much farther," Lucien said. "And there are Jeeps at both houses, in case you want to get around but don't want to use your car." I let this sink in for a second, just how different this way of living was from anything else I'd even heard of, let alone experienced. "Here we are," he said, and Roger pulled to a stop in front of what would have been considered a normal-size house in Raven Rock. It was two stories and seemed more cabinlike than the main house. It was made of dark wood, with a peaked roof, glass windows that went from floor to ceiling, and a wraparound porch.

"Yeah," said Roger with a short laugh, killing the engine, "I think this will do." We got out of the car, and Lucien grabbed my suitcase from the back before I could get to it, then unlocked the guesthouse and let us in.

Inside, it was cozy but very decorated. Everything seemed to match, and since it was a guesthouse, there were no personalized touches anywhere. But it was a real house, with a functioning kitchen, one bedroom downstairs, and two upstairs. Lucien showed us where the snacks were and how to use the air-conditioning unit, while I mostly just looked around, trying to take it all in.

"So I think that's it. Just give me a call if you have any questions," he said, writing down his cell number on the pristine whiteboard on the fridge. "And I guess I'll see y'all tomorrow morning. If you want to come by the main house, breakfast is normally around nine."

"This is great, man," Roger said, looking as shell-shocked as I felt. "Thanks."

"Sure," he said, and was heading for the door when I spotted a thin silver laptop sitting on the kitchen table.

"Lucien," I said. "Is that yours, or . . . ?"

He turned back to look at it, and shook his head. "It's the house's," he said. "But feel free to use it." He made a vague gesture upward. "We've got Wi-Fi."

"I'll drive you back to the house," said Roger, grabbing the keys.

"It's okay," Lucien said. "I'll just grab one of the Jeeps, if that's cool. See you tomorrow." He lifted one hand in a wave and shut the door behind him.

In the silence that followed, I looked around, still a little stunned, then turned to Roger. "Remind me again how we got here?"

"I don't know," he said with a yawn. "I think you invited him to dinner." He headed up the stairs, and I followed.

I grabbed my suitcase from where it had been left on the landing and gestured to the room closest to me. "I'll take this one?"

"Sounds good," Roger said, yawning again. He slung his duffel bag over his shoulder and headed for the bedroom a little ways down the hall. "I'm spent. 'Night, Hillary."

I smiled at that. "'Night, Edmund." I watched him disappear into his room and then headed for my own. Roger might have been exhausted—driving all day probably had something to do with it—but I was feeling strangely restless. I changed into gray sweatpants with COLORADO COLLEGE printed in blue on one leg, and a navy tank top, marveling at how even Bronwyn's loungewear was nicer than anything of mine. I headed downstairs, figuring that maybe I would go online, or watch the flat-screen, or make some popcorn. But when I saw the moonlight flooding in through the windows, I knew the only place I wanted to be was outside.

I stepped barefoot out into the still warm night and sat on the porch steps. I leaned back on my hands and looked up. The only light was coming from inside the house. There were no streetlights or city lights visible, and as a result, the stars just took over the sky. There was a riot of them, incredibly clear and seemingly closer than usual. The moon was almost full and seemed twice as big as normal. It provided so much light that the path back to the main house was still visible.

As I stared at the stars, I realized that there were always this many of them. It was only when the other lights were removed that I could see what had been there all along.

I don't know how long I sat there, staring up at the sky, but it must have been a while, because I began to feel my neck developing a crick. As I stretched and stood up, I noticed a pair of headlights rounding the curve in the road, heading toward the guesthouse. As the car got closer, I saw it was an open Jeep painted white, with Lucien in the driver's seat. He was steering with one hand, the other arm thrown over the back of the bench seat next to him. The Jeep drove past the guesthouse, then screeched to a stop and reversed until the car was in front of me.

"Hey," he said, his expression surprised. Then he smiled at me. "Want to go for a ride?"

I looked at him, and the car idling. My first instinct was to say no. It was late, we were going to have to get up early, I wasn't wearing a bra, and I didn't have any shoes on. But I hesitated for only a second before heading down the stairs. Maybe this was a chance to find out where my sense of adventure was. "Sure," I said. I pulled open the passenger door and climbed in. "Let's go."

I said, blue moon of Kentucky, keep on shining.
—*Elvis Presley*

We bounced along the road in silence. The Jeep was certainly bumpier than a car, and I held tightly to the roll bar above my head. There was something great, though, about being in an open-air vehicle and seeing all those stars above us as we moved along underneath them.

"Couldn't sleep?" I asked after a moment.

"Nah," he said. He rested the hand that wasn't on the wheel on the roll bar. He seemed to drive exclusively with one hand, but was totally in control of the car. Which wasn't surprising, since he'd told us at dinner that he'd learned to drive on the property when he was ten. "I don't know. There's just something about being in an empty house. . . ."

"I know," I said automatically. He looked over at me, eyebrows raised in surprise. I thought about backing down, muttering some half-baked explanation and pretending I hadn't said anything. But I had said something. I took a breath. "I, um, was alone in my house for all of May. So I know what it's like."

"For a month?" Lucien asked, and I nodded. "Where was your family?"

The question should have been expected. But it hit me hard, as I had been wondering pretty much the same thing for the past three months. "Well," I said, looking out at the grounds and not at him, "my brother was . . ." I hadn't told anyone that Charlie was in rehab, sticking to my mother's story. My mother had never even said the word aloud to me, always just calling it "the facility." "He went to North Carolina," I said, hoping Lucien wouldn't ask why and forcing myself to keep going. Like the sharks that died when they stopped swimming, I knew I wouldn't be able to keep talking if I stopped to hear what I was saying. "And my mother had to go to Connecticut to get our new house set up. And my father . . . my father died." I pressed my lips together hard after saying that, feeling my chin trembling after just saying the word.

"I am so sorry," Lucien said. And like before, he seemed to really mean what he said.

"Thank you," I said, meaning that, too. "I'm just trying to . . ."

"Get through it?"

"Something like that," I said, and we drove on in silence. "It was a car accident," I added after a moment, just so Lucien wouldn't ask and the *how* wouldn't hang between us.

"Is that why you're not driving?" he asked after a small pause.

"Yeah," I said. We drove on, and I felt the threat of tears recede a little. I closed my eyes for a moment and felt the warm night air on my face.

"Are you ever going to drive again?" he asked.

I opened my eyes and looked over at him. "Well, probably someday," I said, realizing that I hadn't thought about an end point. Just as I hadn't realized until this morning that if I didn't go to Graceland with my father, I would never get there. "I just . . . every time I think about driving, I start to panic."

"I can see that. But you can't let it stop you, right?"

I wasn't sure I wanted to answer that, so I looked out at the scenery. We seemed to be somewhat closer to the main house, but I was so turned around at this point, I couldn't be sure. "Where are we headed?" I asked.

"Almost there," he said. "You'll see." We hit a pothole, and both of us were jolted in our seats. I grabbed onto the roll bar tightly. "It's all right," he said. "I've got it under control." He smiled. "But you might want to hold on for this next part."

With that, he swung the Jeep off the road and onto the grass.

"Um, can we do this?" I asked.

"Sure," he said. "All the way back here, my mother doesn't care what the grass looks like."

We crossed the field, hitting some very deep holes that Lucien explained had been made by gophers. He pulled to a stop at the edge of what was probably properly called a meadow, a huge open expanse of grass. But it wasn't empty. It was filled with a menagerie of the animal-shaped topiaries we'd seen along the roads and then closer to the house. There were at least fifteen that I could see, and some that seemed to still be in hedge form, with pieces of what they would become beginning to take shape.

"Wow," I murmured, getting out of the car as Lucien killed the engine. I walked up to the nearest one, which was a life-size horse with a garland around his neck.

"That one was for the Derby last month," Lucien said. "It made the paper."

"These are incredible," I said, looking around at the creatures surrounding us.

"You really like them?" he asked.

"Of course," I said, then registered his tone of voice. I crouched down to look at an alligator that had its jaws wide open, a tiny bird perched on its teeth. "How long did this one take you?" I asked, looking up at him.

He gave a short, embarrassed laugh. "Is it obvious?"

"You just seemed a little invested in what I thought," I said, smiling at him. "But I can't believe you can do this. It's amazing."

"It's just a hobby," he said, following along a few steps behind me as I walked around, watching my expression as I looked at all of them.

"This isn't a hobby," I said. "It's like you're a sculptor. You should be proud of these." I saw a small handsaw lying next to a piece that was still half in hedge form, and something clicked into place. "Are these why you were carrying a chain saw earlier?"

"Yeah," he said. "I was working on a few around back when I heard a car. I didn't scare you, did I?"

I pretended to be very interested in a duck and a line of ducklings behind her. "Maybe just a little." The ducks were incredibly detailed—they even had ridges for feathers carved into them. "How does this even happen?" I asked, looking around at all of them. "How did you learn to do this?"

"It's not a very interesting story," he said. "Like I told you, they're kind of a tradition around here. I'd always liked them. And then a few years ago, we hired a gardener who was really great at it. He taught me what he knew, and that was that." He rested his hand on the back of a wildcat with one paw raised. "There's this quote by Michelangelo that I always liked. He said that he could see the angel in the marble, and was carving to set him free. I guess it's the same thing with me. Except I see the wildcat in the shrubbery." He smiled, but then shrugged. "But like I said, it's just a hobby."

I shook my head. "I don't think people spend this much time or energy on their hobbies." I turned away from a bear—bears seemed to be a motif—and looked at him, shoulders hunched in the moonlight. "You're an artist," I said.

He gave a short laugh. "Artists don't make money. And gardeners certainly don't make money. My parents put up with this as long as they think it's just for fun. I looked at a few colleges that had landscaping programs, and you should have heard them. It was like I had betrayed them."

"But you can't let that stop you," I said. "I mean, if you have a gift for something, I think it's wrong not to work at it, just because it gets hard, or because you're scared." I paused after saying this, wondering why these words sounded so familiar.

"Look, never mind," said Lucien, his face, what I could see of it in the dark, more closed off than I'd yet seen it. "I guess I shouldn't have expected you to understand."

"God," I said, getting frustrated. Getting mad. I could feel my pulse quickening, but it didn't feel scary and out of control, like when I'd been talking to my mother. Weirdly, it felt good. "I do understand. You think my parents want me to be an actress?" I paused, a little stunned, when I realized I'd used the plural—and the present tense. "I mean, they didn't. My mother still doesn't. Whatever," I said, trying to push on past this and get back to what was at hand. "My father was a history professor." I stumbled over the "was" for just a moment. "My mother's a PhD in English. They don't understand. They think that what I want to do is crazy. And maybe it is, but that doesn't mean I'm going to stop because they don't want me to do it. Because they *didn't* want me to. . . ." I sighed, giving up on trying to make my tenses match. "I'm just saying," I said.

Lucien nodded, looking at the ground, shoulders hunched.

"I just . . ." I looked up at the sky for a moment, then pressed on. "I thought I was going to die," I said. "For one really long second during the accident, I thought it was all over. And then, obviously, I didn't, but . . . it was like I went the opposite way. Like I stopped living entirely, so I wouldn't have to feel anything again. Because feeling had led to it hurting so, so much. . . ." My voice caught again, but I took a breath and continued saying these things I hadn't even realized until a second ago that I felt. "But since I've been out here, on this trip . . . it's like I've started to remember what it's like. To feel alive. To feel anything. And all I'm saying is that you never know how much time you have."

"I see what you're saying," he said, giving me a sad smile. "And it sounds easy. But I don't know if I can do it."

"Well, there's only one way to find out," I said, getting frustrated again. I looked across the meadow and saw the Jeep, keys dangling from the ignition, glinting a little in the moonlight. Without stopping to think, I crossed to the car, breaking into a half run as I got closer.

"Uh," Lucien called to me. "Amy?"

"Someone just told me," I said, "that you can't let things stop you because you're afraid." I walked around to the driver's-side door and climbed in.

"Right," he said. "But—"

I ignored him and placed my hands on the wheel. "Okay," I murmured to myself. It was the first time I'd been in the driver's seat since the accident. I remembered how it had felt that morning, when I'd grabbed the keys from my father and gotten behind the wheel without a second thought. I put my hand on the keys but didn't turn on the ignition yet. I closed my eyes and took a deep breath, fighting down the panic that was threatening to rise up, the panic that was telling me that I shouldn't be sitting there, that bad things would happen if I did. I opened them and looked around.

I wasn't at home, wherever that was. I wasn't in California, at any rate, and I wasn't back at the intersection at University. I was, improbably, in a meadow in Kentucky, on a warm, starry night. There weren't any other cars around to run reds. It was okay. I turned the key in the ignition.

Before I could talk myself out of it, I shifted out of park and put my foot on the gas. The Jeep jolted forward, and I stepped on the brake, slamming back into the seat. It occurred to me now that I'd never driven one of these before, and they seemed to handle differently from regular cars. Also, the act of driving felt a little rusty. I knew all the things I had to do, but they weren't working together in harmony the way they had a few months ago. I placed my hands at ten and two and pressed on the gas more gently this time. The car eased forward, and I pressed a little harder and slowly began doing a wide circle around the meadow.

Lucien was standing in the middle, next to his wildcat, and he rotated with me, smiling. "You're driving," he called.

"I'm driving!" I yelled back, pressing harder on the gas, speeding up a little. Driving in an open Jeep was fantastic. The wind was lifting my hair as I went, making it seem like I was going much faster than I actually was. When I'd gone around in a circle once, I turned around and started going the other way, making Lucien laugh. As I braked and then sped up again, I realized how much I had missed this, how free I felt, even when I wasn't actually going anywhere.

"Amy, watch out—," Lucien called suddenly, his voice sharp.

"What?" I called, a second before the car dropped down suddenly on the left side, causing me to accidentally hit the gas harder than I'd meant to. The Jeep jolted forward, and suddenly it was out of my control, and for one horrible second, I was back three months ago. A second later I came back to myself and stepped hard on the brake—but not in time to avoid a looming green figure in front of me. There was a *crunch* and the car slammed to a stop.

"Are you okay?" Lucien asked, hustling over to the car.

I could hear the blood pounding in my head, and I felt nauseous. I could feel real panic rising up, threatening to take over. I forced myself to open my eyes and shift the car into park. I took my hands, which were shaking, off the steering wheel. I killed the engine and dropped my hand quickly from the keys. What had I been thinking? Why had I even tried to do this? I stood up, trying to see over the hood. "What happened?" I asked, trying hard to keep my voice from shaking.

"Well, I think the car's okay," Lucien said from the ground, where he was kneeling. "It looks like you hit a gopher hole. But I think Maurice is a goner." He stood up, holding the head—with antlers—of a topiary moose.

"Oh God," I said, staring at it. "I'm so sorry—I broke your moose?" I don't know why this seemed, suddenly, to be funny. But it was. I could feel slightly desperate laughter threatening to get out, and I bit my lip hard against it.

"*Maurice,*" Lucien said mournfully, and that did it. I burst out in hysterical laughter. When it petered out, I got out of the Jeep and walked around to the passenger seat, trying to avoid looking at the severed moose body, thinking it was not quite so funny anymore.

Needless to say, Lucien drove back to the guesthouse. Maurice's head rested between us on the seat. "Sorry, again," I said.

"Oh, he probably had it coming," he said, looking down at the head. "In fact, you might be onto something here. This would look great above a mantel. You know, for people who want the decoration but don't want to kill an actual moose."

"I like that idea," I said. "I think there's a future in it." He glanced over at me, and I just raised my eyebrows at him.

He pulled in front of the guesthouse, and I looked up at the windows. The downstairs was all lit up, the second floor dark. "It looks like Roger went to sleep," I said.

"Yeah," said Lucien, looking at the house. A moment passed with no sounds but the crickets chirping and the rumbling of the engine. "So what's the deal with you two?" he asked, breaking the silence.

I looked at him. "What do you mean?" I asked, knowing what he meant. Lucien killed the engine and turned in the seat so that he was leaning back against the door and facing me head-on. Then, maybe realizing that Maurice was in the way, he lifted up the head and placed it in the back. "There's no deal," I said, looking up at the second floor. "Roger's in love with your sister."

He shook his head. "I'm not so sure about that."

I was about to contradict him when I realized that Roger had said basically the same thing in the car only a few hours ago. "Well . . . I know he's still hung up on her. I mean, that's why we're here."

"So there's nothing going on between you two?" Lucien asked.

I blinked at him. My first instinct was to be incredulous that he would even think that. But . . . I ran my hand through my hair, trying not to pull on it too much. This was *Roger*. And although I'd noticed how cute he was when I first saw him, that wasn't how I thought of him anymore. Then, completely unbidden, a series of images flashed through my mind. Roger drumming on the steering wheel. Roger sleeping next to me in bed, the blanket falling off his shoulder. Watching me carefully as we drove through a rain-soaked Kansas night, asking me to talk to him. Offering me the last french fry.

"Amy?" Lucien prompted.

"No," I said quickly. "No, there's nothing going on. No."

"That's a lot of no's," Lucien said.

"Yeah," I agreed, having heard that myself. I leaned back against my seat, a little shaken by this conversation.

"I just wasn't sure," he said. "What the situation was, I mean."

I shook my head. "Nothing is happening." I paused after saying this. Was that even entirely right? "I mean, nothing has happened," I corrected, secure in the knowledge that this, at least, was true. "I mean, we're here for Hadley. Because Roger still has feelings for her."

"I'm not sure how that's going to go, then. I think Had's going to take one look at him and run. That's what she does. I'm the opposite. I like to stick around."

"You grow things," I reminded him. "You're putting down roots. Literally. People who run off don't tend to do that."

"No," Lucien said with a smile. "I guess not. But I suppose I learned to do it because *someone* had to be here. And Hadley has spent her entire life running away. She runs from everything. Things, people, feelings. Family. I've watched her do it forever. Why do you think she rides horses? She's been trying to escape since she was little. The thing I don't think she's realized is that eventually you have to stop. And what happens when you do?"

Something in what Lucien said was ringing a loud bell, and I had a quick flash of Charlie, seeing his head disappear over the porch railing as he snuck out, night after night. "I think my brother does the same thing," I said slowly. "I don't know if he runs away from stuff. But I think he likes to go places where people can't follow him."

"Yeah?" Lucien asked.

"Yeah," I said, feeling the absence of my brother. I had spent so long carefully not talking about him. But suddenly I wanted to.

I knew without being able to say why that Lucien would under-stand. "He's in rehab," I said out loud, for the first time.

He looked at me for a long moment, then up at the sky with a short laugh. "So's my mother," he said. He shook his head. "She goes almost every summer and dries out. She and my father tell everyone that they're just on a trip, so they can get some golf in. I even believed it until a few years ago, when Had set me straight."

"I'm sorry," I said, hoping he would know that I meant it.

"Me too," he said, looking at me with a smile. "God, we're a regular Norman Rockwell painting, aren't we?"

"Happy families are all alike," I said, quoting from a book I'd once overheard my mother and Charlie talking about.

Lucien nodded. "Exactly."

I leaned my head against the back of the seat and looked up at the sky. "Hey, do you know the Kansas state motto?"

"I don't. Enlighten me."

"It's *Ad astra per aspera*—that's the Latin. In English, it means 'To the stars'—"

"Through adversity," Lucien finished. I glanced over at him, impressed, and he knocked on his skull. "Not just a hat rack."

"Impressive," I said, leaning my head back again. "I just thought of it tonight. It's beautiful out."

"It is," he murmured. "Amy . . ." I turned my head to look at him and saw that he had slid a little closer to me. As I watched, surprised, he slid even closer, reached out, and tucked a stray lock of hair behind my ear. His hand lingered there for a second, and then traced the curve of my cheek, stopping at my chin.

"Oh," I murmured. "*Oh*. Um . . ." I had not been expecting this. And it felt like it had been a long time since I'd had to deal with something like this. I liked Lucien, sure, he was really nice, but . . .

He slid a little closer, his arm resting along the back of the seat, and now right behind my shoulders. And as he did this, I did feel a little thrill. Here was a boy who liked me, who seemed to want to kiss me under the stars. I was still trying to figure out what I was feeling, and what I was going to do, when he leaned even closer and tipped his head toward mine.

At that instant, the light in Roger's window came on, and I looked up at it, effectively ruining the moment. Lucien looked toward the light as well and slid back a little bit to his side of the car. "Looks like Roger's awake," I said, stating the obvious, just trying to cover some of the awkwardness.

"Looks that way," Lucien said, with an embarrassed smile.

I smiled back and slid away. "I'd better go to bed," I said, getting out of the car. I closed the door and leaned over the open window. "But I'll see you tomorrow."

"See you tomorrow," Lucien said easily, though I noticed that he was blushing a little—at least, his sunburn appeared more pronounced. "You drove tonight," he said, looking at me. "That's huge."

"Yeah," I said, feeling the panic begin to rise when I thought about it, the moment when the car had slipped out of my control once again. I pushed the feeling away as best I could and tried to tell myself that I was okay. Unfortunately, the same could not be said of Maurice. I turned and headed to the guesthouse.

"One thing," he called to quietly to me, and I turned back to him. "Do you have a favorite animal?"

I was not prepared for this question. I don't think I'd been asked it since the age of eight, at any rate. Amy! would have known the answer immediately. It was probably kittens. Or unicorns. But she never would have had this night—she wouldn't have taken a chance and gone out barefoot to drive a Jeep around a meadow. And I had. "I don't know," I said, considering the question. "I've always liked owls, I guess."

"Owls?" he asked. "Really?"

"Yeah," I said, with a laugh. "But that might just be because I like lollipops. And potato chips. The ones with glasses, I guess. Why?"

"No reason," he said, backing the car up and turning in the direction of the main house. He gave a little honk, then disappeared down the road, leaving stillness and darkness behind him. I looked up at the house and saw that Roger's light was back off.

I walked inside, unable to keep a smile off my face. Lucien liked me. He wanted to kiss me. After Michael, and so much time alone, and so much time not connecting, I'd thought that it might never happen again. But it had.

As I headed into my room, I saw my cell lying on top of the perfectly made bed. I picked it up, thinking about Lucien's mother drying out in some rehab, not wanting him to damage her grass with his creations. My mother had come to see all my shows, until this last one. She'd always brought me flowers. And though it had embarrassed me at the time, I could always hear her cheers, separate from anyone else's, when we took our curtain call.

I called her cell, pressing in the code to send a message directly. "Hi, Mom," I said, after the beep. "I, um, just wanted to say hi. We're in Kentucky. And I'm okay. So you don't need to worry." I hung up and looked down at the screen. I had been trying not to think about this, but she probably was worried. So maybe that had helped a little. I went to bed feeling like a small weight had been lifted.

In the morning, when I went downstairs to see if Roger was awake and, if so, whether he had made coffee, I saw something on the front porch and went out to investigate. And there it was, sitting on the top step—a very small topiary owl. I picked it up and looked at it closely. It was amazing. There were ridges over its nose and around its eyes, and I realized after a moment that it was wearing a pair of glasses.

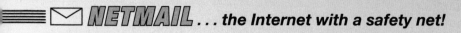
FROM	SUBJECT	STATUS
Charlie Curry	hey	READ
Julia Andersen	**Last Email**	**UNREAD**

FROM: Charlie Curry (charliecurry@netmail.com)
TO: Amy Curry (amycurry@netmail.com)
SUBJECT: hey
DATE: June 10
TIME: 4:45 p.m.

hey—

just wanted to say hi & make sure you're okay. i wrote and
asked mom & she said that she didn't want to talk about it,
but that you were "greatly disappointing her."

it doesn't sound like you, but well done!

anyway, hope you're good.

charlie

FROM: Me (amycurry@netmail.com)
TO: Charlie Curry (charliecurry@netmail.com)
SUBJECT: Re: hey
DATE: June 10
TIME: 11:45 p.m.

Hey—nice to hear from you.

I hope you're doing well and that things are going okay with you.

I'm in Kentucky right now. (It's a long story.) Let's just say that Mom is furious with me, but the feeling is mutual. I'll have to tell you all about it someday. I kind of wish you had phones there, actually. I think it's an in-person story.

Talk to you soon, hopefully.

—Amy

She met a boy up in Kentucky.
—*Steve Earle*

"She's home," Lucien told us. He had arrived at the guesthouse shortly after I'd found the owl. Roger had emerged just as Lucien came in, and now poured himself a glass of water in silence.

"Just now?" I asked.

"Just now," he said, crossing into the kitchen and taking a banana out of the fruit basket he'd brought with him that morning. "She's probably going to bring the horse trailer around to the stables, get them settled in, and then go back to the main house." By this point, I shouldn't have been surprised that they had stables, but I was. "So here's what I think," he continued to Roger. "Why don't Amy and I make ourselves scarce, and you can drive around to the house, and that way Had won't have to know that you two stayed here last night?"

Roger just shrugged. "I don't care if she knows," he said a little sharply. "I'm not going to lie about it."

"Okay," I said, looking at him and trying to gauge what he was feeling. I'd woken up early, checked my e-mail, and done some research on Charlie's facility. I hadn't opened Julia's e-mail, but I had looked at the subject line for a long moment before shutting the guesthouse laptop down. Roger had been holed up in his room that morning, and I hadn't gotten a chance to talk to him about the night before. He seemed to be preoccupied—which was understandable, considering that he was about to see Hadley. "But it's probably best that I'm not in the car with you, right?"

Roger looked at me for a moment, then nodded. "Right." Maybe picking up on Roger's tense vibe, Lucien left to load the bags into the car. When the door slammed shut behind him, I turned to Roger, trying to figure out what was going on with him.

"You feeling okay about this?" I asked.

"Fine," he said, a little shortly. He glanced outside, then asked without looking at me, "Where did that owl come from?"

"Oh," I said, smiling at it. "Lucien made it. Isn't it cute?"

"Yeah," he said hollowly. "Cute."

"Are you okay?" I asked. I hadn't ever seen him this withdrawn and couldn't put my finger on what exactly was wrong.

"Fine," he said again. "I'm fine." He took a breath and looked at me. "Are you—," he started, as Lucien came back in.

"Bags in the car," he said. "All set?"

"Yep," said Roger, causing me to smile. I took a last look back at the guesthouse, and we headed out to the cars. I placed the owl carefully in the backseat, and Roger glanced back at it, shook his head, and got in the driver's side.

"Okay," I said. "So I guess just call when you're . . ." I wasn't sure how to end this sentence. "When you want me to come meet you," I finished. I pressed my lips together and looked at Roger in the car, my spot beside him empty. I was trying not to think about it, but I knew that our trip as we'd been taking it might well be over in a few minutes. Hadley had been his objective this whole time. And now that he'd reached it, what did that mean? If he and Hadley got back together—a thought that made my stomach clench a little bit—I had a feeling he wouldn't be continuing this trip with me.

"Right," he said.

"Amy, you want to drive again?" Lucien called to me from where he was standing by the Jeep.

Roger looked up at me, startled. "What?" he asked, staring at me. "When did you—"

"I haven't had a chance to tell you yet," I said, feeling like there was a lot to catch up on, and wishing that we could do it without Lucien there, and without the audience with Hadley looming. "But yeah, last night. I drove the Jeep for about a minute."

"Until she decapitated a moose," Lucien called.

"It was just shrubbery," I said by way of explanation, wishing that I could have told Roger myself.

"Wow," he said, still looking at me. "That's . . . that's great. Good for you."

"Thanks," I said. Silence fell, and it seemed like there was something off, or a little bit strained, between us.

"Well, I should go," Roger said, starting the engine. "I'll give you a call."

"Good luck," I said, then immediately worried that that wasn't the right thing to say. "I mean, I hope it goes well. I mean . . ." My voice trailed off as he continued to stare straight ahead, and I realized I had no idea what I was really trying to say anyway.

"Right," he said. Then he backed the car out of the guesthouse driveway, heading off to Hadley.

Lucien ended up driving, and we headed around the back of the property and up a hill that seemed to be the highest point on the grounds—the main house was below us, and around the back of it, I could have sworn I saw tennis courts. We were right above the stables, and I could see, in addition to the main building, several different rings, with jumps set up, and what I assumed was an indoor ring in a huge, circular building.

"Wow," I said, taking it all in. It was warm out already, with the promise that it would be really hot around noon. But right now, it just felt good. I breathed in the scent of sweet grass, looked over the expanse of green all around me, and wondered just how I'd gotten there. "What is that?" I asked, pointing to a building near to what looked like a pond. It was so far off in the distance I wasn't even sure if it was still part of the Armstrong estate.

"That's the hunting camp," Lucien said, looking to where I was pointing. He sighed. "My father's favorite thing to do. He can't understand why I want to make fake ducks when we can just shoot the real thing."

"Oh," I said, feeling how clearly we were no longer in California. I'd never met anyone who hunted before.

"Yeah," he said. "He's planned this whole trip for him and me this November, in Canada. Which is probably going to be right in the middle of midterms. I'm trying to get out of it."

I turned to say something to him just as I saw the Liberty pull up in front of the main building. Roger got out and slammed the door behind him, shutting his phone. He looked around, ran his hands through his hair, and then, as though it was an afterthought, smoothed it down the way I'd done for him the day before.

I looked at Lucien, then slid down a little in the seat, which was completely futile, since I was still totally exposed. But it still made me feel a little less like I was spying on someone. "Why is he here?" I asked, just as I got my answer.

The door to the main building opened and out walked the prettiest girl I'd ever seen in my life. Even though we were a ways away, she seemed to have that aura. The one you could sense from celebrities when you saw them in person. In Los Angeles, this happened with some regularity—normally nothing more than a quick glance before you were hustled out of the way by a pack of paparazzi. But a glance was usually long enough to show you that specialness, that glow that the truly beautiful seemed to have. This girl had it. In spades. "Hadley?" I asked, knowing the answer.

"Hadley," Lucien confirmed.

The picture Bronwyn had shown me hadn't done her justice. She was tall and lanky, and had the kind of perfect features that made you wonder why some modeling scout hadn't discovered her years before. She was wearing jeans and a polo shirt, but it might as well have been couture, the way she was wearing them. As I saw her, and saw Roger looking at her, I understood why we'd come all this way. I understood why he'd be willing to put up with me, a stupid high schooler, just for a chance to see her again. I watched as he walked up to her, the same feeling in my stomach as whenever I watched a horror movie. I didn't want to look, but at the same time, I knew I wouldn't be able to look away. I thought for a moment that they were going to hug, but then he took a step back and just raised a hand in a wave.

"What do you think is going to happen?" I whispered to Lucien. He smiled and rolled his eyes.

"Amy, we're about thirty feet away. I don't think they can hear us."

"I know," I said. "But still." I watched them talking, Roger with his hands in his pockets, nodding to the car. Hadley nodded, then motioned to her left, and the two of them walked around the stable building and out of sight. "Damn," I murmured.

"You know," said Lucien. "Depending on what goes on over there"—he gestured in the direction they had gone—"you guys are welcome to stay on for few days if you want. It's been great having you around."

I looked over at him. "That's really nice of you," I said. "But you've already done way too much. And I think I need to get back on the road."

He nodded, as though he'd been expecting this response. "Where y'all headed next?"

"We haven't talked about it," I said. "But . . ." I thought about the trip my father had wanted to take with me and Charlie, and how right now I was just a few hours from Memphis. But now I didn't know what the status of this trip was. For all I knew, it could be ending, right at this moment. I stopped and sat up a little straighter when I saw Hadley stalking out from where she and Roger had disappeared. She didn't look happy; her mouth was twisted and her posture seemed stiffer. She didn't look quite so pretty anymore. Roger followed a moment later. He was walking more slowly and had his head down; it was hard to read his expression. Hadley walked through the stable door and slammed it with such force that even thirty or so feet away, I flinched. "Well," I said.

"Yeah," Lucien agreed.

I watched as Roger leaned against the Liberty, still looking down at the ground. "So I guess I'd better be going," I said to Lucien.

"I guess so," he agreed. "Want me to drive you over there?"

"It's okay," I said, getting out of the car. "It's just down the hill. I'll walk." Lucien got out of the driver's side and met me in front of the hood. "I know this is none of my business," I said, the words coming a little haltingly. "But you should go on that trip with your father."

He blinked, like this wasn't what he had expected me to say. "The thing is—," he started.

I shook my head, interrupting him. "Just do it," I said. "It'll make him happy. And because at some point, you might . . . might not be able to." Lucien nodded, his expression more serious, and I knew he understood what I was saying. I looked at his face for another moment, making sure I'd remember it and realizing that I was going to miss this person I hadn't even known this time yesterday. "Thank you for everything."

"It was fun," he said a little wistfully. He looked down at me and smiled. "You're great. You know that, right?"

I wasn't sure how to respond to that, so I just let out a little embarrassed laugh. "And you should keep making the animals," I said. "Really. I'll be mad if you don't."

"Well, we don't want that," Lucien said. And then, before I even had a chance to register that it was going to happen, he leaned down and kissed me.

It was quick; I only just had time to respond before he broke away and walked back to the driver's side. "Stay in touch," he called to me, and thinking of the fact that I'd put his cell number into my phone when he wrote it on the whiteboard, I nodded and waved as he started the car and backed it onto the main road. Possibly on his way to make something. Maybe another owl. But more likely, a replacement moose. I watched until there was only the dust the Jeep had left behind, then turned and headed down the hill, doing that stumble-run that was inevitable when trying to maneuver down steep hills.

Roger looked up as I jogged down the last part of the hill. "Where did you come from?"

I gestured to the top of the hill. "We were just looking around when we saw you. . . ."

"Oh," Roger said. "Yeah." I looked at him, trying to see if I could register what the outcome of the conversation was, but his face was oddly blank. "Well," he said after a moment, "ready to go?"

"I am," I said. "Are you okay?"

Roger nodded. "You know," he said, giving me the first smile of that morning, "I think I am." I walked around to my side of the car, and just as I tried to open the door, I heard the *beep* of the doors being locked with the clicker. Sure enough, I couldn't open the door.

"Roger," I said. "Come on."

"What?" he said, smiling at me across the hood. "Are you sure you don't want to *drive?*" The emphasis he put on the last word let me know that he hadn't forgotten what Lucien had said. And that I'd been right in thinking he wasn't thrilled about it.

"No," I said, trying not to laugh. "Let me in."

"Okay," he said, clicking the lock open and then clicking it closed again just as I lunged for the handle.

"Stop it!"

"What? Just because you're not fast enough—" The stable door rolled open again, and Hadley stood there, looking at us. Judging from her expression, she had not been expecting to see me.

"Oh," she said, looking from me to Roger.

"We were just going," Roger said, beeping the car unlocked once again. I had a feeling it would stay open this time.

"Is this her?" Hadley asked, looking at me. I blinked at her, stunned. She and Roger had discussed *me?*

"Hello," I said, not sure what the proper response to that question was. *Yes?* "I'm Amy—"

"You're bothering the horses," she said, interrupting me. "If you could just . . ."

"We're leaving," Roger said quietly.

"Yes, well," she said, but didn't seem to have anything to follow this. She gave me a long look, and I looked right back at her, glad once again for Bronwyn's clothes and trying to remember to stand up straight. Then she turned sharply and headed back into the stable, the door rolling shut with a bang.

I got into the car quickly. Roger got in as well, and we buckled our seat belts in unison. "What happened?" I asked. "What did you say?"

Roger put the key in the ignition and looked over at me. "I told her good-bye," he said. Then he started the car and put it in gear, and we headed out.

State #9: Kentucky—The Bluegrass State

motto: United We Stand, Divided We Fall

Size: Not as big as the other states! Finally getting to normal-size states!

Facts: Roger was deeply disappointed that we did not eat KFC in Kentucky. He wanted to know if they just call it "FC" here, because the Kentucky part is understood.

Notes: Kentucky EXCELS at food. Thumbs-up to sweet tea, Hot Browns, and derby pie. Thumbs-down to drinks that taste like stumps.

Travel Scrapbook

I love Waffle House!

WAFFLE HOUSE
Munfordville, KY
6/11
Server: Elle

Waffle Meal #1
Scrambled Eggs &   5.99
Cheese Grits   2.99
Side bacon, crisp   1.50
Sweet Tea

Waffle Meal #3   3.99
Double Stack   2.99
Side bacon, crisp   1.50
Root Beer

                       18.96

TOTAL:

Louisville to
memphis:
5 hours

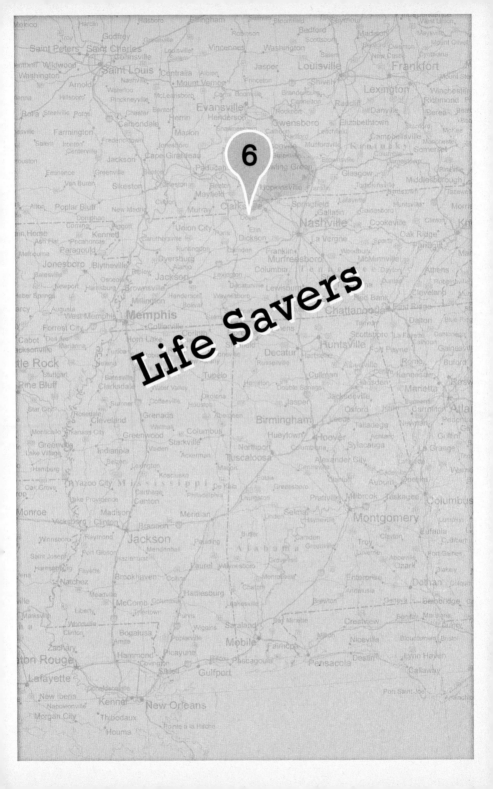

6

Life Savers

We both will be received in Graceland.
—*Paul Simon*

"But I thought you didn't like Elvis," Roger said as we drove down Interstate 65, backtracking, heading to Tennessee. It wasn't too hot out yet, and we had all four windows down, the breeze tossing my ponytail and hopefully not pulling too much of my hair out.

"I love Elvis," I said, thinking of all the lyrics that had just always been a part of my life, all the songs I'd known without even remembering learning them. I suddenly realized these few months were probably the longest I'd ever gone without listening to him.

"But you didn't want to hear him," Roger said, his brow furrowing as he glanced in his mirror and switched to the left-hand lane. "I remember. You put a moratorium on all things Elvis."

"My father," I said, taking a breath before I could get myself to say those words. It hit me that because it hurt so much to talk about him, I'd stopped talking about him altogether. Which suddenly seemed like the worst kind of betrayal. I had just been trying not to remember what had happened. But that didn't mean that I had wanted to forget him. "He loved Elvis."

"Oh," Roger said, glancing at me.

I nodded and looked out the window. But to my surprise, I wasn't done talking yet. And it felt like the talking might be okay. A little shakily, I continued. "We were supposed to go to Graceland in July. Charlie, my father, and me."

Roger looked over at me and smiled. "Then we should get you there, I think."

I turned to him, about to apologize for how out of the way it was, how we were backtracking, but I stopped myself. Maybe I was on a quest of my own.

←——→

"So?" I asked, after we'd been driving through Kentucky for two hours and I couldn't stand the suspense anymore. Even on the interstate, there were green rolling hills on either side of the car, for as far as the eye could see. It looked like pictures I'd seen of Ireland, but I had no idea that parts of my own country looked like this. It hit me once again just how big America was, and until now, how little of it I'd seen.

"I like it," Roger said, his fingers keeping time to the first song of *Avenue Q*. "I didn't know musicals could be funny." He glanced over at me, his sunglasses already on. But for once hadn't commented on the fact that mine were AWOL.

"No," I said, though I was relieved that he actually seemed to like my music and wasn't just pretending. "I mean, what happened with Hadley?" I asked.

Roger didn't say anything for a moment, just switched on the cruise control, causing the car to lurch forward a little before it settled into its steady speed. I glanced over at the speedometer and saw it was exactly at seventy. "It wasn't what I was expecting," he finally said.

"What had you been expecting?" I asked, dreading the answer but needing to hear it.

"I guess . . . in the beginning," Roger said, choosing his words carefully, "I'd been hoping that we could get back together." As soon as he said it, I realized that was exactly the answer I hadn't wanted to hear. Which, coupled with what Lucien said, made me realize that at some point, without my knowing it, the way I'd been thinking about Roger had changed.

"Oh," I said, trying to sound as neutral as possible.

✮ Amy Playlist #1 ✮

"Going to Graceland" or "Roger Gets an Introduction to Musical Theater"

SONG TITLE	ARTIST
"Avenue Q"	Avenue Q
"One Short Day"	Wicked
"All That's Known"	Spring Awakening
"Someone Like You"	Jekyll & Hyde
"When I Look at You"	The Scarlet Pimpernel
"All the Wasted Time"	Parade
"I'd Give it All for You"	Songs for a New World
"I Believe"	Spring Awakening
"I Can Do Better Than That"	The Last Five Years
"The Best of All Possible Worlds"	Candide
"Bill"	Show Boat
"Consider Yourself"	Oliver!
"This Night"	Movin' Out
"Where Did We Go Right?"	The Producers
"Wheels of a Dream"	Ragtime
"Still Hurting"	The Last Five Years
"You Can't Stop the Beat"	Hairspray
"For Now"	Avenue Q
"Nothing in Common"	Wearing Someone Else's Clothes
"Remember?"	A Little Night Music

"But then—I don't know," he said, changing lanes again, even though there wasn't any reason to. "I'd stopped thinking about that in the last few days. And then when I saw her, it was like she didn't even look the same to me."

I had seen Hadley; I found this hard to believe. "Really."

"I know it sounds weird," he said, with a little smile. "But it was like I was seeing someone I used to know, a long time ago. And while she was talking, I kept thinking about things I'd forgotten— like how she hated my music and how she used to keep me waiting for hours to call me back, and how she never got along with my friends. And . . . I don't know. I kept thinking back to the way she ended things. And just like that, I didn't need to know why it had ended. I just knew it was done. That it had been done for a while."

"Wow." I remembered how she had looked after the conversation. "I take it she wasn't too happy with that?"

"No," Roger said. "I think you could safely say that."

"So now what?" I asked.

"I don't know," he said, looking at me. "Now what?"

I looked over at him, and my heart began to beat a little more quickly. I was pretty sure that he meant the trip. We were both talking about the trip. Weren't we? I looked out the window. He was single now in a way he hadn't been before. I was suddenly very aware of the fact I had just thrown my hair up into a ponytail that morning without brushing it. "I don't know," I said, turning back to him. Our eyes met for a long moment before he moved his back to the road.

"Graceland, right?" he asked, looking straight ahead.

"Graceland," I confirmed.

Roger glanced over at me quickly and smiled, then stepped on the gas, taking the car out of cruise control and up to seventy-five.

←——→

It would have been impossible to miss Graceland once in Memphis—it had its own exit off the highway. And once we got off the interstate, we had clearly entered Elvis country. A Days

273

Inn promised a guitar-shaped pool and Elvis movies on demand, twenty-four hours a day. Ahead of us on the road, bizarrely, were two pink Cadillacs driving side by side. And next to the turn for the Graceland parking lot was the Heartbreak Hotel, advertising reduced rates. We paid ten dollars and drove into the lot, but we weren't at Graceland yet. The mansion, as it was referred to on my ticket, was across the street from the parking lot, Elvis's airplanes, three gift shops, and restaurant.

We went with the mansion tour. The VIP package included access to the "jumpsuit room," which I didn't think I needed. After we'd gotten our tickets, we stood on line for the bus behind a German couple and in front of what looked like three generations of a family—grandfather, father, and son. As the line curved around, every group was directed to stand in front of a Graceland backdrop to get their pictures taken. It seemed that this was compulsory— the woman taking the pictures kept explaining, her voice tired, that if you didn't want the pictures, you didn't have to buy them. When Roger and I reached the wall, we stood side by side, a little awkwardly. "Closer," the picture-taking woman said with a weary sigh, hoisting her camera. Roger took a step closer to me and then slowly—as though making sure I'd be okay with it—put his arm around my shoulders.

It was like every nerve in my body was suddenly awake. I smiled for the flash, but was really thinking about how I'd never noticed how sensitive my shoulder was before, how I was hyper-aware of his arm resting across it. How I could feel his breath rising and falling where our sides were touching. "Next!" she called, and we moved apart, not looking at each other, both of us paying a lot of attention to our audio guides. We boarded the small bus that would take us across the street, and after we got on, the driver closed the door and started it up. We drove out from the parking lot, and the driver signaled to turn up the driveway. I looked out the bus window and saw the open Graceland gates, decorated with Elvis with his guitar and musical notes, and the brick wall that led up to the gates—the one that was totally covered in the famous graffiti. And then we pulled up the driveway, and there it was, on top of the hill, and smaller than I expected: Graceland.

We had to follow the audio guide's path through the house and weren't allowed to retrace our steps, but we were permitted to go at our own pace. Roger, seeing that I was taking more time—and pictures—than he was, went on ahead as I walked through the mansion. The house itself was incredible. Every room was overdecorated, and every room had a motif—many, my audio guide told me, chosen by Elvis himself. The whole place was a shrine to sixties decorating.

I stayed in the Jungle Room the longest. And it wasn't like I was really expecting anything to be there—of course not. And yet, I still stood there, waiting. Just in case. But I didn't see anything except an empty room, a family room that nobody had used for years, Lisa Marie's stuffed panda sharing a chair with an unplayed guitar. As I walked through the mansion, looking at the perfectly arranged rooms that nobody lived in any longer, I thought of my own house, standing empty, welcoming strangers HOME!

After the first few prompts, I turned the audio guide off as I made my way through the house and into the office, and then the studio and building dedicated to memorabilia—costumes, an entire room full of records, jumpsuits standing upright and empty, and Elvis, Elvis everywhere.

I took my pictures, I looked around, but as I continued with the tour, it felt like my vision was narrowing, like the Elvis-bedecked walls were closing in on me. I wondered what my father had thought of the exhibits, and what trivia he could have told me, all the little details I was missing. I realized I didn't even know how old he'd been when he'd visited. But I'd never asked him. I'd never asked him a lot of things. And now I'd never know. Coming to Graceland had been a mistake, I felt, as I looked at all the Elvisness that surrounded me. It was a shrine to what my father had loved, and I should not have been there alone. It was just wrong. I was at Graceland, and my father wasn't with me. And he wasn't ever going to make the trip. He was never going to get to come here again. He was done listening to Elvis and driving to Tennessee and taking souvenir pictures. And it was all because of me.

The tour finished out by the pool, and I raised my camera to take a picture, until I realized what was at the end of the pool. Elvis's grave.

It was surrounded by flowers and wreaths and teddy bears, in front of an eternal flame and flanked by the graves of his parents. I stepped closer and read the inscription on top in raised bronze lettering. I stared down at it, feeling my breath get ragged. There was one part that I couldn't look away from. GOD SAW THAT HE NEEDED SOME REST AND CALLED HIM HOME TO BE WITH HIM. WE MISS YOU SON AND DADDY.

My vision swam with tears, the eternal flame in its Plexiglas blurring in front of me. Home? How could he be called home? *This* was his home. But at least he'd been buried here, by the house he loved so much. At least he wasn't alone, and far away from everyone in his family. At least people were doing their best to remember him. At least he hadn't been abandoned in Orange County.

*Well they've been so long on Lonely Street they
ain't ever going to look back.*

—*Elvis Presley*

Two months earlier

My mother, Charlie, and I stood in a line, looking down at the small brass marker in the ground. The overly solicitous funeral director had shown us the plot, then backed away, telling us he'd be nearby if we needed anything.

I couldn't think of anything we'd need that he could provide, so I'd just glared at him while he talked, then felt bad about it as he left and waited a respectful distance away. The cemetery, Pacific View, was beautiful—we'd been informed on our drive up to the plot that John Wayne was buried there. But we were in Orange County, an hour and a half away from Raven Rock. And I didn't like to think of my father alone out here, so far away from home.

I didn't want to think about him at all, and it seemed impossible to me, as I looked down at the small brass marker—BENJAMIN CURRY. BELOVED HUSBAND, FATHER, AND EDUCATOR—that my father was in there. He had always been too tall for things, complaining about tiny movie theater and airplane seats. How could he fit below a marker the size of my hand? How was that possible? And as I looked at my mother and my brother, both staring down at the ground, nobody saying anything, the whole thing just felt wrong. We shouldn't have been putting him in the cold, dark ground. We should have scattered his ashes in the Jungle Room or over the fields of Gettysburg or even on our lawn he loved so much. He shouldn't have been in Orange County, surrounded by strangers, most of whom were probably old and had died peacefully of natural causes.

My mother cleared her throat, then looked at Charlie and me. I looked back at her, not wanting to, telling myself that I'd learned by now, but still waiting for her to say something. Or put her arms around us. Just to somehow make this better. But she turned and walked away, heading toward the funeral director. I looked at Charlie, who was still staring down at the ground. His eyes were red, and I actually had no idea what the cause was today. We were standing fairly close—I could have extended my arm and touched him—but it felt like we were miles apart. Why weren't we talking about this? Why weren't we reaching out to each other?

Charlie left as well, heading toward my mother, leaving me alone. Alone with the small piece of ground that held what was left of my father, I reached into my pocket and took out what I'd brought him. When I'd been in the 7-Eleven that morning, looking down at the candy display, I'd suddenly panicked, because I couldn't remember what his favorite flavors were. Why hadn't I paid more attention? Why hadn't I realized that one day he wouldn't be there to ask?

I'd finally gone with Butter Rum and Wint-O-Green. I took them out and placed them on top of the marker, where they rolled back until they hit the raised *B* of his name and stopped. It had always been my job to give him Life Savers. And now this was the only way I could do it. I looked at the candy, knowing it would be taken away, uneaten, when the flowers were thrown away every week.

Then I turned away too, leaving him all alone.

Where I've Been . . .

State #10: Tennessee—The Volunteer State

motto: I don't know.

Facts: Don't know.

Notes: Don't care.

(Not actually Elvis)

POST CARD

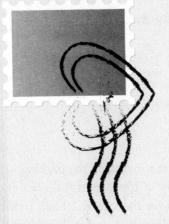

Benjamin Curry
Pacific View
Orange County, CA

Hi, Daddy—

Well, I made it to Graceland, after all. I'm sorry we never got to take our trip. And I'm sorry that I never read your book. I'm just sorry—for everything.

I hope you're happy. I hope that there's lots of Elvis and lots of unmown lawn and lots of people to talk about Reconstruction with.

I know people always say this on postcards, but it's really, really true this time.

I wish you were here.

I took a trip while I was gone. I cashed in all my savings and bought an El Dorado, drove to Tennessee.
—*Jason Robert Brown*

"Are you okay?" Roger asked.

I nodded, looking straight ahead as we crossed the parking lot to the car. I'd left the postcard on top of the graffiti wall, underneath the heaviest rock I could find on the street. I hadn't said much when I'd met Roger by the middle gift shop. I still didn't feel like saying much.

We got into the car, and Roger reached into his pocket and pulled out a small tissue-wrapped object. "I know you're probably not going to want them," he said as I looked at him, surprised, "but they seemed too good to pass up."

I tore off the tissue paper and saw that he'd bought me sunglasses—Elvis-style gold-rimmed sunglasses. I looked down at them in my hands and thought about my own sunglasses, shattered in the impact—I'd seen one of the lenses on the ground, mixed with all the auto glass. It was stupid to refuse to get new ones. It wasn't like it was going to do anything. I gave Roger the best approximation of a smile I could. "Thank you," I said, slipping them on. "What do you think?"

He gave me a real smile in return. "Lovely," he said. He started the car. "Lunch?"

⟷

Roger had discovered his own version of heaven, and it was Krystal, a fast-food chain neither of us had heard of before. And it was good—the burgers were mini-burgers, and the fries were extra salty. And there was sweet tea as a drink option. We ate sitting in the way-back, the door raised, our legs dangling over the edge. We had the view of the Tennessee-Alabama Fireworks emporium across the street, and I noticed Roger looking at it a little too interestedly, when not exclaiming over the perfection of the burgers.

I held the atlas on my lap, looking down at the country, amazed by how far we'd come. We still had a little ways to go, but it seemed like most of the country was behind us.

"What's the plan?" Roger asked, holding out the fries to me. I took one and dipped it in the barbecue sauce container sitting between us, while he made a face. He did not approve of barbecue sauce on fries, I'd found out.

"I don't know," I said, even though, as I looked down at the map, I could see where I wanted to go. We weren't that far from it either. Just one state away. "I should tell you something." Roger put the fry that was halfway to his mouth down and looked at me. "My brother's not at an academic enrichment camp," I said. "He's in rehab." The word, ugly and loaded, hung between us in the car for a moment.

"Oh," Roger said quietly.

"Yeah," I said with a short laugh. "And I was thinking . . ." I traced my finger across Tennessee and to North Carolina. To Asheville. "I think that I need to see him."

←——→

Around one a.m. we were outside of Asheville. We hadn't talked much on this drive. We'd listened to Walcott's demo, which made up in volume what the lead singer lacked in pitch. Roger had put on one of his mixes, but then asked if he could listen to some of my musicals in their entirety, since he was having trouble following the stories, hearing the songs out of context. He'd liked *The Producers* so much, he'd listened to it twice.

We were here. But I'd realized, as we drove across Tennessee and the time got later and later, that we'd have to wait until the morning to see Charlie. While Roger had been humming along

♡ Amy Playlist #2 ♡

Pay No Attention to the Boys Behind the Curtain/The Henry Gales

TRACK LIST

1. New Way of Thinking
2. South of Lincoln, West of You
3. Surrender, Dorothy
4. Fields of Poppies in Technicolor Red
5. Late Last Nite
6. Tell me How
7. Where I Am Is Where I'm From

with Nathan Lane, I'd been thinking about my brother. After all those months of not speaking, suddenly talking to him was the only thing I wanted to do. It seemed like it was time.

We pulled into the parking lot of a Wal-Mart so we could take stock of how much money we had for a hotel tonight and figure out where we were going to stay. I'd just assumed it would be closed—everything else around seemed to be—but the parking lot was strangely full of RVs and semi trucks, the lights on tall metal poles still on. "Is Wal-Mart open?" I asked, as Roger pulled into a parking spot. Three spots away was a huge silver Airstream trailer, glinting in the floodlights.

"Maybe," he said with a yawn. "It might be one of those twenty-four-hour ones."

I took out my wallet and counted our remaining money. We had only three hundred dollars now. It was mostly the cost of gas that was depleting our money so quickly. Three hundred dollars felt a lot less safe than four hundred dollars, particularly if we had to spend a hundred dollars on a hotel room tonight. "Want to go in?" I asked, putting the money back in my wallet. "We could probably get some snacks cheaper than in mini-marts."

"Sure," he said, opening his door and getting out. I got out as well, and Roger pressed his hands against the back of the car and stretched out his legs before walking to the store.

The Wal-Mart was open. There was even a greeter in a blue vest who wished us a good evening and welcomed us to Wal-Mart. I found myself blinking at the fluorescent brightness of the store. It was absolutely massive, utterly quiet, and appeared pretty deserted—which made no sense, since the parking lot was so full. We headed to the snack aisle, and I stocked up on soda and chips. When I turned to ask Roger if he wanted Reese's Pieces or peanut butter M&M's, he was no longer there. I left our cart in the middle of the snack aisle—I didn't think it'd be in anyone's way—and went looking for him. It was a little eerie, as I didn't see any other shoppers. It was like I was all alone in that huge, silent store. I was relieved when I spotted Roger heading back to grocery from the apparel section. "Roger," I called, hearing how loud my voice sounded. He ran over to me, and as he did, I saw that he had a pack of white tube socks in his hand. When he reached me, he ripped the package open. "I think you have to pay for those first," I said, completely confused as to why he needed socks *right now*. As I watched, baffled, he kicked off his flip-flops and pulled on a pair of the socks. Then he handed a pair to me. I looked down at the tube socks. "I don't understand," I said.

"Put them on," he said, and he no longer seemed tired at all. He seemed more excited that I had ever seen before.

"But I'm wearing flip-flops," I explained, wondering if maybe Roger had been driving too long.

"Just do it," he said, smiling at me. "Seriously." I shrugged and took off my flip-flops. I pulled on the socks, hoping we wouldn't get in trouble for wearing them without buying them first. "Ready?" he asked, as I straightened up.

"For what—," I started. But Roger grabbed my hand and began running down one of the gleaming aisles, pulling me behind him. I stopped protesting and just ran with him, tightening my fingers around his for just a second. Then he let go of my hand, stopped running, and slid down the length of empty aisle in his socks.

He turned back to me, grinning. "You have got to try this," he called.

I didn't worry about how it was dangerous, how one of us might get hurt. I just took off at a run down the toothpaste aisle. I didn't think about what I was doing. I just ran full-out, then stopped and let momentum carry me down the rest of the aisle, faster than I'd been expecting. It was scary and thrilling and it felt, slipping on new socks down an empty Wal-Mart aisle, like I was free. Roger, laughing, slid to my side and took my hands in his. He spun me around and I let go, letting myself twirl, the brightly colored displays all around me turning to a blur. Roger turned in the other direction and started running, then sliding, almost falling, windmilling his arms to stay upright. By the time I caught up with him, almost crashing into a Crest display, I was laughing harder than I had in a long, long time.

←———→

"These too," Roger said, handing the empty sock package to the one cashier still open. She raised her eyebrows, but just scanned it without comment. I put my flip-flops back on, still a little out of breath. In the glass opposite the cashier's station, I caught sight of my reflection and almost didn't recognize myself. My hair was messed up, my shirt was wrinkled, and I looked happy. I looked like I'd just been having fun. Which was exactly, I realized, what I'd been doing.

"What's with all the RVs out there?" Roger asked, as she bagged our items.

"Wal-Mart policy," she said. "Free overnight parking. That'll be thirty forty-five."

Roger met my eyes as I pulled out the money we had left to pay for our snacks and socks. I had a feeling we'd both just had the same thought.

I hadn't folded down the backseats in a while, but after a few tries, I got them down, turning the whole back of the Jeep into an open area, one that would hopefully give us enough room to sleep comfortably. Roger had gone back inside to buy a blanket and two pillows. While he was gone, I'd changed in the front seat, pulling on the tank top I'd worn the night before. But since it was still warm out, I'd grabbed a pair of Bronwyn's shorts. They had looked okay from the front, but when I held them up I saw that TEXAS FOREVER was printed across the butt. They also were a little shorter than I might have preferred, but I figured I could deal with it for one night. After I got changed, I took out my phone and saw I had a missed call from my mother. She hadn't left a message, but she had called. I punched in the number for her cell, and at the last moment, added the code to send a message right to voice mail.

"Hi, Mom," I said. "I, um, saw you called. I'm fine. We're in

Asheville right now. I'm going to try to see Charlie tomorrow." I stopped and took a breath before continuing. "I went to Graceland today. I was wondering—did you know how old Dad was when he went there?" I paused again, feeling like I'd just pushed open a door. We hadn't talked about my father at all. Not even the good stuff that we remembered. Not even the stuff we wanted to celebrate. "I was just wondering. Anyway, I just wanted to let you know that I'm doing okay."

I closed my phone, my throat feeling tight. I held the phone in my hand for just a minute longer, in case she called back. But it was late, and she was probably asleep, alone in our new house. It struck me for the first time that my mother had also spent the past month alone. I hadn't really been able to think beyond myself—I hadn't even realized we'd been in the same situation. I saw Roger heading up from the store and shut my phone off to conserve the battery, dropping it next to my father's book in my purse.

Roger must have changed in the Wal-Mart bathroom, as he was back in his T-shirt and shorts that I now knew well. He opened the back door and tossed me the blanket and pillows. I placed the pillows by the door, so our feet would face the front seats. Julia, who'd gone through a big "energy healing" phase last year, could have told me if this was the proper car feng shui. But Julia was finally giving up on me, if the title of her last e-mail was anything to go by.

Roger started the car, shaking me out of these thoughts, and cracked all four windows. Even so, it was hot in the back. Clearly we could have saved the $9.99 he'd spent on the blanket. I passed him the suitcases from the back, and he piled our bags on the passenger seat, my owl resting on top. Then he killed the engine, locked the car from the inside, and climbed over the driver's seat and into the back. I moved over to the left side—my side—to try and give him room. But it was really close quarters in the back, something I hadn't really thought through. I lay down, resting my head on the brand-new pillow and seeing that Roger was now nearer to me than he had been in any of the beds we'd shared. But I found that I didn't mind so much this time. The blanket was down by our feet, and I was really aware of him next to me, without a sheet or blanket covering us, his bare legs just a handspan away from mine.

I rolled onto my back and looked up, through the back window, trying to see the stars. But the parking lot floodlights must have been too bright, and all I could see was the inside of the car, reflected back at me. "'Night," I said, turning my head to look at Roger, expecting him to be half-asleep already, as usual.

But he was turning from side to side, and kicking the blanket even farther away from him. "I'm hot," he said, pulling at his T-shirt. "Aren't you?"

"Yeah," I said. Now that we were both in the back, it seemed even hotter back there. And the air felt still, like the heat was pressing down on us. "But then, I'm not the space heater."

"I know," he groaned. "It's like an oven in here."

"We could open the windows more," I suggested.

"It's so warm out there, it probably wouldn't make a difference," he said. "Plus, I'd be worried someone would break in." He rolled from side to side again, then sat up. "Would it bother you," he started, then cleared his throat. "I mean, would you mind if I took my shirt off?"

"Oh," I said, and I could feel my cheeks growing warm. "No, that's fine."

"Really?" he asked.

"Absolutely," I assured him, then hoped I hadn't sounded too enthusiastic. "I mean, sure." Roger sat up and pulled off his Colorado College T-shirt, and I tried to keep my eyes fixed on the window. But when he lay down again, I glanced over and could feel myself start to blush harder. Because, um . . . yeah. Roger had a great body. It was lean and not too muscley, but he did have really nice stomach muscles, and . . . I looked back up to the ceiling quickly, feeling suddenly even warmer in the car.

"'Night, Hillary," Roger said with a yawn.

"'Night, Edmund," I said, as breezily as possible. I looked over at him a moment later, once his breathing had grown long and even. He had rolled on his side, facing me, and I turned onto mine, facing him. I closed my eyes but had a feeling I wouldn't be able to sleep. I had slept last night, but that was in Lucien's luxury accommodations. It wasn't in a car in a Wal-Mart parking lot, with a half-naked Roger next to me.

But when I opened my eyes again, it was light out—the cool light of early dawn. And at some point during the night, we had started sharing a pillow.

I was on your porch last night.

—The Format

I was sitting outside on the left-hand porch, and according to the faint green glow of the numbers on my watch, I'd been waiting for two hours. The mosquitoes had taken advantage of this and had been slowly devouring me. It was the Amy all-you-can-eat buffet. I'd given up the fight, choosing instead nonviolent resistance, simply scratching the bites every now and then.

My father said this porch was one of the architect's many follies. Our house was designed with two porches on the second story that faced the street. They looked nice. And the second porch, the one to the right of the one I was currently being eaten alive on, was functional. It was connected to the guest room by a set of French doors, giving our theoretical guests a lovely view of the driveway. But the left-hand porch wasn't connected to anything—it was purely decorative. However, Charlie and I had discovered long ago that both of our windows—which flanked the porch—were close enough to it that you could climb out your window and make it onto the porch, if you did it quickly and without looking down. When we were younger, we used to sneak out at night occasionally, at a predetermined time. We'd eat candy, or play handheld video games, or just stay up and talk, reveling in the fact that we were breaking the rules, that we were awake when we shouldn't have been. It had been one of the few times we were united in something.

I scratched at my ankle hard enough to draw blood just as a pair of headlights rounded the cul-de-sac. As usual, they went too far past our house and then just swung around the circle again, stopping in front of our driveway. The driver of the car— it looked like an SUV—turned off the headlights, but left the engine running. I looked toward Charlie's window and waited. Sure enough, I heard the rasp of the sill being pushed up, and a second later Charlie's leg emerged from the window, stretching over the railing, and then the rest of him followed, backing out of his window. I waited until he was all the way on the porch before I spoke.

"Hey."

Charlie whirled around while simultaneously making a high-pitched squeaking noise that I wished I'd somehow been able to record. "Amy, what the fuck," he said, talking in low tones, his breath coming quickly. "Don't do that. Jesus." He glanced down to the waiting car, then back at me. My eyes had adjusted enough to the darkness that I could see he was calculating how to try and spin this. "What are you doing out here?"

"I could ask you the same thing," I said.

"Come on, don't be naive," he said, glancing out toward the car again, and when he looked back at me it was with a smile. Clearly he had decided to go for charm. "I'm just going out with my friends. Is that such a crime? Hey, you want to come?"

For a second I thought about saying yes, just to freak him out and see how he would try to dance around the fact that our social circles didn't exactly intersect. "You've been going out with your friends a lot lately," I said, then rolled my eyes at myself. You would have thought that after waiting for two hours, I'd have come up with a better way to say this. But apparently not. "Look, Charlie, I'm just worried."

"Worried?" Charlie frowned, the picture of innocence. "What about?"

"Cut the crap," I said. "I just think that maybe you should slow down or something. Or at least limit this stuff to the weekends. You do realize it's a Tuesday night?"

"Hey, my GPA was better than yours last semester, if I recall. And just because you don't know how to party—" The SUV at the bottom of the driveway flashed its lights on and off, causing both of us to look in its direction. "My friends are waiting," he said, shouldering his backpack.

"I just think you should cut this back a little," I said, my voice getting louder. I saw Charlie glance back to the house and realized I held some cards here.

"Amy, Jesus," he said, his voice low. "Keep it down. I'm fine. You didn't have to—"

"I'll tell Mom and Dad," I said, interrupting him.

He stared at me for a long moment. "No, you won't."

I looked up at him. "I will, I—" I slapped at my leg, knowing it was futile.

"No," he said, crossing the porch to where, I saw, he'd attached a rope ladder. It looked like the one that used to be on our old tree house before it was torn down; I wondered where he'd found it. "If you were going to tell them, you'd have told already. And it's not like they'd be able to do anything anyway. The only thing that would accomplish would be that I'd be pissed at you, and Mom and Dad wouldn't trust either of us."

"Why wouldn't they trust me?"

"How long have you known about this?" he asked. "Without telling them?" It had been a few months. Maybe four. The answer hung between us for a moment, unsaid. "Exactly," he said. "So don't be a narc, okay? Just try to be cool, for once in your life." He tossed the rope ladder over the railing and threw one leg over, then the other. Then I watched as his head disappeared, and a second later I heard a soft thump as he hit the ground and hustled over to the rumbling car. He got in, and the car peeled away, not putting its headlights on until it was all the way around the cul-de-sac.

While I Breathe, I Hope.
—*South Carolina state motto*

"Ready?" Roger asked me. I nodded, then looked up at the window five feet above me. I wasn't sure this was going to work. In fact, it seemed much more likely that it would fail. But as Roger might have said, we'd come this far.

"Ready," I said. He made a cradle with his hands, and I stepped one foot into it. Roger bent his knees, and I put my hands on his shoulders. His T-shirt was warm from driving in the sun. For just a moment, I let my hands rest on his shoulders, feeling the muscle underneath the warm cotton, realizing how close together we were.

"Okay," I said, trying to focus on the task ahead. I nodded and pushed off Roger's hand as he hoisted me up, giving me the leverage I needed to grasp onto the sill of the window above me. I dangled there for a moment, then felt him grab my feet and give them another push. This extra momentum gave me enough forward motion to pull myself up and over, and I tumbled into the room.

←——→

The original plan had been to walk in and ask to see him. The original plan hadn't involved any sort of forced entry. But the original plan had been foiled. We'd gotten breakfast at a Cracker Barrel near the Wal-Mart, where Roger declared the pancakes the best he'd ever eaten, then headed into Asheville and arrived at Promises Kept around ten. The building looked more like a mansion than a rehab center. The only indication that it wasn't were the parking spaces, clearly labeled VISITORS, MEDICAL PRACTITIONERS, and DROP-OFF. Roger had gone in with me, but we hadn't gotten very far before we were stopped by a woman wearing white scrubs who introduced herself as Courtney. Even though the website of this place had seemed very welcoming, we were led back outside. She told us how the guests at Promises Kept were currently in the middle of their treatment plan, and that no contact with family members—except by e-mail—was permitted until the treatment plan was completed. Then she told us to have a blessed day and shut the door firmly behind her.

We had been heading back to the car when I happened to look around the side of the building. That's when I spotted the low(ish) window and the white curtains blowing out of it, letting me know that it was open, and screenless.

We moved quickly, and I hadn't really had time to come up with a plan, which hit me just as I hit the floor. I pushed myself to my feet and looked around. The room was large, with two beds, and seemed to be decorated all in white. There was a girl lying on each bed, both of whom looked very surprised to see me.

"Hi," I said, trying not to speak too loudly. "Um. Hi."

"Can I help you?" the girl on the bed nearest to me asked. She had brown curly hair and looked all of twelve, and for a second I wondered what she could possibly be doing in here.

"Yes," I said. "I'm Charlie Curry's sister? I was looking for him?"

"You're Amy?" the other girl asked. She had hair that was probably platinum blond most of the time, but now had a good three inches of black roots growing in. Even from a distance, I could see what looked like burns on her lips.

I looked at her in surprise. "I am," I said. "But how did you—"

"We have Group," she said. "We all share things."

"Oh." I realized that Charlie had been talking about me. About our family. I immediately wanted to know what he'd been saying. And then I felt a flash of anger, so intense it scared me. Charlie could talk to strangers, but he couldn't talk to me? "Well, do you know where I could find him?" I asked. They both just looked at me in silence. "Please?" I added.

"I don't know," the curly-haired girl said. "Are you here to make him feel bad? He feels guilty enough already, you know."

"What?" I asked, confused. Charlie had never felt guilty about anything in his life. "No. I just want to talk to him."

The two girls looked at each other and seemed to be having some kind of silent conversation. Finally the blond girl nodded. "He's three doors down," she said, indicating that I should head to the left. "Him and Muz."

"Muz?" I asked, just as a chime played loudly. I looked around and saw that both girls had looked over to the wall, where an intercom was mounted.

"Good afternoon," a soothing voice said in soft tones. "I hope that your morning reflection been pleasant and fulfilling. Reflection time will be ending in twenty minutes. In twenty minutes, please make your way to your designated prelunch activity. Thank you." Then the chime sounded again, and the intercom clicked off.

I stared up at it for a moment. *This* was how Charlie had been spending the last month—in luxury accommodations, talking though his feelings and reflecting? Meanwhile, I'd been getting pizza delivered and rattling around in the house alone, trying to fall asleep to the Weather Channel. "Thanks," I said to the girls as I headed for the door.

"Sure," the curly-haired girl said.

The blonde just looked at me for a moment. "You should call your mother," she said. "Really."

I wanted to ask her what she meant, but I didn't have time to. But what just happened? I stepped out into the hallway, which was decorated in an Asian theme. Julia would have approved. There was a potted bamboo in front of every room and a quietly trickling fountain at the end of the hallway, which was softly lit. I looked around to make sure that the coast was clear, and then hurried past three rooms, catching glances from people as I passed open doors—and all the doors seemed to be open.

I stopped in front of a door that was ajar, but not as much as the others. CHARLIE AND ZACH was written on a laminated sign attached to the door in a little slot that was clearly designed so the sign could be changed frequently. I took a breath, pushed the door open, and stepped inside.

The first thing I saw was a guy in his underwear doing a headstand against the wall. A guy who was, thankfully, not my brother. His upside-down eyes widened, and he gave a little yelp before tumbling over. "Um, what?" he asked, scrambling to his feet. He was a little chunky, with thick brown curly hair.

"That's why I've told you, Muz, put some damn clothes on if you're going to do yoga." I looked across the room and saw my brother sitting in an armchair, as though he had been expecting me. "After all, you never know when my sister might decide to drop by."

I turned and faced Charlie, both because I wanted to get a better look at him, and because I wanted to give Muz some privacy while he—hopefully—put some pants on. Charlie looked much better than he had the last time I'd seen him, though it probably would have been hard for him to look worse. But he looked healthier, and tan, and more in focus. It was like seeing the slides at the optometrist, when you didn't even realize how blurry something was until you got to see the clearer version, and you could see what had been obscured before.

"Hey," I said, coming a little farther into the room.

"This is a surprise," Charlie said. He sounded casual, but I knew him well enough to see that I had rattled him. "Were you just in the neighborhood?"

"Kind of," I said. I glanced up at the intercom. "Um, I heard the announcement. You have to leave in twenty minutes?"

"More like fifteen," Muz said from behind me, and I turned a little cautiously. But thankfully, he had put on shorts and a T-shirt, and was extending his hand to me. "Zach Tyler," he said.

"Amy Curry," I said, and we shook quickly. At this point, it might have surprised me if we hadn't shaken hands.

"Oh, I know," he said. "*Believe* me."

I turned to look at Charlie, who just smiled and said, "Amy, meet Zach, more commonly known as Muz."

"Messed-Up Zach," Muz translated. "But, you know, for brevity's sake, we usually went with the acronym."

"Muz is from Richmond, Virginia, and until recently, his hobbies included freebasing."

"Hi," I said to Muz, then looked back at my brother. "So you have to go in fifteen minutes?"

Charlie glanced over at the clock between the two beds. "Yeah," he said.

"Do you have to?" I asked. "I mean, can you get out of it?"

"No, I can't get out of it," Charlie said sharply. "This is rehab, Amy, not homeroom."

Muz cleared his throat and murmured, "I think maybe I'll just go wait in the hallway now, okay?"

"Thanks," said Charlie. Muz shuffled out and pulled the door a little farther shut—though he still didn't close it—behind him.

"This is a nice setup here," I said, looking around the room. I could tell Charlie's side because there were stacks of books around his bed, and a tennis racket with a can of tennis balls next to it. I wondered if he'd started playing again while he'd been here. In his leisure time. I could feel myself beginning to get angry again.

"Amy, what are you doing here?" Charlie asked, staring at me.

"I went to Graceland yesterday," I said, looking right back at him.

Charlie's face seemed to close off a little. "Oh," he said.

"Yeah," I said, and I could hear that my voice was shaking. "You know, the trip you didn't want to go on? The trip that you told Dad was stupid?" Charlie looked down at the ground. He picked up a tennis ball and gripped it hard. "I thought that one of us should go on it."

"Why did you come?" Charlie asked, looking up at me, his face drawn. "Seriously. Was it just to make me feel bad?"

"No," I said. I hadn't intended that, but seeing him here was just feeding an anger that I'd been holding back for a long time. A little of it had slipped out in my conversation with my mother, but clearly there was more where that had come from. "But I'm sure that if I do, you can discuss it in your *group*."

Charlie looked at me sharply. "How do you know about that?"

"Oh, I just climbed in the window of two girls who seemed to know all about me. That's all."

"We talk about things here," Charlie said defensively. "It's part of their whole philosophy."

"Then why——," I started, and could hear my voice crack. "Why couldn't we have done that? Why did we just . . ." I searched for the word, but it wasn't coming. I wanted to know why we had retreated to different parts of the house, and then to different parts of the country, scattering when we should have been coming together. I sat down on the edge of Muz's bed and looked at my brother. "Maybe I needed you," I said. "But you were always high, and——"

"Oh, is that what this is about?" Charlie asked, some anger coming back into his voice. There was an expression on his face I recognized, one I'd never liked, one I'd always backed down from. "You're here to tell me what a fuckup I am?"

"No," I said, standing my ground this time. "But I have been completely alone, until this week. You've been here. You've had people to talk to."

"You could have talked to me," he said.

"It wouldn't have done any good!" I yelled, surprising myself. Charlie glanced toward the open door, and I lowered my volume a little. "You were never there. You haven't been there for almost a year." I stared at him hard. "I should have told Mom and Dad. You were right when you said I wouldn't. But if I had, then maybe . . ." I couldn't finish the sentence. It was just one more way in which I'd brought this about, one more reason it was my fault. One more thing I couldn't undo.

Charlie turned the tennis ball in his hands and gave a short, bitter laugh. "You think I don't ask myself that every fucking day?" he asked. "You think I don't wish that I could do things differently?"

"I don't believe you," I said, hearing my voice shake. "What, you've been here for a month and suddenly you've grown a conscience?" Charlie looked at me like I'd just slapped him without warning—that surprised, that hurt. "I was always covering for you," I said, the words spilling out of me in a torrent. "For *years*. And you never had to take any responsibility. And if you'd thought about someone else other than yourself just *once* in your fucking life, this wouldn't have happened." The sentence was out before I could weigh its consequences, or take it back.

Charlie was gripping the tennis ball hard, looking down at it, his lip twisted, his chin trembling.

"I shouldn't have said that," I said, feeling I'd gone too far.

Charlie shrugged. "It's the truth," he said thickly, still looking down.

"I just wish . . . ," I started. I took a breath and made myself keep going. "I just wish things could have been different."

Charlie looked up at me. "Me too," he said. Without warning, he tossed me the tennis ball. I caught it, and this surprised me so much that I almost dropped it again.

"Do you talk about him?" I asked, running my hand over the yellow felt. "About Daddy?"

Charlie nodded. "I'm starting to," he said, his voice a little hoarse. "Are you?"

I shook my head. "Not yet." I looked up at my brother—my twin—and saw that he looked like I currently felt. We'd both lost the same father. Why weren't *we* talking about it? "I miss him," I said, feeling my own chin start to tremble. The words were nothing compared to the feeling behind them. It was so much more than just missing. It was waiting, always, for the phone call that wouldn't come. Waiting to hear a voice that I never would, ever again.

Charlie looked at me, his lip trembling. "Me too."

"I keep waiting for him to show up again. It's like I can't believe that it's real. That this is real life now."

"How do you think I feel?" Charlie asked. "I'm not entirely convinced you showing up here isn't an acid flashback."

"I'm real," I said. I tossed him the ball, and he caught it with one hand.

"But what are you doing in North Carolina? I thought you were supposed have made it to Connecticut days ago."

"Well, that was the plan," I said, feeling a small smile begin to form. "But Roger and I kind of took a detour."

"Roger?"

"Roger Sullivan. You remember him. We used to play Spud with him in the cul-de-sac."

"I remember that," said Charlie. "So you went rogue?" I nodded. "That's why Mom is mad?"

"Oh, more than mad," I said.

"Wow," he said, leaning back in the chair and looking at me as though he'd never seen me before. "And you . . . you came to see me? You climbed in a window?"

"I did," I said. "I just . . . thought we should talk."

"I'm glad you did," he said after a pause.

"Hey, Chuck." We both turned to see Muz lurking in the doorway. "We better get going, man, it's five minutes to—"

"Yeah," Charlie said, though he didn't move.

I stood, and as I did so, I saw a familiar book on the bedside table: *Food, Gas, and Lodging.* "Are you reading this?" I asked, looking up at Charlie, a little stunned, and hoping it wasn't Muz's. He nodded. "Me too," I said, staring down at it.

"Yeah?" he asked, looking surprised. "I know it was one of Dad's favorites, and I thought I should check it out." I just nodded, looking down at the familiar cover, wishing we could have all done this a few months ago. When we both could have talked to him about it, when he would have still been around to have the conversation.

"Chuck?" Muz asked again, and Charlie nodded and stood up,

and we all headed for the door. It seemed like there was suddenly so much to say, it was impossible to say anything.

"Hey," said Muz, looking at both of us. "Are you going to be going by Richmond at all?"

"I'm pretty sure he means you," Charlie said.

"Um, I don't know," I said. I had thought as far ahead as seeing Charlie, and the fact that there was no plan beyond that was a little disconcerting.

"But you might? You might be going that way?" Muz asked, growing more excited.

"Maybe," I said. "I don't know."

Muz nodded, bent down, and fished around in a backpack that was hanging on the knob of the closet door. "Well, if you do," he said, standing and holding a crumpled envelope in his hand, "would you give this to Corey who hangs out at the Dairy Queen?"

"Are you serious?" asked Charlie.

"I need you to," Muz said, extending the envelope toward me. "Please. You can just give it to one of the counter staff, they'll get it to him. He needs to know why I never showed up when I said I was going to. I wasn't holding out on him, I just got sent here. If he doesn't find out, he's going to kill my fish."

"Your fish?" I asked.

"God, enough about the fish," Charlie muttered. "Why don't you just e-mail him?"

"Oh yeah, that's a great idea," Muz said. "Should I just send it to Corey who hangs out at the Dairy Queen dot com?"

"I'll see if I can," I said, taking the envelope from Muz and smoothing out some of the wrinkles. "I'll try."

"Thanks," he said, smiling at me. "I knew you would. Chuck's always talking about how you're always there for him, and—"

"We have to go," Charlie said, pulling the door farther open. "I'll help you get back down." We stepped out into the hallway and found it deserted, the only sound the gentle trickling of the water.

"Are we late?" asked Muz.

"Oh, yeah," Charlie said, and we all hustled down to the room I'd entered from.

"Thanks again," Muz shout-whispered to me before heading down the corridor. He raised a hand in a wave, which I returned before following Charlie into the room. It was empty—presumably the two girls had headed out to their next activity.

"That one?" asked Charlie, pointing to the open window. I nodded, and we headed over to it. "Well, I guess this is it, then," he said, twisting his hands together.

"Are you okay?" I asked, knowing that we were out of time, but not feeling ready to leave yet. "I mean, you look better. But this place . . . are you okay here?"

Charlie looked down a the white carpet and rocked back and forth on his flip-flops. "I think I am," he said. "I think so."

"Amy," I heard whispered loudly from outside. I stuck my head out the window and saw Roger looking up. He looked incredibly relieved when he saw me, and I wondered how long he'd been calling for me.

"I'm coming right down," I called back, and he nodded. I pulled my head back into the room and looked at my brother. "How long are you here?" I asked. "I mean, when do you get to leave?" I hadn't realized until I saw this old version of him, one I hadn't seen in a very long time, how much I'd missed my brother. But it was hitting me now, when I was leaving him again.

"Another month," he said. He gave me a small smile. "Not so long."

"Amy," Roger called from out the window, a little louder this time, just as the chime sounded again. Charlie and I looked to the intercom.

The soothing voice, sounding a little less calm this time, announced, "The prelunch session has now begun. Please conduct yourself as quickly as possible to your designated activity, if you have not already done so."

"Okay," I said. Charlie nodded, and we looked at each other. My brother and I were not huggers. I couldn't actually remember the last time we'd hugged. But I wasn't about to shake hands with him. I started to wave when Charlie reached out and hugged me hard. I hugged him back, and it felt exactly right—and something we should have done a while ago.

"Thanks for coming," he mumbled into my shoulder. I nodded, and we separated. "You should talk to Mom," he said. "I've been getting her e-mails, and she's worried about you. I think she's kind of lost without you."

I stared at him. "What are you talking about?" I asked. "She's not lost without me. She left me for a month and barely—"

"*Amy,* " Roger called again.

"Talk to her," Charlie said. "But good for you for doing all this. I'd have barely recognized you."

"In a good way?" I asked.

"In a good way," he said. He smiled, then looked at the window. "Need a hand?"

"I think I might," I said. Holding on to the sill, my arms stretching over it, I swung a leg outside it, and saw Roger waiting down below, reaching for me. I took a breath and swung my other leg over. I looked down, and suddenly Roger and the ground seemed very far away. "Um," I said. "I'm not sure . . ."

"You have to extend your arms," Charlie said. "Give me your hand." I looked up at him, and he nodded. "It's okay." I unhooked my arm from around the sill, and Charlie took my hand. He placed it on the edge of the sill, and then helped me do it with the other hand. I extended my arms, and was hanging there in space. I felt someone grab my foot, and I knew Roger was there.

"Just drop," he called. "I've got you."

I looked up at my brother, who was looking right at me. "You have to let go," Charlie said. "It's okay."

"Take care, okay?" I asked. He nodded, and I smiled at him. Then I let go of the sill and dropped straight down, landing on something soft—Roger. "Sorry," I gasped, rolling off of him and standing up, brushing myself off. "Are you all right?"

"I'm fine," he said, taking the hand that I extended to help him up. "But I think we have to get out of here, like, now." He started speed-walking toward the car, still holding on to my hand, pulling me along behind him.

"Why's that?" I asked as I struggled to keep up.

"I think there's a possibility that we may have attracted some attention," he said. "I was trying to look as inconspicuous as possible, but that's hard to do when you're talking to a window. People kept walking by and looking at me."

We hustled toward the car, and sure enough, I noticed a lot more white-scrubs-clad people hanging around the entrance than had been there before. And I noticed that now they were all carrying walkie-talkies. "Let's just make it to the car," I mumbled under my breath, and Roger squeezed my hand once in answer.

"Excuse me," a voice behind us said. We turned to see Courtney walking toward us. "I have to speak with you two."

Roger and I looked at each other and then, without discussing anything, still holding hands, we both bolted for the car, running flat out. "Keys?" I asked him breathlessly as we crossed the parking lot.

"Yeah," he gasped. I turned and noticed that Courtney was also jogging toward us. We reached the car, Roger beeped it open, and we threw ourselves inside. He started it and backed up with record speed, and we peeled out of the parking lot.

Roger didn't slow down until we'd been driving for five minutes and it became clear that Promises Kept wasn't sending someone after us to give chase. "Close one," he said, and I watched as the speedometer dropped to his normal non-interstate speed.

I stared out the window at the other cars rushing by, trying to sort out what I was feeling. I had been trying with everything I had to avoid thinking about that morning, trying not to play the memory out to its conclusion. But seeing Charlie, and talking about it . . .

"You okay?" I could hear Roger ask from a place that sounded very far away.

I nodded, but turned more toward my window, and closed my eyes. But it wasn't going away this time. It was like I no longer had the strength anymore to hold this back.

"Amy?" I opened my eyes and saw Roger looking over at me, worried. "Are you okay?"

I started to nod, but gave it up halfway through, and shook my head. "I just . . . ," I started to say, and heard my voice crack. "I'm not okay," I said. He looked over at me and turned down the music. I could feel the memories of that morning swelling behind me. I knew Roger wouldn't look at me the same way once he knew the truth. But I was tired of fighting to hold it back.

"What is it?" he asked quietly, looking at me, then back at the road.

"The Elvis thing," I started. "Why I didn't want to hear it."

"Because of your father," Roger said. "Right?"

I nodded. "We were listening to Elvis in the car," I said. "I mean, we were always listening to Elvis in the car. But we were listening to him when it happened." I swallowed hard and forced the word out. "The accident."

"Oh," he said softly. It was like this wasn't even a word. It felt more like he was laying out a stone for me to step on, so that I could keep going.

I felt my breathing speed up, and I knew I was circling around what I could no longer not say. "The accident," I said, trying to force my voice to stay audible. I took a shaky breath and said it. "It was my fault. It's my fault that he died."

"Amy," Roger said, looking over at me sharply. "Of course it wasn't your fault."

Other people had said the same thing. But this was just what you said to people. And none of them knew. None of them had actually been there. "But it was," I whispered. And I took another breath and told him why.

I'll be right here with you, come what may.

—*Elvis Presley*

MARCH 8—THREE MONTHS EARLIER

I stepped out into the sunlight and slipped on my new sunglasses. I couldn't help wondering what my mother was going to do to Charlie. Being picked up by the police for sleeping on a park bench, still stoned, had to merit some kind of punishment. Maybe this would make my parents finally see what was happening with him. I walked down the driveway, toward the garage, and looked back to the house, where I could hear my mother's voice, still sharply edged with worry and anger.

"And then once you've gotten him," she said as she stepped outside, my father following, letting the screen door slam behind him, "I'm going to need you to stop at the store. So just give me a call when you get there and I'll tell you what we need."

My father gave her a look as he slipped on his ancient sunglasses, aviators with lenses so scratched I was always amazed that he could see through them. "Or you could tell me now," he said, a smile in his voice. "That's always an option."

"Right," my mother said, shaking her head. "We've been through that before."

"I'll be back soon," he said, kissing her quickly, causing me to automatically avert my eyes.

"Call if there's a problem," she called to us.

"We will," my father and I called back in unison, and we exchanged a smile when we realized this.

"Amy, where are your shoes?" my mother yelled to me, sounding exasperated.

"Oh." I looked down at my bare feet. "Just a second," I said to my father, dashing across the lawn. It was still wet, and freshly mowed—an unfortunate combination, and as I looked down, I could see that grass clippings were sticking to my feet. I ran up the steps to the house and around my mother, still standing in the doorway, to grab my flip-flops from the basket in the mudroom.

I slipped them on and headed outside again, where my mother was holding the car keys in her hand. "Ben, keys," she said in what my father referred to as her Exasperated Voice.

"I've got them," I said, grabbing them from her hand and giving her a quick wave. I ran across the lawn to the garage, and headed around to the driver's side. I tossed the keys in my hand and gave my father my most convincing smile. "I'll drive."

He smiled and walked around to the passenger side as I opened the driver's door and adjusted the seat. I buckled my seat belt, and pointed at my father. "Buckle up," I said. My father hated wearing seat belts, and the only way Charlie and I had ever gotten him to wear one was by refusing to put ours on until he buckled up too.

"Come on, pumpkin," my father said in his best persuasive voice. "We're in a hurry. Why don't we just go?"

"Fine," I said, unbuckling my own seat belt and turning the key in the ignition the ignition. "Let's go."

My father grumbled and pulled on his seat belt. "Happy now?" he asked.

"Very," I said, snapping my own back in. "Thank you. I'm telling you, you'll thank me someday." I looked into the rearview mirror and began to back slowly down the driveway.

"Music?" my father asked as I pulled the car around the cul-de-sac.

I'd had my license for three months now, but I still had to

concentrate when I drove, and was just recently becoming okay with having music playing in the car. When I just had my permit, and found the three-point turn to be on par with quantum physics in terms of difficulty, I'd needed total silence at all times. "Sure," I said as I braked at a stop sign. "You want to hear the King?"

"You need to ask?" my father asked, flipping through the CDs. "Ah," he said, taking one out of its case and sliding it into the player.

"Which one is that?" I asked. When I was driving, I reserved the right to be picky about the Elvis that was played. None of the Hawaii stuff was permitted, for example.

"I think you'll approve," he said, skipping through the tracks. A moment later, "All That I Am" began to play.

"Nice," I said, smiling at him. "I like this song."

"I know you do," my father said. "That's because you are my daughter, and the child of my heart." We drove for a minute, listening to the King croon. "And as a matter of fact," my father added after a moment, "I think we should dance to this at your wedding. Sound like a plan?"

"Dad," I said, rolling my eyes. "Gross. Plus, I think that's a few years away. You know, just a couple."

"Sorry," he said, but he was still chuckling, and I had a feeling that he didn't mean it. "Hand," he said, and I carefully took one off the wheel. He turned my palm up, placed something inside, and then folded my fingers over again. When I opened my palm, there was a Life Saver sitting there. It looked like Butter Rum, and I glanced over to see my father tossing back one of his own.

"Thank you," I said, popping it in my mouth.

I pulled up to the intersection at Campus Drive, and realized I didn't know the way from here. "Right? Left?" I asked. It was odd to have to need directions in a car I was so used to navigating in.

"Left," my father said. "Take University." He sighed and looked out the window. "Let's get this over with."

As I put on my turn signal, I saw him crunch down on another

Life Saver. "Have you known about this?" he asked, interrupting the King. "About your brother, I mean?"

I glanced over at him, then back at the road, wondering how much to tell him, and wondering if there was any point now in still trying to cover for Charlie. "I knew something was going on," I said. I thought of the failed intervention I'd tried to stage, and wished now that I'd just told my parents about it then. I pulled up to the intersection and braked when the light turned yellow, making some people behind me, who must have been hoping for me to run it, honk unhappily.

"I knew something wasn't right with him," my father said, looking out the window. "I just didn't think it had gone this far."

"I know," I said. "But I think it'll be okay."

My father shook his head. "I hope so, kid." He glanced over at me. "Thanks for coming along."

"Sure," I said, eyes on the light. I took them off for a second, looked over and smiled at him.

"Green," my father said, pointing.

I returned my eyes to the road and stepped on the gas, going through the intersection, when I saw something out of the corner of my eye that wasn't right. It was a flash of red, coming toward me when there shouldn't have been anything coming toward me.

"Amy —" I heard my father say, before everything slowed down. It's a cliché, but it was true. And I think it only happened when there was no point to having things slow down. I knew, somehow, that I wasn't going to be able to do anything about it. It was like I was just getting extra time to see what was coming.

And what was coming was a red SUV running the light, trying to get through the intersection that I was currently in the middle of. There was more honking behind me, and then the other car slammed into us with such force I was thrown back against the seat, my teeth knocking together, and we were spinning around the intersection, and I kept my hands on the wheel the entire time, and I kept pressing my foot down on the brake, as though that would stop all of this from happening. There was a horrible scraping sound, metal on metal, and I saw the pole about a second before we slammed into it, on my father's side. And that's when the car finally stopped. But my father had stopped moving and my forehead felt like it was burning, and someone was screaming and they wouldn't stop. And it wasn't until the ambulance came and a paramedic pulled me out of the car and shook my shoulders firmly, that I realized it had been me.

If you don't mind, North Carolina is
where I want to be.
—*Eddie from Ohio*

I got back into the passenger seat and slammed the door, staring
ahead at the dashboard. After I'd finished telling Roger what had
happened, it had looked like he was about to say something, but
I wasn't ready to hear it yet. I'd just pointed to a roadside diner,
and we'd headed in to eat an almost silent meal. I didn't know
what was going to happen now. But slowly, I was beginning to feel
lighter, like I'd just put down something that I'd been carrying for
so long, I hadn't realized how heavy it had grown.

Roger slammed the driver's door shut and looked at me.
"Amy —," he started.

"How would you feel about Richmond?" I interrupted.

Roger blinked, looking a little thrown by this. "What's in
Richmond?"

"Charlie's roommate, Muz," I said. "He was from there, and
gave me a note to give to this guy Corey who hangs out at the
Dairy Queen. Apparently, the life of a fish hangs in the balance."

"A fish?"

"I know," I said, as Roger started the car up. "I didn't understand that part either."

"And what kind of name is Muz?"

"It's an acronym," I said. "It stands for Messed-Up Zach."

"Ah," Roger said. "Naturally. Well, we can go to Richmond.
Why should a fish die in vain?"

Looking down at the atlas, I gave him directions, then took out the envelope that Muz had given me and smoothed out some of its creases.

"How's the money holding out?" Roger asked, after he'd pulled back onto the highway.

"We have one hundred and eighty-five dollars," I said. Hopefully, it would be enough to take us to Richmond, and then Connecticut.

I looked at him sitting across the car from me. At some point it had become the sight I'd gotten accustomed to. I couldn't believe that so soon, I wouldn't be seeing it anymore.

We drove on I-40 for a few miles in silence. Roger kept looking over at me, and I knew him well enough by now to know he wanted to say something. Every time I saw him take a breath, I turned up the volume on his mix. After this had happened three times, and the music was blasting in the car loud enough to rattle the windows, Roger reached over and turned the music off.

"I need to say something," he said.

I looked out the window, bracing myself. I had known that things would change once I told him what had happened. And it looked like I wasn't going to be able to put off finding out how any longer. "Okay," I said. I looked back at him. He was looking out at the road, but glanced over at me before beginning.

"It wasn't your fault," he said.

I shook my head. This was like saying that the sky wasn't blue. Saying something like that didn't make it true. "Of course it was," I said. "I was driving the car."

"That doesn't mean it was your fault," he said.

"You don't have to do this," I said.

"I'm serious," he said, in a voice that was free of all humor. He took one hand off the wheel and pointed at a blue van that had switched lanes and was driving next to us. "If that van suddenly swerved and plowed into us, would that be my fault?"

"No," I admitted. "But—"

"So it wasn't your fault," Roger said. "I'm not just saying that."

"It's not just the driving," I said. "I overheard two of the para-medics talking at the scene. They were saying that it was one of the very rare instances. But that if he hadn't had his seat belt on, he most likely would have been thrown into the backseat and suf-fered only minor bruising. But I made him put it on. And so he was trapped in his seat, and a streetlight pole crushed his skull."

I expected Roger to flinch at this, but he didn't. "No," he said in the same serious tone. "That was just speculation. Nobody knows. He might have not had it on, and been thrown forward through the windshield. Or he might have had it off and not gone into the backseat. There's no way of knowing. But it was an accident. It wasn't your fault."

I shook my head against these words, not wanting to let them in. This fact was what I had been living with for the past three months. I had ceased to believe in a world where it wasn't true. "But if I'd run the yellow," I said. "If I hadn't forgotten my shoes—"

"You can't think that way. It wasn't your fault," Roger repeated, softly but distinctly. "It wasn't."

"You don't know that," I whispered.

"You don't know that it was," he said. "It was an accident," he said. "A terrible accident. There's nothing you could have done. You didn't do it. It wasn't your fault."

"It was," I said hoarsely, not wanting to believe in this reprieve that he was offering me. Because it seemed almost too much to begin to believe in, what he was telling me. And what if he was wrong?

"No," he said simply. "I don't lie. I promise you, it wasn't your fault."

It was this that finally got through. Roger hadn't lied to me this whole time. I knew I could trust him. He wouldn't start lying now, not about something this important. The thought that this hadn't been my fault, that I wasn't to blame, that it had been nothing but back luck and a chain of events I had no control over, was what finally did it. The last few straining boards on the dam burst open, and I started really crying, letting out everything I'd been holding tightly inside. I was relieved, but mostly I was just sad. Sad that I'd been holding on to this when I didn't have to.

Roger slowed the car down, signaled, and pulled off the highway and into a rest stop. He parked the car in front of the picnic tables and killed the engine. Then he unbuckled his seat belt, pressed the button to undo mine, and slid to the edge of his seat. The center console was between us, but he leaned across it and put his arms around me, as easily as if he'd always been doing it. And I didn't think about anything else but how nice it felt to have someone holding me, someone who wasn't going to let go any time soon. And I turned my face into his T-shirt and just let myself cry, past the point of caring if I got snot all over it, just finally feeling like I could let go, that I could do this. Knowing that he could handle it, and would be there for as long as I needed him to be.

As cars sped by on the Interstate just out the window, Roger smoothed my hair away from my forehead and rocked me back and forth slowly.

←——→

"Virginia!" Roger called, two mixes and four rounds of Twenty Questions (Eleanor of Aquitaine, Jonathan Larson, Sir Francis Drake, and Bernadette Peters) later. He pointed out the window at the sign passing us by and smiled at me.

I looked over at him, still reeling a bit that I had told him, and that he had been okay with it. He wasn't looking at me differently, as far as I could see. I couldn't quite believe that it was true. But if it was . . . it was like another weight had been taken from my shoulders. And it was a relief, now that he knew. Now that there were no secrets between us. Just in time for the trip to end.

"Do you know the Virginia motto?" he asked. "It's *Sic semper tyrannis*, which means—"

"'Thus always to tyrants'," I finished for him. Roger glanced over at me, eyebrows raised. "And," I continued, "it's what Booth yelled after he shot Lincoln."

315

"Impressive," he said, smiling at me.

I took a breath and told him what I hadn't been able to tell him five days ago. "My father was a history professor," I said, barely getting caught up on the past tense this time. "And that was his time period."

"That's a good period," Roger said. He glanced over at me, as though making sure I was okay with this. "Did he like Lincoln?"

I smiled at that, thinking about the Lincoln facts on the note card in my father's favorite book, the one that had come with me across the country. "Almost as much as Elvis."

"So," Roger said two hours later, turning down *Into the Woods* on my mix and looking out the window, "we're looking for a DQ."

"We are," I said, as we pulled onto the main street. We drove up and down a few streets that seemed much too nice to have Dairy Queens on them. We only found it, twenty minutes later, because I ran into a gas station to ask for directions. We were directed to an area of town that was a little seedier, with check-cashing places and liquor stores replacing the boutiques and coffee shops we'd seen when we first got into town.

"There," said Roger, pointing. The Dairy Queen, its red and white sign not yet lit, was next to a Greyhound bus terminal. He pulled into the parking lot and looked at the sign that hung just a few feet before us, clearly above where the buses pulled in and left. It looked like there was only one place for both, since the sign read ARRIVALS DEPARTURES, without anything even separating the words.

"All right," I said. Roger killed the engine and we both got out, Roger stretching his legs. "I'll be right back," I said. "Want anything?"

"A Blizzard would be amazing," he said.

"What kind?"

He smiled. "Surprise me."

"You got it," I said. I looked at the Dairy Queen and realized

that it was a takeout-only franchise, with just a counter for ordering, but no place to sit inside. This explained the inordinately high
number of people eating ice cream in their cars or sitting on their
back bumpers.

I headed over to the DQ window, pulling Muz's letter out of
my pocket. I hoped he knew what he was talking about, because
I didn't want to have to be on the lookout for people who looked
like they might be named Corey, or to have to try and explain this
situation to the counter workers.

I looked back at the car as I crossed the parking lot and saw
Roger sitting in our usual spot in the way-back, legs hanging over
the edge.

"Hi," I said as I approached the Dairy Queen ordering window
to speak to the bored-looking attendant, who was wearing his DQ
hat turned to the side.

"Help you?" he asked with a deep sigh.

"Yes," I said. "Muz gave me this to give to Corey? He said you
could get it to him?" I slid the envelope across the counter, looking
at him closely to see if this code meant something to him.

"Fine," he said, taking the envelope, his expression not even
changing, as though he constantly intercepted mail for people
in between taking sundae orders. Who knows, maybe he did.
"Anything else?"

"Um, yeah," I said, a little amazed that the transaction had gone
so smoothly. "Um . . ." I looked up at the menu boards and knew
exactly what Roger would want—a Reese's Pieces Blizzard with
half vanilla ice cream and half chocolate. After a moment of delib-
eration, I ordered, choosing an Oreo Blizzard for myself. I paid
and walked the treats over to the car, still shocked that the hardest
part of that process had been figuring out what to order.

I walked around to the back and saw Roger, feet dangling, sunglasses on, even though it was cloudy. And I felt something within
me shift. It was the same way I'd felt when I'd proposed we go to
Yosemite. The way I'd felt when I'd run to the Jeep and gotten

behind the wheel. The feeling right before I threw my leg over the window and tumbled into the room at Promises Kept. The feeling that I was about to do something without being sure of the outcome. The feeling of just jumping off something and hoping that the ground would be there when I landed.

I sat next to Roger in the back, setting the big Styrofoam cups to the side, near the wheel well.

"Hey," he said, smiling at me, pulling off his sunglasses. "Did you get me something good?"

"I think so," I said, trying to ignore how hard my heart was beating. Then, before I could think about it, or analyze, or consider what I was doing, I leaned over and kissed him.

Travel Scrapbook

Loves

199⁹ 219⁹

SUBWAY
SUBWAY

BLUE RIDGE DINER
Asheville, NC
"GO HEELS!"

Table #7
Customers: 2
Server: Jennie

2 orders pancakes $3.99/ ea.
1 side bacon
1 root beer $2.00
1 cream soda $1.50
                     $1.50

Total: $12.98

THANK YOU
FOR YOUR BUSINESS

Where I've Been . . .

State #11: North Carolina—The Tar Heel State

motto: Esse Quam Videri (To Be Rather Than to Seem)

Size: It's certainly no Utah.

Facts: Blue Ridge mountains are beautiful.

Notes: Rehab center employees are overly suspicious.

State #12: Virginia—The Old Dominion

motto: Sic Semper Tyrannis (Thus Always to Tyrants)

Size: Bigger than West Virginia.

Facts: Still smaller than Utah. EVERYTHING feels smaller than Utah.

Notes: No word on whether the state, in fact, believes there is a Santa Claus.

*Country roads, take me home to
the place I belong.*
—*John Denver*

He kissed me back. For just a moment, but he kissed me back, as though it was an automatic response, as though we had been kissing for a long time. But then he pulled away and looked at me. "Amy," he said softly. He'd never said my name that way before, and even though he'd pulled back, it was the answer that I needed. He touched my face, tracing his hand down my cheek and cupping it under my chin. "I'm not sure . . ."

But I was. And I leaned over and kissed him again. And this time he really kissed me back, moving his hand from under my chin to my hair, and then down my back, and then under my chin again. And we were kissing like drowning people breathe—like suddenly we'd discovered something that has never been so sweet before that moment.

And as we slowed for just a breath, to a kiss that was sweeter and more lingering, I understood in a flash why, on the Greyhound sign, Arrivals and Departures were right next to each other. Because sometimes, like in that moment, they can mean exactly the same thing.

"God," he murmured into my hair when we broke away. It might have been ten minutes. It might have been an hour. I was past the point of being able to judge such things. He smoothed down my hair. "I've been wanting to do that for a long time."

"Really?" I asked, almost afraid to believe this.

"Oh yes," he said. "Since Kansas. At *least*."

"Blizzard?" I asked, handing him his drink.

He took it, kissed me again, then took a sip. "Perfect," he said, smiling at me. "Reese's with a swirl?" I nodded. He smiled and took another sip, his hand resting on my knee.

I took a breath, leaned over, and kissed him again. This time he tasted like ice cream, and I could have stayed there forever, the taste of Roger's kiss on my lips, whatever was going to happen stretching out before us like the paths of the highways—the road open, the routes endless.

And that's when it started to rain.

Roger and I broke apart, and I looked at the sky, which had darkened rapidly, and showed signs of getting worse. We were starting to get rained on, sitting in the back, and we jumped up, and Roger slammed the door. We ran around to the front seats and closed the doors just as the sky opened up and started pouring down water on us. "Wow," I said, looking out at it.

"I know," Roger said. He reached across his seat to rest his hand on my knee, and I felt my heart begin to pound, still not quite able to believe this was happening. "So I guess we should get going?" he asked.

I stared out at the parking lot, which was now nearly deserted. The DQ employee had pulled his sweatshirt hood over his cap. "I guess so," I said. I brushed my wet hair away from my face. It hit me that we were almost out of time together—that the trip was ending just when things were beginning. But I didn't see anything we could do about it.

Roger touched my cheek for a moment. Then he started the car and we pulled out of the parking lot.

Where I've Been . . .

<u>State #13</u>: maryland—The Old Line State

<u>motto</u>: Fatti maschii, parole femine (manly Deeds, Womanly Words)

<u>Size</u>: SMALL!

<u>Facts</u>: The state beverage is milk. Who knew that states get beverages??

<u>Notes:</u> DO NOT let Roger talk about <u>The Wire</u> while you are driving through maryland. YOU WILL REGRET THIS.

TOWSON INN
TOWSON, MARYLAND

"Welcome!"

Date:
6/12

Name:
Mr. Edmund Udell & Ms. Hillary Udell

Stay Duration:
1 Night

Cost of Room:
$89

Cost of room includes dinner at the Inn Resta

DO NOT DISTURB

Maybe this time with all this much to lose and all this much to gain: Pennsylvania, Maryland, the world.
—*William Faulkner*

The rain had gotten worse by the time we'd reached Maryland. I had never experienced a sudden thunderstorm like this—not in the summer—but maybe they were common on the East Coast. I'd have to learn a whole new set of weather norms. It also occurred to me that I'd have winter for the first time too. I might even see snow.

But the rain was just hammering the car. Roger had the wipers turned up to full speed, and his headlights on, and still I could barely see the lines on the road in front of us.

"This is bad," I said, handing him his glasses.

"Thank you," he said, smiling without taking his eyes off the road and putting them on. He squinted out the windshield. "I keep hoping it's going to let up, but that doesn't seem to be happening."

I looked to the food/gas/lodging signs on the side of the highway. It looked like we were going to hit a biggish town soon. And there were at least three hotels listed on the lodging sign. "You know," I said, careful not to look at him, feeling my cheeks heat up, "this really does seem like tough going."

"I know," Roger said, shaking his head.

"So maybe," I said, speaking quickly, "we should get off the road before it gets too bad. Find a cheap place to stay for the night."

Roger looked over at me, then back at the road, a smile forming on his lips. "Really?" he asked. "Are you sure?"

"I am very sure," I said, feeling myself smile as well.

"Can we afford it, though?"

"I think it's possible," I said. It would be barely possible, but doable. And if we did run out of gas, that's what AAA was for. Roger looked over at me, and I nodded. He put on his turn signal and took the first exit.

←——→

After the Udells checked in, we headed to our room and opened the door with the key card. It was one of the least-nicest places we had stayed, but I didn't care at all. The bed was king-size, and covered with what we had been assured by the front desk clerk was an authentic reproduction of a Pennsylvania Dutch quilt, from nearby Lancaster County. But I knew, and I was sure Roger knew, that the fact that there was just one bed meant something very different than it had before.

"I'm going to take a quick bath," I said, trying to defuse the tension I suddenly felt in the room. "I feel like I haven't had one in about a year."

"Great," Roger said, sticking his hands in his pockets, then taking them out and folding them awkwardly. It made me feel a lot better to see that he was nervous too.

I pulled my suitcase into the bathroom with me, not wanting to have to get ready in front of him. It was ridiculous, since after spending almost every waking minute together for as long as we had, Roger had seen me in every possible state, including first thing in the morning. But even though it didn't make any sense, I wanted to look nice tonight. We had a inclusive dinner, after all. And it felt, to me, like our first date.

I took a long, hot bath, using the products I'd stolen from hotels across America. I blow-dried my hair afterward, being gentle with it. Maybe it was just wishful thinking, but there didn't seem to be quite as much falling out as there had been before. I dug through my suitcase, looking for something special to wear. Bronwyn had organized the suitcase by type of clothing—the T-shirts and tank tops were on top, and I'd mostly been sticking to them. But I was pretty sure I'd seen a dress folded along the bottom. I rummaged to the lowest layer, and there it was, all alone, taking up the length of the suitcase. I held it up, thankful one more time for Bronwyn and all she had given me. The dress was long and periwinkle blue with a sweetheart neckline. It was an incredibly soft material, and when I looked closer I saw that it had a slight sheen to it. Even though it was much, much too fancy for the hotel restaurant, it was exactly the right dress to wear tonight. As I pulled it out, I saw the green lingerie set that she'd insisted on giving me as well. I looked at the bra and underwear for a moment, then put them on.

I finished getting ready, putting on a little more makeup than usual, and even adding some mascara. Then I looked at my reflection one last time, took a breath, and stepped out into the bedroom.

Roger was sitting on the edge of the bed, and he stood up when he saw me. He had dressed up too, I saw. He was wearing khakis and a button-down shirt. "Hey," I said. "You look nice."

"You too," he said, smiling at me.

I was about to brush this off, or tell him that it was Bronwyn's dress, or make a joke. But I just smiled back and said, "Thank you."

"Shall we?" he asked, holding out his hand to me. I took it, interlacing my fingers with his.

"Yep," I said.

Behind closed doors . . .
—*Charlie Rich*

There was a fire in the fireplace of the Towson Inn lobby, and Roger and I were sitting on the couch in front of it. Dinner had been great, even though the food had only been okay and we had been the most dressed-up people in the restaurant. But that hadn't mattered. We'd held hands under the table.

But as we sat there together, the pauses in our conversation stretched longer and longer, and I leaned my head into Roger's chest for a moment. He rested his chin on top of my head, and I squeezed his hand once and stood up. I did so carefully, since there was much more fabric to this dress than I was used to, and I didn't want to wreck the moment by falling down. He looked up at me, and I held out my hand to him. "Ready to go up?" I asked.

Roger took my hand in both of his, but stayed sitting. "Look," he said, tracing a slow circle on the back of my hand. "I don't want you to feel any pressure, like that we have to . . . I mean, I just want to make sure you know that I—"

"Roger," I said. He stopped talking and looked up at me. "Ready to go up?" I asked again, smiling at him. My heart was pounding, and I was incredibly nervous. But in a good way. The kind of nervous you get before something really good happens.

He smiled and stood up, still holding on to my hand. "You sure?"

I nodded, and kissed him. He kissed me back, and we stayed like that for a moment. But then getting to the room, and quickly, seemed like a good idea to both of us. We stumbled into the elevator together, kissing until it reached our floor, then hurried out, laughing and trying to walk all at the same time. We got the room open after only three tries, and made it inside. He was trying to figure out my straps, and I had untucked his shirt from his pants and was already starting to undo his shirt buttons while we kissed—and I nearly tripped over my dress. And before going over to join him on the bed, I locked the door and drew the shades.

◄———►

"Hey," I murmured, several hours later. I stretched over and kissed him on his bare shoulder. "You up?"

"Nope," he said, smiling without opening his eyes. He rolled onto his back and I rolled into him, resting my head on his chest. After I moment, I realized that I could feel his heartbeat. I closed my eyes, and he smoothed his hand over my hair. "Five Questions?" he asked. I shook my head against his chest. "One?" he amended.

"That counts, you know," I said, propping myself up a little bit and turning to face him.

"You're not playing fair," he said.

"I learned from the best. Okay, fine," I relented. "One."

He traced the line of my chin, his expression growing serious. "Right now," he said. "This minute. Are you happy?"

I stretched up to kiss him before nodding. "Yes," I said. "Very much so." I looked at him, at the serious expression still on his face. "Are you?"

He nodded and stretched out the arm I had been lying on. He rolled onto his side, and I did the same, facing him. We twined our feet together, as though we'd always been doing it. It happened just that easily. "I am," he said. "A little too much, I think."

I moved closer to him. I knew that at some point, we were going to have to talk about things. We were going to have to say good-bye. And even if Roger refused to call it that, that's what it would be. But I didn't want to think about that just yet. I closed my eyes and wrapped my hand around his.

You've Got a Friend in Pennsylvania.
—PA license plate slogan

"Are you sure?" Roger asked me, from the passenger seat.

I adjusted the rearview mirror and made sure I was close enough to the pedals. I let out a breath and caught my smile reflected in my side mirror. "Yes," I said. When we'd headed out of the Towson Inn that morning, I'd walked around to the driver's side. I wanted to give it a try, at least. I wanted to see if I could do it.

"Feeling okay?" he asked.

"I think so," I said, and placed my hands on the wheel, at ten and two. Roger reached over and squeezed the hand at two.

"You'll be great," he said. "Just take it slow. And I'm right here."

"Okay," I said. "Okay." I pressed my lips together, then started the car. That felt all right, so I put it in gear and slowly exited the hotel parking lot.

"You okay?" he asked as I carefully merged onto the main road.

"I think so," I said. I braked at the stoplight, aware of how hard I was concentrating, but feeling like I had it under control. I thought that it might actually be easier once we got on the highway, when there would be less stopping and starting.

"Want me to be the DJ?" Roger asked, looking down at the iPod.

"Maybe in just a minute," I said, realizing that I'd gone back to the way I used to need silence in the car when I was first learning. "I'm concentrating here."

"No problem," he said, leaning back in the passenger seat. "I actually like it over here. It's very peaceful. You might be driving for the rest of the trip."

The sentence hung in the air between us, and I felt the weight of it. There was no more rest of the trip. The trip was over.

I pulled onto the highway and merged into the middle lane, which had always been my preferred lane. I never wanted to go as fast as the drivers in the left lane, and in the right lane there were always too many people merging. Once I hit seventy, I was doing the same speed as the rest of the cars and was able to relax a little. It was okay. It wasn't a joy like it had once been, but it was okay. I was driving. And I was fine.

← →

Roger had offered to stop at one of the many roadside diners we'd seen advertised on the highway—it seemed that Pennsylvania was diner country. But when I'd seen the sign for the burger place, I'd known that's where we had to stop for lunch.

We had gotten the burgers to go, then parked in the farthest space in the parking lot. We were eating in the way-back, containers of fries sitting between us, our legs dangling over the edge.

"This is great," Roger said, and I saw that his burger was almost gone. "Maybe there's something good about Pennsylvania after all."

I smiled and took a bite of my own burger, which really was excellent, and adjusted my new sunglasses. And I realized that we'd sat in this same place and eaten burgers from the

BURGERTOWN, USA
Linwood, Pennsylvania
6/13

2 burgers/
2 fries/   5.50
Cream soda/Root beer/ 3.00
                            2.95

TO GO

Total: 11.45

Thank you!!
Come back soon!

In-N-Out in California on the very first day of the trip. The day we'd decided to take a detour. Just a small one. I looked across at Roger, who was so familiar to me now.

"Last one?" Roger asked, angling the fries toward me.

I shook my head. "All yours."

He finished the fries and stood up as I stuffed the trash into the Burgertown bag. Roger shut the back door, then turned to me and took my hand in his carefully, like he was still getting used to doing this. "Want me to take over driving, Hillary?" he asked.

With my other hand, I took the keys out of my pocket and shook my head, smiling at him. "I've got it, Edmund."

←——→

After I'd been driving for another hour, I could handle having music on again. Roger made his last mix, and I recognized some of his repeat bands, some of my favorites – bands I hadn't even heard of a few days ago. I sang along to the words that I knew, and Roger kept time, drumming on the dashboard.

As I drove, I tried to picture what the rest of the day would be like. I played out the scenarios of Roger coming back with me and facing my mother's anger. Roger standing around while she yelled at me in some kitchen I couldn't even picture, with a fridge free from magnets. I thought about someone else watching our goodbye, even if we didn't use those exact words.

I glanced down at the gas gauge, which was hovering close to empty. Pulling off at the next exit, I headed for a Sunoco. "Here's a thought," I said as I carefully pulled forward to the pump and killed the engine. Roger turned to look at me. "What if I dropped you off in Philadelphia and drove myself to Connecticut?"

Roger shook his head. "I don't think that's such a good idea."

"I'll be okay," I promised. "Really. And it makes more sense this way." Roger got out of the car and unscrewed the gas cap. I could tell he was thinking it over. I walked inside the mini-mart to prepay with cash, hoping it would be enough to get us to Philly. When I got back to the car, Roger was pumping gas.

"I'm okay with driving," I assured him, as I squeegeed the dead-bug graveyard off our windshield. "Really. And it doesn't make any sense for you to drive with me to Connecticut only to get back on a train to Philadelphia."

"But you just started driving again," Roger said, replacing the gas cap and shutting the fuel door. "I don't know if you should drive alone yet."

I replaced the squeegee and walked over to him. "I'm going to be fine," I said. "And this way, I can spare you the wrath of my mother."

Roger put his arms around me and I leaned my head into his chest. We stayed that way until a honk behind us let us know that people were waiting for the pump. I passed him the keys. He got behind the wheel and I got back into the passenger side, and we headed to the last leg of our journey.

Where I've Been . . .

State #14: Pennsylvania—The Keystone State

motto: Virtue, Liberty, and Independence

Size: Surprisingly big, actually. Luckily, we didn't have to cross the whole thing.

Facts: The state beverage is ALSO milk. Time for a showdown with maryland?

Notes: Where are all these so-called friends that the license plates keep promising?

ROGER'S LAST PLAYLIST

"Pennsylvania, Here We Come" aka "Journey's End"

SONG TITLE	ARTIST
"How to Say Goodbye"	Paul Tiernan
"It'll All Work Out"	Tom Petty and the Heartbreakers
"The Trees and the Wild"	Matt Pond PA
"No Myth"	Michael Penn
"Slow Pony Home"	The Weepies
"How We Roll"	Plushgun
"The Resolution"	Jack's Mannequin
"World Spins Madly On"	The Weepies
"Signal Fire"	Snow Patrol
"Live to Tell the Tale"	Passion Pit
"What's So Bad (About Feeling Good)?"	Ben Lee
"Young Folks"	Peter, Bjorn & John

The famous explorers Edmund and Hillary

Good-bye, so long, farewell . . .
—*Paul Tiernan*

Twenty miles outside of Philadelphia, I began to break down. It seemed that all too soon, there were signs every few feet, telling me just how close Philadelphia was. Roger was holding my hand between our seats, but I was having trouble even looking at him, choosing instead to stare out the window, and not able to think about anything except how in a very few minutes, he'd be gone.

"You okay?" Roger asked, as he turned down a residential street.

"I don't think so," I said, still looking out my window.

"Well, I think we're almost there," he said, slowing down and squinting at the numbers on his side.

"That's not really helping," I said, trying to keep my voice light and utterly failing. Roger looked over at me for a moment, then pulled to the side of the road. I looked around—we were between two houses. "Are we here?" I asked, confused.

"I think it's up there," he said, looking from the address in his phone to a driveway a few feet away. "I just wanted a little privacy." He killed the engine, left the keys in the ignition, and turned to me, unbuckling his seat belt and then mine.

"What now?" I asked, hoping that he had some sort of a plan.

"Well," he said, sliding to the edge of his seat, "I'm going to go in and you're going to drive to Connecticut. And then I'm going to call you later tonight and we'll talk."

"No," I said. "I mean, what's going to happen? With us?" I asked, heart hammering.

He smiled at me. "You're the navigator," he said. "You want to know where we're going, and the exact route."

"Well, yes," I said. "I mean . . ."

"But what if we hadn't taken the detour?" he asked. "We'd have been back a long time ago. And we would only have seen Tulsa."

"I know," I said, thinking about the trip my mother had wanted me to take, and the trip we'd ended up taking, and how much better ours had been.

"So I think we have to be open to what happens," he said. "We can't know exactly what's coming."

"But I just want to know if . . ." I stopped when I realized I couldn't finish the sentence. What I wanted was some kind of guarantee, and he couldn't give that to me. Nobody could.

"Amy," Roger said. I looked at him, hearing just how he'd said my name. Like it contained only the good letters. "I didn't expect this to happen. Did you?"

"Well, of course not."

"Exactly. So I'm just trying to figure it out myself. We can't know what's going to happen. We can just try to figure it out as we go along. Right?"

"Right," I said slowly. "But . . ."

"I mean, I should have known," he said, leaning back a little and smiling at me. "It always happens this way."

"What does?"

"The best discoveries always happened to the people who weren't looking for them. Columbus and America. Pinzón, who stumbled on Brazil while looking for the West Indies. Stanley happening on Victoria Falls. And you. Amy Curry, when I was least expecting her."

I smiled back at him, while feeling sharply just how much I was going to miss him. It was almost a physical pain. "I'm on that list?"

"You're at the top of that list." He leaned over and kissed me, and I kissed back, and we stayed that way until we switched to just holding each other. He pulled away after a long moment, and

I nodded. We both got out of the car, and I walked around to the driver's side as Roger grabbed his backpack and duffel.

"Okay," I said. We kissed again, and he hugged me so tightly that my feet lifted off the ground.

"I'm calling you tonight," he whispered into my ear. "And we'll figure it out. I promise." I nodded again, and Roger set me down, and I felt him slip something into the front pocket of my jeans. "Don't open it until you get to Connecticut, okay?" He stepped back, smiling at me sadly. "We're not going to say good-bye."

"Of course not," I said, trying my best to smile back at him.

"I'm just going to say . . . see you around," he said, taking a few steps toward his dad's house.

"Don't be a stranger," I said.

"Take care," he said, stepping away.

"So long," I said.

"Talk to you later," he said, walking away, still facing me.

"See you soon," I called.

He was now at the base of his driveway, and he raised a hand in a wave to me. I raised a hand back. And then he shouldered his duffel and headed up the driveway, leaving me standing by the car, alone.

✳ Amy Playlist #3 ✳

"The End of the Road" or "The Beginning"

SONG TITLE	ARTIST
"All Shook Up"	Elvis Presley
"I Guess This Is Goodbye"	Into the Woods
"New Music"	Ragtime
"The Joy You Feel"	The Light in the Piazza
"I'd Do Anything"	Oliver!
"Goodbye Until Tomorrow"	The Last Five Years
"All That I Am"	Elvis Presley
"It Would Have Been Wonderful"	A Little Night Music
"We're Okay"	Rent
"With So Little to Be Sure Of"	Anyone Can Whistle
"Come What May"	Elvis Presley

Into the woods, then out of the woods,
and home before dark.
—*Stephen Sondheim*

Three hours later I passed the sign that told me I'd just entered Connecticut, and I pulled off into the first rest station that I saw. I killed the engine and pulled out of my pocket what Roger had given me—an object, wrapped in a note.

The magnet had AMERICA written across it. I turned it in my hand, thinking about the trip. Thinking about the people we had met, and everything that we had seen.

I read his words over again. I wasn't sure what would happen with us. I knew that there were no guarantees. Terrible things happened when you were least expecting them, on sunny Saturday mornings, and the consequences just had to be lived with, every day. But it seemed that wonderful things could happen too. You could be forced to take a trip, not knowing who you would meet. Not knowing that it would change your life.

I got out of the car and stretched my legs, taking in my first real view of Connecticut. It was pretty, I realized with some surprise, even at the rest station.

I took out the Connecticut map I'd bought at a gas station and unfolded it when I realized that I didn't have the address of my mother's—our—new house. I began to think about the house as a real place, one that I would be at in under an hour. I couldn't picture it, but I hoped it had Internet access. I owed Julia a long-overdue e-mail. I took out my phone and dialed my mother's cell, expecting it to go straight to voice mail, as all my other calls had.

She answered after the second ring. "Amy?" she asked, her voice a little hesitant.

"Hi, Mom," I said, trying to speak around the lump in my throat that had formed just hearing her voice.

"Are you okay?" my mother asked, and I could hear how tense she sounded. "Is everything all right?"

"I'm fine," I said quickly, and I could hear her let out a breath. "I'm okay. I'm in Connecticut."

"You're—here?" she asked, the worry in her voice replaced by surprise. "Now? With Roger?"

"No, just me," I said, still a little surprised that it was true. "I dropped Roger off at his father's a few hours ago."

"You dropped him off?" my mother was sounding more and more confused. "You mean—you're driving?"

"I am," I said. And I felt, in the silence that followed, everything that had happened on the trip to bring me to this place.

"Well," she said, sounding a little stunned. "That . . . that's great. I mean, that you . . . ," her voice trailed off. "Not that I'm not upset with you," she said, in a tone that was probably meant to be stern. But she didn't quite pull it off. "I am. And we're going to talk about consequences."

"We're going to have to talk about a lot," I said. "I hope."

"Well . . . yes," my mother said slowly, probably trying to figure out what I was talking about. But if she didn't get it now, it was okay. I could tell her later.

"Can I have the address?" I asked. "I just crossed the state line."

"Oh, of course," my mother said. She read me the address and gave me basic directions, and then silence fell between us.

"Okay," I said after a moment. "So—"

"Are you hungry?" my mother asked, a little abruptly. "I was just about to get dinner started. But if you haven't eaten, I'll wait."

"I haven't eaten," I said. As I said, this I realized that I actually was hungry. And that a home-cooked meal sounded pretty good.

"Well, I'll start it now," my mother said. "And you'll drive safe?"

"I will," I promised. "I'll see you soon." I hung up the phone and got back into the car. I placed Roger's magnet carefully in my purse. As I did, I saw the copy of *Food, Gas, and Lodging*—the book that had come with me across the country. I pulled it out and opened it up to the note card, to the last page my father had read. As I looked at it, I knew I was going to be able to read beyond page sixty-two. Otherwise, I was never going to find out what happened next. I would read through to the end, even though I knew that I wouldn't be able to discuss it with my father. But maybe Charlie and I could talk about it when he came back.

As I smoothed out the Connecticut map, the state motto on the cover caught my eye. *He who transplanted sustains.*

I looked at it for a long time. Even though that had obviously been Connecticut's motto for a long time—since 1622, the map helpfully told me—it felt like a sign. It felt like it meant that maybe I was going to be okay here. That transplanted as I was, I might find a way to thrive here.

I looked at it for a moment longer, then realized that if I didn't leave soon, I was going to be late for dinner. I turned on the car and scrolled through my mix until I found an Elvis song. Then I signaled, turned up the volume, and pulled back out onto the highway.

Philly's Best Cheesesteak!
Liberty Place
Philadelphia, PA

July 19
Table: 5
Server: Ron
Customers: 2

1 Cheesesteak	
1 Deluxe Cheesesteak	6.25
2 orders fries	6.75
Root Beer/med	4.00
Cream Soda	1.25
	1.25
Total:	
	19.50

Thank you!!
Come back soon!